CANINE

CANINE

DAMIAN PRYCE

CANINE

ISBN: 979-8-9934081-2-5 (Hardcover)

ISBN: 979-8-9934081-1-8 (Paperback)

ISBN: 979-8-9934081-0-1 (eBook)

First Edition: February 2026

10 9 8 7 6 5 4 3 2 1

TRIGGER WARNING

This novel is an extreme horror work and includes graphic content that may not be suitable for all readers. It contains depictions of extreme violence, gore, torture, sexual assault, rape, substance abuse, child abuse, necrophilia, cannibalism, self-harm, suicide, exploitation, and animal abuse. Reader discretion is strongly advised.

DEDICATION

For all the men that have used my dick as a coin slot: this is your prize.

CHAPTERS

BRUISE

I sell them pounds of meat—if they last longer than a cigarette. My body decays into melting pumpkin rinds, and they scrape me of my pulp. They thread my stringy tangles between their fingernails, winding them around clenched fists.

But no one cares to pay attention to what's inside when it takes more effort than a lubricated finger to get there. I let them penetrate me—cattle guns prying into cavities, fishing, coax out some emotion. When they retract, all they lap up is discounted entertainment. If it's worth something, it has a price. No one's interested in worthless things.

I dredge their gutters, exhuming coils of filth, sucking their rot. This numbing, carnal seepage slides down the back of my throat. I want them to split my teeth into fissures, crust them with their humid drip. These pangs satiate my appetite for arousal. I degrade my physique into a shell of hollow innuendos.

It's no wonder I feel nothing at all.

PAIN

There was a time in my life when I had often thought about dying on the side of a desert highway. Not to make a suicidal spectacle—more with the intent of inputting myself into some harsh environment and walking until I couldn't anymore. More passive than erratic, I suppose. I thought about tracing my eyes along my shoes, cotton socks clinging between sweat-slick toes. I thought about shuffling through copper pebbles, air sharp with salt, stinging my skin. Eventually, I'd collapse—disintegrate—my body flattening, melting into dirt. I'd become a puddle of mud, back into what I was made from, or whatever that scripture said.

I once told that to a man who worked at the liquor store down the street. It was a block from a funeral home. As a kid, I thought it was strange—a liquor store that close to a haven for the dead. But I get it now. Good for business—both ways. He always sold me liquor underage. I think he had some kind of affinity for me—for my body. He had these pallid eyes that stared past their sockets. Detached, floating in an empty well—wet, cold, hissing for my body to crumple into them. He told me once he'd always wanted to kill someone. I was fourteen at the time and it was my first erection, hearing him say that. Or it was the first time I noticed it and truly knew what it meant—jeans tightening at the front. A couple months later, the liquor store burned down with him inside. It was a shame. Not that I felt sad, or even an irking in my chest. Just this pulsing irritation, like heartburn. Something had changed—and I missed it. And I didn't deserve another chance to feel it.

RESTORATION

Stewart rolls in a woman with a bruised neckline and an insectile, masculine visage. Her new bed is cold metal—stainless. According to him, she was raped and beaten. More poetically, he calls her *another victim of unfortunate circumstances*. He slides up his gloves and begins reviewing the *restoration process* as he calls it. I'm a spectator in his lecture of death. Like we're connected, him and I. The corpse is an excuse to initiate. This ritual is chronic for him—he doesn't think I'm listening. I'm not. I'm more interested in the way her neck snapped than the anguish-soaked narrative. I've never cared for trivial things.

"Fabrication is what people love about funerals," Stewart says. "Exhuming beauty from an otherwise pale pound of meat. Or rather, restoring that pound of meat back into something more than what it's become."

To Stewart, there's something ethereal in every mundane object. It makes the unruly aspects of his profession more intriguing—or frightening—depending on his state of mind. I don't see it. I just glare into the casket while he blotches more foundation on her stale cheeks. They're shriveled like sun-charred pears, and the makeup gives them a musk I can taste—it soaks into my saliva. "When I was in Berlin," he continues, "I lived across from a church that was put through a restoration project. The end result was quite elegant—but it wasn't the original church." He presses a thumb into her chest. A crisp crack follows. I can't tell if it's his worn joints or her worn body. Her chest deflates like a balloon. He adjusts his glasses with two fingers. "I'm in the business to provide a sense of serenity," he says, "however false that may be."

I don't care.

He motions for me to move to his side. I do. He pinches my bottom lip between two fingers. My jaw jitters like an anxious crustacean, and he begins to probe, fingers morphing into the calves of a back-alley prostitute—her legs wedging my mouth open. The salty web between her legs reminds me of rain fizzling out in a lightbulb's heat—of moth hearts sizzling when they die. In this moment, he holds my skin as collateral. He wants to bend my gummy body and fester in his wet sheets. In the morning, I'll relish a bath and feel pain when I surface unclean. Pain is knowing something is ugly and doing nothing about it.

SWOLLEN

Next day. Different cadaver.

Her body's a vanilla clamshell—breasts sticky, hard. The casket wood seems to shrivel like how skin wrinkles in a sauna. I press into her form—it melts into gelatinous folds. Stewart notices. Says nothing. She's scheduled for display in fifteen minutes. I want to have last contact.

Stewart presses the brim of his glasses into the crook of his nose and leaves the room. I wonder if he knows I'm coming down from a vigorous high. If he knows this monstrosity excites me—the way it feels between my fingers.

I wash my hands and scrape off leftover makeup. The casket seals around her like a smooth cocoon—adorned with crude carvings and cheap gold trim. I push the casket out. Metallic tangs pool in my spit as I scan the steel fixtures and exit. My reflection scrapes my tongue. The wheels scream.

DEATH

I stand next to Stewart at the back of the room. White gold rings adorn his fingers, leaving a pink tint in his swollen knuckles. I think about his fingers in my mouth and wonder if feeding sour worms to pigs counts as cannibalism. Our hands are crossed. He still hasn't said a word to me. One guy looks about my age—argyle slacks that fit like capris, hair slicked to the side in bulky strands, bolstered by a cowlick hugging the crown of his head.

The mourners move forward, lumpy suits—secondhand, oversized, or too tight. Weeping. Shivering limbs. Crumpling knees. Collect, compose, continue. Deconstruction. Reconstruction. Exit. People take living so seriously. As if it isn't long enough for most of us. I would've killed myself too, if I had to watch this kind of aftermath wail over me—over my body. But when the guy approaches, his expression is vacant. He stands still, hands folded. Then moves on.

I scrunch my eyebrows. I wonder if I left the bruise showing—if the makeup's cracking, too caked, or too thick. He shakes hands, fingers closing like a Venus flytrap, excreting sweat to suck in their remorse. He's drawing a lot of attention. People's mouths curve with looks that seem accusatory or apologetic—I can't tell which. Stewart remains still, stiff— like one of the faux marble pillars littering the room. He hasn't acknowledged me once.

Whatever.

I reach into my slacks for cigarettes. The guy glances in my direction. Then, a hunched, old woman with rat teeth bobs into his view. His gaze snaps forward, startled, like she's just encroached on his last cheese wedge. He raises his brows and steps back, offering a short, toothy smile to whatever she's mouthing. He rests a hand on her hunch, gesturing with the other. He says something fast—I think he intends it to be comical. But she scowls, scrunches back. I slide out my cigarette pack and step through the side door.

The parking lot is littered with cars. Some expensive, some beaters. You can tell who cares about the dead by what they show up to a funeral in. A classic car catches my eye—wooden doors, a peeling sticker of a biblical fish. Old people get bored of their money. They find God to pass the time. I peel the sticker off. It leaves a streak of residue, outlining where the fish once was.

The door behind me clacks open. The guy steps out, suit tight across his chest, too short in the sleeves. His argyle slacks vibrate behind my glassy vision. He presses his fingers through his hair and fishes in his pocket. He pulls out a cigarette and places it between his lips. I crush the sticker in my fist, drop it, and it crinkles. He fumbles for a lighter. My shoes crunch on the asphalt. He turns and sees me walking back toward the door.

"Do you have a lighter?" he asks, passing a car with a duct-taped bumper. I shuffle in my pocket and exhale a ribbon of smoke. A slight weight builds in my temple. I nod, hand him a lighter. He leans near my shoulder, shielding the flame from the wind. Greased strands flutter across my suit breast, and his cheek nearly brushes me. He lights the cigarette, exhales a cloud, and hands the lighter back.

"I appreciate it. I'm not much of a smoker, but with these kinds of events, old habits kick in." I don't reply. My eyes scan the lot. Then return to him. "Funny how death brings people out. Strangers telling me how much I've grown. Stories I don't remember. Don't care to either." He pauses. Looks at me like I don't belong here. Or like I'm meat. I'd prefer the latter, but I would understand the former too. "You're the guy who works with Stewart, right?"

"Yeah." I take another drag.

"Stewart's a good man," he says. "He knew I was on a tight budget. Honestly, I couldn't afford much, but he made it work. I should've just thrown her in a bonfire and called it a day." That must've been what spooked the rat woman—heretic energy and lackluster quips. "You his grandson or something?"

"No." I shake my head. "I help him out. He's teaching me the business."

"Well, everything's been very good, considering."

"I did the makeup. Dressed the body and such," I say.

He nods. Quiet for a moment.

"Cool."

"It seems like you're pretty popular."

"Yeah," he replies. "Comes with the territory of being her son."

I don't say anything. We watch our smoke drift into the hum of the street. The wind batters the car frames. The parking lot is haunted by a graveyard of cigarette butts.

"I'm Percy, by the way," he says.

I introduce myself with a name that's not mine.

He nods and slides out his cellphone, then fidgets with the screen. Portable isolation. I don't know if I'm boring him or if he's just insipid in nature.

"Does any of this bother you?" I ask. My vision films. The air glosses my eyes in dew. He keeps tapping the phone, then looks up.

"Not particularly," he says, and hits his cigarette again. "Maybe it should. Maybe it will later. My brain feels like it's stuck in quicksand. Hard to find the right words for someone's life when they didn't find much value in it themselves."

"The funeral business feeds into flattery," I say. "Gives people an excuse to circle jerk their grief all over each other."

"You say that like it's a bad thing," Percy grins.

"It's irritating. It's such a waste, isn't it?"

"Probably," he shrugs. "Sounds like you're in the wrong business."

"Yeah," I reply. "Or I should be doing it differently."

"Either way." He taps the screen a few more times, then holds his phone out. "I could use company that doesn't see me as an opportunity to ejaculate their sentiments over. You seem... more constructive."

"Yeah." I type in my number.

His eyes thaw into pale bursts—graying at the irises, docile but rigid. Like they're guarding an inner sanctum I want to slosh around in. Vacant. Bare. My chest climaxes.

"I've got to head back in," he says. I break the stare—realize how long I'd been locked into it. "Hopefully I don't drown. It'd be a waste."

REVULSION

I pick up a man in a gas station restroom.

He unzips his jeans and stands at the urinal, but doesn't piss. A damp, earthy cologne clings to his clothes and claws at my nostrils. He starts panting—mouth open, eyes flitting. I catch him glancing my cock, so I tell him about this local park tucked deep behind the trees. I tell him it's like another world back there. That provokes him. It means when he crosses that threshold, he doesn't have to be who he is now. No one really wants to live inside the suits they've been assigned to. They just pretend they do. Because if they can find even a sliver of comfort in their own skin, it gives them the upper hand over you.

I slide my hand into his waistband and whisper for him to take me to his car. Precum sticks between my fingers and dries against the crotch of his jeans. The zipper scratches my wrist. He massages his fingers into my collar and breathes heavy—booze dragging from his throat—and agrees. He says he'll even open the door for me.

I guide him to an old service road, winding through the pitch night. Bushes crawl over the edges of his headlights. The glow casts perverse shadows that sway along the gravel and stain the dusk. We're diving into a narrow underworld. Glimmers of animal eyes stalk us from the trees, paving the path. Breadcrumbs to follow.

He pulls off into a flattened clearing, kills the engine, and rolls the windows down. I get out, stuffing my fists into my jacket pockets. The air bites at my neck and the wind combs through my hair. The clearing is barren except for mold-eaten stumps and bark chunks scattered like bones in the dirt. He rummages through his backseat while I light a cigarette. The ember blisters in the dark. His feet crunch behind me. Then, his fingers hook into my belt loops, breath brushing the nape of my neck, warm and pulsing. His mouth presses into my skin, sucking my neck like a gasping pufferfish. I tilt my head slightly toward him, a dull chemical prickle fluttering under my skin from the last of the high. I drag my cigarette again. Molten glow. I push off and face him. The open car windows whistle. A high, rattling note cuts through the breeze—like a chalkboard flapping against a wall.

"Was that fine?" he asks, voice tentative, as if he's done something wrong.

I wish he had.

"Yeah," I murmur. I step in, tongue grazing the sharp curve of his jaw. His words curdle something in me. His voice is a mask, asking permission for what he wants to do. That kind of permission sours me. It makes me want to smother the part of him that asked.

We stumble through the dirt, locked together, legs fumbling as we devour each other's mouths. At the back door, I press him into the metal lip and bite his neck. He gasps, exhales in bursts. I guide him down through the frame—spine folded into the car seats and spreading him like a sacrifice. I take one last drag and flick the cigarette aside. It dies in the gravel. I climb in after him. His body twists—shirt grinding against the upholstery. He turns over, writhing. My hands grip his hips, his belt, his back, his shoulders—pulling, pressing, controlling the angles. Unbuckle his belt, pull down the back of his jeans. I spread his blemished ass between my palms and work my thumbs into its puckered flesh. Hook my fingers around his chin, rub his cheek into the door handle. He sucks his rectal dew from my fingertips. Unbuckle my jeans, pull.

There's a moment—stillness, tension. I reach into my pocket and find the handle. The click is subtle, clean. The switchblade lacerates his bottom lip, slashes across the mouth. His gumline tears, jaw jerks, cranks loose from its tendons. His jowl muscles weep stringy taffy threads and wrap their sticky strands around my knuckles. Blood slips in thin ropes across my fingers and wrists. His voice breaks into wet, broken animal sounds. He seizes, writhes. His legs kick the seats and his body shudders under me. I prop his head up, out the window. It's easier to clean dirt than upholstery. His naked thighs sound hollow, thumping the leather. I roll up the window. Slowly. Until the pressure builds at his throat and the glass crushes it into the car frame. He begins to go limp. Newborn deer, tensing. Body warm, still pliable. Bruises blossom later—I trace the heat of them before the color's had time to rise. His hips reflex and vibrate against my lips. When I chew his cock head, he comes blood.

BLEED

I grip the sink between shaky fingers, knuckles tightening around the porcelain. Pain shoots through their joints. Water surges from the faucet, flecked with calcium deposits, and swirls down the drain. Grime stains the bowl, clinging to hairline cracks that vein outward like fractures in glass. I run my fingers through damp hair, pushing it back from my eyes, and glare at the film of steam coating the mirror. The layers breathe with me. I wipe my hand across the surface—zigzagging—until my portrait emerges from behind the fog, gasping back at me from the reflective abyss.

My eyes strain in scaly, grayed sockets—poached trophies. My body shows wear. It's carved into the pockmarks etched across my cheeks and the taut skin stretched over my bones. It's not youthful anymore— but there's still a hunger in it, a yearning to return to form. My face has sunken into soft curvatures where fat used to sit—scooped out like ice cream and fed to voracious street rats. My skin tents over cave dwellings in my skull. Their prominence swells into broken monoliths. The perks of snorting amphetamines. Movie star simplicities.

Water rolls down my torso and ripples in the sink. I drag my fingers through my hair again, matting down the flattened porcupine style. Grease it. Slick it back, like sealing a wound. I rinse the residue from my hands and grab the towel from the bar above the toilet. Burgundy, with a black stripe along the bottom. Splotched in faded black from the last time I bled. I dry down my chest and study my ribs—jutting through my skin like skeletal wings. They contract and release beneath my scars. And the scars are deep. Sometimes I run a fingernail—or a paperclip—through the crevices to scrape out dried fluid or caked filth. The worst are across my chest—never healed right. I like to think they add a kind of attraction. Sometimes an erection surges up when I smooth my fingers between them. I like to think they add character.

As I'm admiring this, immersed in the language of my own skin, a bead of blood falls into the sink. It splatters in crimson webbing, dissolving into a rosé swirl down the drain. My nose again. I press the towel to it—let it soak, let it scar, let it add another dark spot to its already desecrated landscape.

STATIC

The tea kettle screams in the other room—steam hissing from its lip, lid rattling against metal. I lean back into the sofa cushions and gaze at my scarred chest in the reflection of the television screen. Color gradients flicker across the image, its corners eroded in white noise—melting me in its place. Stewart owns an old TV with a bulbous screen that juts out like a tumor. It shocks my fingers every time I touch it.

My arms feel hollow—like paper towel rolls—crinkling with every twitch. My stomach echoes the same sensation. Like the blood from my nose didn't just leave—it drained me empty. Like my sanctuary cage is dissolving, making room for the inner fluids to rise and drown their bars beneath cold foam.

The screen pulsates, buzzing behind my temples. I take a drag of my cigarette. Ash flecks drift down across the scars and abrasions carved into my sternum. My skin stiffens like tanned tarp—leathery, yellowed.

"You know, the entire time, I don't think that guy cried once," I say. My eyes don't leave the screen, bleeding sanguine with gradual distortion. I'm thinking about Percy. I interject this sentiment like I'm hoping Stewart will give me something back, some answer. He doesn't know about my other endeavors—the other guys. It's not that I want to hide it. He just wouldn't understand—not like I do.

I'm still trying to figure that out myself. What I'm trying to accomplish. Whatever that means. Stewart's feet shuffle behind me. The coffee maker clicks off. Water pouring. Silence. The hush of the TV takes over again.

"I didn't notice," he says. I hear the clink of a lid. "People show grief in different ways."

"People like that aren't memorable to the right audience. That's the danger—they blend in." The pour stops. I glance down at my chest. Stewart's gaunt figure appears beside me. He slides two bony fingers into the edge of my shoulder blade. One of his nails catches on a trench carved deep into my collar. It feels like an intrusion. I don't know if that's the right word. The feeling is welcome—it just doesn't belong there. "Sometimes I think blending in is good. Sometimes I think the worst thing is to be forgotten. Either way, eventually the wrong audience notices."

I look back at the screen. Blimps float through—weightless, bobbing. I take another drag. My cheeks collapse in, cratering, then billow back into a razed landscape with each exhale. Stewart doesn't reply. I wonder if I even said anything at all. I glance back at the scars across my chest. Blood wells up in the ravines—my scars drink—and my nose begins to throb again.

PIERCE: RETURN

The glass panes breathe as I pass, my reflection dispersing and recollecting in haunting wisps beneath the surface. My body appears thinner, ghastly, moving autonomously from my perception—like I'm crawling behind the frame, pressed flat into the misted glass. I pull the cold handle and step inside, watching my reflection move with me.

The foyer is bare. My boots clack against the tile, their echoes rebounding like I'm being followed. I glance back. The sun overtakes the glass, reflecting the parking lot. I turn to the counter and slide my fingers across its surface. A woman with a thin face and puckered lips glances up. Her hair is pulled into a taut ponytail, inky curls fanning at the end.

"Hello," I say, eyeing the paperwork under her folded hands. "I'm here to see Gus Cameron. I have an appointment." I don't know where to train my eyes. Her shirt gapes above her cleavage, a raisin birthmark peeking from behind the fabric. I force myself to look elsewhere, but catch her eyebrows rise in my periphery. I've been tapping my fingers. I stuff them into my jacket pockets.

"You must be Detective Pierce?" she asks, voice clipped. Her lips don't move much—botched filler clasps her mouth stationary. "I've heard plenty about you, and not just from Chief Cameron. You're a bit of a celebrity around here. Or at least you were." She stands and adjusts the badge hooked to her pocket

"I can find his office," I say, assuming her intention to direct me. "Unless it's moved."

"Same place," she replies. "I keep telling him to change the carpet, rearrange a little. But we're creatures of habit, aren't we? What happens if you replace the carpet and suddenly everything feels wrong?"

I tap my knuckle on Cameron's office door. He glances up from a manila folder, shuts it, and waves me in. A wiry smile crosses his face as he stands and opens his arms wide—like he's offering an embrace or presenting something ceremonial.

"James," he says, moving from behind the desk. His eyes scan me, catch my flushed cheeks, and his smile fades. I keep my hands in my pockets. He settles for a palm grip on my shoulder. "I trust our receptionist didn't badger you too much for an autograph. You've been the talk of the office, not just from my praises."

"Looks like time hasn't treated you particularly well," I reply, averting ghosts. He shrugs, circles back to his chair, and motions for me to sit. The fan on his desk whirs beside the keyboard, metal clinking in its revolutions. The office still holds its worn bookshelves. I remember closing our last case here—clinking bourbon glasses, leaving water rings on the wood. The scratches in the veneer look like constellations eroded from time. Something about that aging wood makes me feel like I should be aging with it. "It's strange being back here," I say, glancing from the bookshelf to Cameron. He opens the manila folder again, holding it between his stubby sausage fingers. His hair's thinner now and the grease he uses to slick it is more obvious. The skin beneath his chin sags like a rooster wattle.

"I should bring you up to speed," he says. "Before we get too deep into pleasantries." He peers at me from behind his glasses. The cavernous wrinkles around his mouth crease deeper. "This case has gotten complicated." He slides the folder across the desk. Inside are paperclipped pages and several photocopied photographs marked up with notes. I press my fingers to the paper, narrowing my eyes.

"These are dogs," I say. "I thought this was a homicide case."

"It started with a string of mutilations," Cameron says. "Someone was breaking into yards, killing pets—dogs mostly. He'd either jump the fence or break the locks, maim the animals, and leave the bodies. He probably watched the houses for a few days, figured out routines. Or he was very lucky."

"And now it's humans."

He nods. "Same style." He points to a photo near my hand. A close-up of a dog's muzzle, torn open. Raw gums exposed, meat peeled back. Jaw broken, chunks of tissue soaking the grass, pooling blood. "He took the dogs' teeth. All of them."

"Christ," I mutter, rubbing my forehead. Sweat beads collecting around my hairline. The fan's whirring sounds are soothing in the stale warmth.

"The human victims were missing teeth too, but just the canines. We held a press conference after a pattern emerged. That's when the media named him: the *Canine Killer*. Shortly after, we got a tip—guy with a schizophrenia diagnosis. He confessed to the mutilations, but not the human victims. We booked him anyway—figured it had to be him."

"Clearly not."

Cameron opens a drawer and produces two new manila folders clipped together. He hands one to me. Inside: a man's jaw split, unhinged like an abused puppet. Eyes sunken, pupils glazed. Final moments intact in his irises. I wipe the sweat from my neck.

"After the arrest, another victim turned up. Same mutilations. Canines missing." He slides the next folder over. "Detective Stanton nearly blew the case," he says. "Got reckless. Pushed suspects too hard in interrogations. She's good, but this case got under her skin."

"Stanton's a detective now?" I ask. "Good for her. Always had a fiery temper."

"That temper is exactly why I need your help." Cameron glares at me. "She was obsessed with the Canine Killer. I don't want to remove her—she's got insight we need. But we have to keep the case on track. I need someone steady."

"I respect Stanton," I say. "I'll do what I can."

"She reminds me of you," Cameron says. "In more ways than one."

I don't respond. I flip a page in the file, and it tears slightly at the corner. Cameron watches me read the toxicology report and the writing scratched in the margins. The office is stifling hot and the fan clatters, sings louder.

"How've you been holding up since your last case?" he asks. He wants to address the proverbial elephant in the room.

I push my hair back, sweat clinging to my scalp. "It's strange being here," I repeat. I clench my jaw and the pressure echoes images of pliers scraping enamel.

Cameron pauses, then turns and reaches for a crystal decanter on the shelf. It's like he's realizing things exist outside of crime, cases, death. He spins his chair and pours two glasses of bourbon. The liquid gurgles like an aquarium pump.

"I wish I could've made the funeral," he says, handing me a glass.

"It's fine," I say. "I didn't either."

He doesn't acknowledge the comment. "She was lovely," he says. "Always reminded me of a pinup girl. Shame she didn't do more with that beauty." I throw the drink back and bare my teeth through the bitter searing. Cameron watches, eyebrow raised, then does the same. "I usually save that for special occasions," he says. I scan the room like I've never seen it before. It could be my imagination, but the heat thickens. "You still haven't seen your son, have you?"

"No," I say. A silverfish creeps across the carpet. I think of our old bathroom. Her hand-painted tiles in the backsplash. Abstract. "I'm dead to him too. Probably better that way."

"James," Cameron says, tone softening. "You're blood. That means something. Percy will come around."

"Blood only matters in crime scenes." I stand and give Cameron a parting nod. The silverfish darts toward the door. I smear it into the carpet with my heel and leave. Cameron doesn't stop me. My reflection follows as I leave. I don't know whether it comforts me or disgusts me. Probably a bit of both.

SANCTUM

I'm thinking about Percy when I approach the man's car. It's an older model, bruised in streaks and scratches that carve across its butterscotch finish. It reminds me of my body—invites me to trace the damage with my fingers. I don't. He leans against the door with his arms crossed, trying to look slick. But his hands give him away—fingers clamped around his forearms, nails dimpling the skin. It's all performative.

I step across the gravel lot. The neon bar sign pulses through the windshield, painting the leather seats a soft lime. Above the door, the curved bulbs spell out the bar name and flies hurl themselves into the glow. Their collisions are violent. Each strike releases a sharp fizz, wings sizzling against the glass like faulty wires.

A lamppost light angles down across his jawline, casting it in sterile white. He's wearing a slim-fit denim vest over a sleeveless white shirt. The vest is frayed and stained in smeared blotches. I don't like it on him. It reminds me of my scars. It's not that I hate my scars—I don't. But seeing pieces of myself echoed on strangers becomes threatening. It feels like something is trying to crawl out of them—like I'm being replaced.

I think his name is Samuel, but I can't remember for sure. Doesn't matter. We met here last week. He pinned me against a bathroom stall, and I told him I'd charge him less if he bought me a few drinks first. It scratched his itch, and something inside me.

Now, he runs a hand through his sandy hair and tries to smile—meant to come off coy, but it lands crooked. Indecisive. His hands twitch again, fingers flexing like he's rehearsing how to touch something. I don't smile back. It'd look unnatural on me, and I don't think I can curve my lips like that without lying. And I'm a terrible liar.

He pushes the bar door open, and an echo of mariachi music spills out, enveloping my ears in an invasive fog. The air is humid with sweat and stale limes. He grabs a stool at the bar and gestures toward the one beside it. I follow suit.

The bartender waddles toward us with a fistful of rags and a gut slumping over his waistband. His stained polo shirt is stretched taut, its bottom seam puckering against his stomach like it's trying to stillbirth embryo secretions. A waxed mustache curls above a toothpick pinned between his lips. His baseball cap bears the bar's name in graffitied, bubble lettering. Samuel—or whatever—orders two gin and tonics and leans over the counter to whisper something about pouring generously. He doesn't ask what I want. He doesn't think to. I can already taste the bitterness rising in my throat.

"I'm not, well, you know," he starts, glancing sideways at me, then down at his drink. "I'm not into this kind of thing. With men, I mean. I don't swing that way, if you get me. But a man's got needs."

"I don't care," I say.

"Sure." He nods, takes a long sip. "I guess I don't pay you to talk. That's what you pay a shrink for, right?" He sets the glass down gently, fingers circling the rim. "I told my shrink once that my life's like this long stretch of road. At first there're turns, choices, different ways to go. But somewhere along the way, all of that just collapses into one narrow lane. And that lane keeps tightening. You can't go back—the road behind you is already sealed by every decision you've made. The oncoming road is worse. You see what's ahead and realize you're damned anyway. So, you freeze. You just stand there, in the middle of that shrinking road, too scared to move forward, too late to turn around. You wait. And eventually, something comes along and flattens you. What do you do with that?" He shakes his head, exacerbated. "He said I was too difficult of a client—can you believe that?"

I think that's what he says—the words trail off, limp and distorted. My mind's elsewhere—past his hairline, locked onto the broken dartboard hanging on the back wall. It looks like a plastic beehive, warped and painted by someone with no sense of symmetry. The colors are mismatched, but I doubt they ever aligned. A patio door creaks open nearby. Chili pepper string lights buzz along the frame and spill outside like a cheap artery. Samuel—or whatever—keeps talking. I don't listen.

After a couple drinks, I walk him out, my arm latched around his forearm as he stumbles. I'm fine. I'd been feeding the artificial floral décor behind us whenever he vanished to empty his bladder. I never cared for gin. At his car, he starts patting himself down in a frantic mime of concern, tracing his waist and back pockets like his wallet might have wriggled free and scurried into the dirt.

"I think I left my wallet," he stammers, head swiveling around and scanning the dirt. His legs wobble beneath him like bent flamingo stilts. I pause, recalibrating. Plans shift.

"I'll wait here," I say, sparking a cigarette. "Go check with the bartender."

He nods and lurches back toward the door.

The night air clings cold to the leather of my jacket, but the lining's weight draws sweat from under my arms. My hands are clammy, fists tightening with a mechanical stiffness, like the joints need oil. I watch him trip against the doorframe, pause to recompose, and vanish inside. My boots crunch the gravel as I crouch by his front tire, pretending to adjust a lace. I scan the lot. Empty. I fish out the switchblade, lean in under the chassis, and feel around for the brake lines. When I find them, I slice. The blade punctures their tubing and fluid spurts across the back of my hand, warm and slick. The rubber parts into wet lips.

I lean casually against the hood once it's done, scanning again. The bar door clacks open. He stumbles out, waving his hand like his wrist is broken. I notice an inch of ash dangling from my cigarette—flick it. He twirls his keys between his fingers and approaches with a sketchy grin, slack-jawed and unsteady. Bared teeth, drooling like I'm a pickled pork shoulder. He collapses against my side and lets the stubble of his cheek drag along my neck, his breath warm and sour.

"You want to follow me?" he slurs, nodding vaguely toward some imagined destination. He rounds the hood and splays his palms across the metal for balance. The car groans under his weight, and the hood pops just slightly—like cartilage under pressure.

"Yeah," I say. I drop the butt, grind it out under my heel, and hold out my hand. His brow knits in sluggish confusion. He stares, then sighs, annoyed. "I'm a businessman first," I remind him. He fumbles out his wallet, peels off a wad of folded bills, and slaps them into my palm before staggering toward the driver's side. I tuck the money into my pocket and turn away, heading for my own car. His headlights flare behind me, stretching my shadow across the lot—fraying and splintering, like the silhouette of some emaciated cryptid. I reach my hearse, and its sharp bumper taunts me with its chrome mouth. I pull the door open and glance back as his headlights sweep the pavement like a lighthouse beam retracting from shore.

The bar is settled on the outskirts of town, distant enough that reaching anything resembling civilization takes time. We're winding down a desolate stretch of highway. Its asphalt cracks like flaked skin. The road is lined with sagging fences—barbed wire gnarled in uneven patches, beginning and ending with no clear intention. Under the moonless sky, they glint when the headlights skim their backs, like the ribs of tinfoil skeletons.

His car rattles further ahead, wheezing as it lumbers through the dark. It's a beast of a thing, coughing like it has fluid in its lungs. I bet it could flatten moose bones. I glance at my rearview mirror. The road is empty except for the occasional crooked telephone pole. Some are still standing, but others lean back like they've given up. He keeps checking his mirrors—rearview, side, back again. Nervous. Good. He leans out his window to spit, a habit he repeats every few minutes like he's on a timer. It's another assertion of his collected, synthetic attitude. People drive the bodies they truly want. And each time, the car veers slightly, grazes the centerline, then swings back. Head, spit, careen, correct. Again. And again. Like watching a metronome lose rhythm.

I flash my headlights once. The next swerve is more aggressive. He jerks the wheel, scrambling to correct. Before he can settle, I clip him—just enough. The front corner of the hearse catches his rear bumper and sends him lurching off the road in a scraping arc. His grille crumples into a light pole, steel buckling around steel with a final screech. I don't give him the option of lingering in the road—I move him forward to finality.

I coast forward, easing the hearse to a stop. Then reverse. The hearse idles in the center of the road as I peer out the passenger window at the wreckage. His front end is wrapped around the pole, radiator hissing steam and seeping into the dirt. The hood is buckled, choking in a billow of smoke. His head slumps sideways, chin dipping over his shoulder with a boneless, slack motion—his neck crumpling in folds like a crushed accordion. Torn cartilage has ruptured through the skin in serrated ridges—throat split in uneven seams. Blood leaks from the corner of his mouth in languid, syrupy strands, tracking down his collarbone and soaking into his shoulder crook. His scalp is torn in raw patches, shredded where the windshield flayed it open—wet flesh puckered and clinging in uneven flaps. I kill the engine.

When I step out, the night inhales.

Glass crunches under my boots as I approach. It smells like burnt plastic and iron. I tug his door open and the remaining glass shards rattle to the ground.

His body has slumped forward. The cartilage in his neck bulges through torn skin like bone scaffolding—wet, ridged, trying to hold shape. Blood mats his scalp in thick ropes, clumping into his hair in a brittle, merlot-crusted shell. His mouth gapes slack, lips split and sagging into a softened expression—something vacant. It's better this way—absent of performance. No smirk, no pretense. Honest. Just ruined symmetry that feels serene in its ugliness. Like his face was waiting to be emptied. There's something almost beautiful about the stillness. Not the man, but the shape of him now. The way his body and his car form a single broken vessel. Man and machine, paused in the moment of transformation—aborted from automotive utero.

I place two fingers gently on the side of his neck. Cold. The skin slips beneath my touch, tissue softened, cartilage pliable where it's torn. I slip my fingers past his broken lips, dragging them along the slick gums. Warm, pulpy, like overripe fruit rotting. My other hand presses against his chest, flattening the blood-wetted fabric, gaining traction. There's no rise. No movement. Just the static hush of cooling metal and a faint drip from the broken radiator. His lips cling to my fingers—sluggish suction, like soft gristle trying to pull them back in as I drag them out. Spittle gloves my hand in a gunky coating.

I linger. It's not desire. Not exactly. It's curiosity. Detachment. A kind of reverence for the vacancy left behind. It's less about the person, more about the orifice. I unbuckle my belt and smear my fingers along the inside of my cheeks until they're slick with spit. Then, I wrestle my jeans down my thighs and choke my cock in a shaky, pasty palm. Reach in, fist a tangle of his matted hair, and drag his head to my navel. Pinch— between finger and thumb. I press my cock between his slack lips and carve out a new inner sanctum within his carcass. The lips chafe from the punishing rhythm and become rubbery. I want to give him one final, malformed rebirth before his last breath folds into nothing.

In the silence, the night folds inward.

STANTON: INSTINCT

The laptop washes me in a stark white pulse. I shift against the couch, legs numb from being folded under me, stiff from hunching over the coffee table and combing through case files. Behind the glow of the screen, the rest of the room has sunk into darkness. The floor lamp in the corner flickers again, briefly warping the edges of my focus—a signal to wind down for the night. I don't. I adjust my glasses on the bridge of my nose and resume scrolling through crime scene photos. The evidence only seems to get murkier. It's terrifying to swim in a river when you can't see the bottom. Anything could be down there. I just need a glimmer—some shape, some sign—paving a path through the algae.

I toss my glasses onto the table and rub my temples. The flickering lamp stares back at me from its reflection in an empty bourbon glass, still stuck to a dried ring on the wood. It goads me to refill it. I ignore it, lean back, and tilt my head toward the ceiling, tracing shadows in the popcorn texture. Their patterns come alive behind the fan's droning revolutions.

A newspaper flutters at the end of the couch. The latest article confirms what the public hadn't wanted to believe: the killer is still out there. The report paints a fresh tableau of carnage, feeding the public's hunger for drama, justice, or whatever it is they're hoping to see when they read this kind of thing.

How lucky am I to have landed a case this outlandish?

I lean forward again, grab a manila folder from the stack, and flip through the photos. Dogs, gutted. Bowed into horseshoe shapes, bodies piled against backyard fences like snapped branches. Jowls shattered. Bones pushing through matted fur. One report details a dog found beheaded, ears torn from its skull. The teeth removed. Always the teeth.

The lamp flickers again. And I'm back there. Rewind. The interrogation room. My memory rolls like old film. Fast-forward. There's something about their modus operandi that ties them together. Pause. Something in the conversation. A thread I haven't followed. Play:

The interrogation room screamed when the steel door opened, hinges shrieking in protest. A single bulb hung overhead in a metal canopy, flickering. The light painted razor shadows across the concrete walls, harsh and dizzying. It reminded me of the nightlight projector I had as a kid, except this one cast barbs instead of constellations. I had a knot in my chest about this arrest, and I couldn't place it. Something felt wrong. Maybe that's just instinct, some primordial muscle flexing in the background of my brain.

I took my seat, opened the folder, and spread photos and documents across the table. The man across from me sat crooked, eyes on the wall, fingers scraping his scalp. His hair had been shaved close, leaving patchy spots and visible scabs that he rubbed until they bled. His legs jittered under the table, steady pulse. He could feel me watching. He looked down at his shackled feet, his twitching intensifying. The metal chair screeched as it shifted—like scraping a chalkboard. Goosebumps pinpricked my flesh, pinched my arms. The orange jumpsuit hung on his frame like wet cloth, accentuating his skeletal form. Too big. Too empty. He leaned into his cuff chain and dragged it across his cheek like it might undo something.

"I want to ask you a few questions," I said, laying a photo down between us. It was a male victim. Jaw crudely shattered, incisions carved in the corners of the mouth, and lips pulled back like a withered anglerfish. The face was more blood than expression. Facial nuances misconstrued. "Do you know this man? Is he familiar?"

He glanced at the photograph, then shrank into himself. The chain rattled again. Eyes squeezed shut. I thought I heard a whisper—low, unintelligible—but I couldn't tell if it was for me or someone else that only he could see. So, I let the silence hold.

"The dogs you mutilated," I said, trying to keep my voice even, though my anger was beginning to catch in my throat. "Why remove their teeth?"

He whispered something again. This time his legs began to slow. He swallowed, tilted his head, and finally looked at me—holding a glare at my chest.

"I wanted to make them beautiful," he said softly. "They deserved that. To be beautiful. To be fixed. To be loved."

"That's what you call it?" I snapped. "Is that why you mutilated those men? They needed to be fixed too?"

"People can't be fixed," he said. "Even if you were to remove everything."

My pulse stilled.

"What do you mean by that?"

"If you remove everything, there's still a trail," he said. "You cut off an arm, what they did with it doesn't disappear. Take their tongue, the things they said still exist in someone else. Take their teeth, their bites still bleed."

He was later diagnosed with schizophrenia and substance-induced psychosis. By the time I sat across from him, he'd started to detox. The hallucinations had lessened, according to the medical team. Still, he insisted the voice wasn't gone. That it wasn't something they could cure. It wasn't separate from him. It was him. I didn't want to believe that. But I did.

I skim the newspaper again. This time, I notice something new—something small that hadn't registered before. It's the way the article refers to him—not the man behind bars, the one still prowling the city.

Just one word: *Canine.*

I reread the line. Then again. It's jarring how language can distort a person's image—how fast humanity is stripped away when you name someone after an animal. It reduces him to something feral—an absence, not a name, something else.

The hallway door opens, and a small shape stumbles into the room. I jolt—then exhale when I see it's Lainey, shuffling in with weary eyes and sheep-print pajamas. I glance at the laptop, at the case files spread around me, then back at her.

"There's a man in my room," she whispers.

"A man?" I keep my voice calm. "What does he look like?"

"I don't know," she says. "He's all shadowy."

"Mom?" Preston's voice breaks the silence as he emerges from his room. He's already taller than me. Shoulders wide. Somewhere along the line he became a man while I wasn't looking. I don't like that thought.

"You two go back to sleep," I say, smiling gently. "I've still got some work." I pause. Remind myself: these moments matter. Even if they're interruptions. Maybe especially because they are. "Will you take Lainey back to her room and look around? She says there's a shadowy man in there."

"Sure," he sighs, reluctant but soft. "Everything okay?"

I nod and fold the paper aside.

"Promise. Your dad will be back from his work trip in a couple days. Think about something fun we can all do together, alright?"

"Sure," he says, and guides Lainey by her shoulders back toward her room.

He flicks on the light, peeks inside, and guides her in. "See?" he says. "No one here. Monsters aren't real unless you let them be."

MIRAGE

I'm lying on a plastic, teal chaise lounge by the pool. The frayed edges itch my back whenever I shift, the plastic sticking to my sweat-slicked skin beneath the sun's relentless glare. I'm wearing scratched sunglasses. The sun fractures through their lenses, splintering across a thin veil of clouds.

Next to me, Casey lies face down on another chaise lounge, one cheek poking through the plastic bands. Her sunglasses sit askew and she's wearing a ragged straw hat we once pulled from a dumpster behind her apartment complex.

A stray cat had been curled inside it, probably no older than a few months. Its neck was thin, like an uncooked spaghetti noodle. I remember lifting it from the hat by the scruff, cradling it in my hand, and dropping it into the hollow belly of the dumpster. The lip of the bin had scorched my arms—sunbaked metal branding raw skin. My flesh blistered in pale, swollen pockets. While I nursed the burn, Casey had picked up the hat by its crumpled brim and scrunched it in her hands. She shot me a half-smile through cracked lips, flashing her degraded teeth. The cat started whining, then crying. She placed the hat on my head and told me to pose like one of those musicians people always say I look like—ignoring the petty yelping. But that's Casey—aloof, distant, tuning out the sound of anything outside of her attention. I think that's what I like most about her. She doesn't notice much of anything. Especially me.

She raises her arm steadily, her bones realigning beneath the skin. Her body's a milky mannequin, ambiguous in its hollow outlines. She scratches at a sore below her ear, splitting it open again. Dried blood cakes beneath a chipped fingernail, her teal polish eroded and oxidized like a leaking battery. Cheese grater scabs flake from her skin.

"I met this guy at the open casket," I say. The words hang in the heat for a second. I don't know why I bring him up—maybe it's the heat, maybe it's Casey. With her, there's a kind of quiet. An emptiness that feels safe to echo in.

"Loverboy?" she jokes, still picking at her skin.

"He didn't cry," I say. "Not once. Or—I don't think he did." I glance down at my wrist. The watch face is fractured, but I try to read it anyway. My skin's starting to tan, but under the band, there's a sickly strip of pale lemon flesh. It reminds me I'm still rotting—that my body is fucked.

"And what does that say about him?" she asks. She shifts again, her body tightening and relaxing under her seaweed-toned swimsuit. It sucks up into her rectal cavity and I imagine it making an airy pop when her clench releases. "Or does that say something about you?"

I recoil slightly. The question feels intrusive. "I don't know. I think I just need to talk to him again, you know? Get this rumination out of me, or whatever."

"You should," she says.

When Casey and I first met, she had a thing for me. Back then, the scabs were new, fewer. She used to hold on to that infatuation. I never gave her much back, but she still clung to the idea of me like it meant something. She probably still does. People cling to the things they'll never obtain because letting go means their time was wasted. Now, she's all sores and silence. Maybe it's the heroin, maybe it's just who she became. Either way, her vacancy keeps pulling me back. Not because I want to fuck it, not exactly. But because I like the idea of being inside something so far gone it can't feel me there.

"Hey," she rasps, then clears her throat. "What do you make of this?"

"What do you mean?" I tilt my head toward her. She shifts onto her back, joints dangling over the sides of the chaise lounge like a broken windchime.

"Sometimes I feel like I'm not here," she says. Her jaw moves in sluggish, grinding ticks. "Like I'm in a different place. I see these shadows. I know, I sound crazy, but sometimes they're full of people. Watching. Talking. I feel them when I'm working—when I'm spread open for men. And they are too—spread open. Like they're copying me. Mimicking. Mocking. And I think—I belong with them. Like this body isn't really mine, and something's holding it hostage. I think about that other place— what it's like over there instead of here."

I stare down at the end of the chaise lounge. My toenails are bruised with soft purples and yellows. I want to tell her she's not making sense. But I don't. Fact is, while she's rambling about shadow people, I can see my own—a figure kneeling at the edge of the pool. It doesn't move. I can't tell if it's looking at me, through me, or at nothing at all. The water behind it sloshes quietly over the tile.

"Our bodies are all collateral," I say. "If not one way, another."

Casey doesn't respond. Her face slackens like she's drifted off. Then she stirs. "Hey," she says, like she's remembering her place again. "Did you hear about that guy they found out in the woods?" She rolls, places the hat over her face like she's hiding from the sun—or the thought. "Grisly story, Mackey says." Mackey is either her client or her pimp depending on his mood. Neither is preferable. "They found him torn up. Hanging out of his car. Died fast, I guess."

"I don't know. Stewart might've mentioned it."

"They thought it was random at first—some crime of passion or whatever. But Mackey says two of his teeth were gone. Same as the others."

The shadow at the edge of the pool is gone.

"Same person, then," I say. "Same as the others."

"Yeah," she says. "But why would you stop at just two?"

"I don't know, seems like taking them all out would be better head."

It's a joke. Sort of. She doesn't laugh. I glance over and her head's started to tilt, her jaw slack. The heroin's kicked in. She's gone again.

PIERCE: CONTACT

I release my grip on the steering wheel, noticing how tightly I've been clutching it—white-knuckled, suffocating the lining beneath my fingers. Heat pulses through the windshield, cooking the fabric of my suit and baking into my thighs. My eyelids are tender, heavy from lack of sleep. I replay the call in my head, picking through the details Cameron gave about the scene I'm approaching. Then my thoughts drift—Stanton. What she looks like now. Whether she'll recognize me. Whether I'll recognize myself.

I rub at the razor burn under my chin like I'm reading braille in its bumpy irritation. Up ahead, shapes along the roadside start to sharpen—lumps growing into forms. I ease off the gas and guide the car toward the shoulder, pulling in behind a warped heap of steel.

Officers wade through withered grass, dusting their boots with gravel. One points a gloved hand and calls to another. A forensic photographer crosses in front of the hood. He tilts his chin toward the telephone pole like he's watching clouds rearrange into God.

I step out. Wind slices across my face—dry, sharp—deafening gusts biting the muted landscape. The wrecked vehicle is more contorted than I'd pictured. The bumper's been crushed inward, metal torqued into thorns, loose panels littered around the chassis in molted shells. Yellow tape crisscrosses the site. Evidence placards punctuate the soil. The photographer circles the car, limbs rotating in exaggerated vulture revolutions—taunting the wreckage. I cross to the trunk of a patrol cruiser and pull on a pair of latex gloves. They pinch at my wrists, choking their circulation and dampening them in sweat. The lightbar pulses in cadence with the throb behind my eyes.

Up ahead, another forensic technician crouches beside the open driver's door. The corpse is bloated, its skin distended from heat and the oppressive churning of maggots beneath ruptured tissue. I fish a notepad and pen from my jacket and inch around the front of the vehicle, ducking low for a moment for a better view.

Stanton rises into frame on the far side of the car. Her head appears above the roofline. She hasn't seen me yet. Another photographer stands beside her, angling the camera screen in her vision. She points toward the rear bumper, says something indistinct, then follows the man's movement with her eyes. Then her gaze jumps—locks on mine. She smiles, just a flicker, lips pale and brief in their curve. Her ponytail is gone, replaced with a short bob that curls beneath her ears. It's darker now—or dyed. She circles the pole and approaches, gravel crunching beneath her boots.

"I just got here," she says, raising her voice over the wind and low murmur of the scene. "About thirty minutes ago."

"What do we know?" I ask. The photographer backs away from the body, clearing a path.

"Doesn't look like an accident," she says.

I crouch beside the doorframe. Her voice dulls beneath the roof. The smell is immediate—dense, sour. It grips the inside of my throat and tastes of rotten egg and singed fur. There's an acidic sharpness that turns my stomach before my mind can name it.

"He was repositioned postmortem," she says.

I don't understand until my gaze lands on the head. The jaw dangles unhinged and sagging from torn sockets. His upper lip is flayed open, peeled back in jagged ribbons like shredded beef. The top row of teeth is rammed into the steering wheel, embedded deep in the vinyl. Blood clots along the gumline, dark and crusting. It takes a moment before I realize—some of the teeth are gone.

"He's lost teeth," I say, standing upright.

"Two, to be exact," Stanton replies. She glances into the car again, then meets my eyes. She doesn't look surprised. "We're running DNA now. Forensics thinks we can lift a few clean prints from the interior— off the steering column or gear shift. Best case, we match them to other scenes. Worst case, we hit the same wall."

"No hits so far?" I ask.

"Only on the victims." She pinches the bridge of her nose. "This guy's not in any database. No prints, no DNA match, not even a misdemeanor."

"That's rare," I say.

Her eyes are ringed with exhaustion—or something closer to corrosion. She looks like she hasn't slept in days. I recognize an edge in her voice—a harshness. Not directed at me, just everything at once. She stares at the body. Sunlight slips across her jaw, catching the curve of her cheek and fine strands of hair twitching under her ears. "There's a bar a few miles back," she says. "Off the highway. Not much else out here besides the interstate. Might be nothing, but I'm heading there next. Someone might've seen them."

"Makes sense," I say. I consider offering to handle it myself—but stop short. She's sharp enough to catch condescension even when it's not there, and if she thinks I'm undermining her now, I'll lose any chance of earning her trust. "I'll stick around a little longer," I add. "See what else turns up. I'll run the plate, get a name." She watches me for a beat—eyes steady, measuring something. Then the wind cuts through again, broad and biting.

"I know we didn't work closely before," she says, her voice softening, "but I'm glad you came back, sir."

The *sir* lands sharp. I might outrank her on paper, but hearing it out loud underscores the distance time's put between us.

"I'm about ready to lose this jacket," I say, shifting the subject. "Didn't think I'd shed my lizard skin."

"That's what a few years on the East Coast will do to you," she says, heading back to her car.

I don't think she's ever been to the East Coast.

CONSUMPTION

I crane my neck back against the sofa, mouth slack, eyes locked on the flickering television. Red streamers crawl across the screen and dissolve into vapor at the edges. My arms dangle limp beside my bare torso, numb hoses stretched over cracked leather. Every so often, a rush shivers through my body—spiking through my chest and lighting my nerves with stinging pressure. I exhale hard. Pleasure blooms into euphoric etchings. My anatomy sloughs off its casing, sucked toward the television's glow, tangled in its static. The scars running down my chest and waist rise with each breath—inhale, swell, deflate. Their pencil-thin lips beckon mine to align into theirs—into some communal maw of hunger. I stare into them and my nose throbs again. Blood trickles over my lip. I plug my nostrils with two fingers, painting them in a velour sheen. The taste of salt and tin coats my tongue. An amphetamine shiver sinks into my gums. I work it in with my fingers, massaging the tender lining, feeling the pressure behind my teeth. My neck pulses, jaw tightens. Another indulgent breath escapes me, and my cock worms with a hard pulse against my jeans.

"What happened to the car now?" Stewart groans, appearing behind the couch. He shuffles into the room and braces one ragged arm against the leather. I turn my face slightly, cheek grazing the headrest, dragging a squeak from the material. It sounds frightened. The stiff leather drives a cold needle into my neck and cheek, prying my mouth ajar and honing each exhale into something sharp between my bared teeth. Stewart staggers beside me, knees bent at wrong angles, posture collapsing—scarecrow puppet. He hovers over my flaccid torso, waist level with my eyes. His body quivers like it might splinter. My skin buzzes. Blood vessels seed and wilt synchronously within my meat. Dried blood hardens across my lip and clots in my nose—webbed in a porous seal, stiff and obstructive.

"Are you high?" he says in a debatably rhetorical tone, crouching closer. His bony fingers clamp my face, pressing into my cheeks, skin clumping around his joints. His bones dig into mine. He pulls my lips into a warped grin, puckering them grotesquely, and jerks my head up to face him. His breath reeks of onion and coffee. Burst vessels spiderweb across the whites of his eyes and his skin flakes from their corners. And then I see myself reflected, pupils stretched wide, swimming in black. My pupils flood past their sockets, dilated into pulped saucers and dissolving into spongy halos. Their waterlogged rings smear a damp film over my vision and dull my sight into an unformed blur devoid of color.

"Jesus," he mutters, letting my head drop. My neck flops over the back of the couch. The leather hisses again. So does my throat. "What did you hit? The headlight's smashed and the passenger side's dented. What if you'd gotten killed? Driving around spun out like this?"

My head is concrete. Inside, my mind sprawls—hollow, expansive—and my vision is glassy, feathered along its edges.

I chew my bottom lip and try to look up at him, but my gaze barely rises to his belt buckle—rusted chrome etched in cursive script. Outline craggy, smoldering metal. I reach out, fingers crawling along his jeans, clutching at the stiff fabric. His thighs twitch under my palms, brittle as dry bark, like I'm going to rupture his groin. Drip sap.

"I'm high," I admit, attempting seduction, but struggling to orchestrate language. The words drag in a sluggish drawl. "I need things. You like that I need things." I slide my fingers to his belt, tug at the buckle. I'm not fully aware of what I'm doing. I reach for the top button on his jeans. His hand clamps down on my wrist. The pressure shoots through my arm like fire, seeping pleasure. My breath hitches, saliva froths. My cock throbs again, straining against denim. I pin it down, palm firm against the denim like it's gnawing at the zipper—restraining the impulse. Clamp it shut. Muzzle the hunger.

"I need you to be careful," he says. "You need to treat my things with the same respect you treat me." His words swirl. I barely hear them.

"This is transactional," I remind him. I hate the way he sounds sentimental. Whatever charge was lingering in my tone burns off. The atmosphere curdles, tightens. His nose wrinkles, jaw clenched, like he's winding up for a retort. But we both know he doesn't have one. He says nothing. He knows I'm right. He drags his thumb across my crusted lip to clean my face, then walks out of the room. I slump deeper into the couch, the television's static swimming in and out of spatial haze.

It's night when the high finally thins out. My body hums with a sour ache, the crash settling in. I can feel my limbs again—stretched rubber, pulled taut from the inside. My skeleton scrapes against skin—straining to come out, exit. I'm still slouched on the couch, head tilted back. I might've passed out, but if I did, I wouldn't have noticed. My vision's mostly cleared, though something still blurry, muddled—like a film over glass. I glance down. My jeans are half-undone. At some point, I must've masturbated. My jeans hang low on my hips, and my cock flops limp like a dehydrated earthworm—shriveled like it's baked in the sun too long. My pocked ass stings raw, skin flaring as I shift upright. A crusted come smear along my stomach flakes off into milky, curdled bits that collect into my navel. I shift upright, joints creaking, and realize the sun has drowned—darkness pooling across the room, unnoticed until it had swallowed everything. I rub my face, pressing the pitted trenches beneath my eyes. The skin is tender, thin as paper, and bruised by every hour I haven't slept.

There's an incongruity between my aching limbs and the stillness in my chest. I move like I'm wired into a body I didn't build—joysticks plugged into wet meat, reacting half a second behind thought. It's a vessel underneath this sallow husk. I'm not bloated in rage, contrary to reactionary lashings. It's vacancy with an edge—the default presentation when you're internally devoid. Amphetamine wet dreams run on collusion—some gutted conspiracy clawing for an outcome. I don't know if it even exists. People say temptation is a feeling. They're wrong. It's a function. It calcifies, sharpens when you fall back into the old rhythm. Observe. Mimic. Mirror. Manipulate. Imagine how much power a praying mantis would hold if it asphyxiated its lover in a noose—sustained control, watched the life fade—rather than just biting off its head. That's real authority. It could inspire religion. Control is my omen—the locusts await instruction. Execution is mundane outside of the human sheath. I want to crawl into omnipotence from the inside out—wrap their organ sheets inside me, contort myself into what it truly means to walk in someone's skin. I wish it were practical to peel flesh like a tarp, but there's never a clean break. All I ever get is their bite—their heat slick on my tongue, their scream like gristle. I won't spit it out.

But then there's Percy. There's something unmoving, fortified in him. Some impenetrable boundary I haven't figured out how to erode. Albeit, a perception, my proficiency in translating absent character expositions is immaculate. Still, the absence of intrusion is loud. I read people well. I dissect their physique. But with him, I get nothing. There's no clarity when I imagine deconstructing him. No blueprint. There's a barricade between my intention and his intramural governance. Just static between want and will. That makes him different. That makes me need it more. He can pulverize my cavities into mulch, and I'd be compelled to drown in them. I'd let him turn me inside out and feed on the pulp. He can devour my ashes under his violating tongue and interbreed their flecks with my come. He can choke down my spermicide paste. If I let him.

STANTON: LATENCY

I slide into a booth tucked in the far back of the café, close to the kitchen doors. Crumbs scatter across the table—flaky remnants of pastries half-forgotten. My forehead pulses, feverish, and the crumbs blur behind my vision, flickering like the ruins of sandcastles. Fragments of something once constructed, now crumbled.

The entrance chimes. I glance up and catch the bell above it jangle as Pierce walks in. His hair's parted down the center, which sharpens his boxy features—makes him look older. He stalls awkwardly near the entrance, fists shoved into his jacket pockets, scanning the café. A stray dog on the shoulder of the highway, gauging whether the oncoming traffic is worth it. I consider waving him over, but the migraine's behind my eyes now, thudding too hard for generosity. So, I just stare, willing him to see me. Part of me is curious if the dog will take the risk, part of me wonders if he'll bolt—part of me hopes he will.

Eventually, he clocks my slouched silhouette and approaches, weaving past a server who's obviously stoned. His boots clap against the laminate floor, the sound peeling ribbons from the inside of my skull. He slides into the booth across from me and offers a faint grin. It only sharpens the pressure at my temples. I ignore it. I shift my focus to my messenger bag and start sorting through the case files. I pull what's relevant, stack it, spread it across the table.

"I trust you've got something," Pierce says. His harsh smoker's voice is hoarse and sounds like my father's—perpetually hushed, like a confessional cadence.

"I do." I pass him a folder. "Bartender remembered seeing the victim a few times. He said he was with a man—mid-twenties, slim, hair waxed back like porcupine quills. He didn't recognize him. Said he wasn't the usual type that came in. Cameron's working on getting a warrant for the camera feed. He'll pull whatever footage he can."

Pierce finally frees his fists from his pockets and flips through the folder. He squints, attempting to read my jumbled chicken scratch in the margins. Then, he lingers too long on a page, gaze sliding off the text, staring like it's revealing something beyond the words. Like the victim's mangled ligaments expose a deep-seeded clandestine allegory. A streak of sunlight pushes through the window and cuts across my face. The pressure behind my eyes surges, migraine intensifying.

"Pierce?" I break in, sharper than I intend to. He blinks, recalibrating from the trance. "You following me?"

"Right. Yeah. Sorry," he mutters, shifting his gaze back down to the paper.

A server stops at our table—heels, black polo, hair in a tight ponytail that looks a little like mine used to. She's got a cleft lip that exaggerates her toothy smile. We place our orders. I can't help but think her face belongs intermingled with the disfigured victims.

"It sounds like the bartender might be worth a second pass," Pierce says.

The server returns with our coffee, and a silence settles between us. Plates clatter. Conversations swirl in the background. Everything grows louder—like the soundscape itself is pulling away from me. Pierce watches the steam waft off his cup. It ripples like the surface of a hot spring. I think of my honeymoon. My husband's skin after hours soaking—soft, dissolving at the edges. I remember touching his shoulder and thinking it might come away in my hand. I don't remember the last time I had a moment like that.

"I'll check with toxicology," I say, swallowing the memory. "They recovered paint chips from the other vehicle. We've got tire tread impressions too—might help us narrow down the type of vehicle. Probably not an exact match, but it's a start."

"The car was hit hard on the back left. The bumper's a mess. There's black paint scuffed near the fuel cap," he says. "Odontologist pulled a mold of the bite marks in the steering wheel. They're taking a closer look at the victim's remaining teeth and checking for trace fluids in what's left of the victim's mouth."

"Good." I watch his attention slip again. "Pierce, you're not here."

He doesn't deny it. Just breathes in, then says, "My wife killed herself." He pauses. "Ex-wife, technically. That's why I came back. To try to fix what's left. You remember how I transferred back to New York after the last case?"

I nod. I remember whispers, muttered theories in the hallways. I didn't engage. I never cared much for the gossip. We weren't close—

some overlap in police work, the occasional shared elevator ride. I respected him. He was one of the few who seemed to care about the job. Too much, perhaps. That's what the whispers always said.

"She hated me by the end. My son, too." He sips from his mug. "I didn't come back for the funeral. I sent him a check for the expenses—figured that was what he would've wanted. But the guilt hit later, like it always does, so I bought a plane ticket. I've been trying to act like this is just about work, but I've got to bite the bullet."

"I take it your son didn't give you the warmest welcome back?"

He shakes his head. "I haven't mustered the willpower to call him yet. I think about it—then I stare at the ceiling and drink instead. Work helps distract. Bourbon helps more."

"Call him," I urge.

He doesn't answer that. Just sips again. "Cameron called right as I was boarding, told me about this case. He said it wasn't like anything he's seen. Someone who slips through the cracks so seamlessly." He pauses, watching the last ribbons of steam unravel from his mug. "Out here, crimes don't feel curated. They're blunt, sloppy. This one… this one's different. So, what am I doing here? Pretending this is a job and not a distraction. Pretending if I ignore the mess behind me, it'll stop growing."

I clench my jaw. I've never been good at this kind of talk. I envy how direct he can be, how little he seems to care what anyone thinks. But I'm not the one he should be unpacking with. I glance toward the walkway. "I'm going to hit the restroom before we go."

The door creaks shut behind me. The restroom is as worn out as I feel. Smooth jazz drones from a speaker above the mirror. The sink is chipped and the faucet is coated in water stains. I splash my face. My cheeks are raw and warm—tight under my eyes. I try to smooth the bags out with my fingers. It doesn't work. My shoulders ache. I roll them, hear the pop of tight joints. I duck into a stall despite the putrid smell. The music bubbles louder, saxophone humming. The walls are littered in graffiti—obscene sketches, hearted initials, stick drawings, things that meant something to someone at some time. Near the bottom of the stall door, a carving catches my eye. Cut deep. Red marker bleeds across the letters: *fuck the Canine Killer*. Crude teeth are drawn around it.

When I return, Pierce stands. He folds his napkin and sets it down, eyes already somewhere else. We head toward the front. I mention the bathroom scrawl. I hope it'll snap him back. It doesn't.

"Call me when you've got something new," he says. "I'm going to stop by the office and update Cameron, just so he knows we're not standing around with our dicks in the wind."

"Go see your son," I say, cutting in abruptly. He nods, then walks to his car.

A weight settles in my chest—an unease that he's opening another door without closing the last. He's not here with me, not really. There's only so many doors a person can leave swinging before they all slam shut at once. What happens to everyone still standing in the threshold? And at what junction does fear finally convince the body to collapse?

CONSTRICT

I drag the paintbrush along the warped windowsill, laying down a thick coat of white over its splintered edge. The ladder trembles as I shift, hanging on its fiberglass spine like an aloof sloth. I'm perched outside the funeral home, arms looped around the rungs, wondering how much force it would take to snap my neck against the asphalt if I fell just right.

The sill has rotted, flaking in withered strips that crumble like dry mulch. Stewart's latest directive wrangles my attention toward another half-assed restoration. Hardwood concealment. Atonement for his—or our—battered hearse. Reasonable enough. I grunt my acceptance through clenched teeth, lips tacky with heat. These are the junctures that test my edges, moments when even the most menial task feels like an autopsy of my own deficiencies. Truth is, I need him too. And that truth feels repulsive in my mouth. I won't let him know it. I barely let myself believe it.

I wipe the sweat back through my hair, bite down on the paintbrush, and hang there for a moment—one arm fumbling in my jeans pocket for a cigarette. I descend, step by step, and spit the brush into the bucket at my feet. A glob of paint splashes across a parking stall, cream-slicking the faded white lines and trailing over the concrete marker like spilt milk.

As I light up, a car creeps around the corner and slows to a stop at the side of the building. I don't recognize it—probably some blubber-faced mourner circling back for a forgotten keepsake. I drift toward the lot's edge and step into the sun, squaring off with the grille. It lets out a throaty hum—old engine, reconditioned—while condensation leaks from the front like it's salivating. The hood ornament is clearly aftermarket, a cheap knockoff pretending to be something classic. The discoloration gives it away. The passenger window rolls down as I approach.

"I thought I'd find you here," Percy says, lowering his sunglasses and staring at me from above the rim. The bridge of his nose is rosy and peeling, sunburned raw. Greasy strands fall over the lenses, and the rest of his hair is matted into a sandy wave.

It feels like an interruption. The paint drying across my skin, crusting in the hairs on my arms, makes me think of his pale flesh—what it might feel like to retract from him—elbow-deep, wrist trapped in some tight, clenching place. The thought knots something in my gut. The context disrupts my body. I know I offered the proverbial handshake.

"Yeah," I say, exhaling a ribbon of smoke across the hood of his car. I lean into the window, and the trim is scalding hot. "Just cleaning up. Stewart's inside doing detail work on the next client—checking for blemishes I might've missed. The guy was crushed under tractor wheels—flattened his legs. They look like kettle chips."

Percy glances through the windshield at my brushwork, eyes trailing the frame. "It's a good thing no one will care to remember what got him there," he says. "Stewart doesn't give you a break, does he?"

"No," I shrug. "He wants me to learn the ropes—get comfortable, or whatever. I guess the idea is I'll take over someday. Not unrealistic of a prospect, given his age."

Percy nods, but there's something in the way his lip curves—hinting at confusion or disinterest.

I'd prefer the latter.

"Is he your father or something?" he asks. Déjà vu. We've done this dance.

"No. Both my parents are dead." I blow another smoke stream past his mirror. "Part of why I have an affinity for this kind of work, I guess. Stewart's the closest thing I've had to a father. That's probably why I hate him. Comes with the territory."

He starts to smile, then catches himself. I can't tell if he doesn't believe me or doesn't want to believe me. Either way, it fractures the moment—or it's just the setting. I should smear his stupid grin with the dried paint cracking in my palms.

"What are you doing here?" I ask, flicking the cigarette to the pavement and grinding its tobacco innards until it wheezes out its last breath.

"I thought we could pick up where we left off," Percy says. "I don't know. You've got to start somewhere when things change, don't you?"

"No," I say, pulling open the passenger door. "But I'll go along for the ride."

Percy doesn't speak much. When he does, his words are careful—robust in flavor, like each syllable's been handpicked from a curated platter. His lexicon is a charcuterie board, and he lays it out like it costs him something. Sentences accrue interest. I'll collect on the debt. That restraint, that economy, builds a cold precision in him that draws me closer. Goosebumps rise along my arms, subtle cues alluding to entanglement. His expression mimics the sensation—unreadable. I think it's rare. Then again, my perception is prone to being skewed. The closest liaisons between myself and genuine connection are a junkie whore and a dementia-shelled senior with pudding thoughts. Maybe this is how "normal" manifests.

"I want to take you into the marina," he says. "I watch people there. The way they weave in and out—it's how I imagine the inside of a sewing machine might look. They wind together, and if you tug hard enough, the threads snap."

The sentiment lands clumsy. My attraction flinches. I expect his verbiage to blossom further into metaphor, but he doesn't. It ends there—flat. Something in me recoils. His vocal floridity decomposes, and for the first time, I question what he means. I find myself parsing him again, imagining phantasmic needle-thin strands tugged through his body. His pores are like orange peel shavings glued to his bones—dimpled, sun-stained. I picture his cherry nipples pinched until they bruise and burst. His cock erect and twitching, balls taut and covered in fine hair like kiwi skin. I imagine baring them in my teeth, splitting the membrane beneath with a scrape and lapping up their scrotal mucus. I want to press our bodies into the horn of some vile cornucopia—cheeks parted like spoiled plums, devoured until there's nothing left but spit-polished pulp. Ass presented for mastication—I engorge on his delectable constitution.

The seatbelt digs into my sternum, clamps my chest—restraint. I can feel my organs strumming with my heartbeat, a throb echoing beneath the tension. I glance over and see the slight rise of his sternum beneath his tight shirt. He swallows, and the movement in his throat clicks like a shotgun being pumped. My jeans pull tight across my lap, heat pools in my groin, and tender pangs flex my hardening cock.

He pulls into a gravel lot and kills the engine.

Salt air floods in as I step out. I shift my jeans, peel them from where they cling to my sweated thighs, and palm myself through the fabric, repositioning. I slam the door. A second later, Percy's door slams too. I wait—just a beat—for the pressure in my jeans to subside before turning toward him. He's perched on the hood of the car, looking out over the marina. He lifts his shirt to blot sweat from his face, dragging it up over tight abdominals glazed in sweat. The fabric clings to his back, drenched through. His body gleams in the sunlight, cut into hard lines. My neck burns. My forehead prickles and dampens. I light a cigarette.

He scans the docks, eyes flitting like they're tracking something.

"What are you looking for?" I ask, watching him from the corner of my eye.

"My mother keeps her boat here," he says. "Present tense. Because even dead, she still has a stranglehold on the better part of me."

The ocean laps against the docks. Gulls shriek and waddle through crowds, pecking at crumbs. Metal clanks against metal in the distance—steel beams, rigging, the hum of a wind-churned marina. People cluster in loose groups and shuffle around the squawking birds.

"If I remember right," Percy mutters, nodding toward a far dock, "it's down that way." He starts walking. I stay still a moment, watching his body dissolve into sunlight. His shape burns against my vision. I clench my jaw, trying to pull the heat down from where it pulses in my lap and engorges my cock. Then I follow.

A man bumps my shoulder. I'm a few paces behind Percy, and the jolt knocks me slightly off balance. The man catches my sleeve instinctively, his grip clumsy and warm. A multicolored peace sign keychain dangles from his car keys, and one of the jagged ends presses into my forearm. He twists his wrist in a twitchy, effeminate motion— nervous, uncertain of the right response.

My ears flush hot. I can feel the blood rushing to them in waves, swelling up in a deep flush. I don't know if he notices—if he's gauging my reaction or just surviving it. Inflamed images flare—sharp, brief, impossible to interpret. Percy hasn't turned around. I don't think he's realized I've fallen behind. The man starts to straighten up, his posture loosening like he's been released from my grip. Relief floods him too quickly. It makes me wonder if he's hoping for something. His mouth curves awkwardly, like he's trying to smile, but there's something else beneath it—some flicker of acquiescence. His eyes are shallow tide pools, reflective and bottomless. It feels like he's surrendering himself.

"You good?" I ask. I don't care. My palm slides along the small of his back, steady and intentional, accepting the submission. I let it linger there, like I'm calming him. Or claiming him. His button-down is tucked neatly into his waistband, patterned in hammerhead sharks that match the washed-out gray of his eyes. I pull my hand away and it leaves a damp imprint. His skin glows a warm, olive tone—sun-glossed and enviable, like a bronzed basketball smoothed of its texture. My skin is weakened, prone to sunbeam abuse, peeling like the flesh of a roasted, eviscerated potato.

"I'm sorry," he says, fidgeting with his keychain. "Yeah, I'm fine."

"What's your name?" I ask. The words come out sudden, a little too forward.

"Max," he says. I take the keychain from his hand and turn it in mine, pretending to study it. It's a cheap souvenir from the local welcome center—the kind of place that milks tourists dry with faux charm and inflated pricing. "Got it down the way," he offers. "If you're looking for one."

I let the keychain fall back into his hand and glance past him. Percy's crouched near a dock, coaxing a seagull to converse with him. It doesn't flinch. He whispers something to it and leans in. It lets him. The bird doesn't seem to recognize that it should fear him. Maybe it's right. I turn back to Max.

"I'm actually just visiting," I lie. "I'm looking for a hotel nearby. Know any?"

He nods, pulling his phone from his pocket. He adjusts his baseball cap—beige, fraying at the edges, a sun-faded sports logo ghosting the front. Whatever mascot it used to display is nearly rubbed off, but the outline resembles a piñata.

"Here's where I'm staying," he says, holding out his phone. "It's called The Blue Mist. More motel than hotel, but it's just a few miles north of the marina."

I place my hand on his lower back again and lean in, studying the screen. My hair grazes the brim of his hat, the waxed strands wilting under the contact. I hear the hitch in his breath.

"I'll see you later, then," I say, beginning to turn. "What room number?"

It's a five-minute transaction. My flushed skin begins to cool, ears retreating from their flush back into pale, numb flaps. Mundane—but there's a beauty in vacant exchanges, in meaningless collisions. Obsession recedes for a moment. I detach, and Percy reclaims the vacancy like a leash snapping taut again. Sorry, Percy. He was begging for it.

I meet Percy at the edge of the docks, still crouched low. As I approach, I notice the bird he's watching is suffocating. It isn't a seagull— it's a pigeon. Its neck is jammed inside an empty beer bottle. It flails in erratic shudders, trying to rip free, but the bottle rolls with every movement, dragging its body across the deck. Percy's arms hang loosely over his knees. He doesn't touch the bird. He doesn't attempt to aid it—pull it free. He doesn't snap its neck—kill it. He's just kind of looking at it—watching. The glass glints under the sun, shifting with the bird's frantic movements. I temper my steps. Percy hears me, surely, but doesn't turn.

"Make a new friend?" he asks, calm and distant. I didn't think he'd noticed. My ears heat up again. "The boat's this way." He nods down the dock toward a cream-colored vessel, meshed with algae, crusted in salt.

The pigeon is a foot from the edge. Its wings beat the boards in a chaotic rhythm. My anticipation tongue-kisses moribund gratification.

"I'm going to smoke another cigarette," I lie. "I'll follow in a minute."

He doesn't respond. Just shoves his fists into his pockets, offers a sideways smirk—casual, knowing—and walks away. I watch him disappear down the dock.

I stay. I don't light a cigarette. I stare down at the pigeon as it jerks and spasms, caught in its own reflection. I think Percy liked watching it. I do too. It draws something out of me—pulls a wire between us, stretches it thin. I want to do this together. But not now. In this moment, I'm more selfish. I want to savor the moment for myself. I press my heel against the bottle. Push. There's a low *thunk* as it slips off the dock, a sloshing gulp, then bubbles. I lean over the edge and watch.

When I climb onto the boat, Percy is perched at the bow, legs dangling over the edge. The hull's a faded cream—probably once white, before the sun pressed its breath deep into the fiberglass. He lifts a beer to his lips, throat worming as he swallows. The sunlight catches his sunglasses and refracts back at me, like a mirror translating my movements into something he can parse and consume. Like what I did wasn't private at all. And if he saw it—God, I hope he did—I hope he took it as something meant for him.

"I've got another," Percy calls, lifting a second bottle over his head. "Looks like she left me something half-decent after all. Cheap shit, but you don't drink beer for the taste, right?"

I shuffle forward, gripping the railings, still trying to find my sea legs. He turns, watches me struggle. Raises his eyebrows. Smiles. It's off. Too casual. Like he's hiding something.

DEHISCENCE

"I need you to drop me off somewhere," I say. We've left the marina and are winding back toward the city. My eyes sag in their sockets, and my stomach is churning, constricting my ribs. Hunger has caught up to me— I don't think I've eaten in a day or two. I wonder if it's obvious to Percy that I'm strung out on amphetamines. My shirt clings to me, damp and itchy, stuck to my torso like flypaper. I glance at my arm—it's turning a splotchy pink, creased against jaundiced skin. My neck is probably burnt, too. I feel like a drying onion. Peel me apart, Percy. Strip this flaking suit—I'll make you cry. "It's just a few blocks over."

Percy pulls to the side of the road, just before the apartment complex entrance. I hope he doesn't ask to come with me. I don't want him to meet Casey. Her place is always wrecked. She's always wrecked. I dread the trek across the parking lot, past the pool where we lounge in better weather. But I also dread whatever this thing is that we're continuing. I need to air out my head—this hollow basin balanced on my neck.

I pull the handle and crack the door, slide a cigarette between my teeth. The door creaks open. I stare at the dashboard for a moment, then glance over at Percy. He turns away, stares out his window.

I sit there with the unlit cigarette dangling from my mouth, not sure how to end this. I look at him again, through the windshield, then step out. I'm not used to being dismissed so bluntly.

"Hey—" Percy starts. His sunglasses slide an inch down his nose. He leans over the console, seatbelt stretching across his chest. "I'll call next time," he says, peering through the open door. I place the cigarette between my fingers and crouch, kneeling to meet him at eye level. His skin glistens, salt-slick from the heat. I want to touch it, see if it gives under pressure. My lips feel like they might split if I try to speak. I nod instead, grip the doorframe, and push the door shut. The engine hums louder for a second, and then he drives off—his muffler coughing out a puff of smoke. I open my jaw wide and roll it in my palm, working circulation back into my face. It's gone a bit numb. As the car fades, I think of the pigeon again. I would've liked to see it crushed under his tires, too.

There's a distinction between drowning and crushing. Drowning allows for a final exhale—an involuntary surrender that discharges some flicker of complacency from a man's ungrateful existence. Crushing doesn't concede the same opportunity. It doesn't give you time to ruminate on your being. It blatantly eliminates you under compression— pure, mechanical eradication. The vicissitude between survival and extermination is pulchritudinous regardless of expiration method. I'm not just thinking about animals anymore.

I bang on Casey's door with the side of my fist. The paint is chipped and weathered, flakes drifting down to the doormat like dead skin. The craving's rising—tight and sharp. My throat burns. Muscles cramp into knots. This doesn't happen often. I'm usually too high too often to notice the distance between highs. But now the pressure behind my eyes builds like it's being dredged up by ethereal ladles—scraping against my retinas and teasing the blood vessels to rupture. I need a fresh jolt. Something now.

The curtains are drawn. I watch them stir—just slightly, like breath has slipped through the room. I hear soft footfalls, then shuffling. Then, Casey cracks the door, nudges it open just enough for her to peer through like she always does. It's routine. She motions me in with a twitchy hand from behind the door, swallowed in the apartment's dark. I glance over my shoulder—a habit by now—but something in her movements is wrong. Off-rhythm. The parking lot's empty, except for a few parked cars. When she jerks the door open wider, it leaves a fresh dent in the drywall. She grabs my belt buckle, yanks me inside, then slams the door shut behind us. Her bony finger rises to her lips and her eyes dart back and forth in broken circuits, shoulders hunched like she's hiding. It's more erratic than usual. She's more paranoid than I've seen her in a while. I watch her scuttle to the window, peel back the curtain, then cower back into the room—then do it again. I don't interrupt. The last time I saw her like this she slammed my head into the wall. The dent's probably still here somewhere. It left half my face molted purple for two weeks.

"You shouldn't be here," she whispers. Her pupils are pinpricks, bouncing like jacks. I never liked heroin. "You can't be here." Her fingers start crawling across my shoulders—thin and cold, spiderlike. They creep around my waist, down my back, across my arms. Like she's trying to position me. Or considering where to hide me.

"What's going on, Casey?" I ask.

"Mackey," she says, voice strangled.

"What about him?"

Her head retracts into her shoulders like it's trying to disappear. I scan the apartment. It reeks—acrid, piss—garbage and rot. It could be leaking from the heaps of trash, could be the bathtub again—choking on sewage, painting its porcelain in flecks of shit. That wouldn't be unusual. But it's worse this time. Everything's more gutted. Like she stirred the debris and something came alive—something fungal and buttery—like rupturing spores.

"Look, Casey, I don't have time for this shit," I mutter. "I just need to pick up. That's it."

"Mackey's going to be here any minute," she hisses. "I thought you were him knocking."

"Fuck," I mutter, gritting my teeth. I should be thinking with my head—not my dick. But whatever instinct I'm supposed to have— whatever fear complex—is dulled. Maybe I was born that way, or maybe I've swallowed so many rails of amphetamines that it's just burned out now—melted into some dull ember I can't access anymore. I don't remember if it was ever there. All I remember are the residuals—

sensations my body stores. Anyway, there's always a thrill imagining what Mackey would do inside of me. "Can I still fit in your closet?" I ask. This isn't the first time, and it won't be the last. "You haven't crammed more shit in there? I can still feel the last needle I sat on." I stamp out my cigarette in her curtain. It's starting to look like a hunk of molding cheese—yellowed, pocked with burn holes, frayed at the seams.

"Good idea," she stammers, like we haven't rehearsed this dance a dozen times before. I envy how blissfully oblivious she can get. "Mackey will drop off more." She raises her hands like I might pounce, skittish and twitching.

Then, pounding rattles the door, followed by a low, husky voice—too muffled to make out, but it coils through the room, threatening. Casey startles, then snaps her head toward me, eyes wide and commanding. She waves me back. I slink around the corner without protest. The closet door groans as I pull it open. I duck inside, crouching low and folding in like a cocooned caterpillar. Shirts dangle overhead, and I wedge myself between their polyester husks, buried in scent, dust, and fabric. The front door squeals open. Mackey's hefty footfalls rattle the floor. His voice doesn't need volume to carry. It's built into him—a throaty boom, soaked in smoke and contempt. I can't delineate his words, but I can feel the tone. It's not good. I light another cigarette.

I don't think he'll notice. And if he does? I'm not sure I care. He'd brutalize me into pulp, maybe to death, maybe not. He'd smack Casey around too, but only bruise places she can make up halfway decent excuses for. Like her arms—swell them into violet discs. Her usual excuse is "fucked up slamming again." I don't believe it. I know it's a lie, because I've fantasized doing it myself—pummeling her naked body. Sometimes it seems like Mackey hits her just for the hell of it. Like it's fun. I'm sure it is.

I take a drag from my cigarette, filling the closet with smoke—humid and stale with sweat. A wet smack echoes through the apartment. It sounds like a butcher slapping Casey's splayed ass across a cutting board—flesh splitting into ribbons, meat bleeding under his hand. I peel off my sweat-slicked shirt, beads rolling down my chest like condensation on a meat locker wall. Her yelping chokes off into smothered groans, and the noise dulls into something distant, ambient, almost rhythmic.

I trace the sweaty grooves of my scars and fantasize about Percy. The cuts engraved through my stomach bulge beneath my nails, and my nose pulses, swelling with blood. Droplets streak down my sternum, pooling in my navel. Watching it collect sends a swell of pressure through my cock. It stiffens—aches against my jeans. My forehead pulses. The pain is dizzying, euphoric.

I slip into the memory of us on the boat—backs to the wet deck, heatwaves branding tan lines in our collarbones. He spills beer on his neck—lets it trail in amber lines into the sweat along his chest. There's something holy about it, radiant and glistening, like a syrupy offering. I picture dragging his throat across the deck boards, the sound of his cartilage bending beneath my grip like reeds in a storm. I can strum a ballad and gorge myself on his sap. I can hook my fingers in his jaw, squeeze the breath from his chest, force it out in one long, guttural note.

I smear the blood up from my navel, paint it into the creases of my abdomen, massaging it in like oil. My body slumps—boneless, plastic, shriveled like heat-warped packaging.

A soft tapping hits the closet door. I blink. Still crouched on the carpet. I reach for the knob and turn it open.

"He's gone," Casey whispers, peeling back the door. Her bruises are new—though I can't recall where the old ones stopped and the fresh ones started. "I've got some for you," she adds. "Not much, but Mackey will bring more."

"Okay," I say, using the wall to pull myself upright.

"He hit me again," she says. "Harder this time." Her arms tremble erratically.

"Okay," I repeat. My eyes flit over her—only half-listening. I'm more interested in the baggie. She holds it out and I take it between two fingers. It's a quarter full, and I don't think it'll last long.

"Here." I hand her a crumpled wad of bills from my pocket. "I'm not getting enough business for him," she says. "I'm scared. Next time he might not stop. My body's falling apart. Sometimes I don't know if it's even mine anymore."

"Yeah," I say, dragging smoke from my cigarette. "We mistreat our bodies all our lives, which is weird considering the emphasis people put on the human experience—like it's something sacred—like there's some divine tether between what's inside and what's outside. But we're just flesh sacks. Mobile meat. We move from one location to the next. That's it. And we still act surprised when our bodies fail us."

"You remember telling me our bodies are collateral?"

"Yeah," I lie.

"What happens when it has nothing left to give?"

"That's subjective, isn't it?" I grind my cigarette into the wall and drag it down, leaving a burn mark across the paint. "I don't think you had much to give in the first place."

PIERCE: RESIDUAL

I fold the duvet around my waist, lean back against the headboard, and stare up at the popcorn ceiling. A dried water spot blooms above me, swollen in a spiral beneath the paint. There's a tear in it where a bubble of water used to hang. The air conditioner is broken. Without ventilation, the air settles stagnant. A swampy film clings to my skin. Every few minutes, the unit sputters, like it's trying to come alive. It groans into a whirr, then dies again. The room hums with a low, ambient decay. I rub my eyes and notice a splitting headache blooming at my temples.

She's at the foot of the bed, shuffling through a pile of clothes. Silent now. The sweet, fake murmurings are gone. Her face has stiffened, stale with post-coital detachment. Our transaction's done, but I continue watching her. Her pale ass rises as she bends to step her chopstick legs into her jeans. Her strawberry-blonde hair falls over her face, veiling her eyes. There's some mystique restored in her as her features blur behind the strands. I like finding beauty where I can.

"There's a money clip in the top drawer," I say, breaking my gaze and realizing I might be too mesmerized in her ass. I gesture toward the dresser. Her head swivels, eyes darting to me, then to the drawer. Her lip lines are drawn wide and vacant over her plump lip filler. The wood lets out a hollow groan as she opens it. She crosses into the bathroom and runs the sink.

She reappears, jeans pulled halfway up her hips, wriggling them into place. I scan her again. Her stomach is smooth, milky. Freckles scatter her lower back and break across the edge of a snake tattoo rising from her waistband. I've never liked tattoos. I've stopped asking what they mean. The answers are always the same—*there is none.* It's better to invent meaning myself.

"You have kids?" I ask.

She stands in front of the dead television, pushing her hair behind her ears. She picks up her spiral hoop earrings from the dresser and leans toward her reflection in the black screen—not the mirror in the bathroom. I don't ask why. I already feel like I've overstepped, and another question would cross a line. Apologizing would be worse. My gut drops. All of this—this room, this moment—is something I shouldn't be doing, but it's another form of escape.

It delays the moment I have to confront my reflection—the one that glared at me through the fogged shower mirror. That version of me pressed her against the shower tiles, glimpsing our bodies through the torrenting nozzle and steam. It mouthed things I didn't want to hear, taunting me like I haven't learned anything. I guess I haven't. When I stepped out, the glass was still clouded. That murky veil between us let me disconnect for a little longer—at least until the fog dissipated again.

"Yes," she says. The answer startles my wandering mind, jolting me back. She's drawing the shape of her eyebrows with a makeup pencil. "I've got a son. He's five, turning six next month."

"They usually do," I reply. I bite my lip, wince. I've lumped her in with the others. Like after this, she'll dissolve into the rest, a droplet lost in some anonymous pool. It's like telling an artist their work looks like everything else. Her expression doesn't shift. She either expected it or stopped listening. Why should she care? Our transaction is done. Anything else we say now is just filling empty space. She's letting me have that.

"You have a son too," she says. Not a question—an observation.

"I do," I answer, unmoving, watching her reflection instead of her directly. I'm just another broken cog in the machinery. She's patched up scrap like me before.

"They usually do," she says. It stings. My headache flares, vibrating behind my eyes. "I bet you're a cop too."

"Something like that." Should I help her gather her things or is that too invasive?

"You seem like a good man. Most of them do." She slings her purse over her shoulder and packs her makeup into the center compartment. It's a cheap leather bag with a gold emblem—scratched, latch broken. "People like you get stuck. You veer off—swerve, divert, drive into traffic—anything to regain control of your direction. But you don't. I've learned a lot about your line of work. You all end up in the same place. Underground. You stay stuck—you like it. That's why cops are rarely repeat customers. You can't fuck underground."

"Your line of work isn't much different."

"No, it's not," she says, placing a hand on the doorknob. She stares down at a vague patch of carpet, thinking, then clicks her nails against the metal as she turns the handle. "We'll both end up there. The only difference is your type doesn't see it coming."

STANTON: SEDIMENT

I open the door and Pierce steps in. My eyes are puffy, waterlogged, the skin beneath them sagging from the night before. I haven't slept. He follows me inside and I return to the coffee table. The mug in my hands has gone cold and the ceramic sends a chill through my clammy palms. Pierce scans the clutter and furrows his brow at the papers and folders spilled onto the floor. He shrugs off his jacket, folds it once, and drapes it over a kitchen barstool. I say nothing, hoping he'll ignore the mess. Silence stretches between us, heavy and awkward. We're alone. I glance at my watch and realize I hadn't noticed the kids leave for school. Vanished—like ghosts—or I'm the ghost.

"You're still dredging through this?" Pierce questions, tone sharp. He hovers over me while I flip through the next manila folder. His eyes drift to the glowing laptop screen, reviewing the tabs I've left open on articles detailing dental anatomy. He turns back to me. "Have you even slept?" he asks. There's something ingenuine in the concern, like he's assessing my competency more than my wellbeing.

"Did you see your son?" I snap, locking eyes with him. It comes out too harsh—a flare of defensiveness. It doesn't help my case. My headache pulses, bourbon still clinging to my bloodstream. He doesn't answer, just tenses, like he grits his teeth—but I can't quite tell.

My vision blurs, just slightly, then comes back. He lets the question dissolve into silence.

"The victim had a wife," he says finally. "No kids. She says they'd grown distant, and he wasn't socializing much. It was hard to get him out of his room, let alone out of the house. Claimed he was close with a few people, but—" he shrugs, "—not sure how accurate that is."

"What makes you say that?" I ask, eyes leveling with his as I reorganize the stack of papers.

"He told her he was going downtown to watch a film at the local cinema with some friends," Pierce says. "I checked with the theater. The security footage doesn't show that he was ever there."

"She didn't know he'd gone to the bar?"

"She didn't even know he'd *ever* been there," Pierce says. "The bartender recognized him, though. He claims the guy had been coming in for months—always alone. This was the first time he'd ever seen him with someone else. He gave me the same rundown he gave you."

"What about the bar's cameras?"

"Nothing," Pierce replies with a shrug. "The owner says he's upgrading the system. The cameras have just been for show the past week. He said the place doesn't get much trouble, so he figured he could go without surveillance for a bit. That's his story, anyway. Makes you wonder if they were ever working to begin with."

"Did the bartender give a description?"

"Yeah," Pierce says, settling on the arm of the couch. "Same as before—slender guy, strung-out look, black spiked hair—could be anyone. Sounds like your average gas station tweaker."

"We don't have much," I mutter, pressing my fingers to my hairline.

"Any luck identifying the other car?" he asks.

"Not really," I say, shaking my head. "Large vehicle, front passenger-side damage, black, likely has a busted headlight. We got decent tread marks at the scene, so that'll help narrow the search. I've called a few local body shops, but nothing's come up yet. Still more to check."

Pierce nods, reaches over, and picks up a photo of the victim's car bumper.

"Forensics managed to lift a few complete prints," I continue. "They also collected semen from the victim's gumline. Nothing in the database."

"Jesus," Pierce mutters, gritting his teeth and tightening his jaw until the tendons stand out. "He was sexually assaulted?"

"It was post-mortem."

Pierce rubs his palms over his face, pressing his fingertips into his eyes in leaden, circular motions. Then, he stands and walks into the kitchen, grabbing the open bottle of bourbon on the counter. The glow from the laptop screen reflects faintly off the glass. He pours himself a drink, knocks it back, and hisses through his teeth at the burn.

"What do we have to work with?" he asks, staring into the empty glass before refilling it.

"We can get a decent composite sketch from the bartender," I say. "It appears the Canine is a homosexual man who targets men in their mid-twenties to late thirties." He pauses, glass halfway to his lips. It's the first time I've used the nickname out loud, and I think it unsettles him—just for a moment. I glance over the files strewn across the floor while he pulls himself back together. There's a sharp inhale, another hiss, and the glass clinks back onto the counter. I take it as permission to continue. "We were originally linking the dog mutilations to him," I say. "But that was a misdirection—coincidence. This guy's pattern is different. He doesn't take all the teeth. He only removes the upper canines. Why?"

"You said the original suspect removed the dogs' teeth because something about their bared mouths unsettled him—like they looked vicious, threatening."

"Right."

"Maybe the human version of that sets something off in him, too. The canines specifically—they're primal, symbolic. It could be that's what he's reacting to."

I nod, turning the idea over in my head. There's something else behind it, something I can't quite articulate. I pull a photo from the mess—its corner folded, poking out between pages. It's a crime scene still from the car. It's a profile shot of the victim's head, jaw dislocated, the top of his mouth crushed against the steering wheel. Splattered fluids streak the interior in a moss of gore, clinging to the bones like vines.

"There's a big difference between an animal and a human," I say, eyes drifting across the photo. "Why do people own dogs?"

"Companionship, I guess," Pierce mutters, circling a finger around the rim of his empty glass.

"Sure. But deeper than that." I look up at him. "They're protectors. Emotional, physical—doesn't matter. You take out their teeth, you take away their bite. But people aren't that simple." My mind is racing. It's a longshot, but I open a browser and start typing.

"How does that help us?" Pierce asks.

"For humans, the canine teeth symbolize force. Power," I say, gesturing for him to come over. He leaves the glass on the counter. "Look—this article says the shape and size of the canines are tied to dominance—strength of personality. Symbolically. Visually." I spin the laptop toward him. He kneels to skim the page while my thoughts fire like pistons. "There's a reason why he's not interested in dogs—we're not like them," I say. "What makes us different is our conscious experience. It's what makes us more interesting to him. If he pulled all of the victims' teeth, they'd bleed out fast—die quick. But two? Just the canines? That's slow. That's intentional. He wants them awake. Aware. He's stripping them of their power, making them feel it while he takes control of their bodies."

Pierce stands, walks back to the kitchen, pours another glass. "And again—how does that help us?" he says, tone flat. "It feels like a bit of a reach."

"Maybe it is," I admit, sharper than I mean to be. "But it gives us something. A window into his head. Something to stand on while we wade through whatever fantasy he's living in." I flip through the folders again. My vision blurs, hands twitching—too fast, too erratic, like cockroach limbs scuttling across paper.

"Stanton," Pierce says evenly. "Give it a rest. You're starting to look like a raccoon tearing through that mess." I think it's meant as a joke, but it lands flat. He's already pouring another drink. Maybe he doesn't notice. Maybe he doesn't care. I know I spiral. I know I go too far—get too deep. But I can't stop. Time keeps ticking and the clocks continue to chime louder even when their batteries are dead.

"It's seven in the morning, Pierce," I say, unable to mask the irritation. Sometimes I wonder if he's really taking any of this seriously. He doesn't answer. Just knocks back the bourbon with a wince, hissing through his teeth like it's a punishment. He rinses the glass, sets it in the sink, then pulls a clean one and fills it with water. He returns and holds it out to me. The water ripples faintly in my hands, reacting to the churn in my empty stomach. I trace the etched ridges with my thumb, letting the cool seep into my skin. The water stings my cracked lips, flooding their coarse surface. I drag the back of my hand across my mouth, pressing moisture into the split skin. My eyes begin to blur from strain. Too many hours staring into that screen. Still, the first sip hits like a signal to return to my body, and with it comes an ache that fills my limbs everywhere at once. Pierce doesn't say anything. He's mastered dodging my blunt interjections.

"Is this what it's always going to be?" I ask. But it's not really a question. "We're janitors cleaning what's left behind. Only these stains don't fade. They multiply. Sometimes I get this fear that there'll come a point where the sludge thickens so much that I won't be able to wade through it anymore. It's like walking in quicksand. The more you try to move forward, the more you get stuck." My hand trembles. The water ripples inside the glass, tiny waves catching the light. Something in me says to leave the rest.

Pierce stands. "I'm heading back to the office," he says, voice low, worn thin. "Get some rest. Termites eat themselves to the surface, eventually."

I open my eyes. Afternoon light filters in. My head throbs, the base of my skull burning like I've been grinding it against concrete. I lift my gaze—papers and folders are scattered on the floor, caught in the idle churn of the ceiling fan. I stare up at its rotations—blank. My jeans are damp with sweat. So is my sweater, clinging to every inch of me. The house isn't quiet anymore—footsteps creak, a guitar riff stabs through Preston's door. The kids must be home. Somehow, I missed it. I groan and reach for my laptop, tapping the keys. The browser lights back up. The article's still open, surrounded by other half-read tabs. I check my phone. No texts. No emails. Nothing.

In the kitchen, I pull the fridge open. Inside is a carton of milk that's probably expired, a stained takeout box, and a few molding strawberries bleeding from their plastic containers. Some carrots have gone limp, and other buttery smears of something sticky has left a dried trail in the corner, like a slug's path. The filter light blinks red. I can't remember the last time I cleaned the fridge, much less changed the filter.

"Guys," I call out, voice raspy, straining to regain my voice. "What do you want for dinner? We're ordering out again." I glare into the fridge like it owes me something. I was never a good cook, and I don't know if I'd be able to prepare a meal if I had fresh ingredients in front of me. Their father handled that when he was around—not travelling for business conferences. He was supposed to be back from his trip days ago. Now I don't even know when he's coming back. He probably doesn't either. Then I remember the four voicemails on my phone that I haven't listened to. It's probably the school again. I already know what they say— same scripts, different days.

"Can we get pizza for once?" Preston says, appearing across from me at the counter. "None of that Thailand shit."

"Fine," I say. A flicker of warmth catches in my chest when I hear his voice and see his face. His hair's a mess, flopping over his forehead in uneven waves. Sometimes I worry I'm starting to forget what he even looks like. "Watch the language," I add, offering him a smile. "Save the profanity for the other foul-mouthed man in our lives. And don't talk like that to girls."

"Mom, you're not a girl," he grins, sliding onto a barstool. "You're practically a dinosaur."

"My bones definitely feel like fossils," I say, stretching my arms out. "Will you order it on your computer? My wallet's in my bag—on the other barstool."

"Sure, Mom."

"Wait," I say, remembering the voicemails. "Are you skipping school again?"

"Yeah," he says casually. It's not the admission that shocks me—it's how unbothered he is about it. I wasn't much better at his age. "The theater downtown was showing this indie horror movie I've been dying to see. All the guys were going, so I had to. I know I shouldn't have. But don't worry, Jed and Tim are good guys."

"It's nice that you had company, but that doesn't mean it's safe."

"Mom, no one's going to mess with a cop's kid."

"That's not the point," I start—but the buzzing of my phone cuts me off. It skitters against the countertop, a vibrating pulse that makes my stomach drop. I watch it bounce—the longer I don't answer, the longer it doesn't exist. "You'd be surprised what some people will do, if given the chance," I mutter, more to myself than to him.

I answer the call, and something tightens inside me the second I hear Pierce's voice.

"Stanton," I say.

"I need you to meet me at The Blue Mist," he says. His voice is taut, frayed. "It's a motel a few miles north of the marina. Streets are being blocked off. I've got officers sweeping the area. A few are already headed into the marina."

"What's going on?"

There's a beat of silence.

"We've got another body," he says. "It's getting worse."

COMMUNION

I slink into the dip of his lower back, sliding my stomach along his ridge of muscle, leaving salamander sweat trails in my wake. His feet are knotted in pillowcases—legs splayed toward the headboard. Both arms hang limp around the lower bedposts, fingers twitching like they're still trying to grip something. Our sweat mingles, merging into beads that thread down the sheets. I take the crevice of his shoulder blade into my mouth, teeth closing until the flesh bunches between my lips. The muscle tightens, sending pressure into my jaw. My fingers creep up his neck and prod into his mouth. The mouth exudes wet, corrosive gurgles that froth against my skin. I hook his jaw and feel the resistance shudder through my palms. The tendons are roped tight—cheeks bloated with a fatty swell that makes the bone harder to pry loose. My thumbs work the base of his skull, tremoring with the strain, while my fingers crank at his lower lip. His muscles protest, and heat blooms through me, all pliant flesh and tightening grip. A guttural rumble seeps from his throat, breath clinging damp around my fingers. Either the high is fading, or I hadn't dosed him enough. A grind starts deep in the hinge of his jaw, the bone working against itself. I squeeze the slick bulge of his cheeks, grappling the defiant clench until—snap—like knuckles cracking. I slam the underside of his chin into the bedpost. The joint gives with a dull, wet crack—cartilage detaching under the skin like breaking a glowstick.

Blood floods forward in a thick, spitting surge, coating his tongue, pooling along the gumline, and drowning the gaps between his teeth before it spills over his chin. The growl in his throat collapses into thin, fractured whines. His mashed head slumps limp against the post, the back of his neck already welting in a buttery surge of bruising.

I dig into my jeans pocket, smearing the lining with blood, and pull pliers free. The metal is crusted in boy-residual—dried spit, skin, secretions. The bedpost is drinking deep from the slurry spilling out of him, teeth hidden under the taffy drag of gore. The pliers hum up my wrist as enamel scrapes metal. I clamp down on the first canine, goosebumps shivering my skin like I've bitten tinfoil. Pressure. Bend. Tremor. Snap. The tooth tears from the gum like a stump yanked from wet soil, a splinter of root still embedded in jagged spikes. I leave it. The next gum is swollen, bloated like rotten tomato. I lean, reaching for my boot toppled beside the bed—switchblade winking from the fold. My fingers hook the handle. I palm it, sink the blade into the pink mound. Ripping through the gum loosens the root but floods the cavity with sticky clots. I push deeper. The slick surface splits, coating the pliers, gloving my hands in a warm sheen. Chalkboard-shiver. Goosebumps rise, fade. Clamp. Enamel grinds. Crack. This time, I procure the whole thing. I still haven't perfected the art. Strands of tacky meat cling to my skin, thickening between my fingers until they glue together. I pocket the teeth and gummy debris.

My belt buckle bites cold into the smooth waistline of my stomach, and my hipbones carve a "V" that dips into the waistband of my jeans. Across the room, the bathroom mirror is spidered with cracks. My emaciated torso catches in the fractured glass—thin, gleaming—turns me on. I stumble across the room to meet my reflection. The top corner juts outward, frame chipped away. Jagged. Glistening. I lift the pliers, chip at the fault line. Glass breaks off in chunks, splintering into the sink. I imagine watching myself. I gather the shards into my palm, the pieces clicking together, and return to the bed.

His torso wrenches in repressed, stifled spasms—final reflexes twitching, expelling. Almost methodical, like the body is trying to do something, anything—whether that's comprehension, surrender, some half-formed instinct, or whatever. I crouch in front of him, centerfold to his face, balanced in a gargoyle hunch. Blood has dried into clotted ribbons in the hair on my arms. I stretch his mouth around the bedpost, pulling at the taut cheeks that strain over the broken jaw—forcing him to deep-throat the stake. His tongue folds over itself like a suffocating leech, bumpy and pulsing. The lips peel back, and his head vibrates faintly under my fingers, throat coughing out its last spasms. I press a shard of mirror into his gumline. The first piece saws a cavern between his teeth, fixing itself there. The second cuts through gum and lip, and the swelling grips it like a mouth suckling breastmilk. I drive the opposite ends of each shard into the bedpost, locking them in place. His face warps into a jagged, vampiric grin. Careful, I cup the back of his head in both palms—then slam. A crunch. The shards bite deeper into the wood, slice deeper into the mouth. The gape of his expression stirs heat low in my gut, sharp and unblinking—eroticizes my cock.

I smear caked blood across my face, flecks of tissue clinging to my chin. The mirror shards catch the splatter, each one flashing back slivers of me—skin purpling beneath my eyes, not just from lack of sleep but from something more beaten-in. I trace my jawline in the reflection, note the cheekbone's cut, lick at the corner of my mouth. His earring flickers in my periphery. The sight pulls the room into focus, like filters burning off. It makes me wonder what else I've missed—and whether I can trust the things I do notice.

The remaining shards arc into sharp crescents. I fold the tip of his ear, drive glass through cartilage. There's a satisfying give—like puncturing a sealed plastic lid. The skin parts in papery threads as I slide the other point under the cheek's flesh. The new structure gives him bat-like ears, refracting the light in jittery shimmers. Foamy residue blooms around the wounds, yellowed cream pooling in the torn skin. I smear it with my thumb, taste it—salted tea.

I meet my own gaze in the glass, my fingers grazing his nose. Copper brine hangs heavy in the air and spills across my tongue. His face has shifted into something cryptid, inhuman. So has mine. A sudden jerk—he's still here. With my head framed between the splayed mirror shards, I drag my mouth over the shredded nostril cartilage, the doughy swell of upper lip. My breath rebounds off him in hot bursts, folding back into my own mouth, choking me on my own fog.

Stand, maneuver. The wooden bedframe groans under the shift of weight. I straddle his back, fingers pressing into the flesh just above his waistband. The girthy ridges of bone feel clammy, skin fever-hot and drawn tight over the frame of his ribcage. I massage them apart, like kneading stiff clay, feeling the resistance give in small, reluctant increments. A cord of saliva slips from my lip, landing across the shallow trench of his spine, spreading into the pores like it's sealing them shut. My hands move to his belt loops, tugging the fabric down over the sharp hooks of his hipbones. His ass is mottled in splotches and raised lesions, scattered across their curve of muscle and fat and deeper into the pucker of his rectum. I press into the blemished skin until it swells and deepens in color, then fades back toward its olive tone. The heat radiating from his body rises into my chest, sticking to my skin in an almost resinous way. My palms explore the hollows and ridges, tracing the uneven terrain of spine, scar, and welt, mapping each imperfection like landmarks. The lesions have their own topography—some puffed, others cratered—each one pulling faintly against the pad of my thumb. The shape is wrong—disproportionate and too abrupt in some places, too soft in others—yet both sides mirror each other in their flawed symmetry. I drag my nails along the outer edge of a bruise and watch the skin pale under the pressure before flooding back with color. Every surface feels swollen with its own history, as if the body is still trying to tell me something long after the voice has gone quiet.

I unzip my jeans and careen my hips out, the movement scraping denim against skin, and wrench my cock from my waistband, probing his rectum between my fingers with the other hand. My torso drags over the ridge of his spine, the heat of his sweat-slicked skin sucking at my nipples. His pubic rectal bristles brush my navel. I cup a hand beneath the slack hinge of his jaw, collecting the spill that drips in syrupy strands from his maw. It slicks my palm, clinging in a tacky film. I smear my cock in its thick lather and sleeve it in its wet lubrication. The warmth of his blood exudes a pressurized throb that radiates upward through my crotch, the seepage hardens me further. I brace my knees against the mattress and drag my fingernails into the meat of his thighs, pulling his legs wider, bones creaking at the shift. My cock worms against his ass, and I guide its shaft into his interior. Each movement grates against the dried crust along his skin, flaking and cracking under the pressure. My grip forces him open, the tension in his muscles grinding against my hold. Each thrust dries the blood, each puncture more abrasive. The mattress dips and groans with the motion, its stained fabric puckering under my weight. His rectal sleeve tightens around my head, and I come. My tender cock flops from his cavity. It spurts silky substances, fluids both mine and his. I lean down to paste mine across my lips—his are kind of everywhere. The dampness returns, and I probe hungrily in the orifice—panting, lapping expulsing drippage. The gush from his wounds thickens into sluggish ribbons, stringing between my fingers. I follow them, tracing their path as they gather into dark pools against the sheets. I breathe through the smell rising from him—an acrid sweetness, metallic and humid—that coats the back of my throat. It clings there, tenacious to fade, a presence that makes the air feel heavier.

I scratch at flecks of dried blood caked in the cuts etched across my knuckles. The sink swirls with a thin red film, staining the porcelain, scabbing it in charcoal-tinted flecks. Loose meat clings to the sides. The faucet gurgles—then only a trickle, sputter, drip—collecting in a shallow pool. My knuckles sting under the water as I scrub away clotted secretions, indistinguishably mine or other. My vision tunnels into them, skin raw and pink, until I realize they're not getting clean because the cuts are still bleeding—profusely, insistently. Here's my sacrament.

The bathroom light flickers, and my body stutters in the shattered remnants of the mirror. Amphetamine tremors curve the backs of my wrists. I shove limp strands of hair off my forehead. The wax has congealed into greasy masses, collapsed from their urchin spikes. Sweat beads on my scalp, slicking the strands into curls. Another flicker—the bulb shadows a graveyard of withered moth bodies in its dome. My reflection jitters in the shards. Burial in fragments. Flicker again: the moth husks shift, eyes swelling black, twitching in silent laughter. Glitch—distorting glow—until the tiles ripple like muscle under skin. The grout seams pulse, stretching wider, as if the walls are breathing with me, or against me. I press my palm to the mirror, but the glass feels warm, almost damp, like there's something on the other side leaning back. Another flicker, and for an instant, I'm not sure which one of us is the reflection and which is a shell of broken innuendos.

I blink hard, thumb the plastic stopper in the drain, and watch the water whirl away—vision clearing as the pool disappears into the pipes, leaving behind splotches in grainy constellations. My chest drips—outside and in—and I drag my fingernails across it, catching on a scar. It runs from the notch of my collarbone down the sternum, a fissure that opens like a vaginal maw, its lips widening, closing, beathing with me. Peel it back, feel the shift. The scars tracing my ribcage accentuate my sunken skin and cling tight to the frame of my bones. My ribs tent against me like they might break through at any second—massive in their tautness, as if someone shoved broken bones into a garbage bag.

A sudden pressure blooms behind my nose, ready to burst. I tip my head back, swallow, pinch. Copper saliva slides ropy down my throat in a drip, then spills from my lip. After a few minutes it begins to clot. I swallow again, the sound ragged, wet—like a bird drowning mid-breath. I grab my sweatshirt from the shower rod and step out.

His contorted face waits—an indistinct, perfect mass. Firm. The kind of beauty you could starve for. I feel my tongue press to my teeth, the saliva rising like it's preparing for communion.

I throw my sweatshirt over my torso and rub the backs of my hands—now searing, now clean, cleansed, or whatever. His limp form exhales a fouler stench from his evacuated bowels, seepage tracking down the meat of his thighs and bleeding into the sheets. That sign of finality folds my arousal inward, collapsing my erection. The ceiling fan stirs the stench, its blades the only movement, the only sound fluttering through the room. The air feels denser now, as if even it has begun to rot.

At the dresser, I thumb through his wallet. In the black glass of the dead television, his eyes still watch me. They look more alert in reflection than they did when he was breathing. The wallet's leather is stamped with initials, stitching cheap and crooked. Inside, a water-stained photo of Max, arm around another man—Max is younger here, slimmer, hair bushy, acne bristling across his cheeks. Prom picture. Ugly then too. There are a few crumpled bills and an old movie ticket. I liked the film. Sometimes I imagine recording these moments. Would they hold the same weight if they existed beyond the present, or would the permanence rot them? Part of the allure is the finite experience—it ends. Why mar perfect art? A thing can only be purified once.

The itch builds, splitting primal satiation from some poised, self-styled clarity. My mind veers, deterring into chaotic ferocity. His defunct physique feels like mockery—like he knows something I haven't learned yet. Something in my chest tightens, an internal hinge shifting to its next state, a click I can't unhear. And then Percy fills the frame. He lures me in like sirens on a shoreline, reeling my lips forward on fishhooks. That enigmatic, inchoate attraction—infatuation brewed from obsessive speculation. I try to picture him, but his image keeps shifting in my head, like he's trying to keep from being caught. Most people are easy to read: you take in their skin and immediately see the point of entry. How they'll fold, how they'll bend, the seams you can work your fingers into. With Percy, the entry point blurs, drifts, refuses to settle. Imagining him stirs me. The idea of compressing a hollowed-out body, filling that vacancy with my own presence, excites me. I already know the problem and refuse to name it. Naming it means finality. It means conclusion. If I wore Percy's skin, if I roamed around his flesh pockets, I'd have to kill him too. And that would mean ending the only thing I can't yet fully picture. It isn't that I don't yearn to devour every inch of his body—it's that I know I'd only get to do it once.

STANTON: REFRACTIONS

I cross the parking lot toward the yellow tape. The night breeze breathes a chill across my collarbones, tightening around my throat. A row of thin lampposts spills light in fractured pools, insects flitting in erratic spirals around their glow. The shimmer catches in puddles gathered in the empty spaces, trembling with each gust. Beyond the lot, the city glows in muted contours along the skyline. Saltwater humidity drifts in from the marina, its briny weight settling in my lungs. Water laps the docks in hushed, rhythmic moans. The doorway pulses with alternating red and blue strobes from the cruisers parked out front, each flash briefly blinding the scene, then drowning it in shadow. A forensic technician stationed at the threshold glances up as I approach.

"Stanton," he says, fishing into his pocket. His fingers wrestle with something before producing a small, circular tin of petroleum jelly. "You're going to want this."

"It's that bad?" I ask, turning the container over in my palm, thumb tracing the tacky residue clinging to its rim.

"I don't know what to make of it," he says, eyes flicking toward the room before settling on me again. There's a faint wince at the corner of his mouth. "Best if you see for yourself."

I unscrew the cap, drag two fingers across the waxy surface, and smear the balm inside my nostrils. The menthol influx is immediate, tingling the edges of my sinuses. He turns, and I follow him past the pulsing lights and into the dim interior. My vision adjusts gradually, shapes bleeding into clarity. In the far corner, the body resolves—or what's left of it. Husked facial features, tissue, and muscle spread in clumps over the sheets. For a moment, I'm not sure what I'm looking at. Goosebumps prickle up my arms as the features assemble themselves in my mind: a man, face grotesquely mutilated, flayed, and fixed in place, head pinned to the bedpost in a grotesque display. The eyes—still intact—stare unblinking, the only part of him left whole. His body hangs half off the bed, shoulders splayed and flattened like a stiffened animal hide drying on a line.

Up close, his skin has a hardened, leathery quality, the throat swollen and distended. A floorboard creaks in the corner, and I register the faint murmur of voices. The background presses forward in a haze, the details of the room surfacing in fragments—stale air, the tang of metal, the slow drip of water from somewhere unseen. A sliver of movement catches in my periphery. A door at the back of the room eases open, spilling harsh fluorescent light across the scene. Pierce steps out of what appears to be a bathroom, one gloved hand braced on the doorframe. He pushes the door fully wide, and the light floods the room, bleaching the gore into stark brilliance. The heat presses down in heavy waves. I skirt the foot of the bed, aware of the victim's eyes seeming to track my path as I join Pierce at the bathroom threshold. He meets my gaze, gives a short nod.

"How long has the victim been dead?" I ask. The bathroom air clings damp against my collar, sticky and stale, like it's been steeping in sweat.

"Hard to say," Pierce says. "The body has already stiffened drastically. Rigor mortis has set in. At first, the tech estimated fifteen to twenty-four hours." He brushes past me toward the window, gesturing for me to follow. Beneath the sill is a squat, rust-freckled air-conditioning unit. Its vents gape open and it hums faintly, dust layered over the panels—except for the row of buttons, worn clean. Pale numbers flicker on the digital display. Pierce lays a palm over the vents. "Feel this. Tell me what you think."

I mimic the motion, turning my hand over in the breath of the machine. A wave of heat rolls across my glove, dampening the latex until it sticks to my skin—latex sauna. No wonder the room feels suffocating. I glance at the display. "It's set to ninety degrees."

"He cranked it up to accelerate the rigor mortis process," Pierce says.

"Meaning he was still here a few hours ago," I reply, eyes fixed on the numbers.

"Exactly. It'll make nailing down the time of death harder."

"He knows what he's doing," I say. Goosebumps rise along my arms. My gaze shifts back to the body. Blood has hardened into dark meres—glossy pools engorged in a bathhouse of maggots. The scalp is webbed in clotted strands, flies drilling into the wet seams. A flash of light catches on the mirror shards beside the bed, dragging my attention.

"I also found some black filaments in the bathroom," Pierce says. "Could be fabric from whatever he was wearing."

"Any witnesses?"

"None. We've got officers sweeping the marina and talking to the motel manager. There are two cameras—one covering the room doors, the other aimed at the office entrance."

"There's a chance we'll be able to put a face to a name then?"

"Possibly," he says, but the edge in his voice is frayed, doubtful. "It's a start."

The menthol burns faintly at the rim of my nostrils. I wipe at it with my wrist, and a vein of the decay cuts through—sweeter than animal rot and fouled further by whatever fluids have soaked into the victim's skin. Light refracts off the shards, catching on the victim's slack mouth. My peripheral vision seems to widen, distorting the edges of the room.

"The victim was sexually assaulted before death," Pierce says evenly. "The light test lit up the rectal area. Swabs will likely confirm semen."

I crouch to study how the glass is seated in the gumline, how it punctures the flesh. The reflection in the shards leers back, swallowing the edges of the room. Pierce says something, but the words distort— drain—until all I hear is my own breathing. I meet my eyes in the fractured mirror.

"This is different," I cut in, silencing whatever he was saying. "He's evolving."

Pierce shifts, uneasy. "Yeah. He's gotten more brutal."

"Not just that." My jaw tightens, heat prickling under my lids. "It's like he's growing into himself. Emerging."

"What do you mean?" His tone balances between confusion and scrutiny.

"The larva grows to form—the moth splits the cocoon. He's crossing a new threshold. Before, it was about dominance—stripping away autonomy, forcing submission, controlling the narrative. That's what fed him. But this—" I gesture toward the jagged halo of mirror shards embedded around the face. "This is more than voyeurism from the outside. He wants to be inside it."

"You're saying he wants to watch himself?"

"Removing their teeth isn't enough. Making them watch isn't either." I lean in until the shards frame me, reflecting every angle of my head. "He wants to inhabit the pain. Be part of it too."

The blacktop outside hums under the lamplight, wet and shifting in puddled reflections. My legs feel unsteady—whether from fatigue or from their appearance in the rippling reflections, I'm not sure. My fingers find my cigarette pack in my pocket, knuckles whitening as I crush the cardboard. The lighter sparks—I inhale until the ember glows, heat bleeding tension out through my lungs. The night air swallows my pulse, gnaws at the walls of my skull, and lets the pressure leak from my throat. I flick the cigarette. The photographs roll through my head—jowls split, ears torn loose—my mind gnashing like an animal behind glass, mouth frothing. Death doesn't wait for age. Neither does life. Both are driven by the same hunger, the same voyeurism. Maybe Cameron was right—I'm not built for this work.

"Stanton." The sound of my name cuts through the static. I turn. Pierce is stepping out of the motel room, his tone sharp with concern. "Everything okay?"

"Yeah." I sniff, rub at my nose. The shift in air makes my eyes sting—or it's just exhaustion. His boots crunch on the asphalt as he crosses to me.

"I value our partnership," he says, "but only if you're honest." I nod, teeth clenched. I'm not honest. "Otherwise, you're a liability."

I'll eat it if it comes to it.

"The motel manager is turning over the camera footage," he continues. My mind drifts, and I realize too late. I haven't answered. He doesn't push—he lets the silence hang like bait in water. "Looks like we've got him on film. I'll go through it at the office, see if we can pull any identifiers. I'll let you know."

"The victim's ID was still in his wallet," I say. His brow lifts. "The face is too mangled—we'll need dental records to confirm. I'll start contacting next of kin, see if we can shake out a lead." I draw on the cigarette and the ash hisses as it drops into a puddle, dissolving into the water. "Did the employees notice anything unusual?"

"No," Pierce says. I drag on the cigarette again, and a curtain of smoke folds over the air. "But I imagine they see some wild things here— things the rest of the world would call strange."

"Does the hotel manager have any leads?" I ask. "Anyone who owns property in the marina we can check in with? A regular who might've seen someone acting cagey?"

"No, but I do." His lips press thin. "Percy."

"Your son?"

He nods without looking at me. "It's a long shot. My wife kept a boat in the marina. Percy spent more time there than at home—reading on the bow until dark, drinking until dawn. We didn't notice much, and that was for the best, given the way she and I treated each other." His eyes track the waterline. "The things we do to the people we love." He gestures for my cigarette, takes a drag, passes it back. Somewhere in the marina, a boat horn moans. "I would've fucked him up worse if I'd paid more attention to him."

I weigh my response, then ask, "Do you want me to come with you?" The offer tastes wrong the second I say it. I think of my son and almost take it back. Empty pizza box politics.

"No," he says. "I'll track him down in the morning. Call me when you've got something. I'll do the same."

I nod and crush the cigarette in the puddle. The thought I'd been chasing slips away.

INTERVAL

We pass a metal rack stacked with plastic bottles of cinnamon whiskey shots. It reminds me of the old liquor store and the fire, the charred cedar and the burnt hair. That smell carries a kind of alluring nostalgia, unfurling gradually through my inhalations. I think about the desert highway speckled under the orange sunset. A flicker snaps it away—a fluorescent bulb flashes, pus-tinted, casting its sickly stain across the linoleum. The faint backdrop of grocery-store chatter surges in my ears. Casey walks ahead, her ass arched back, upper body draped over the shopping cart handle like she's been poured there. The light washes her flesh into a pale mustard—or the heroin is just catching up with her now. Sometimes when she gets a cut, the blood is so thick I half-believe it's tar. Her hips swivel in jerky, gear-like arcs inside her jeans. A rhinestone-pink belt, its flowers dulled and discolored, bites into her waist. Her thong rides up her ass and her jeans slouch lower.

The cart scrapes against the metal railing by the vegetable display. She leans over the damp peppers first, working them between her dirt-caked fingernails before putting them back. Then she lifts a small carton of mushrooms—oddly pointed, like her clitoris. Little hardened papier-mâché tepees. She replaces them, then molests a bushel of parsley. The sprinkler sputters to life, misting the back of her hand, glistening the vegetables in a thin dew. She bites her lip, startled, and retracts her hand. It's kind of arousing. She doesn't know what she's looking for.

"It doesn't matter, Casey," I tell her. "He's going to hit you for cooking like shit."

"I can try," she mutters. "What does basil look like?" She smooths a glossy catalog page—the recipe printed there barely holding her attention as she circles her thumb across its surface. "Is it leafier, or more of a stalk?"

I check the clock. Its revolutions move quicker than it should.

I don't answer. There's a spider tracing quick, surgical steps along the fluorescent tubing above the vegetables. The legs work like a sewing machine, threading heat. I wonder if the bulb burns it, and then I feel a burn of my own. Casey keeps muttering, tossing random items into the cart. The misters spit a heavier fog, and the spider freezes mid-step.

"Are you going to help me?" she asks.

The clock ticks. My chest syncs to it—tick—my neck pulsing with the second hand.

"I think it's a waste of time," I snap. The cuts across the backs of my hands pulse too. I flex my fingers to quiet them. She turns toward me, arms folded. I glance back at the clock. Tick.

"You're always looking at time like you're running out of it," she says—quiet, almost bored, like my existence is exhausting to her. It probably is. The background noise swells again, carts rolling like distant thunder. "I wonder what would happen if you didn't set a time limit on every aspect of your existence." Tick.

I think that's what she says.

"Grab the fucking basil," I hiss, teeth bared. She jerks back a step—I lock my hand around her forearm, squeezing until the skin blooms a beet-red flush. The jolt startles her—my grip only tightens. Tick.

"Excuse me," a voice cuts in. I turn. A few feet away, a woman stands by her cart glaring—I hadn't seen her approach. The interruption jars my attention, and the grocery store's noise snaps back into focus. Our eyes lock. Her hair is a dark brunette, pushed behind her ears, and hangs in greasy coils like it hasn't been washed in days. A black coat drapes her frame. Her face is bare, lips set in a hard, unbroken line. She breaks the stare, leans into the vegetable case, and selects a saran-wrapped head of iceberg lettuce. I shove Casey aside, step in front of the woman's cart, and wrap my fists around the metal grille. Tick.

"Is this supposed to be threatening?" she says, setting the lettuce into her shopping cart. It's packed with microwave dinners. "If not, you're wasting my time." She pushes her jacket back to show the pistol on her hip and the badge clipped beside it. She rests her hand on the grip. "Otherwise—try me."

I grit my teeth, reach into my jacket, and pull my cigarettes. The spider's gone. Casey lingers at the edge of my vision. I slide one free, thumb my lighter, and cup the flame. The ember flares behind my palms. I exhale a stream of smoke in her direction. We hold each other's gaze. I draw again, the smoke trailing toward the ceiling. She unbuckles her holster. The misters shut off, and the store's hum flattens into a dull, industrial drone. I lean in, hands sinking into her cart. The cigarette dangles from my lips as I cradle the lettuce in the crook of my arm. Back between my fingers, the cigarette breathes smoke over its pale, tight leaves—the thing seems to cough in my grip. I press the ember into the saranwrap. It hisses. The plastic splits, blackening the top layer of leaves. I drop it back into her cart and it thuds against the metal, crushing the boxes of microwave dinners. Her eyes never leave mine. The ash fizzles out. I let the cigarette fall to the linoleum and walk past her. Tick.

STANTON: STALLED

The clock isn't working.

I crack open a freezer door and load the cart with pre-cooked TV dinners. I try to pick a variety—Preston and Lainey are both picky—but remind myself that at least I'm feeding them. That counts for something. I wheel into the vegetable aisle. The misters hiss on, fogging the air and beading the produce in fine dew. Under the wrap, every sphere of green looks the same, and I can't tell one from another. My husband's the cook in the family. When he's away on business, I'm left guessing. I study the prepackaged salads—they all look identical. I'll grab one at random. The kids will drown it in ranch dressing anyway.

"Grab the fucking basil," a voice cuts through the mist. I glance down the aisle. A man looms over a woman, his fingers digging into her forearm hard enough to raise the skin. His hair juts back in greasy quills, and the bulk of his leather jacket only makes his frame look thinner. He jerks his chin toward the vegetables, profile catching in the light—eyes sunken, bruised, like someone clocked him not long ago. I move down the aisle until my cart intrudes upon theirs.

"Excuse me," I say, cutting in. Our eyes lock—his stare crawls into a provocative leer. I break it, reach into the mist, and pull out a head of lettuce. I turn back to my cart just as he grips the front grille and gives it a jolt. "Is this supposed to be threatening?" My voice stays level. "If not, you're wasting my time." I push my jacket aside, showing the pistol on my hip and the badge clipped beside it. My hand rests on the grip, thumb brushing the holster latch. "Otherwise—try me."

He slips a hand into his jacket pocket, and my grip tightens on the holster. A pack of cigarettes emerges—he shakes one free, lights it. The ember flares, then he exhales a stream of smoke over my cart. The stale burn churns my stomach. My thumb flicks the holster latch. He leans in, plucks the lettuce from the bottom of my cart, tucks it under his arm like a helmet, and grinds the cigarette into its plastic skin. The wrap hisses and the plastic puckers—a hole shrivels into a charred crater, the ember burning the patch of leaves beneath.

He drops it back into the cart. Smoke seeps from the blackened crater and over the rim. The woman with him gives me a thin, uneasy grin—something caught between pride and shame. We hold the stare a moment too long before she turns away, abandoning her cart in the aisle like it never belonged to her.

PIERCE: WAKE

A silhouette darts across the bow, the sun warping it into something spectral as it moves. The dock sways under my boots, planks groaning under each step. At the boat, I brace a heel against its side, grip the railing, and haul myself up. The hull jerks with the current, the motion sloshing my stomach and rattling my head in sync with the waves. I've never liked boats. Crossing to the bow, I find the figure folded in on himself—hunched tight like a clamshell. Percy is wearing a teal flat-brim hat stitched with purple rectangles and tortoiseshell sunglasses tinted red. My reflection looms in the lenses, pale and malnourished. A bottle dangles from his fingers, glass tapping out a private rhythm as his gaze fixes somewhere beyond the marina. My hands are bowling balls, weighty and klutzy dangling at my sides. I shove them into my jacket pockets because I don't know where else they belong. Percy glances over his shoulder, eyes passing through me like I'm a ghost. He tips the bottle back and the shadow of his arm elongates across the bow, creeping over salt-stained lacquer. The boat rocks with the uneven current. I drop to one knee beside him, then sit.

"You're starting to look old," he says. The shift of the boat makes my movements look unsteady, betraying my vulnerabilities. "I didn't think the next time I saw you that you would have changed this much." He drinks. Amber foam catches the light.

"Can we talk?" My voice comes out rough, stammering.

"I don't have much of a choice," he says. His eyes flick to the badge hanging from my neck, and he tilts the bottle toward it. "What's the point in asking?"

"Can we walk?" I try again. The wind tugs strands of hair across my forehead. The boat's sway keeps my stomach on edge. "Down the marina?"

Percy doesn't answer at first—just lets the silence sit. The boat groans against the dock, hollow knocks thudding through the hull. Overhead, gulls rasp out harsh, throaty cries. My jaw tightens. The sounds conglomerate together into one irregular, droning note.

"No," Percy says, flat.

"I should've come for the funeral," I tell him. My throat feels raw, parched. The silence swells again. "I loved her—regardless of the things I said, regardless of the things I did."

He exhales through his nose in a sharp, mocking huff.

"I was sitting there flipping through catalogs of caskets, trying to figure out what I could even afford. Then there's the assets to deal with. I barely even know what assets are." He tips the bottle, draining it. "And then what? What am I supposed to do next?"

I don't answer. Anything I say will only cut deeper, and the silence is already its own wound. I want to speak—he doesn't deserve more pain—but I'm useless here. I stay quiet. That hurts him too. Every road ends the same.

"Do you know what it's like to bury your mother alone?" he says. "You may have gone numb to death, but some of us still shudder when we see a car crash on the news."

"It's like death's glued to me—closer than the sunlight on my back," I say. "Every road I take leaves me burned and blistered, no matter where it leads." The words taste dry in my mouth, and for a moment I weigh whether they'll reach him at all. I pause, searching his face for some softening, some sign he's letting me in—but my mind slips to the image of a black carnation resting on her pillow. The sheets around it are rumpled, hollow where her head should have been, and the flower's shadow bleeds in the afternoon light. The quiet in my head is deafening. His jaw tightens. "Look," I say, trying to pull back to solid ground, "I dove into this case and—"

"Right," he cuts in. "For a second there, I almost forgot who you were."

"I didn't want to leave you or your mother. It drove me into dark corners—ate at me. I'm still trying to steady myself from that. It doesn't make it right, and I know it doesn't make it better."

"I'm sure it was tough," Percy snaps, "between drug-fueled binges, back-alley prostitutes, and vomiting up last night's regrets behind slummy gas stations. I'm guessing your police buddies never caught wind of that—or you just picked that badge up at a dollar store."

I don't respond. I let his rage hang in the summer heat, a static buzz warping the air between us. Any attempt at reconciliation now would burn up before it reached him, so I let him steam. The harder part will be steering us to the real reason I came. I can feel the corners of my mouth threatening to curve into something that might read as indifference.

"Percy, I need to ask you something."

"You should go," he blurts.

I grit my teeth and an ache shoots through my jaw. My throat feels like sandpaper, every imperfection scraping as I swallow. He won't meet my eyes—his head hangs low, shutting me out.

"I need to ask you a few questions about the marina—if you've noticed anything unusual." The words come out rougher than I want, but there's no elegant way to broach this. He stays quiet, so I press on. "I'm working the Canine case. It's getting dodgy."

"There's always a fucking case," he mutters.

"Last night, the motel manager at The Blue Mist called in a complaint of a foul odor. He checked a room and found the body. We think the person responsible might frequent the marina, own a boat here, or have passed through in the last few days. Have you seen anything unusual? Anyone out of place or acting strange?"

"No, I don't think so." His voice is low, almost swallowed by the water lapping against the hull. "Faces blur together after a while. You stop knowing who's worth remembering because there's no way to tell who's going stick around."

I nod, pull a card from my jacket, and hand it to him. "Call me if anything comes up. My cellphone number is at the bottom. It's a new number since I moved back."

"Just for the case?" he asks, taking the card. His tone is still flat, harsh, but the question loosens something in my chest.

"Anything," I tell him. "I'm staying downtown until I find a place."

"Thanks, James." That lands heavier than I expect—it's the first time he's used my name, and I'm not sure how to take it. "I met this guy at the funeral. Pretty sure he's on something, but he's decent. Seems like the only one who actually gives a shit about me right now. Sometimes I wonder what it'd be like to be blasted out of my head like that. Push it all down. At least the pain of being strung out is pain you can control." He turns the card over in his fingers. Silence stretches. I push my palms against the deck and rise, knees bent against the boat's sway, making my way toward the bow. "I'm still trying to resemble the person I was," Percy says behind me. "Reconfigure. Figure out who I am or where I go now."

"Yeah," I say. "Me too."

I step down the dock, boots clacking against the warped planks. The marina smells of brine and stale fuel. My phone buzzes in my jacket pocket. It's Stanton.

"Pierce," I say, clearing my throat as I bring it to my ear. The tension in my muscles has started to ease, though my throat feels clotted again, coated in saliva. Stanton's voice cuts in—sharp, quick, like she's riding a spike of adrenaline.

"The victim's ID matches his license," she says. "The autopsy is in progress. He was under the influence of some illicit substances."

"Or drugged," I answer, scanning the marina as I keep walking.

"Exactly." There's an edge of enthusiasm in her tone. "While we wait for the toxicology analysis to return, I'm going to meet the victim's parents and deliver the news. He was visiting from out of town, but they still live here. They might know who he was close to—places he hung out or anyone he could have met up with."

"I'll join you. I reviewed the motel's camera footage. It's mostly static and snow—you couldn't tell bigfoot from a man in a suit—but you can at least make out two figures."

"What exactly does it show?"

"A side profile of two men. One matches the victim—same clothes, same build. The other's in a black hoodie with the hood up. Stature matches the bartender's description. His features are too blurred or covered to get anything solid. If he was drugged, it probably happened after they entered the room—they both look steady on their feet in the footage."

"Damn," Stanton says, then pauses. "I'll be there in twenty."

TRANSACTIONAL

I'm high, and Percy is calling. I shot up an hour ago, maybe two—time drains into a liquid blur, so I'm not too sure. I'm spread out on the couch, my body hollow, like a sewer tunnel draining—emptying itself, leaking my weight. My jeans are pushed low on my hips, and I'm tracing the shaft of my cock. Rhythmless—just chasing the tension. There's a pressure—cool, electric—buzzing deep under my skin and rippling through my veins. My shirt is drenched in sweat and sticks to my back. It drips down my neck in beads, slick and hot. The moisture clings to my hairline, grease sticking to my scalp. My vision fractures, pupils vibrating into a glassy hum that warps and blurs. I groan, zip up my jeans, and fumble to clasp my belt. The fabric drags against my skin and my belt snaps together with a sickly, muted click. Sweat leaves oily trails across my phone screen when I pick it up to answer.

"Hey," I mutter, voice scraping my throat.

"You free?" Percy spits, sharp, insistent. I narrow my eyes, listening. "I kind of need someone. I don't know… seems right to ask you," he says, voice wavering at the edges. I choke back mucus, swallow. I don't like this. There's a quiver under his words—a panicked undertone, like it's difficult for him to string together a coherent sentence.

"Sure," I say, propping myself upright against the cushions. My clothes suck at the contours of my skin like they want to keep it.

My thighs feel like they're sinking into warm pudding with how moisture cakes the hairs down my legs. "When?"

"I'm on my way over," he says. The words bubble up, almost obscene, like pustules splitting beneath my sternum. "I need to get out of town for the afternoon." There's a pause, breath jagged through the receiver, small tremors running along the line. He hesitates, uncertain. "My parents own a summer home a few miles out of the city," he continues. "It's got an ocean view, but looks more like a cabin. It's nestled back between trees, high on the side of a ridge. The foliage swallows it whole and shades it from the sun."

I don't hear much of what he's saying—just a motor whirring, grinding in my skull, his words chugging past me. My chest heaves, bones bending outward, skin slick with white froth. My skull burns from the inside, wax melting, dripping into nothing. Then his voice vanishes. I squint, as if forcing my eyes might dredge me back from the blur, as if I could chase the drone through the glassy haze of my vision.

"Sure," I say again. He hangs up. I don't know what I'm doing. Mouth foamed, filmed in sweat. I wish I wasn't high. I wish I were dead. One of those is a lie.

I climb into the shower, and the water licks my body, warm and urgent, tracing my shoulders, sliding down my chest, smoothing over my navel. I picture Percy's stale breath, his saliva searing my muscles, soaking into my hip bones. My cock stiffens, and I press my stomach against the cool shower tiles. The icy shock runs through me, tingling at my navel, spreading into my stomach, sinking into my thighs, rising in my throat. Soap flakes cling to my chest, gritty and slick, and I imagine him there, his presence pressing into my skin, filling me from the inside out. Tart come welling in my pores.

Then screeching—car brakes. The horn blares, shrill. I turn the shower knob, pressing my forehead into the tiles, letting the remaining water drip from the shower head and trickle down my torso. The glass fogs over, plastered with mist. My cock shrivels as the cold tiles bite at my forehead. My skin absorbs the humid air—heavy, soaked. The horn blares again, relentless.

I fling open the front door, letting it slam behind me, tugging a fresh shirt over my head. He's there, sunglasses low, eyes locked on the blacktop like he's counting the pockmarks in its asphalt flesh. I rake my fingers through my hair, shaking damp strands free. The heat clings, already pulling them back into slick ribbons of sweat.

The passenger door pops, and I slide into the leather seat. The leather exhales, breathes, something, as my ass settles into it. I close the door, inhale sharp. Percy's hand snakes to my thigh, warm, firm. The fabric of my jeans bunches, tightening over my skin, quivering along my muscles. I wonder if he can make out the imprint of my cock against the denim—pressing, straining.

"Are you okay?" Percy asks, tilting his head. The sunglasses hide his eyes, but his lips tilt in a wave of concern. I blink hard, forcing my eyes open wider. I'm a damned, drugged deer caught in the reflection of his sunglasses—his buzzing headlights. We're both waiting for me to give him some kind of response. Freeze or run—get hit.

"I'm fine," I say, nodding, swallowing hard. He stares for a moment longer before returning his hand to the stick shift. My smirk is either too expensive or too cheap—either way, he doesn't buy it.

"Sure," he says. He knows I'm lying. I'm not trying hard enough to hide it. He ignores it because he feels it too. It scares him. Whatever—get your head straight. My other head pulses, autonomous. My jeans try to clench it back. Fuck. A rush vibrates through my forehead, stringy, like strands of semen quivering beneath my skull. My brain is sopping in milky cords under my skin, leaking, seeping out of my scalp. The denim tightens over my crotch. I press my palm into it, and an ecstatic lurch snakes up my throat. Percy notices. Then it hits me—we're moving. The car rolls beneath us, the tires spinning, my body revolving with them, suspended in the blur of motion and sensation. I'm caught between the high and the drive, suspended.

"I'm glad you could come. I needed someone to tag along," he says. "I haven't been up to our summer home since my mother died. It was my parents' place, but we all knew it was really hers at heart. It feels like some kind of specter—like something hovering over me since she died. I don't know what to do with it."

"Sell it," I blurt. It's all I can manage in the moment, but it doesn't feel like enough. Like I owe him more—some other words I haven't said, something I should have. He doesn't respond, and I realize it wasn't the right thing to say. Good.

We hit bumps in the road, and my legs shiver against the seats. The leather presses into me like wet, naked bodies, thudding against my back and ass, dragging me into their caress. I run fingers along my neck, a shiver crawling through me. He's talking, I think, but I'm not paying attention. I'm holding a moan behind my teeth, eyes fixed on his lap below the belt buckle, tracing the taut line of his stomach straining against the seatbelt. Tension from the seatbelt molds to his sticky torso, highlighting the sculpted ridges of his stomach through the creases of his shirt. I want to climb over, around, into him.

"You're the only person I know that's kind of wavering," Percy says, and somehow it jerks my focus. Wavering—such a pliable word, like it could bend around anything. Like I'm augmented into a banal lump. "Not in a bad way, but you kind of exist around me without a bias. People say a lot from their expressions. Somone raises an eyebrow, and you know that suddenly whatever you said is on trial. They purse their lips and it's judgment, like you're grotesque. You don't do that. Your mannerisms are all the same. I guess that's comfortable." Whatever he's unpacking contradicts what my jeans are trying to contain. "Don't get me wrong, it's not a bad thing. They just don't change. I'm attracted to the ambivalence in that, or maybe I'm attracted to how you hide it. It makes me comfortable that I don't have to deal with whatever you're really feeling." People say things they don't buy into because dishonesty is more comfortable than silence. The road jostles us again. The leather presses closer, closing in, tight.

"That doesn't bother you?" I ask, trying to tether myself to whatever this is, though my body has its own agenda. I want his tongue dragging over a cheese grater, shredding saturated mucus clumps across my bare chest, smearing into my oiled skin.

"If I think about it too long, it might," he says.

Outside the driver's window, the city melts into a jagged mural—stones spiking from dirt like fractured teeth. Time thins—I can't say how long we've been moving, or how much of it I've truly existed in. My eyes snap back to the seatbelt, his waist pressed against mine, and I feel him everywhere at once. His tongue burrows into my throat—swollen, greedy, fat, sliding into my stomach like molten rope. I swallow, muscles contracting, straining against the pulse. Choke. I break my gaze, glaze over the hollow of his neckline, the arch of his back, then tilt my head toward the windshield. It's plastered with insect ruin, sticky streaks of dismembered wings and shells—making my stomach flip. I lean my head out the passenger window, letting the air claw at me.

The seatbelt massages into my sternum and navel, dragging a line of heat through me that hums down my thighs. We're climbing, or falling—maybe both—through a winding blacktop canyon, jagged mural frozen along his side. The ocean glimmers below, its whitecaps milky—my mouth floods with saliva and I can't hold it back. My mind is a single fiber back to him: Percy bent, spread, skin glistening, impossibly close. Every imagined brush of his body sends electric tremors slithering through my veins—ties slicked knots under my skin.

He turns the wheel, veers onto a dirt road. Gravel jolts from beneath the tires, and the chassis quakes, groaning as it grinds its way through the dirt. Shadows claw over the car from the trees above, brushing the roof, whispering—inaudible voices teasing through the hum of the engine. My fingers grip the seat, knuckles white, hips pressing toward him instinctively, pulling him into all the nerve endings I can still feel. Every bump, jolt, and shadow becomes a pulse in my body, a resonance within him, a tide that I ride and can't escape.

"We're here," Percy says, pulling the car to a stop in front of the cabin. It's rustic with fake wood-painted patterns smeared in muddy layers, the porch the same, stairs worn at the corners like cracking bones. Chips peel back to reveal a rubbery underlayer.

I follow behind him, stepping up warped boards that groan beneath our weight. Ice-jagged sparks lacerate my joints, veins inflating with tension, footfalls hammering my skull. My gaze is fixed on his ass, the slight sway as he moves ahead, the fabric of his jeans hugging muscle and rippling over the tiny tear at his thigh. Threads stretch in loose webs, and I imagine my fingers weaving through them, fingernails scraping over skin, tiny goosebumps rising like static across his body. I can feel my palms tighten, imagining tracing the fine hairs along his thighs, pressing into the warmth beneath, and my body hums with a lurching, seething energy that wants to collapse, consume, and fold around him entirely.

Percy moves ahead, unaware, or pretending, and I follow. The creaks and tremors are a rhythm that mirrors the tightening ache of anticipation winding in my chest. The cabin looms above, shadowed and indifferent. Inside, the air presses heavy with desire and obsession, and I can't decide whether I want to sink into it—or into him.

He opens the door, and I slip inside behind him, the cabin swallowing us whole. The air is warm against my skin. Patinaed metal sculptures jut from the walls, edges dull yet sharp in my imagination, like teeth waiting to unfurl—to bite. Between them, photographs bloom in jagged, blown-out squares—pixelated chaos. I can't stop staring, imagining each dot as a tiny painting, a secret world hiding some fragment of him. Then I see him. Percy. With his mother. The boat. Other men I don't know. His face is always crisp, everything else blurred. My chest clenches, muscles tightening, veins pulsing, a wire wound tight around my spine. Empty hooks punctuate the walls where pictures used to hang. I want to fill them, press him into their vacant spaces.

The kitchen opens into the living area, divided by a bar top with neon checkered stools—lime and yellow, alien against the washed wood—intrusive, demanding attention. The color sears behind my eyes, igniting something raw and tight in my pelvis, nerves buzzing, chest rising, falling, wanting. I don't belong here. Across from the bar, the black licorice leather sofa gleams, cushions taut and slick. The faux brick wall circling the living room is spongy, inviting, daring me to press my fists into it so it can suck on my knuckles. And then I notice the painting. It's hung in the place of the television—floral frame coated in gold lacquered trim, thick and smothering. It juts forward. Insistent, aggressive. I can feel it in my teeth, in my fingertips, in the pressure constricting my pelvis, like the cabin itself is aware of my gaze. The painting breathes, the frame hissing over the edges, and I think of Percy bending over it, bending over me, and the room hums with possibilities—hot, firm, risky. My gaze lingers. Obsessive, imagining his hands, the curve of his fingers over the frame, pressing into the wood, the paint, his nails catching the edge. My pulse syncs with the imagined compression—body tightening, stomach knotting, cock aching, veins screaming with need. The cabin hums around me, walls pulse with heat. Surfaces absorb me. The shadows brush every corner in textures that harden my body. Percy moves, brushing by, and I feel him everywhere—the dip of his shoulder, the tension in his jeans, the warmth spilling from his body. My own muscles clench in response, pelvis rocking, hands itching to explore, claim, devour. His breath slides through me, into me, making me tremor, ache. I could dissolve into it, into him, into the smell of wood, metal, fabric, skin. My tongue presses against my teeth, drool pooling thick in my mouth. The cabin waits. Percy waits. And I wait inside the snare trembling—electric, drenched in want, undone, consumed by the hum of desire moaning through the space and through my body alike.

I stand with my back to the bar top, my back to Percy. He opens the refrigerator and begins rifling through it, the faint clink of glass echoing. I step forward, pressing against the back of the sofa, angling for a better look at the painting. My fingers trail along the sofa leather, knuckles whitening, jeans tight, heart hammering. The belt of my jeans presses against the edge of the leather, and I rub against it, trying to stop myself from hungrily massaging my cock.

The painting dominates my vision, swollen with grotesque muscle and hollowed innards. It's layered in pale tans, maroons, and blacks, and depicts a monstrous cattle corpse. The carcass stretches across the canvas, fat and bulging, the stomach hollow and glistening. Its sides bulge like stuffed, lumpy garbage bags. The head is removed, the stomach carved open, innards meticulously cleaned out. Two hooves are tied taut to the corners of the frame—the rear hooves mirror the restraint. The ribcage is rendered in intense detail, bones stretched around the hollowed stomach, pink tissue and sticky sinews strung across its frame. Tendons swell, tissues warp—this isn't just tanning, it's a display of anatomy, grotesque yet precise, and it pulls me in. I imagine sliding my hands across the rope, feeling its tautness press into my palms, imagining wrapping my fingers around the taut sinews. Staring at the muscles, I feel my own body respond, veins throbbing in my arms and neck, a rush of heat and pulse. I want to inhabit that space, swim inside its vast cavity, lose myself in the secretions and folds, to drown in the intimate, terrible expanse of it.

"There's a couple left in here," Percy calls over, breaking my fantasizing grip on the carcass. Heat floods my ears—I wonder if he can tell. "She always made sure the fridge was stocked just enough." I hear glass bottles clink against the bar top. I stay in place, swiveling my head to follow him. He pops lids with a bottle opener, then steps out from behind the counter, crossing the kitchen toward me. My gaze tracks him mechanically. My palms dig into the headboard, and when he leans against it, his side grazes my hand. Percy's presence weaves heat into my spine. He brushes my shoulder and his warmth seeps through the thin fabric of our shirts. Percy shifts, his leg brushing mine, and the contact sends shivers along my spine—each touch a tether between reality and hallucination. My cock strains in my jeans, every nerve alight. I snap my eyes back to the painting, but Percy doesn't look away from me. He's scanning, from my eyes down to my chest, then back up. I can't tell if it's flirtation or judgment. Either way, my chest tightens. I stay silent, staring at the painting, wondering if he notices my dilated pupils.

"It's a fucking weird painting, isn't it?" Percy says.

"I like it." I love it. The tendons in the painting seem to pulse, ribcage creaking, its hollow swollen with viscera, and I imagine sinking into it, curling inside that cavernous flesh while Percy's body presses against me, teasing me, grounding me.

"My mother got it at an art auction downtown. She paid a boatload for it. I mean, considering what it is." Percy takes a swig, glares at the painting, and jabs at it with the lip of the beer bottle. "I feel like I get art," he continues. "I really do. But some art… just isn't art."

"That's subjective," I snap. My fingers bunch tighter around the headboard, the fire in my chest crawling into my knuckles, inflaming my fists. I glance at the space between us, then back to the painting. He leans closer and his shoulder grazes mine. I taste iron, the imagined blood of the carcass, and the faint salt of him sharp against my tongue. My veins pulse, scalp tingling, every detail in the painting mirrored in the heat of his hand against mine. His leg brushes mine, and I absorb the tension of his presence.

"Nothing's subjective," he replies. "Everything's transactional." He peers over my cheek, into me. "The only thing that matters is how much it's worth." He tilts back, lifts the bottle to his lips, and I hear the soft swallow of beer. His wet lips pucker around the glass. He lowers it, taps his finger against the bottle. "I don't think this abstract, brown blob is art. Or worth much of anything."

"You don't think it's fairly realistic?" I ask. I wriggle closer, sink deeper into the imagined cavity, my palms grazing the slick walls, feeling its hollowed curves and sticky tendons. Percy shifts behind me, silent but insistent, his shoulder, his warmth blistering through the hallucination. "I mean, I don't know cattle anatomy, but there's a lot of detail here. That's got to count for something."

"You see cattle?"

"What do you mean?"

"Maybe value is in the creativity behind the eye," he says, light, mocking. I catch a curved smile at the corner of his mouth from my periphery. Like I missed a punchline. I don't get it. "I just see a canvas of splotchy brown lines."

A ripple of confusion stings my forehead. And yet—somehow— I'm lost, submerged in the grotesque flesh and his body at once, the pulse of the painting mirrored in the pulse of his skin, my mind and body fusing together, desperate, consuming, swallowed entirely by the visceral, living canvas. My cock presses hard against the side of my jeans, throbbing, restless. We stand in silence, taut and fragile. Our breaths mingle, heavy in the humid air. His exhalations brush my cheek. Percy's eyes trace the curve of the bottle, sharp and watchful. The heat between us lingers unspoken, dangerous.

"My father came to visit me," Percy blurts, breaking the silence.

"Yeah," I say, letting the words bubble up without thinking, pretending to be curious. I want him to stop, but a part of me leans closer, aching to trace the tension in his body, wanting to massage gristly strips of his skin around my fingers and wrap his meat rinds around my cock.

"He's moving back," he continues. "I don't know what to make of it."

"Why?" I ask, though my voice is flatter than curiosity demands. Something rises in him, an edge I can't read, and it pulls at me, restless and unpredictable. I feel it wrap my chest, spinning outward in shivers that race down my arms. I want to spit in his gashes.

"He works for the city," Percy says, his voice wavering. He's not being entirely upfront. "Odd jobs. Business stuff I don't really understand." He's lying—just enough. "He moved back for work, possibly for me too. I don't know."

"He must get paid well to afford this place. Or your mother did," I murmur, voice low, eyes catching the line of his jaw as he shifts.

"He does," he admits, a nervous tremor shaking his words. "He's good at his job. Sees patterns others don't, finds solutions others wouldn't. Doesn't seem easy." There's honesty in it now, but the uncertainty gnaws at me—friction I can't ignore.

"Sounds like you admire him."

Percy's gaze lingers on the bottle, and for a moment, the quiet stretches—fragile, humming, charged. The air between us pulls at something deep inside, something I can't quite name.

"Do you ever feel like you're living outside of your body?" he asks. "Like you're interacting with people from a third-person perspective and everything—everyone—looks strange?"

"Yeah," I say, "but probably much different than you."

His eyes well up, and he pinches the bridge of his nose. He rubs at them, and they grow bloodshot. This is what he's been hiding. He leans his head into my shoulder blade, and strands of hair curl against my skin, tickling the brim of my nose. The absence he portrayed was a cover-up—everything before was fabricated. His body trembles against me, and the dampness of his skin transfers onto my shirt. My throat tightens. I don't move him. I let him collapse into me, let him release whatever he's been holding. My own body hums with tension, nerves strung tight. He's a weight against me, heavy and unpredictable, and I want to hold him, press against him, feel him entirely. The heat of his presence winds around me, and I can't look away. His movements press against something buried in me—a chaotic, obsessive need to feel, to contain. My ribcage feels bound in electric cords, nerves taut and strung in knots. I want to engulf him, fold him into the weight of my presence, consume the space he occupies. He's not unique—there's nothing different about him from the rest of the men I've devoured, dissected. Weak. My hands clench. I want to crush his throat like a soda can—bend tin. Ache to breed his bones in ejaculate and crawl inside his tendons. Press closer, merge with him, wrap obsession over me like a second skin, a leathery suit of fixation that clings to my chest and spine.

He lifts his head, pressing his lips to the side of my mouth, then to mine. The touch sends an ecstatic prick through my lips, crawling into my gums and along the roof of my mouth. His tongue traces mine—like they're interlocking slugs shriveling and dying into each other. I grip his face in both hands and pull him closer. He doesn't shock these sensations through me, it's the drugs. My chest presses into his, the warmth of him, his weight, crushes my hunger. His hand slides along my side, brushing over my ribs, tracing my waist. My muscles tense, straining toward him, my body humming with the electric charge of proximity. Our breaths, the tilting of our heads, shared pulsations, all feel amplified—like the world has shrunk to this moment, this closeness, and nothing else exists. I lean into him harder, desperate for more, and the rush swells until it's unbearable. Chaotic, intoxicating.

He pulls back for a moment, his eyes searching mine, and I let out a sharp, involuntary exhale. Our gazes lock, and I feel the weight of him pressing through the space between us. A grin curves at the edge of his mouth—uneasy, unreadable.

"Are you high?" he asks—even, flat. Not a question so much as a declaration. Our bodies part.

"Yeah," I whisper, blinking. Foggy slits slice through my glassy vision. "I didn't intend to be. Or, like, intend on being anywhere outside of myself—I guess."

"I get it," he says, retreating to the kitchen. He drains his bottle, tosses it in the trash, and grabs another from the fridge, the pop of the cap is sharp in the silence. I still haven't touched mine, so he hands it to me on his return.

"Thanks," I mutter, taking the bottle.

"It's easier to ignore pain than deal with it," he says. The thought of bending the bottle, forcing it against him, tasting him again—hovers in my mind, jagged and insistent. Carve underneath his chin, cut my tongue on the shards skewered through his tongue. "It's always there, and it always will be. You choose whether to manage it or shove it aside."

"That's subjective," I murmur, but my chest tightens, my knuckles whitening against the bottle. I might break it.

"You either make your bed on a mattress or under the dirt," he says, lifting the bottle to his lips. Preachy. Disappointing. I watch him drink, the world narrowing to the angle of his jaw, the tilt of his head. "I won't stick around for the latter."

I don't answer. I don't move. All I feel is pressure in my chest— the slow, suffocating urge of wanting to undo him. Whatever. I'm going to kill him.

CLOT

It's three in the morning. I'm slumped over the bathroom sink, arms stiff, knuckles pressed raw against the porcelain. Warm water dribbles from the faucet, hissing faintly as it hits the basin. My head pulses, hollow and airy, thoughts shrieking, jagged and bleating like trapped animals.

Sheets shift behind me. Stewart rolls over. I glance at my reflection in the vanity mirror. My eyes are halos of bruised black, darkening into swollen purple crescents. I pull my bottom lip down with a fingernail. It's puffy like an engorged larva, red and splitting, flaking at the edges. Time fractures. Days dissolve into one endless, dragging scene. My consciousness lurches through it in slow motion, stop-motion, picturesque snapshots—fixating on his body. They're relentless, jabbing, repeating. I can't tell what's real anymore. Sleep might be behind me—or this might *be* sleep. Hollow. Empty. Shell. I hear Stewart shuffle under the sheets. Again. The sound yanks me back, something about him always yanks me back. I flex my fingers, tense, and stare into the mirror again. His bathroom smells of lavender and milk, sickly sweet and cloying. It latches onto my stomach, my throat, makes my head swim. It smells like him—all his edges, distilled and nauseating. My reflection flickers. My eyes, my bruises, the cracking lip—I can't tell where I end and the glass begins. The emptiness in me stretches, yawns, and I feel it want to consume the room, the light, him, all of it.

I remember Percy dropping me off at some point after we returned to town. We didn't talk much on the way back—I know I didn't. I think he was just tolerating my state of being, which was more than I could say for myself. It boils my stomach bile. Later, I stumbled through Stewart's door, swaying in a haze, moving on autopilot in some drug-addled stupor, like clockwork. He was slouched on the sofa, drumming his bony fingers absently down the front of his jeans—so I fucked him. I guided his frail frame backward into his room, steadying him as he stumbled, bent him over the mattress. My hands gripped the sides of his body, feeling the sharp angles and uneven planes beneath his skin, like the weathered surfaces of cave rock—tanned, discolored, and worn with age. While I was fucking him, I pressed my nails into his wrinkled back, feeling the tautness of his skin ooze beads of clear fluid—pus. I imagined tightening fists around his ankles, contorting his legs backward, and snapping his ligaments. Testing the limits of his frailty like he was an exorcism toy. Each thrust warranted a raspy, childish groan—like my cock was penetrating through his throat and petrifying pain within his creases. Every fragile moan made the room charged with unease. Anytime I do this, I imagine his body might buckle, collapse, or crumple into itself like melting plastic. He never lets me take off my shirt. He hates my scars. He says I look like some mangy, beaten dumpster dog. I don't disagree, but I like them. I had bent him over, beaten him, fucked him, made him bark at me. I came inside of him mid-bark. The motions and sounds he made sharpened the room—something erupted inside me, outside me. A stream of erotic pain had expelled from my cock, like I had excised a demon from my body. I had taken each deflated balloon of his ass, pushed their flabs to either side, directed a fist to caress the cavern of his malleable rectum. Sometimes there's blood.

I stop ruminating and turn the faucet to stop the water flow. I stand there for a moment, my gaze floating over the sink. My bare legs, feet, and limp cock stiffen in my lower peripheral vision. There's a dried splotch of come crusted along my navel. I rub at it, it flakes, and I turn the shower on. The glass is sparkling under the vanity light, beaming through its crisp surface. It reflects my body, my translucent skin shifting over my ribcage, moving with my strained breaths. The bones remain still, the flesh sliding back and forth along them. I stare at the scars in my reflection, tracing them with my fingers, through them, along the entirety of my mutilated body. It looks like I sleep in barbed wire, and the thought arouses me. I start getting erect thinking of those scars melting into the incisions I wanted to line Percy's tender stomach in. A drop of blood lands on the tile. I press the back of my hand against my nose, applying pressure, tilting my head back. It pools there, then dribbles over my chin and down my neck.

"Fuck," I mutter. It takes longer than usual to clot.

"What's going on?" Stewart groans, appearing in the doorway, hunched over, shoulders drooping as if the weight of him might topple forward. He squints, eyes hard to make out in the steam-filled room. His face glows red from the heat, like molten lava.

"Nosebleed," I whisper back, voice groggy.

"When it clots, come back to bed," Stewart says.

I hate him. I nod. He lingers, and I feel his gaze on me, calculating, as if he's waiting for me to falter. When I shift my body and tilt my head, the expression changes. His face tightens, lips drawn into a frown, as if the heat and tension are pressing him inward. I slowly draw my hand from my nose. The bleeding subsides, leaving just a few final drips before it stops. My mouth is a Rorschach blood-blot.

"You never told me what happened to your parents," Stewart says abruptly, catching me off guard. A flare of irritation rises in my chest.

"They're dead," I reply. "You should know that—you were there."

"I thought we'd grown closer. I'm sorry," he apologizes, and it makes the irritation sting sharper. He knows better.

"I thought we made it clear when you took me in," I say. He's breaching our agreement, and I thought we had an understanding. He can have my body if I could have his home—at least until some better option shows up. But years later, I've learned there isn't one. There never was. "Let sleeping dogs lie."

"I know how this all started—our arrangement, or whatever," Stewart says, his tone somber. "Your coldness is fair. I'm partially to blame for that, letting it fester. But you're more to me than just a body to use, you know."

He's staring at my scars, but differently this time. It unsettles me—there's something in the crook of his lips, some shame. I can't tell if it's his own shame, or pity for me. Either way, it's wasting my time.

"My skin has always been collateral," I say, sliding the shower door open and stepping in. This conversation is over. Stewart can draw back into the sheets, retreat into his writhing shell, or wherever he crawled from. "Don't make this out to be more than what it is."

PIERCE: PRESSURE

I'm pressed into an off-white floral couch that's laminated under a plastic sheet. It crinkles and sticks beneath my palms with every shift. Pastel flowers and embroidered branches stretch across the fabric like something meant to be preserved behind glass. The rest of the furniture is wrapped in plastic too. It's a delicate, protective layer that makes the room feel frozen, paranoid. I lift the clay mug in front of me and sip coffee. A fingerprint with initials etched into the side catches my eye, a crude heart carved lopsidedly into the clay. Does the print match the victim's? My throat tightens at the thought.

Stanton stands by the window, her silhouette rigid against the blinds, peering into the oppressive afternoon heat. Sunlight slants into the living room, heavy and viscous, filling the space with a quiet, suffocating glare. Memory slides in with it—Sunday afternoons, returning from church, bells drifting through warm air, calm and ordered. I set the mug down on a cork coaster, press my fingers against my chin, rub the base of my jaw, fold my hands between my legs. A prayer, a futile plea. The memory presses in like a tomb sealing shut.

The oriental rug beneath the coffee table drags my attention, a feeble anchor against the sobs that leak through the room like water from a cracked pipe. Across from me, the mother hunches into a wicker chair, palms covering her face, body crumpled like it could collapse through the frame. I'm glad she can't see me. My own gestures feel intrusive, clumsy, wrong. Her hair is bunched in a messy nest, tangles bouncing against her shoulders in cadence with her sobbing. Her face is sharp, harsh—sunken around the lips, hollowed by grief. It's a stark contrast to her son—his cheeks were pudgy, round, and head a perfect bowl.

She rubs at her eyes, fists moving with frantic insistence. She glares at the back of Stanton's jacket. If this doesn't end soon, I think, she might leap forward. Stanton's words can wound, but usually there's a rhythm, a method behind the bite. Normally, there's a careful method to her bluntness, a passion laced through the harshness. Not now. Now, her tact is absent, and the weight of it feels personal. I bet it's starting to feel personal for her. This time it's reckless and abrasive. Her usual precision is gone.

The woman stops sobbing, and the sudden silence is almost unbearable. I know Stanton hears it too, but she doesn't acknowledge it. She remains at the window, back turned, watching cars drift past as if scrutinizing their every movement too.

"I think that's all the questions we have for you now, ma'am," I say, cutting into the quiet. Her jaw tightens, as if she's weighing whether to snap at Stanton. Or she's sending some unspoken, urgent signal—carving daggers into Stanton's jacket with her piercing eyes. I glance toward Stanton, waiting for her to respond, to intervene. She doesn't. Her fists slide into her pockets, but her gaze stays locked on the window, distant and unyielding. "We'll be in touch. If anything comes up—or if you think of something, even if it seems small—give us a call.

We appreciate your time." I slide my card across the table. The corners of her mouth tremble, a silent concession, a private defeat in her standoff with Stanton. She buries her face in her hands and wails again, her body shuddering and wrenching under the force of grief. The wicker chair groans under her weight, creaking in rhythm with each throaty sob. I take it as my cue to leave.

"Stanton?" I murmur, stepping to her side and tapping her shoulder. She flinches, a flash of irate coldness cutting across her face, then blinks, disoriented, like she's been yanked from some other ethereal plane. For a moment, she seems suspended—lost somewhere between fury and confusion. She doesn't glance at the woman. She nods at me once, then strides out with a relentless resolve. Her boots pound the floorboards, each step a sharp echo that fills the hallway.

I fall in step behind her, trying to match her pace, but she quickens, moving down the driveway like she's chasing down something unseen, propelled by sheer, unthinking determination. I catch her at the passenger door and grip her elbow, tugging. Her body stiffens—her muscles seize, contracting like steel springs. She spins on me, teeth bared in a hard, dangerous snarl. Her eyes burn with a feral rage, and I feel the heat of it radiate outward, contained in a human frame—ready to bite if provoked.

"What the fuck has gotten into you?" I hiss, voice low, firm. My words feel swallowed by the fervor radiating off her. "You're erratic. Unhinged. You look like you haven't slept in days." Her elbow stiffens under my grip, trembles, a live wire of tension. "You're shaking. Foaming at the mouth like some rabid mutt."

Her teeth flash. Her spit lands somewhere between me and the asphalt. "You want to know what's gotten into me?" Every word sparks embers. "We haven't gotten any closer. Someone else is going to die. People like that—they thrive on our time. They twist it like it's our fault. Like we're the ones killing their kids." Her eyes glaze over, a trickle running down her cheek. "We're trying to make it a little safer for their kids—for my kids—and they tell us we don't know pain. We keep doing this, and there's no guarantee we'll ever get closer."

I grit my teeth. "You're not going to get closer if you can't even walk without falling apart."

She laughs—sharp, empty—and it cuts into me. "Yeah?" she snaps. "Well, I'm not willing to risk burying my kid for your apathy. What's it to you to avoid another funeral?"

I take a step closer, and the air between us thickens, charged. "Your obsession isn't helping anyone," I say, jagged. "It's going to bury the case—and you with it." My chest heaves. I press my fingers to the bridge of my nose, exhale, trying to anchor myself. I feel her body shaking through the ground. Silence stretches viscous, almost solid between us. Her eyes burn into me, unyielding. I swallow the heat rising in my throat, try to speak over it, over her fury. "What good is any of this," I say, voice trembling, "if you drive your own sanity into the ground first?"

She doesn't answer. The world feels smaller now, compressed. Her rage presses against my chest, thick as smoke. I know she's waiting for me to break first. I have to hold it together.

She crumples to the sidewalk, knees slamming together, body folding into the car. Screams tear out of her throat—raw, broken, like her jaw might fracture. Fists clutch at her skull, fingers tangling her hair, eyes squeezed shut. Sharp exhales rip from her chest. Then, fumbling in her pocket, she produces a cigarette and lighter. Sparks, inhale, tilt, exhale— smoke sliding along the length of the car.

I kneel in front of her, a flush crawling into my forehead, sweat slicked, fear pressing in from all angles. My throat pulls. She's a mirror: panic flashing in her pupils, poised anger shattering like glass. Every motion is déjà vu—the same terror I felt before. Her eyes bulge, dead-girl-in-the-pool wide. I remember the helplessness, the paralysis. Watching Stanton spiral, obsess, fray—it's me too. My mind, fragile again, disintegrating alongside hers.

"Look, I get it," I say. She blows smoke to the side. Tears have dried to salty residue along her cheeks. "This work—we live in pain. We're lucky to see scraps of anything good, anything whole. We've got to find ways to be okay, to just get by, for the sake of other people. That's the life we signed up for. But it also means we hold a lot of responsibility to ourselves, too. If you lose yourself now, this case isn't the only one that's fucked."

"I'd like it more if we were all still ignorant," she says. I know she's listening, but I can't tell if she's really hearing me. "When we were kids, the world wasn't dark in every corner. We looked at things with curiosity—like behind someone else's door was another dimension. You could disappear, disconnect. Now…depravity finds you everywhere. There's no hiding. When did everything turn into a manic obsession?"

I don't answer. I just watch her, feel the tug of her thought pulling me in. I don't know if she's gone too far, but I know I'll follow anyway.

"Blame whoever bit the fruit," I say, motioning for a drag of the cigarette. "If you believe in that shitty story."

PIERCE: REMEMBERING

Four children were already missing when the call came in—a noise complaint in a quiet rural cul-de-sac. The neighbor said she'd heard shrill screeching, something that might've been a young woman, or possibly a child. She insisted something wasn't right in that house. When she was pressed for specifics, she admitted she didn't much like her neighbor, not since they put up a wooden fence that ruined her view of the lake. At first it sounded petty. Then I saw the fence.

I case the cruiser along the curb and shut the door behind me. The air outside is slick in dense heat—pressing down, damp, unrelenting. Sweat gathers at my collar before I've taken a step. The property stands out against the rest of the block. The fence rises seven feet high, a wall of raw boards circling the perimeter of the property. It's too uniform for simple privacy and too bland to be decorative. It looks intentional—like it's meant to keep something in—or out.

Crossing the front yard, I pass through the mist of sprinklers hissing rhythmically, soaking my pant leg. The boards run straight and tight, but an inch of space between them gives me partial sightlines into the property. Through those slivers of light, I catch impressions: the side of the house, shadows of the back garden, flashes of glass and greenery.

I follow the fence line to the rear, squinting between the slats. The backyard is strange. A clear structure covers it end to end, stretching like a greenhouse pressed against the house itself. Plastic sheeting or perhaps sheets of plexiglass wall it in, distorted in places where sunlight warps the surface. Inside, rows of shrubs and flowering bushes grow dense, their leaves pressed against the barrier like they're trying to escape. At the center, incongruous, sits a swimming pool. Its water glints blue under the enclosure, catching the light in a way that looks unnatural—wrong. Condensation clings to the plastic walls, dripping back down into the soil and pool, recycling itself. I lean closer, trying to parse details through the heat glare, when movement jolts me still. A face appears in the gap—an elderly woman, sudden and sharp in my line of sight.

"Pardon me, are you looking for something?" she asks. Her voice carries a sharp edge.

"Apologies," I say, stepping back and raising my palms, a gesture that feels absurdly defensive. "We received a call from a resident in distress. They reported concerning noises coming from your property."

"Concerning noises?" she repeats, tilting her head, eyes narrowing through the gap in the fence. "So, you don't know what you're listening for—you just know it's concerning?"

"Screaming," I clarify, flattening my tone. "We got a report of possible child endangerment. With the missing kids in the county, we can't afford to be careless. Every potential lead has to be checked."

Her lips pull tight, and then she smiles in a way that doesn't soften her wrinkles. "You must be talking about my Lucy," she says. "Would you like to come in and meet her?"

The invitation jars me. People don't usually offer so quickly, not when there's even a hint of accusation in the air. I nod anyway. "All right. Where's the gate back here?"

"There isn't one," she says, lifting a frail, veined arm and pointing toward the front. We walk in parallel, her shadow trailing me along the other side of the boards. Her voice follows through the slats as we move. "I had to put this fence up after the chicken wire gave out. Too many people snooping—kids tossing their footballs over, neighbors poking around. Some even climbed over and pulled grapefruits right off my tree. Can you imagine—what audacity."

"No, ma'am," I say. The fence creaks faintly as the wind presses against it. "I suppose that explains the fortress. Has anyone checked that it's up to code?"

She ignores the question, her steps carrying her toward a side entrance that bleeds into the kitchen. "I'll open the front door for you, honey. Only one way in and out of this house, and that's through the front."

I cut across the lawn toward the porch, boots leaving impressions in the watered grass. The front door looms, wood weathered to a dull sheen. At its center hangs a brass knocker shaped like a feline. The details blur in the sunlight—could be a cat, but the metal curves around its head suggests a lion. Its mouth is parted just enough to show tiny brass teeth, polished down to nubs from years of wear. I pause for a second, the image catching me off guard. The garage door is worn clean of its paint coat and appears stuck—unmovable.

She opens the door and waves me inside. The air shifts as soon as I cross the threshold—warmer with the scent of baking. Maple, vanilla, something sugary clinging to the walls like it's seeped into the paint. The sweetness is pleasant on its own but overwhelming in this much concentration.

I step onto the entryway tiles. They look like shards of broken pottery reassembled into a mosaic, the pieces uneven and catching light at odd angles. Pale turquoise grout stitches them together, giving the floor a kind of southwestern charm. Photographs run along the hallway in heavy turquoise frames that echo the grout. Family portraits, landscapes, memories—though I don't linger on the images long enough to read them.

As I'm studying the walls, something slinks around my ankle. I freeze, instinct tightening before I register the soft body of a cat brushing against my leg. Orange stripes ripple as it circles me, tail upright, head pressing against the leather of my boot. The purring is abrasive, like it's housing a motor tucked inside its ribs.

"She likes you," the woman says, a smile forming in the corner of her mouth as she watches. "She doesn't take to many people like that. You must be a good man."

"What's its name?" I ask, keeping still. I've never been fond of cats.

"That's Lucy," she replies.

I stare down at the animal. I'd been expecting a child—a face, something more human—something that would've matched a scream. Instead, I'm staring at a cat—rubbing against me like I owe it. The confusion stirs frustration, but before it burns through, I snap my attention away.

"Mind if I look around—or if you'd show me around?" My voice steadies itself and my eyes map the space. The hallway stretches ahead, opening into a living room. Sunlight filters through sliding glass doors at the back, refracted by curtains and casting long, pale beams across the floor. To my left, another hallway branches off. A master bedroom door stands open, curtains drawn back so daylight floods the bedspread in a way that feels curated, like its waiting to be photographed. At the far end, another door sits swallowed in shadows, paint dull, the frame worn. I point toward it. "What's through that door?"

"That's just the garage," she says, casual but quick. "The garage door mechanism broke years ago. Too much money to fix it, so my husband keeps his car in the driveway. Now it's just a glorified storage room." Her tone is dismissive, but her eyes don't leave mine.

"Mind if I take a look?" I ask, letting the question hang, watching how she reacts.

She hesitates, eyes narrowing just slightly, then bends to gather Lucy into the crook of her arm. The cat relaxes against her chest, purring like an engine. "Go ahead then," she says.

I move down the hallway, my steps heavy on the fractured turquoise tile. Passing the master bedroom, I glance inside. The bedspread is pulled taut, curtains drawn back to let in the swelling daylight. The whole room looks staged, arranged as if it isn't lived in anymore. Nothing stirs. The house feels suspended, like it's been waiting. Time refuses to pass within its walls. I reach the end of the hall, grip the knob, and twist it open. The door creaks into darkness.

I flick the switch and a bulb swings to life above, its glow sickly and yellow, hanging bare from the ceiling by a frayed cord. The light exposes raw brick walls—their surfaces stripped down to their bones. The space is choked with clutter—rusted car parts piled in corners, dented toolboxes, half-assembled machines whose purpose I can't place. Every surface wears a film of dust that dulls the outlines of the objects beneath. Even the air feels layered, stale and unmoving. My boots crunch over grit on the concrete floor, and the sound is swallowed instantly, like the walls themselves absorb it. Then something interrupts the uniformity.

A neat row of firearm safes is pushed against one wall. There are several small ones built for handguns, and two tall ones built for rifles. My eyes sweep past them to the back wall where two chest freezers loom side by side, their enamel is chipped and yellowing with age. A refrigerator is tucked in the corner, its seal darkened from years of grime. At first glance, the freezers look untouched, but then I notice the dust across their lids is uneven. There are patches near the rims where fingers or palms have brushed, thinning the gray layer into streaks. Not wiped clean, not obvious, but enough to show the lids have been opened recently.

"Those are mighty large freezers," I say, my voice steady, though my chest tightens.

"Gerald is quite the deer hunter," she replies, repositioning Lucy so the cat's head rests in the crook of her elbow. "Gerald, my husband— you know, I mentioned him."

"Yes, ma'am, I remember." My hand drifts up to the back of my neck, scratching at the heat gathering there. I weigh her answer, eyes still fixed on the dust-scored lids. "When's the last time he used these freezers?"

"He went out hunting at the beginning of the month," she says, rocking the cat gently as if to soothe herself. "Brought home a big buck— we had venison for weeks."

"The beginning of the month?" I echo, watching her face.

"Yes, sir."

"We're nearing the end of April," I say, keeping my voice even. "Deer season ended three months ago."

She falters, glancing toward the freezers before meeting my eyes again. Her hand moves through Lucy's fur with a careful steadiness. The cat curls tighter against her chest, purring in steady pulses. "Has it been that long already?" she asks, half to herself.

I nod once.

Lucy suddenly unleashes a jagged screech that tears through the garage, high-pitched and erratic. The sound is so sharp it almost reads as human, something raw and distressed trapped in a small animal's throat. Her mouth yawns open, teeth flashing in tight rows, scissoring with each ragged cry. My body wants to pull back, but I lock myself still, eyebrows knotting up in confusion.

The woman presses her fingers around the cat's head, massaging behind the ears, cooing as if the noise were nothing. "See? This is the kind of racket she makes." Her smile holds firm, a strange pride in the display. "I think she wants to show you the backyard."

I give a gentle nod and trail her through the house. Her steps are sluggish, and she holds Lucy balanced tightly in her arm. She leads me to the sliding glass door at the rear of the house and eases it open.

The air inside the enclosure is instantly heavier—humid, sweet with soil and faint mildew. Plastic panels arc high above us, ribbed and curved like the frame of an igloo stretched wide enough to cap the entire yard. The structure seals out the world, diffusing the sunlight into a pale, jaundiced haze. The light presses down with sterile warmth, the way hospital fluorescents pretend to be sunlight. Shrubs, flowering bushes, and beds of foliage line the perimeter. A grapefruit tree is tucked against the perimeter. Solar lights spear the ground between them, small plastic heads angled upward. The panels themselves are streaked with dirt and grit, layers of grime softening the outside glare into a veiled glow. Everything feels contained, designed—like a terrarium under glass.

At the far end of the dome, the pool gleams. It's expansive and ringed by faux-rock slabs. The water shimmers, and its rippling refracts against the enclosure. Chlorine sharpens faintly in my nose, crisp and chemical, a discordant note against the humid greenhouse smell. For a moment I expect algae, leaves, a film of green clinging to the surface—

but there's nothing. The water is placid, unblemished. It feels weirdly pristine among the overgrown greenery.

"This is quite the structure," I say, my eyes cataloguing the elements.

She looks up toward the curve of the dome, rubbing Lucy's ears until the cat hums with incessant purring. "We thought about renovating," she says. "Extending this side of the house, potentially adding a skylight. But I didn't want to lose the yard, especially my grapefruit tree." Her gaze lingers on the translucent panels, softened by the filtered light. "I didn't want to sacrifice the sun." I stand beneath the faint glow, feeling the air cling damp against my skin, the pool glinting at the back of the dome.

"Does anyone else live here with you and Gerald?" I ask.

"Jack," she says. "That's where Gerald is now. He takes him out every Saturday—today it's the arcade and ice cream. Jack has special needs. Makes things hard for us sometimes, but we make do." Her tone weakens and becomes more hushed. "And while I know you're just here on business, it is nice to talk to someone new. To show someone around, even if it's only the grass. Conversation doesn't have to matter much to mean something."

A sullen smile tugs at her face. She looks at me with something close to hope, and guilt drops into my gut—sudden, draining me the way a rollercoaster plunge steals empty space from your stomach.

"I don't believe I caught your name, ma'am."

"Bette," she replies. "Like the actress."

"Detective James Pierce," I say, nodding. "I appreciate your openness, and your willingness to help. I may follow up with you in the future. In the meantime, if you notice anything unusual, don't hesitate to reach out."

I hand her my card. She takes it gingerly. Lucy nestles closer, cradled in the crook of her arm. For a moment, Bette seems smaller—fragile and childlike beneath the frame of the doorway.

On the surface, nothing is wrong here. Nothing I can write up, nothing that fits into a report. And yet, the oddities press against me—the fortress fence, the freezers, the greenhouse dome, the pool—all of it lingers like grit at the bottom of my heel. She sees me out, and I step down onto the lawn. The grass is damp, still beading from the sprinklers, and the soil clings to the soles of my boots. The door shuts quietly behind me, and the property seems to settle into itself, sealing itself off again.

I pause at the curb, crossing in front of the cruiser, and look back. The house stands rigid, barricaded, panels of the dome catching dull light. For a moment I can't move, pinned by some quiet insistence that I'm not finished here.

The thought of the missing children edges in. I picture their faces on the flyers back at the station. Their smiles have already begun to fade—lost or forgotten, maybe both. The silence of this cul-de-sac feels like it could swallow them whole, hide anything it wants, never let them be found. When no answer comes to justify why I'm still standing here, I slide my sunglasses back on and open the door of the cruiser. The leather seat breathes back the day's heat as I settle in. I glance once more at the house in the rearview mirror before turning the key. It shrinks as I pull away, but the unease rides with me. It's a feeling I know I'll circle back to.

STANTON: MONSTERS

I open my eyes. The ceiling fan hums above, coated in the pale wash of streetlights spilling through the blinds. The low vibration pulses along the walls, like hummingbird wings brushing against my ears. I shift to the side, repositioning on the couch. The cushions have lost their shape from too many restless nights, uncomfortable against my back. My head aches in a dull thrum behind my eyes. Subtle pangs ripple across my skull as my vision adjusts to the dark. My laptop screen casts a stark white silhouette across my torso, a fractured glow in the otherwise black room. I don't know how long I've been asleep.

Suddenly, a thud echoes from down the hallway, followed by the shuffle of small feet. The hallway stretches unnaturally in my vision, elongated as if the space itself is holding its breath. Something heavy must have hit the floor, rolled, cracked. I tilt my head, questioning whether it happened or if my exhaustion conjured it. Silence follows. The doorknob rattles, then turns, and Lainey slips out, closing the door softly behind her. She freezes when she sees me, small frame recoiling, face pale in the collision of streetlight and shadow. Her steps shuffle across the carpet, careful and hesitant, drawing closer. The details of her face blur in the fractured light, features only half-defined, half-hidden, caught in a dance between shadow and illumination.

"Is everything okay?" I ask. She hovers, fingers fidgeting between her closed hands. She sways, glances at the door, then returns her gaze to me.

"There's a man in my room," she whispers. "I shut the door so he can't get out."

"Is it the same one?" I groan, rubbing at my forehead, bracing myself to stand. "The one from the other night?"

"I think so," she mutters. "He's just… staring at me."

"Okay," I say, nodding. I place my hands on her shoulders and guide her back down the hallway. She shuffles to her door, hesitating. I don't hear anything. "I'll go talk to him and tell him he's bothering you, then he'll leave, okay?"

She nods.

I wrap my palm around the handle and ease the door open a sliver. The hinges whine. I step inside, closing it behind me. Cars hum outside, their beams slicing across the walls. Her lamp lies crooked on the floor, bulb shattered, glass fragments scattered across the carpet. I kneel, lift the base, and peer under the bed. A tangle of shirts and a blanket is stuffed beneath the frame, but no stray shards. I raise my head and lock eyes with him. Across the mattress, behind the ruffled comforter, there's a man hunched over. His shoulders rise sharply toward his ears, palms pressing into the fabric, wiry fingers spread like claws across the bed. I pause, sensation draining from my body, my vision stretching outward as if I'm observing from above. I exhale sharply and stumble backward against the wall, palms catching in the carpet—and a shard of glass. Pain slices through my skin, and I wince, look up, he's gone. My heart hammers, pulsing in my skull. My ears ring. My chest heaves, lungs expanding as if they might burst. I stay frozen, nerve endings tightening, waiting for the next sound, the next movement.

The noise wakes Preston. I hear him shuffle out of his room before he peers through the doorway, his face tense with distress. He steps around the mess and begins helping me gather the shards. I move carefully, trying to control my trembling arms and hands, hoping he doesn't notice. I take the last pieces from him and we return to Lainey, still standing in the hallway. I don't mention the lamp, don't speak of the incident. I kiss her forehead and guide her back into her room, shutting the door behind us.

Preston slides onto a bar stool, swiveling slightly. I pour a glass of water from the sink, set it in front of me, and lean my elbows on the counter, fingers combing back through my hair.

"Did you see anything the other night?" I ask, pressing my thumbs into the sides of my head in small circles, staring at the water.

"What do you mean?"

"In her room?"

"No," he says. He steps into the kitchen, pouring himself a glass with ice. The cubes jangle against the glass, sending a sharp twang through my skull. I sip at my water, gaze drifting through the window at the pulsing lights outside. Everything around me feels distant, muffled, unrecognizable. "When's Dad coming home?" he asks. His voice sounds subdued, like it's coming through a wall.

"I'm not entirely sure," I admit. I haven't talked to him—I haven't called in days. I can't even recall when he was supposed to return. I feel small, lonely, the walls pressing in and stretching at once. Voices echo in the hallways, fragments of my own words bouncing back at me. I feel vacant, vast, yet my mind tightens around itself, claustrophobic and restless.

"I hope he comes home soon," he says, leaving his water untouched. The ice cubes clink sharply against the glass. "I'm worried about you."

"He will," I murmur, though I don't believe it myself. I rub the back of my neck and glance at him. He forces a smile, but it wavers as his eyes linger on the water. "Everything's fine. I've just been wrapped up in work."

"Okay," he says, but the hesitation in his voice presses against me.

I give a weak smile and return to my laptop. The ceiling fan hums above, stirring papers that flutter and shift across the table.

"Do you believe in monsters?" he asks, swiveling to face me. I tap idly at the keyboard, a thought slipping through my fingers before I can grasp it. I mull back over his question in my head for a minute.

"No," I reply. For some reason, the question leaves me feeling uneasy. "Why do you ask?"

"You still act like you do."

I purse my lips and sigh, then slide onto the stool beside him.

"When I was a kid, I did. Monsters under the bed, growling in the closet, crouched in corners. Your imagination conjures up wild things.

They faded as I grew up—crept back into the shadows and kind of disappeared. But then something changed. At some point, in this line of work, there came a point where all I could see was monsters. There's something different in these ones, though. There's a point where you stop imagining them. You *see* them. Only now, they aren't fantastical. They look like us. *They are us.* That's what makes them more terrifying. I'm still learning how to live with that. The difference now is that I don't believe they're real. I *know* they are."

"That doesn't scare you?" His voice is shaking, fragile.

"It does," I admit. "Every day. But we're trained to stop them, to keep people safe."

"No, not that," he says, brow furrowing. "I mean, scared that if you're not careful, spending so much time with them, you might become one, too."

PIERCE: TREAD

An electronic bell buzzes as I push through the door. Cold air blasts from the ceiling vents, rattling against the stillness of the showroom. The air conditioner hums, a low fluttering that scratches at the silence. My boots click against the slick linoleum, cream speckled with smudged rectangles of black and blue. Fluorescent light bounces off the tiles and a small television mounted on the wall. The local news station plays in a soft, distant drone. The room reminds me of the holding areas where inmates wait for arraignments—sterile, controlled. A row of tires in various sizes hang from the wall, metal fixtures glinting in the light. I stuff my fists into my pockets, letting my gaze drift over the rubber treads, noting the differences in depth and pattern. A poster of a cartoon limousine clings to the window, its corner peeling and flapping against the vented breeze. The cartoon's wide, drugged eyes and toothy grin are meant to charm, but they look fevered, hungry—insidious in a way that sets my skin on edge. The showroom is quiet, except for the steady whirr of the air conditioner, the flapping poster, and the muffled chatter of a news anchor on the television. I scan the room again, check my watch, and let the silence settle. Then, metal scraping against linoleum—a door swings open. From the garage, a man barrels into the showroom. He's panting, the sound forced. Not from running, but from carrying the weight of his rounded belly.

"What can I do for you, sir?" He wipes his forehead with a greasy rag, matting down his slicked-back gray hair. He drags the cloth over his fingers, cleaning residue while smearing it across the fabric. His stiff button-down shirt strains against his stomach, and he reeks of bean burritos. A scuffed nametag reads *Lee*. Flecks of brown streak through his bushy mustache, outlining the gray. I catch myself zoning out, taking in the details more than listening.

"My name is Detective James Pierce," I say. I consider a handshake but glance at his sausage fingers and let it go. Leaning over the counter, I glance at the computer and the scattered paperwork. "I need to check your records. Has anyone brought a vehicle in recently—large, black, front passenger side dented, broken headlight? It could have been repaired and may show residual signs around the impact area." I slide my badge onto the counter for him to inspect.

"I don't believe I have any vehicles like that here," he replies, eyebrow raised. "You're not sure what car you're looking for?"

"No," I admit, glancing toward the garage window behind him. Floodlights illuminate several cars being serviced, but the details are obscured. "I know it's black. It would've come through within the past couple weeks. We've checked most other shops. This is one of the last on our list."

"I don't imagine it would come through here, sir," he says, scratching the back of his head. He glances through the window again, frowning as if searching his memory, then returns his gaze to me. His calm manner and honest confusion suggests he's telling the truth—or at least the truth as he knows it. "See, I only work on specialty vehicles. Limousines, classics, unique models. People don't let these puppies get a scratch on them, much less destroy them. Classic car collectors are meticulous, you know."

"I know," I nod. "We've checked every collision center and body shop in town but haven't found anything that matches. Figured checking here was worth a shot. Do you know anyone else in town who could handle something like that? Or anything else that might be relevant?"

"I don't, sir. Nothing the police wouldn't already know."

"Try me," I say, more abrupt than intended. He hesitates for a moment.

"I can show you around the garage, if you like. Otherwise, I can call you if a customer comes through with something that fits your description."

"I'd appreciate that," I say, handing him my card. He picks it up, flipping it back and forth, inspecting the lettering. "Besides limousines and classic cars, what else do you work on?"

"This business is mostly a passion project. Limousines are the bread and butter, but occasionally I see something unique, truly vintage or rare. I have regular customers, but sometimes a diamond in the rough rolls through."

"If you have time, I'd like to see what you're working on currently."

"Of course," he says, a grin of excitement crossing his face. I wonder how many social interactions he has outside work. He motions for me to follow and heads toward the garage door.

He's a foot shorter than me and waddles like a penguin. The moment we step into the humid garage, I feel sweat lining my armpits. Gasoline hits my nostrils and fumes drip down the back of my throat, lining it in the taste of torched metal. Two limousines are cranked up on lifts, and two other vehicles sit on the concrete below. I cross the floor and duck beneath one limousine's underbelly, loose cords dangling from the ceiling. At the back, an old hippie bus sits painted with crude peace signs, circular lights adorned with hearts, its faded teal hood propped up with a plank of wood. Another car gleams under a polished hood, wooden panels on the doors. I circle the back, absorbing the patchwork of materials and parts—a rudder protrudes from beneath the rear bumper, jutting awkwardly from the car.

"What's this supposed to be?" I ask, pointing at the fixture.

"It's an amphibious car," he says. "Only a handful left in the world. They were on the market for a few years—never really caught on. No one wanted a car that could drive in water, but now we've got cars running purely on electricity. Ridiculous. That's what's wrong with the world—skewed priorities."

I nod, not engaging. I get enough political commentary at the office. My attention shifts to a hulking object against a far wall, camouflaged among tools and spare parts. It's constructed of metal pieces fastened together, like a belt of some sort, meant to extend or pull out.

Sliding poles run across it. At first, I think it might be an attachment for a trailer. No hitch or accessory is visible at either end. I step back to take it all in, cocking my head, trying to make sense of it. Nothing clicks.

"What's this for?" I ask, realizing that if fully extended, it would stretch several feet back.

"That's right," he exclaims, pressing his palm to his forehead. "I almost forgot—I need to follow up with this customer. I've been waiting on this part for weeks—it finally arrived a few days ago. He hasn't called, so I guess he's not too worried." He moves closer, pointing at the tracks used for sliding the poles across its width. "His rollers were worn out and had to be replaced. See this section here? Completely broken. There was no way to fix it—you have to replace the whole thing. It kept getting stuck whenever he pulled it out, and it damaged the tracks. Nice guy, though—also into classic cars. This one's for one of his personal vehicles."

"But what is it?" I press, still not connecting the dots.

"They're casket rollers," he says. "You know, for a hearse."

I pause, mesmerized. A hearse. Why would anyone want to own a hearse?

My pocket buzzes. I dig out my phone from my jacket and gesture to him, mouthing a silent *thank. you.* I step toward the garage door, back into the blistering heat. Compared to the scalding sun outside, the humid garage with its oversized fans had been a relief.

"Pierce," I state, making my way across the parking lot.

"We've got another victim, Pierce," Chief Cameron says.

"Is it the Canine?" I ask, clenching my teeth. My car keys rattle between my fingers.

"From what I've gathered—" He pauses, then continues. "I think it would be best for you to see it for yourself."

"Have you informed Stanton?"

"Not yet," he says. "I'm going to call her now."

"Hold on," I cut in. "I'll call her."

"Careful," he mutters. He knows I'm lying.

"I am."

"I mean with her."

I know exactly what he means. Dread bursts through my chest, crawling up my collarbones. My face flushes hot, sweat prickling along my spine. Stanton is exposed, vulnerable. I tap a finger against the back of my phone, silent. She's slipping, focus fraying, and I can feel my grip on her unraveling. I picture her, scratching at her arms in front of the laptop, restless, like a junkie foaming for her next fix. I can't push her further—can't shove her off a bridge. She needs space from this case, at least for now. Long enough to find the surface, to break through, catch a breath.

I pull the car handle and slide in. The leather seat is stiff beneath me, the sun heating it like a skillet. My chest tightens, breath quickening, mingling with the faint scent of gasoline from the lot. My heart hammers in my ears, louder than the distant roar of traffic and the metallic clatter of nearby construction. Louder. And then I realize I haven't answered.

"Send me the address," I say. "I'm on my way."

Silence stretches. Cameron's pause sharpens the unease, and for a moment, I fear he thinks I've gone too far.

"It's roughly thirty minutes southwest of downtown. A rundown house—looks like it's been abandoned for years, except for our perpetrator as of recent." A muffled voice in the background. Shuffling. A pen drops. "Let me know what you gather from the scene. See if it connects to the prior Canine cases."

"Understood," I say, shifting into reverse. Eyes on the rear window.

"Careful," Cameron warns again. I hang up.

Backing out, I notice Lee returning from the garage. He paces the showroom, cellphone wedged between cheek and shoulder, muttering into the phone.

SPIT

"I could kill him," I murmur, watching Mackey reverse his car, sputtering out of the parking lot. I drag on my cigarette, the tip glowing—pulsing in the dark. I hold the curtain ajar, watching the first sunbeams spill across the blacktop, gold morning pouring itself over the asphalt in thin ribbons. My fingers brush the breast pocket of my shirt, caressing the small baggie of amphetamines nestled there, checking again—lingering. The anticipation tightens me, presses heat straight down.

Casey bends into a fetal ball on the corner of the couch, trembling in her shadow. Her calves bloom with bruises, the knotted purples and blues of broken blood vessels rising beneath swollen flesh. Her neck is marked with deep fingerprints, red and swollen against the white canvas of her throat. She folds herself tighter, changes colors like a chameleon— every shiver a new shade. When I'd stepped out of the closet, I'd found her slumped on the floor, wheezing, her breath shallow and rattling— suffocating on her panic.

I settle beside her, close enough to feel the heat rising off her body, close enough to taste the fear. A pale plastic tray sits on the coffee table. I drag the cigarette, watch the ash spiral down, eyes on the amphetamine residue streaked across the surface. I touch the powder— brush my gums, lick, scrape, inhale the faint metallic tang. My skin prickles, taut as a drum. My pores scream with the sour heat of it, sweating beneath their layers. Bones tighten, everything hardens, sharpens. Pores—lambs crying out in a slaughterhouse. Sour—sweat drips where it shouldn't, sliding under layers of skin and cloth, pooling in hollowed spaces between muscle and bone. Everything sharpens—the world contracts to the tray, to the powder, to the rhythm of her breathing. My spine coils like a spring. The anticipation hammers through me, each pulse a little louder, a little hotter.

It enrages me when Casey crumples up, shaking, collapsing into herself. Mackey moves over her so effortlessly, manipulates her like a puppet, bending her body, and she stays there, pliant. One minute she cries out in lust, the next in pain. He touches her, she bites her lip in ecstasy—then, she bites it from teeth pressed into her jaw. It infuriates me—he's trespassing, stepping onto my turf, my property. It creates obstacles between Casey and me. Every touch he gives her, every noise he coaxes out of her, sabotages me. Whatever I'm building, whatever comes next, pauses while she recovers. She folds back into that useless, quivering ball, immobile for hours. And I sit there, cock in hand, snorting lines from the tray, spitting at her just to make her flinch, confirming she's still alive—still mine to mold. This is purely transactional—her and me— always has been. But Mackey can't finish it, can't claim what isn't his. Even if I wanted to be done, the right to touch her, to shape her, to break and remake her—that belongs to me alone. But the transaction isn't finished. And even if it were, it's mine to dictate, not his.

"That's sweet of you," she coughs. I don't remember what I said, but her words pull me back from drifting thoughts and into the present.

The cigarette ash hangs halfway down. I flick it to the floor and glare at her contorted ball. She mutters something between her knees—I don't catch it, and I don't ask her to repeat herself. I wouldn't pay attention to whatever she says anyway—it's irrelevant. She tilts her head, nervous, confused. I wonder if my disdain bleeds through my expression. I don't think I can hide it, not that I care to. It's not like she could see through her puffy, battered eyelids anyway. "Sometimes I wish you would," she says.

I pull the baggie from my pocket and line the tray, snagging the gas station card from the table. It smells like methane. I press my palm to the shards and chunks beneath the card, crushing them into glittering flecks, sniffing. My eye sockets flare, burning, inflamed. I don't reply. I slip into a blank trance, drifting, leaving the base of my skull, snaking into something ethereal. I blink, shake my head, pour more onto the tray. Wet my fingertip, melt the flecks into the crevices of my prints. I imagine snow breaking potholes into my hands and rub it along the inside of my nose, inhaling sharply. A twang slices through my arms, thumping in my veins. Flesh around my legs and waist tightens, suctions ravines together, tears breaking, pores swelling. Layers slit free.

"Casey?" I whisper, glancing back at her trembling mass, lost in a haze of white noise. Come back, snap out of it. I tilt my head back, plug my nose with my fingers and sniff hard—dragging back a lungful of amphetamine residue. My eyes squirm from the strain, writhing like cocoons hatching. Her shaking steadies and her movements relax. I spit on her—a glob of saliva splattering across her shoulder in a web. She winces and buries her head against the sofa. "Shit," I mutter, rubbing my fingers across my forehead. My veins feel feathery under the fevered pressure. Another drag of the cigarette, flick ash into the carpet. I press the stub against her bruised thigh and she winces—stretches, collapses backward onto the floor. She sprawls like a frog carcass, greasy limbs bent into the carpet. She's begging for incision, for my soggy fists digging into her coin purse stomach. Peel her back, swallow the flies caught in her oils.

"Fuck," she yelps, surrendered. Her macaroon eyes squint and her neck cranes back like bent rubber. I glimpse slivers of her pupils—they churn like boiling egg whites. She drifts in and out of consciousness. I don't know why I care. I give up.

I inhale the last of the amphetamines, scrub my gums and tongue with them, then slump back against the sofa, neck resting on the headboard. I peel my shirt over my head, feeling the cloth flutter over my skin. My scars suck at my fingers as I trace them, soft pressure, wet mouths eroding my mind. I release a pleasured moan, my scars moisten, drooling sweat over my hands, tracing rivers down my body, soaking into my jeans and thighs. Faces vanish, replaced by mouths pulsing across my chest, navel, back—puckering, wet, greedy, feeling like Percy's. My cheeks warm, like his stomach presses against them. My legs stiffen, sensing his hands clutching my thighs. My mind lurches under the weight of imagined touch, Percy's fingers worming into my brainstem. I feel my own layers pulling apart—veins snapping into new shapes—breath fracturing. Before he fades, I pry Percy's jaws open above me, climb inside him. His face explodes over my thighs. The cigarette burns down between my fingers, ash crumbling, mixing with scar sweat and drool. I breathe, inhale, taste him, taste her, become soft, liquid—a moaning wet imprint. Memory bleeds over—the man from the liquor store stumbles in. I smell burning.

Then I remember the man I had just killed. His shape mounts me, pressing against the front of me, weightless and yet sharp in my vision. He's inside me, or I'm inside him—there's no distinction, only motion and pressure. His fists wedge between my lips, crushing into my mouth, splitting it, invading me. I gag, the same way I'd gagged him, tongue sliding over his knuckles, grinding his fingers between my teeth. It's mirrored, doubled, a looping echo. He moves with precision, wanting what I want, doing what I would. My tongue drags over his fingers, laps up his gums, tastes the imprint of what I took and what I gave. Every movement was calculated. It was very intentional. I had done it for practice—rehearsal. Everything spins, nothing remains solid. I'm an open wound, and somewhere beneath it all, the echo of transcendence waits for its turn.

INFERNO

I used to sell my body behind gas station dumpsters. I still do sometimes, but I learned that selling yourself always comes with submission in some form. My backside would cling to the chalky asphalt, loose rocks biting into my shoulders, puncturing pockmarks into tiny eruptions under my skin. They'd tear at my thighs like shaved coconut shells and pull handfuls of skin from my hips. I'd frost their lips, smear it down their chins, and let my legs dangle on severed marionette strings. There were times I thought I'd lost all sensation in my legs permanently. It's dulled now, though, and if it's no longer a means to get me ahead, I have no interest.

There was one client—or whatever you'd call him—I'd taken a particular liking to. He didn't hand me cash. He pressed a worn VHS tape between my teeth and said *just watch it.* It was a snuff film—or it appeared to be. It was shot in a bathroom with rough cement walls, the floor tiles scarred and hollowed out where the toilet should have been. Every frame smelled of mildew and fear. By the end, the boy was nothing but shattered bones and mangled flesh, hips and cock jammed into the void in the tiles, limbs folded like a trapped wasp. I could hear the echo of it in my teeth, feel the pressure of the tape against my gums as if it were still breathing. He had more tapes. Soon he became a regular. Each one was a small offering, a puzzle of control. But one night, he betrayed me: an obvious rubber limb. It stung.

I used to fuck him in the basement of my parents' house when they were still alive. The stench of sewer water lingered at the back of my throat, canvased with the ripe, chronic odor of his ass. He was slicked in moisture and layered in other secretions. Since my parents died and I stopped cruising, the house has been abandoned, the basement reduced to a shell of memory. That's why I brought him back. To split open old scabs, to stir the rot. He was asking for it.

We trudged through the uncut grass, each step snagging at weeds and aphid hitchhikers in our wake. The bulkhead doors jutted from the soil, rusted and cobwebbed along their hinges. I kicked debris aside and wrenched the doors open, letting them clang against the earth. The stairs shuddered beneath us, wooden planks creaking and nails loosening with every hesitant footfall he made.

At the bottom, the darkness swallowed us. I slid my fingers along his waistline, tracing the edge of his jeans. The tension in his body relaxed under my touch, and I pulled his stomach closer. When I flicked on the battery lantern on the table, the light stabbed through the shadows. Tension erupted back up his spine. He squinted, adjusting as shapes resolved: the table, the chairs—remnants my mother couldn't bear to part with. After my parents died, they kind of died down there too. That's what being sentimental does, it lets the dead stay present. He glanced around, my fingers lingering along his hipbones, tracing their ridges again. Nostalgia flashed across his eyes, faint and unsteady, memory illuminating with the basement. The walls pressed inward, the shadows breathed, the air thickened, and I felt the pulse of the room in him, in me. The basement was remembering too.

"It's kind of lost its touch since I was here last," he said.

"It still works," I replied, tilting my chin over his shoulder blade. My gaze drifted across the workbench, where power tools hung from hooks and lay scattered against the far wall. The glow from the charging battery lights swelled like a pack of jackal eyes. In the corner, an old cherry cheval mirror loomed under a stained sheet, embodying the form of a hunched phantom. Sometimes I think I'm haunted.

"Yeah," he murmured. I pressed my mouth to the corner of his jaw, tracing the line under my tongue until I found the corner of his lips. He tilted his cheek, sucking my tongue into his mouth, fidgeting his fingers around my waist. His hands crept up my shirt, lifting it, thumbs pressing into my chest scars, tracing them until they wept. I pulled back slightly, biting my bottom lip, feigning coyness. He was panting.

"I want to try something," I said, motioning him to sit in one of the chairs. "You'll like it."

"Sure," he hesitated. I dragged the chair from the table, and it scratched across the floorboards. He sat, and I drew a folded bandana from my pocket, crumpling it before pressing it between his teeth. I traced the side of his face with my tongue, prying his lips apart with my fingers, and tied the bandana behind his head in a knot. He struggled to move his mouth, teeth clamped over the cloth, tongue pressed flat. His jaw clenched and sweat pooled along his hairline.

"Close your eyes," I whispered, wetting his earlobe with the tip of my tongue. My temples throbbed, pupils raw and burning. The walls seemed to breathe. Floorboards creaked under my boots. My hands slicked with sweat. He tapped his fingers against the table—it sounded like music I couldn't place, a rhythm that skated at the edge of my mind.

I dug my fingernails into the nape of his neck, and the skin parted in bloody gills. The nail gun pressed into his tapping palm—bursting, spattering blood up my wrist, coating my fingers in warmth that isn't mine. His muffled barking was swallowed by the cloth, replaced by a trembling vibration that slid into my chest. I nailed his other hand down. His bones crunched, brittle and tearing under my weight. Blood pooled, thick and black, carving grotesque rings into the wood, and his arms flailed in chaotic tremors. I slammed the butt of the nail gun against his temple and it made a hollow crack. The wailing dissolved into chokes, wet whimpers that seemed to echo. I moved to the corner, pulled the sheet from the mirror, and tossed it to the floor. The mirror didn't just reflect him—it reflected me reflecting him. His chair scraped once, twice, clawing across the floor. Through the glass, I watched him collapse, jaw slamming against the table, knees buckling, hands shredded into vaginal gashes. And I watched myself watch him. My reflection blinked when I didn't. It leaned, stretched, moved on its own, merging with him, becoming him—or it had always been me. He began attempting to shift the table, to free his hands, limbs twitching against the floorboards.

I dragged the mirror forward and let it crash into the floor. Its frame splintered, shards scattering across the wood. I gathered stray fragments on my way back to him, watching him kneel at the table like a penitent at an altar. I lowered myself into the chair opposite him, staring at his bruised chin, slick with the blood pooling across the tabletop. His eyes narrowed, glare steeped in burning resentment. I turned my attention to the deck of mirror shards and shuffled them between my fingers, as if dealing a hand. My reflection appeared different in each fragment—fractured, jagged, disjointed—and with every shuffle, his whine warped like the sound of someone unraveling in slow motion.

"I get this rising heat in my body," I said, lifting my head to meet his glare. His cheek lay flat in the blood, and the lantern flickered, throwing his features into a stuttering, tangerine glow. I propped a shard of glass against its point on the table and spun it with my finger. The reflection fractured and shimmered, a disco of light across his face, making him flinch, eyelids snapping shut. In each jagged reflection, I looked worn, my eyes hazy, drool at the corner of my mouth. "I don't know where it comes from, but I have to do something with it. I don't remember if it was there when we used to fuck—I don't remember much anymore. It swells inside me, fills me up, makes my stomach tense and heavy. Maybe it's the amphetamines, but I don't think so." I stopped the shard, pressed it flat on the table, palm against it. "I felt this way once with my father—that's how I know it's not just the junk. But I didn't get the chance then." I lined out the other shards, ordering them by length. "It rises and nothing is ever enough. I need more. I need to be inside. I haven't figured out how yet—but this is a start."

I gathered several inch-long slivers and pressed them under his fingers, tracing the tips. I slid a shard flush against the underside of his fingernail, wedging it between flesh and nail. His growl deepened—bubbled up, guttural and wet. The edges glimmered in the lantern light, and every pulse in his fingers made the shards shiver against his skin, sending a crawling heat up my arms. "I want to be inside of you. You should feel elated."

The first fingernail tore upward, threads of skin peeling along the edge of the glass. Warm blood slicked the shard and caught the lantern's flicker in jagged, slicked reflections. He shook against the table, the fissures in his hands widening into cavernous maws, each movement sending a chorus of wet clicks and slaps across the wood. I moved to the next fingernail, separating it from the gummy surface beneath, leaving it tethered only to the cuticle. The shards gleamed in the orange light, refractions glinting his face and splashing across my hands. When I finished, I leaned back in my chair. His glistening talons scraped the wooden surface. Blood dripped in irregular rhythms from the table and splattered the floorboards. I leaned forward and pressed my bottom lip to a talon, feeling the sharp bite into my chapped skin. The trail of his drying blood clung to my cheek—warm and metallic. I pressed closer, tasting it—gorging it down my throat and feeling it stick and burn—filling the empty spaces in me. His back arched, legs thrashing against the floor, the convulsions quieting to stuttered, irregular pulses. I stood, fingers coated with coagulated warmth, knelt beside him again. My hands traced his waistline, dipping into the front of his jeans, tasting the sweat and dried tears still clinging to him, still marking the remnants of his fear. One hand cupped the navel, my gaze snapping to the workbench above—the tools, the hooks, the suspended shadows—and I felt the pull in my chest, the rising heat that demanded release. His body jerked beneath me, small spasms, quivering but quieter now, and I balled a fist in the flesh of his abdomen. The shards of glass on the table reflected us, splintering the basement into fractals of wet shadows. I traced the first cut I would open, feeling it in my palm, anticipating it, letting the lust for entry curdle in my stomach like a living thing, tethering us together in a web of sensation, light, and blood.

EXCISE

I digress. Snap out of it. My body is nothing but a vessel for streaming the show, something to rewatch fragments of motion through clouded vision. My cock throbs against the leg of my jeans. Casey—the specimen—latches onto breath like a parasite. I unzip my jeans, push them down my thighs, and rub my fingers around my crotch. I'm slick with sweat, and my fingers trace their own path—massaging, tasting myself. Her breasts plead to be parted, folded stomach dissected, flaps of her frame peeled back, begging to be undone. I want to press my chin into the lake of her fluids, let it suffocate me, pour into my mouth, seep into me, drown me through my nose. Absorb.

I think about Percy again. Sliding into his skin, arms like sleeves, hands like gloves, wet and gummy, bare muscle melting into mine. Tongue a hollowed sleeve—I push mine through, swallowing, bathing in his saliva, shoving deeper. Teeth puncture gums, carving fissures, making gullets I can pour ejaculate into, froth in salt. Pain pricks my cock, I excise a rush of come up my stomach, pooling in my navel. Breath ragged, voice shredded. A chill spikes through my shaft, worms down my spine, clenches my chest, licks my throat. Mouth pools, saliva drips, my head fogged. Drool runs over my chin like molten glass.

Exhale. Sharp. My body collapses into limp paralysis, shuddering with the rhythm of heartbeats I can't stop. Glassy eyes stare at the ceiling fan, cold air leaking over sweat-damp skin, burning nothingness on my torso. I prop my head in a haze, faint, staring at my skeleton. Splotches cling to scars, coating the hollows of me. Another pulse rises in my cock, stiffening, aching, swelling again—pain and desire indistinguishable, a living knot, semen engorged.

Time fractures. Casey's scent, Percy's memory, my own fluids—tangle, fuse, drip, seep into the same space. My cock wetted. Every hot drip is a whisper for more. I can feel it climbing, spilling in currents. The ceiling fan spins. The room exhales. And I grow inside myself, lost in warm throbbing, the wanting, fluctuating in soreness—and I get hard again.

PIERCE: SUBMERSION

I walk around the side of the house and through the gravel. My boots crunch the dead leaves, mimicking the compression of my crumpling stomach. Trees bend around the house, their bark cracking into splintered chips. Branches curve like fingers pointing down toward the entrance. I glance up at the roof tiles, noticing debris clogged in the drain gutters. Paint peels from the walls, revealing the pale, weathered shell beneath. The bulkhead doors hang open in the ground. A viscous wind snakes past, licking the doors and rattling their flaps against the soil. I step closer, peering into the descending stairwell. A waft of decay expels from the hole. I smear a small glob of petroleum jelly inside my nostrils—menthol snaps up, stinging the roof of my mouth, anchoring me. The yellow tape whips through a gust, startling me, tugging at my focus. Tunnel vision sets in. Hypervigilance.

I descend the stairs. At the bottom, a forensic technician catches my presence and scrambles toward the shadows like a rodent scuttling up from the floorboards. He starts speaking, but the sound is fragmented— sharp whirring noises slicing through the dim basement air, like an electric razor etching indentations into a ceramic saucepan. The flickering lights make his lips look like they're seizing in the dimness, obstructing his movements into jarring, jerking motions. The background blurs and the corpse is only thing that remains in focus.

"Detective Pierce?" I hear, and he tilts his head, confused. I try to focus. My cellphone buzzes in my pocket.

"What have we got?" I ask, shifting my attention to him.

"It's a man, mid-twenties," he says. "The scene mirrors the previous Canine cases. The canine teeth are removed, and the head has been punctured with soda-lime glass—sections of it, positioned the same way as before. The incisions are cleaner this time… more precise. It looks like he's been practicing."

"Any witnesses?"

"A woman passing by noticed a foul smell. She came onto the property to check it out and called us."

I kneel closer to the body, sliding gloves over my hands. Something feels different about this scene, and for a moment, I can't put my finger on it.

"Do we have an estimate on the time of death?" I ask.

"Several days. Hard to narrow it down more yet," he replies.

I study the victim's contorted hands. "He cut the tips of his fingers," I say. My gaze drifts across the basement, squinting through the dim light. A broken mirror catches my eye in the corner. Shards litter the floor, some still clinging to the frame. I return to the slumping corpse. My reflection glints from fragments embedded under the victim's fingernails—sharp, claw-like points.

I bend closer to the torso. From chest to navel, the body has been sliced open, the cavity turned outward. Entrails spill in knotted ropes, strands swollen and constricted, as if something had been packed inside to widen the tunneling intestines. They writhe in place, glistening under the flickering light, like raw calamari ringlets left to bake in the basement's humid air.

"There were traces of semen in the wound," the forensic technician says, nodding toward the cords of intestines, noticing my fixation. "Hard to tell if the Canine violated the body before death, after, or both."

My cellphone buzzes again, and my head slides back into tunnel vision.

"Is Stanton enroute?" he asks.

"We need to start by identifying the previous owners of this property," I reply, letting my gaze drift over the body again, blinking hard. I'm forcing myself to stay awake, speaking aloud to anchor my focus. "The Canine may have a connection to one of them. Have the forensic odontologist pull the victim's dental records for identification." I rub the back of my wrist against my eye. My words spill out in a messy rhythm, echoing my fraying concentration. "Collect all power tools, soda-lime glass, blood samples, fingerprints—anything, no matter how insignificant it may seem." The technician nods without adding anything, and I scan the basement again, searching for something I haven't seen yet. Something is missing.

I step out into the sun, inhaling sharply, clearing my lungs. I toss my gloves aside and press my fingers against the bridge of my nose. Warm light hits my face, seeping into my skin, making me feel feverish, unsteady. Flashes of the dead girl in the pool, the safes, the arrangement of everything I missed before. My chest tightens. I'm choking. My breaths come faster, shallower, frantic. The pool tiles are pastel, the water dense, suffocating. I pause, inhale, hold, release. I'm above water now, but the panic lingers.

I need stability from Stanton as much as she needs it from me. I'm drowning too, froth rising at my lips, clawing at my throat as if I could scrape pieces from its walls just to pull air into my lungs. We hold pieces of each other's sanity, fragile weights balanced in the dark, knowing if either of us falters, the other might drift into the same suffocating panic.

Blur. The world melts. My cellphone buzzes again, sharp in the haze. I lift my hands, let them hover, and force my gaze to the suede-cream sky above. The clouds roll into their own bodies, warping into shapes of pastel pool tiles, the safes, the girl suspended just out of reach. The sky remembers, recasts the details I missed before. My fingers fumble for the screen, sliding across it. It looks like it could rain.

"Pierce," the voice comes, distant like it's underwater.

"Where are you?" Stanton asks. She already knows.

"There's another victim," I reply, voice splintering. "It's the Canine."

STANTON: PRECIPICE

"There has to be something here," Pierce mutters, shuffling the photographs across the table. He's rearranging them again and again, as though if he moves the pieces differently, whatever pattern that's eluding us will reveal itself. The colors blur, merge, and pool together. His eyes dart over each glossy surface—frantic, desperate. "There has to be something," he repeats, and his pale skin seems to dissolve into the swirls of light and shadow across the prints.

Time stretches. I lift my coffee mug, sip from the rim. Steam drifts around my cheeks, the warmth seeps into my hands. My nose is raw, my lungs tight, each exhale a rasping friction against the dryness of my throat. Pierce slides the photographs again, eyes scanning, head tilting, retracing paths that I can't see. I follow his movements, trying to catch a clue, whatever detail he's scouring the images for. But the room offers nothing. The progression gnaws at me. I see it in my mind even when I can't find it in the photographs. At first, the Canine's work was about thirst—primal, immediate. Now it's sculptural—ceremonial. He forces the victims to watch, to participate as he controls their movements. It's like he's developing his art form, working to refine it further with each victim. Like he's creating sculptures from their bodies.

Pierce nudges another photo across the table. I glance down at the newest victim. The camera lingers on the fingers—the claws, the mimicry. Finished. Perfected. The image curdles in my stomach. This is what I've been dreading: the final touches, the ritualized art of control. But it's incomplete, somehow. The Canine is on the edge, poised to merge the next victim with his ceremony, to combine flesh and will in some grotesque sense of wholeness. I can feel the weight of it pressing in—the next body, the next scene. The thought sickens me—writhes in my gut. The bodies will multiply. They'll heap into each other, and we'll be swallowed by them, tripping through a mass of entangled, coagulating limbs. A lake of blood, viscous and relentless, that no one can escape. I see it, taste it—choke on the thought. I watch Pierce's hands, twitching over the photographs. My mind flares with panic. My chest tightens. And in that endless repetition, I feel it—the fear that we're already too late. The Canine is always one step ahead, always shaping his world while we scramble to decipher it. And the next ritual—God help us—will be unlike anything we could imagine.

"Cameron was able to identify the owner of the property," Pierce says, leaning back from the photographs to nurse his coffee. "The residence was last owned by a couple, but they've been dead for ten years. No children, no relatives, no contacts we can trace. Cameron doesn't want us to focus on the previous owners—he thinks it's a dead end. He couldn't find any connections to the prior cases."

"He's sure?" I ask, unsatisfied. "This is the closest lead we have. And he wants us to abandon it?" Every stone, no matter how small, needs to be overturned, examined, crushed to dust under my fingers before I let it go.

"You know he's working this case as hard as we are behind the scenes," Pierce replies, voice low. "If the horse is already dead, what's the point in beating it?"

I feel a sharp pang of irritation ricochet inside my skull. Part of it is frustration at the apathy in that statement, part of it is resentment that I wasn't called to the scene immediately. I grit my teeth, shove it down. It would be like checking the pulse of a horse after it's already been decapitated. Pierce rubs his eyes. They're raw, puffy, and red. My irritation bleeds into concern. Despite my obsessive tendencies, I sense the weight of his exhaustion pressing against me. He's carrying mine—and still trying to carry his own. It's like we're both drowning, clutching at each other, pulling, sinking, neither of us able to reach solid ground. I glance at Pierce. He looks older, thinner—shadows of the night etched under his eyes. I see the way he holds himself, the invisible pressure. He's trying to process the chaos into something that makes sense. I can feel it in his movements, the micro-pauses between shuffling photographs, the shallow exhalations. I want to reach across and steady him—but I don't.

I return my gaze to the photographs, back to the victims. We sit in silence, a fragile equilibrium of exhaustion and obsession. And somewhere in the space between us, in the stillness punctuated only by shallow breaths and flicking lights, we wait for the Canine to make his next move.

"I think his next step is an actual performance," I break in, staring down at the photographs again. "It's ritualistic now. These victims— they're practice. We can see it in the differences in the incisions, in how he's removed the teeth. We've been looking at these cases through the lens of mutilation, thinking his goal is just to torture them while they watch. But what if there's more? A further purpose beyond that?"

I pause, fingers brushing across the images from the last scene. My hand lingers on the photographs of the victim's torn-open stomach, entrails spilling across the floor. "This is the first victim he's eviscerated. And judging from the way he violated the body, it seems there's something inside them he wants too."

"What exactly are you saying?" Pierce asks.

"He wants to be inside them," I continue, voice measured. "To walk around in their skin. When that happens, he reaches some kind of transcendence. And then—the number of victims multiplies. Fast."

"That's… reaching, don't you think?" Pierce says, eyes fixed on the ripples in his coffee. His jaw tightens, cheekbones sharp under the sunlight slicing through the coffee shop window. I shift my gaze from the photographs and to him. The clatter of silverware and murmurs of other patrons fills the background like static.

"Pierce," I say again, softer this time, "we're treading dangerous territory. For both of us."

He meets my eyes, dazed at first because I'm voicing what we've both been trying to ignore—or because his focus is slipping. "Yeah," he says finally. "We're on a fine line. Nothing to hold onto—no leads, no suspects, bare evidence. What do we do with that?"

"You remember that case you mentioned?" I press, leaning closer. "The one with the girl in the pool?"

"Yeah."

"How did you figure out it was them?"

"Chance," he replies.

PIERCE: REMEMBERING

I'd visited Bette nearly every Saturday since that first call. Over time she grew accustomed to my presence, almost expectant, greeting me with fresh coffee already brewed and pastries still warm from the oven. The visits became a kind of ritual—half courtesy, half watchfulness on my part. This week, though, I decided to break the pattern, hoping the unannounced timing might mean I'd finally catch Gerald and Jack at home as well.

I tap my knuckles against the doorframe, bouquet of rhododendrons held flat against my chest. The petals rustle faintly in the breeze while I wait. The knob turns with a sluggish motion, and the door eases back just enough for a man's face to wedge into the gap. His cheek presses against the frame, eye angled through the mesh of the screen. His skin is ruddy, worn from sun, and his mouth pulls taut as he studies me.

"Can I help you?" he asks. His tone cautious, unwelcoming.

"Yes, I'm James," I reply evenly. "You must be Gerald?"

He doesn't answer. His eyes flicker once, then the door shifts inward as he leans back into the house. "Bette," he calls, his voice carrying through the frame. "There's a man at the door. Says his name's James—do you know him?"

From deeper inside: "Oh." Her voice is quick, sharp—not delight, but something heavier—something tinged with dread. "Gerald, please," she urges, softer.

The door closes fully. For a moment I'm left staring at the brass feline knocker, polished dull in the afternoon light. A trace of spice and roasting meat leaks through the seam before it seals. Then, faintly, muffled words—her voice again. *Put the pool cover on. I'll let him in.* The phrasing is indistinct, like something caught in the kitchen steam.

The knob rattles. This time the door swings wide, and Bette stands framed against the hallway behind her. A smile spreads across her face, but it doesn't settle naturally—it wavers, like it's been strung up in a hurry.

"James," she says brightly, unlatching the screen. "What are you doing here? It's the middle of the week."

"I'm taking Percy camping this weekend," I say, offering her the flowers. "Thought I'd stop by today instead. Figured it'd be nice to finally meet Gerald and Jack."

She takes the bouquet and turns it in her hands, eyes glazing over it without much focus. The blooms sag against her grip, ignored. "Well, you've met Gerald, I see," she says after a pause. "Jack's upstairs in his room, playing." She hesitates, glancing back into the house before waving me in. Her smile returns, smaller this time. "Well—come in, then."

I step across the threshold and into the living area. The scent of roasting meat folds over me stronger, clinging to the air in a film. Beyond the sliding glass doors, Gerald is in the backyard. He stands over the covered pool with his hands on his hips, his head swiveling deliberately as if he's examining the rim. The way he lingers there makes the space feel more like a job site than a yard.

"I'll put these in some water," Bette says, drawing my attention back to her. She moves across the living room with the bouquet in hand. "There's more beer in the refrigerator in the garage. Will you be a dear and grab another pack? Gerald's run out of them in here." She disappears into the kitchen, her voice carrying over the counter as cupboards open and close. "Wait until you see what I've been cooking for dinner tonight. I wish you could stay, but I know you're a busy man."

"Yeah, me too," I say, watching Gerald tug once more at the pool cover. "Does he need help?"

"No," she snaps, quick. Her voice sharpens the air. "He's fine. He's particular about those things—how the backyard is kept." She softens a bit, though it doesn't quite erase the edge. "You remember where the garage is?"

"Yeah." I turn down the hallway. Her voice echoes in my ears.

The garage door resists before giving way, groaning on its hinges. A stale current of air greets me with dust, oil, and something metallic that coats my tongue. A narrow path is cleared through the clutter. The bulb overhead swings faintly, throwing the shadows into restless motion. One of the freezers sits open near the back wall. The lid gapes, inviting inspection. I walk the path toward it, my boots grinding grit into the concrete.

Inside, the cavity is empty except for a smear of moisture and ice chunks stuck to the sides. The residue glistens faintly, as though it hasn't had long to settle. I close the lid, the hinges groaning, and let my gaze sweep the room again. The refrigerator hums steadily in the corner. I crouch, tug open the door, and pull out a box of beers, cradling it under my arm. I press the door closed with my elbow, the suction of the seal breaking with a hollow pop. That's when I notice it. The safes. A section of wall that once held a row of handgun safes now gapes blank. Dust outlines their absence in pale rectangles. The concrete floor bears long, shallow grooves where something heavy was dragged, the marks converging toward the door.

I stand still, the weight of the beer carton settling against my arm, the hum of the refrigerator droning in my ear. The room feels off-kilter now, the clutter suddenly arranged to hide rather than neglect. For a moment, I let the silence press in, trying to hear beyond it. Then, I shift the carton in my arms and start back toward the kitchen.

Through the glass doors, I catch sight of Bette in the yard with Gerald. Their voices drift faintly, but the words are muffled, inaudible. I can't tell if their words are heated or cooperative—either way, they're absorbed in the exchange. They're locked in—turned toward each other, oblivious to me.

I tug the refrigerator open. A rush of cold air spills over me, sharp against the warmth of the kitchen. The shelves are crowded and packed tight. Clear bins brim with vegetables, another with fruit, and a gallon of milk balances near the top. I crouch to the bottom shelf, box of beer cradled against my knee, only to find two twelve-packs already there. I pause, irritated, the carton in my hand suddenly purposeless. I straighten, tap my fingers against the box, and leave it on the counter.

My fists sink into my jacket pockets. I drift toward the stove. A pot hisses softly on the burner, steam curling up and fogging the metal hood. The smell of spice and roasting meat lingers heavy, saturating the air. I lean over the pot but don't lift the lid—I don't need to. Whatever's inside simmers steadily.

I turn away and let my eyes roam the living room. Photographs line the walls in neat rows. Family portraits, candid moments, vacations. Faces stare back, frozen in poses that feel more curated than natural.

When I glance again through the glass, Bette is pointing sharply at the pool's edge—then back at Gerald, then back again.

Then, a dull thud—heavy, stifled—shuffles against the ceiling above me. Soft movements. Several uneven steps trail after. My eyes shift back to the yard. Their conversation continues, swallowed by glass and distance. I move. Crossing the living room, I step into the stairwell, my hand brushing the wall as I climb. The carpet deadens each step, muffling my footfalls into silence. At the landing, the second floor opens into a narrow hallway lined with doors, each propped ajar. Darkness swallows them—except one.

From the far end, a single room glows. Light spills into the hallway in a pale, sharp strip, pooling across the carpet. The rest of the house falls out of focus as if it's been pulled into this one opening. I move toward it, fists buried in my pockets. The doorway brightens as I draw closer, until I'm leaning into the frame. Inside, an eleven year old boy lies on his back across the floor. His arms and legs push and flail in sluggish effort, inching him along in awkward motions. His body bends and arches upward, his face tilted toward the ceiling. He moves like a capsized caterpillar, belly to the sky, dragging himself across the room in a rhythm that feels both mechanical and desperate. Lucy sits on the bedspread nestled asleep.

"Hey, Jack." I kneel in the doorway, keeping my movements cautious, giving him time to notice me before I step closer. His eyes widen briefly, startled, then a crooked, playful smirk flickers across his face. "It's Jack, right?" I ask, returning the smile. He chirps back short, staccato sounds, high-pitched and uneven, his jaw shifting side to side in awkward rhythm. Bette had told me more than once that her son had special needs, but she never offered detail beyond that—just that he didn't talk much, that he understood better through touch. "My name's James," I continue softly. He inches toward me, awkward but determined, rolling his weight across his back. His fists scrape the floorboards as he moves.

Something catches my eye. His hands. They're clamped tight, knuckles whitening with strain. He's holding something. I tilt my head, lowering closer to his level. He stops and looks up at me, gaze blank, expression wide and innocent, though his fists stay rigid at his sides. The light of the room reflects off his skin—his hands look slick, glistening. I stretch my fingers toward him with a faint smile, and his chirps grow louder, more insistent.

"What have you got there, Jack? Can I take a look?"

He nods quickly, his head bobbing with excitement, a strange eagerness flashing across his face. But the moment my own expression falters, the movement stops. He stiffens, body freezing against the floorboards. I ease his small fingers open one by one. The resistance gives way, like prying loose something not meant to be shared. His palms unfurl, and I see it. A sheen of lotion coats his skin, clinging in glossy streaks that glimmer under the light. The smell rises immediately—honey and vanilla, sweet, cloying, out of place in the stale air.

But it's what's inside his hands that disturbs me. Tufts. Clumps of hair wound into knots, matted and tangled, sticky with the same lotion smeared across his palms. I freeze, my fingers still hovering near his. It's not the cat's—it's too thick, too long, too coarse. I glance around the room, my gaze snapping to corners I'd barely registered before. The shadows seem heavier now, the silence sharpened to a hum in my ears. The boy watches me, still smirking faintly, as if he's waiting to see what I'll do with the discovery. My stomach tightens. The realization settles cold and heavy. This isn't from the cat—not from any animal. It's from a person.

I unfasten my holster as I descend the stairs, letting the strap hang loose. At the bottom, Bette is pulling the sliding glass door closed behind her. She startles when she notices me. Her head snaps up, eyes locking into mine, her expression held taut and quiet. She doesn't speak right away—she just watches, measuring me.

"What were you doing up there?" she finally asks.

"Looking for a bathroom," I lie, steady and casual. "Jack seems like a nice kid."

Her lips attempt something that might be a smile. "Oh, you didn't need to go all the way up there." Her words feel rehearsed, lightened for effect. She turns and crosses into the kitchen. Her hand lingers on the refrigerator handle for a moment, fingers settling around it like she's weighing a choice. Then she pulls the door open, the rubber seal peeling back with a hiss. She reaches inside, extracts a full plastic pitcher, and sets it down on the counter with a clunk. "I made fresh lemonade, if you'd like some."

"I'm fine," I answer, eyes still on her hands. "That's not going to fit in the fridge." I nod toward the box of beer still on the counter. "There's already two boxes on the bottom shelf."

For a moment her face stills. Then the corner of her mouth crooks into a nervous smile. "Of course. I should've checked beforehand." She pours a glass for herself, then fills a second. The liquid runs pale yellow against the glass, condensation forming almost instantly. "It's such a hot afternoon."

"Yeah," I say evenly, my voice flat to balance hers. "Mind if we chat out back?"

She hesitates mid-pour, then forces brightness into her voice. "I'll bring this out. You need some of my homemade lemonade—got to keep hydrated in this heat. Especially in that coat of yours."

I step to the sliding glass door and pull it open, the warm breath of the greenhouse air rushing in. I motion for her to go first.

"You sure you want to go outside?" she asks, lingering on the threshold.

"Yes."

Her eyes flicker, then she nods and waddles forward, tray with glasses and pitcher in hand. The moment I step through, the air changes. It's humid and clings to my skin like damp cloth. The faint sweetness of flowers mixes with the acrid bite of chlorine and the heavier, sour smell of earth sealed beneath plastic.

She leads us to a white plastic table and chair set positioned several meters from the pool's edge. The dome above filters sunlight into a hazy gold that coats everything in a false warmth. She lowers herself into a chair, places both glasses on the table, and slides one across to me. Her hands linger on the rim a bit too long, as if reluctant to let go. I stay standing for a moment, the humidity pressing down.

"How long has this greenhouse been here?" I ask. My fingers tighten around the backrest of the chair, the flimsy plastic bending slightly under the pressure. I continue to stand, letting the question hang. Bette folds her hands neatly in her lap as though bracing herself. Gerald sets a watering can down beside a potted plant, then ambles over with the gait of someone reluctant to join.

"Two years now, give or take a few months," she says, her voice strained. "Right, Gerald?"

"Sounds right," he mutters, dropping into the chair beside her. His eyes drift to her, then to the sweating pitcher on the table, then outward again, scanning the length of the dome as though it offers him escape.

"You want some lemonade, Gerald?" I ask, my tone casual—intentional. He doesn't answer right away. Bette doesn't offer it. His forehead gleams with sweat, his chest rises with labored breath. The thirst is obvious, but he only glances sideways at her. The silence stretches. Their eyes meet, a flicker of unease passing between them. Almost imperceptible, but there. "You should hydrate with something," I add, watching the way he shifts in his chair.

He shakes his head faintly. "As much as I'd love to indulge, I'm fine for the moment."

"This doesn't get hot for you?" I ask, gesturing around us.

"What do you mean?" Bette's head tilts, her tone edging defensive.

"The greenhouse," I say, eyes tracing the arc of the panels above us. "The sun pounding through all that plastic—it feels like being an ant under a magnifying glass."

"That's rather morbid, don't you think?" she asks, releasing a clipped chuckle.

I turn from her smile before it can harden further, my eyes catching on the pool. The edge locks my gaze, and I consider my next move. And then, I notice it. Black marks streak the faux-rock rim, jagged and uneven, as though something heavy scraped against it.

I move across the lawn, the grass damp under my shoes, and close the distance. Behind me, there's a sudden scrape—the plastic legs of a chair bending against the ground, followed by the hollow clatter of it tipping. When I glance back, Bette is on her feet. She's risen too fast, her chair knocked sideways, lying askew behind her. Gerald stands after her, not moving closer, but not retreating either. Both watch me, their forms stiffening.

I crouch at the pool's edge, pressing my palm lightly against the scored stone. The scratches are deep, gouged in irregular arcs, like something was dragged over the surface. The black residue clings in the grooves, charred or rubbery—I can't tell which. I look up.

They're still there, both upright, both locked in silence. Bette's hands fidget against her thighs, Gerald's jaw shifts like he's chewing words, but can't swallow. They look like they want to speak but are tethered back by something heavier. The dome presses heat down on us, but a chill runs through me like a cold draft.

"What am I going to find under here?" I ask, pointing at the pool cover.

Neither of them answers. I crouch low, keeping them in my line of sight, and hook my fingers under the vinyl. The material is slick with condensation, warm from the greenhouse air. I start to drag it back, inch by inch, the vinyl squealing in protest. My pulse thrums in my ears. The final fold slaps against itself, and the surface of the pool lies bare.

I draw my pistol and level it on the couple. My hands stay steady, but my chest tightens as I look down. The water distorts but doesn't hide what floats beneath. Small bodies, pale and swollen, tethered in place. Ankles cinched in rope, the lines running taut to the pool floor where heavy shapes anchor them—the missing gun safes. For a moment the whole dome feels like it tilts, the air pressing closer. My throat goes dry.

One face catches me. A girl, turned upward, her wide eyes fixed on the surface. For a moment she almost looks alive, like she's still fighting for air, still begging to be pulled free. The illusion won't let go, even though I know better. Later, when they haul the bodies out one by one, her face stays with me. It follows me in reflections, in the quiet hours between reports, in the hollowness of my dreams. What gnaws at me most is the familiarity. At first, I can't place it—the slope of her cheek, the angle of her mouth—but the recognition builds, steady and merciless. She looks like Percy. The resemblance is enough to hollow me out, a cold crack opening inside my chest. For a second it feels like I lose him—lose everything—in that water.

This is what had happened:

Bette adored her son with a devotion that became obsessive. Everything she did, every decision she made, worked toward keeping him happy. One stormy night, when the wind lashed the siding and rain hammered the cul-de-sac, she opened her front door and found a child huddled on the stoop, soaked and trembling. She pulled the girl inside, wrapped her in dry clothes, and fed her soup and lemonade. In the moment, it was out of compassion.

Jack was elated. He had never been allowed outside, never been permitted to roughhouse with kids his own age. Suddenly, here was a companion under his roof—someone to laugh with, someone to occupy the long hours that usually pressed down like punishment. For a little while, it must have seemed like a miracle.

But days passed. The child began asking to go home. The questions turned into pleading. And Bette—terrified of losing Jack's newfound joy—refused. She found her answer in the same lemonade she had offered in kindness, slipping something into it to keep the girl compliant. The child weakened, her voice fading to whispers, her movements sluggish. Jack didn't mind. To him, it was still play. Even if his partner could no longer keep up.

What happened next was inevitable. One afternoon, in the chaos of play, Jack clutched too hard, wrung too long. Bones cracked, breath faltered, and the girl went limp for good. Bette panicked. Gerald did not. When he came home from work and she told him what had happened, he acted with cold efficiency. He emptied the freezers in the garage, wrapped the body in plastic, and stored it away, telling her they would decide what to do later. But later never came.

Jack's grief was immediate and consuming. He grew restless, moody, inconsolable. And to Bette, his happiness was worth more than anything. When another child passed on the street—headed to school, riding a bike, simply wandering too close—she called out to them with a smile, coaxing them inside. The pattern repeated. A playmate, temporary joy, then silence. Gerald and Bette both knew where it would end, but neither stopped it. They only worked to hide the aftermath.

After Jack crushed the life from a second child, Bette told herself something had to change. She loved him too much to stop the pattern, but she convinced herself she could soften it. She began coating his hands with lotion, rubbing it across the children's clothes and skin as well, believing the slickness would prolong the damage, give him more time with his playmates before the inevitable happened. For a while, it worked. The children lasted longer. But the outcome never changed.

Meanwhile, Bette and Gerald wrestled endlessly with the problem of the bodies. They whispered in the kitchen late at night, spoke in fragments and half-plans, but arrived nowhere. Gerald built fences, stacked wood, went to work, came home. Bette baked, cleaned, waited for me on Saturdays. And still, the same question hung over them: what to do with the growing number of dead children hidden under their roof.

One evening, Bette watched Jack in the glow of the fireplace. He was transfixed by a snow globe, shaking it again and again as a three-headed hellhound drifted underneath the glittering flakes. The image burrowed into her imagination. She thought of the greenhouse, its panels fogged and gleaming, and she pictured another globe, larger and crueler. A sealed world. A place where Jack could gaze into the water and see the companions he loved suspended in glassy permanence.

Gerald provided the solution. He had sold his handguns years before, trading them for hunting rifles, but the safes that once held the pistols remained. They were too heavy to sell, too useless to scrap. Now they had a purpose. He offered them as anchors, dead weight to drag the bodies down and pin them at the bottom of the pool.

That was the design they agreed upon: a snow globe built from grief, fear, and love—perverted into something unrecognizable. A greenhouse dome above, a glassy pool below, and in between, the silent figures of the children Jack couldn't keep alive.

All of this was happening while I sat at her table, while I nodded politely and told myself I was doing my job. I shook her hand, drank her coffee, listened to her talk about the weather—and never saw what was in front of me. What began as a single stormy night of misplaced kindness became a chain of horrors.

By the time we closed the case, nine children were dead. Nine families destroyed. And I was left staring at the wreckage, knowing I had been in their home week after week, blind to the truth. That blindness is what I carry. The deaths are theirs, but the weight of not seeing it—of not stopping it—still belongs to me. And all of it unfolded just behind that fence, under that dome, while I was drinking her coffee and convincing myself nothing was wrong. My conscience has a body count.

STANTON: ABYSS

"It's hard to believe that parents could do that to a child," I say.

"If a parent can do that to a child," Pierce replies, "then what is another person's life actually worth to them?"

I don't answer. Instead, I shuffle through the photographs again, letting my eyes gloss over the details. The gore doesn't faze me anymore—I've grown used to that. You have to in this line of work. What never becomes familiar, what no one could ever truly acclimate to, are the implications. The physicality of the gore remains constant. The meaning behind it shifts with every case, unpredictable and unnerving.

"How much is a human life worth?" I murmur, the words feeling foreign as they leave my mouth. I peer past the crowded café, trying to separate myself from the question. Around me, people laugh, gesture, chatter. My shoulders sag under invisible weights, heavy and unyielding. I can't remember the last time I felt even the faintest touch of ease, of weightlessness.

"I think it's subjective," he says. "In our line of work, people often don't think they've got much worth. Either we're cynical, or they're ignorant."

I shake my head. "I mean for you. Your life. Is what we do worth it?"

"No." He doesn't hesitate. "Someone has to be the martyr, though, right?"

"I don't think it's possible for it not to consume you," I say.

"What about you?"

"No," I reply. "I'm drowning in a fishbowl, and my children are watching from the outside, peering in, wondering if their mother will float belly up or keep swimming. Either way, there's a wall between us—a layer of glass, fogging over, separating us. And I'm the one fogging it, breathing into it, so focused on continuing to swim, to survive, that I can't see a way out."

"I don't know if I have a kid anymore," he says. "That's the sacrifice you make. You don't realize it until it's too late, until the fishbowl's been knocked over. You're flapping on the counter, among the shards of glass, and then down the drain. You end up in a bigger body of water—or torn to bits when someone turns on the garbage disposal. Then you discover you never needed to breathe in the first place. You have gills, after all. But you did it anyway. And you wouldn't change it, because that's what you thought you had to do. You end up forgotten, and the only thing left to cling to is the drain you chose to die in."

"There's no way out," I murmur.

"I lost everything obsessing over that case," Pierce continues, voice low. "I fell into this void of desperation and gluttony. I abused drugs, cheated on my wife, used prostitutes, abused them, abused Percy." He pauses, the words catching in his throat. "I've been pushing this feeling down for a long time—since the first Canine victim. Like we're missing something, the cycle repeating, swirling back, on the edge of the void. I think it could all be prevented if we just looked in the right places. But then the abyss shows up. Looming. Terrifying. Nothing left to lose. And next time—there won't be a chance to turn back."

"We have to be careful," I say. "We may be trapped in the fishbowl, but we can keep it from breaking."

BEG

"I don't know, Casey," I mutter again, the phone trapped between my cheek and shoulder blade. My cheek is damp with sweat, leaving a fine trail where it rests. "I'll be back in a couple of days. I'll call you then. Stewart's on the phone again, and I can barely hear myself think between you two jabbering on."

Harsh colors flash across the television screen, a program blurring beyond my focus. A mahogany hue starts to rot into burnt orange. The bulb behind the screen glares, nauseating, as if the images are growing out of the glass, layering into a gelatinous mass. When I shift my gaze, the burnt orange stretches into smears, lingering in the corners of my vision like residue I can't wipe away.

Stewart is shuffling around in the kitchen behind me. He's been on the phone more than usual these past few days, and I've been mapping it, tracking the rhythm. It's off—something's wrong. At first, I thought he was negotiating with clients, but the more I listen, the more it seems he's the problem, not whoever is on the other end.

I let the colors settle in my vision, let Stewart's movements become coordinates, grids overlaying the mundane. The shifting and scraping of his shoes against the floor becomes data. Something is unraveling. Something is always unraveling.

"Yes, I can drop it off in the next day or two," Stewart says, his voice hushed. I crane my neck over the sofa headboard, treating it like a rolling pin, pressing my ear into the cushions, inching closer to the kitchen. "There's a little problem in the front. Some damage I need you to look at. I don't think it's too excessive, but I'll leave that to you when you see it. You're the expert in these things, not me."

My mind drifts, spinning, trying to pin down what he's talking about. Words tumble into the muffled static of the television, of the phone, of my own thoughts. Wait. The hearse. He's talking about the hearse.

My cellphone buzzes in my pocket, startling me. I groan, expecting Casey.

"Yeah," I answer flatly.

"It's me," Percy says, voice awkward, bright. "Are you busy?"

The body in the basement is still circulating in my mind, and a thin spike of apprehension pierces through me. But something else stirs—something urgent writhing in my chest, demanding attention. My sternum drums with it. I realize I've been holding my breath. I inhale, and the prickling returns, crawling up my ribs, settling hot against my skin, thinking of him, imagining him. The last corpse hasn't stopped whispering into my memories, and still the sensation claws, insisting I ride it a little longer, grant myself one more indulgence. My shirt clings to me, soaked with the fine tremors of my pulse. My stomach feels tender against the cotton. I squirm on the couch, like my limbs need new positions to hold the tension at bay. I sigh a hollow sound, and the high bleeds away in the exhale, leaving a vacuum that hums under my skin.

"No," I say. My breath wanes, humid. I glance toward the kitchen. Stewart taps at his phone, hangs up, slides it into his pocket. He shuffles out of sight. Metal clanks, drawers scrape open and closed. My attention flits back to my thoughts, but the kitchen lights cast the drawers in a jaundiced yellow. I imagine the same sickly hue reflecting in my eyes, staring back at myself.

"Can I pick you up?" Percy's voice cuts through, faint, almost swallowed by the room. My fingers dig into my jeans pocket, stiff, shelled, like crustacean claws I want to crack at the joints. I scrape around and find the baggie lumped at the bottom. Coarse. Feverish.

"Sure," I say, checking my watch, glancing toward the kitchen. The noises have stopped. The coffee machine gurgles somewhere—a weighty, mechanical heartbeat. I don't see Stewart, but I feel him back there, skulking. "Give me an hour. I have to talk to Stewart." I hang up.

Stewart steps into the living room and lingers at the side of the couch. My fingers roll the amphetamines between them, watching the white crystals suckle against one another under my touch. Stewart stares, lips crooked, frown deepening the lines of his face. He doesn't speak, just stands there, wiping a bone china mug with an old rag, the fabric rasping.

"Who was that on the phone?" I ask, my voice hollow. I don't care—I just don't like how he's looking at me.

"A client," he says. Lies, of course. I know him too well. Ten years of shared space, shared rhythms. I know his tone, his mannerisms, the way he bends words around what he's hiding. I know him inside and out—literally. "They had some questions about their arrangements. Nothing special."

"You need help with anything?" I probe. The offer isn't genuine—it's a test. He's hiding something.

"No," he replies. "Not yet, at least."

"I'm going to be gone for a bit," I say. I don't need to report to him, and often I don't. Still, it feels like an obligation sometimes—but only when I'm not high, which is rare. It partially keeps him roped in, lets him feel he has some semblance of power over me. No one likes feeling helpless, like a caged animal, regardless of how succumbed they are to their own bliss. I have to feed him little scraps sometimes, tiny morsels so he won't gnaw through the cage, but never enough that he grows fat and complacent. Never enough to where he doesn't need me anymore. I hate it, because it means showing a trace of weakness. But in a few minutes, I'll be high and won't care—or remember. "Percy's picking me up. I probably won't be back tonight. I don't know."

"Percy—that's the boy from that open casket, right?" Stewart says, a stammer edging through his words. I don't know why he's taking this conversational avenue. "Are you actually fawning over a boy for once, instead of using him like he's your next entrepreneurial endeavor? Or am I reading you wrong?"

"No," I say. A half-lie. I don't know if he's off, or if there's some look on my face he's picking up on that I'm not aware of. I don't think you can fawn over an object. Fawn over the feeling, yeah, but not the thing itself. Fawning is soft, sentimental—not what I do. This is Stewart trying to take a stranglehold on whatever control he thinks he has over me, a subtle word to poke at weakness. "Everything is an entrepreneurial endeavor, isn't it? You just paint faulty perceptions of your interactions to make yourself believe otherwise. There's nothing beyond it but a transactional exchange."

"That's bleak," he murmurs. It's accusatory, harsh—out of character for Stewart. "I don't blame you. Sometimes I think, even though I've lived more than twice your age, you've already been to the end of a life and back. It's weird watching it—I feel like I'm just starting to skirt the edge."

I don't like the direction he's going. My fingers start emptying the amphetamines onto the table, white crystals scattering. I know where this is going, and I need to be high if this conversation is going to continue.

"You think this is helping?" I ask evenly, sprinkling the crystals across the table. The television has melted into a molded purple haze. I don't know what's playing—if anything is—or if the bacteria swimming in my eyes are just swelling up. "You're leering over me like I'm something to get to know. I'm not. I'm some dog that wandered to your doorstep, tongue hanging, lapping at your legs, sucking up your cock. Sometimes I wish I were a dog. I'd have no obligation in this conversation—in whatever kind of relationship this is. I could just be a bitch for you to kick around whenever you want. But because I'm not a dog, you have to care, or satiate some trivial curiosity, whatever. Sometimes our own consciousness is our biggest detriment."

"I get it," Stewart hisses through clenched teeth. Anger festers in him, yet beneath the hiss lies sorrow, pity, or something else entirely. He's holding back, biting down, not letting himself tear into me. I want him to kick my stomach until his shoe cracks my ribs, burrows inside me. "That's all I'm saying—I get it." He inhales, then exhales sharp. "There are other alternatives," he mutters, but I've stopped listening.

I crush the junk under the back of my cellphone, grinding it into the plastic, into the wood. It sticks, abrasively, like this ugly dialogue looping between us. I escape it—escape him trying to assert control, trying to make me fawn after him. Opening a door to let others hold power is dangerous—they'll take it. I hate him in these moments. But the hate is tangled with the knowledge he can, because I need him. He knows I love him, transactionally, like I love the amphetamines. Affection doesn't enter it. Survival is the connection. I hover my nose over the table, inhale sharply, and crystals rise. I crystallize. Turn the phone over, lick the remnants, feel the cold sting ripple through me. My torso arches, my body falls into the sofa cushions, letting them suck on my flesh. I crane my neck over the back of the headboard, waist jerking with the snaking sensation.

"Fuck," I groan, mouth gaping, panting warm. Stewart says nothing. His shadow slides from the corner of my eye, then disappears. My vision fogs, glassy, eyes watering. My throat aches and veins push soft throbs into the base of my jaw, piercing with needle points. I hold my jaw open, letting the drip trail down the back of my throat, tasting the sour seepage slither through my torso, biting at my hips. My chapping lips flake like stale bread. I close my mouth, teeth clenching, securing it. Stewart is gone. The television bleeds.

TRANSCENDENCE

I'm drowning in the ceiling. Its blank slate presses down on my vision—my mind pasted across its popcorn landscape. Blank. A car horn blares outside, dragging me back. I hitch my jeans up over my hips, buckle my belt, and peel off the sweat-logged shirt glued to my skin. I slip on something dry—something clean, and fish for my sunglasses on the arm of the sofa. I slide them on, and the lenses swallow my pupils, hiding them. They shade the sun's glare as I step through the door.

The gate screen screeches shut behind me, metal hot enough to sear my skin from baking in the afternoon heat. Warmth needles into my skin until my pores pucker like wilted buds, then flare open again, sucking my trickling sweat back into them. My stomach is hollow, bile sloshing around when my boots hit concrete.

He leans across the seat and pops the passenger door open. I catch the lip of it and haul myself inside, the frame groaning under the swing of my body. The door slams and nausea heaves up my throat. Vision smears, hazes out. He rolls the window down for me, like he knows. I lean my head through it, staring at weeds sprouting from the cracks of the sidewalk. His fingers slide into my hair, combing back greasy strands. I hear the snap of his seatbelt, then the slow lean—his mouth grazes my cheek, traces my jawline, and settles in the crook of my neck. I swallow hard against the bile burning my throat, but it pushes through.

A syrupy thread leaks between my teeth, caramel-thick, streaking the passenger door. More wells up. I spit it into the weeds, and it clings there, glistening.

"I'm a bit out of it," I mutter, breath snagging, chest tight. His lips pinprick against my skin, needling me in scattered points. I squirm in the seat, let my head loll against the headrest, and angle toward him. Through the blur, he's watching me—caught between fixation and hesitation, caught on the edge of saying something. "Where are we going?"

"I figured I'd take you over to my place," Percy says. He's wearing boxy black sunglasses that hide his eyes. It's unnerving—I'm missing access to that piece of him, like it's locked behind closed doors. Instead, I glare at my reflection, which is looking less like me each time I meet it. "It was my mother's house. I lived with her until she died. I guess it's mine now—or will be soon." I force down another hard swallow, nausea burning as it slides down, and shut my eyes until the nausea ebbs. He watches me, voice tentative. "Are you going to be alright?"

"Yeah." I force myself upright, words sharp, automatic. "I'll be fine."

Silence takes hold, broken only by the hum of the motor. He presses his fingers against his mouth, staring out the window before looking back at me. His face holds some preoccupation I can't pin.

"Everything feels vast," he blurts. I realize I've been staring at my bootlaces and the gummy dirt residue caked into the leather. The streaks resemble constellations. His voice is low, almost apologetic. "Like walls are farther away than they should be. They seem so sunken and distant, like I'm walking down a hallway of catacombs that doesn't seem to have an end."

And I picture bones crushed into dust under my boots. He rubs his eyes, pinches the bridge of his nose—like he's about to weep, but won't allow it.

"I get like that sometimes," I lie. I don't. I just want him to shut the fuck up. My hands drag across my chest, down my thighs, trying to pin myself to my body, but it feels like it's leaking out of me, hostage in a rubber suit. I rake damp hair between my fingers, pushing quilled strands across my forehead, skin coated in dew. The heat is suffocating.

"I don't know what to make of this," he says. I'm not sure what *this* is supposed to mean, and for a second, I wonder if I blacked out, if he's been talking and time kept going without me.

"Does it matter?" I ask, flat.

He goes quiet, then leans back, eyes closed, inhaling deep, head tilted to the car roof. Without responding, he shifts the car into gear. Gravel crunches under the tires as its weight lurches forward.

I can't tell if he's disappointed that I don't want to feed him anything, or if he's disappointed because he understands that's the best answer I'm capable of. Whatever's inside him is boiling over, cracking the soft shell he usually wears. He hasn't changed. It's me. Since that day at the summer house, he's looked different, smelled different. His expressions hang crooked. His voice runs an octave sharper. His skin feels like burnt sandalwood turned to ash.

I'm starting to lose track of what first pulled me toward him, but I remember the unease. Like there was a hollowness to him. He always seemed half-absent, drifting through life like a bystander rather than a character. That's how I'd like to remember myself too—back when I was only watching, before I began carving my mark into men. But being a spectator grew dull. I didn't want the narrative shown to me. I wanted to alter it.

I'm digressing.

What I appreciate about these moments with Percy is that I'm a spectator again. I watch him, study whatever erratic moves he makes, waiting for something uncharacteristic, something to rupture the typical structure of a man. Reel me deeper into the enigma. Yet his tears broke that illusion—the veil dissolved like another forgotten name lost in a graveyard. There's a manipulation in it, how he drew me close. He could have remained a passerby in his own narrative. They always have that choice. He leaves me none now. And in that, it feels impeccable how it's worked out—pieces locking into place—natural regulation. Order.

He wants this too.

The others were practice—fine-tuning. Percy has built a monolith inside himself, a structure that embodies everything I want to embed myself in, to slink into and wrap around my bare torso—his husk a second skin. Peeling my fingernails back and melting their cuticles into fishhooks, grafting onto him, latching into and splaying his rectum. Our bodies liquefy into stains that absorb him, leeching from his core and into my parasitic fluids—dissolving the line between us—intruding on his bodily authority—until his body becomes mine.

"We're almost there," Percy says. He glances over, a shallow smile crooking up in the corner of his mouth. I'm not sure if I drifted asleep or if my mind scattered too far—either way, time has slipped without me.

"Can I ask you something kind of personal?" His voice stutters, and the weight of it seems ominous in its implications. I exhale hard through my nose, turn toward him.

"It depends on what it is," I say, then shift back to the windshield. Shadows of trees pass across the pavement as the car eases. The engine sputters. He eases the brake, pulling to a stop at the end of the cul-de-sac. He kills the engine. The neighborhood is eerie in quiet warmth, vacant of onlookers or parked cars.

"I'm sorry if this is sudden—or a bit too personal too soon," Percy stammers. My throat knots, mucus like wax cooling and hardening in its lining. "Those scars—they're deep. What happened?"

I slide a cigarette between my lips, spark it, let smoke bleed out the open window, and tell him the story. It takes him a few minutes before he musters up a response, and it seems like he wants to climb out of his skin. It makes me wonder how he would react if had I told him the truth.

"I get it," Percy says, nodding. His hand slides across my jeans, fingers tightening around my thigh. His jaw shifts, teeth clenched. "It doesn't matter—I don't expect you to tell me. It's hard enough for me to talk to people I know, let alone people I don't. Honestly, I'm not sure I have an idea of what that means anymore." I stare at his hand gripping the fabric, knuckles hard. He keeps going, voice low and uneven. "I think it started when I lost my father—as a figure of speech. Not just him— trust, too. After that, being vulnerable with anyone felt dangerous. And then when my mother died, I realized I'd already cut myself off from her long before. I've been living like anyone who gets too close will turn into a threat too. I don't know if that means anything to you. We tend to spend most of our lives making things harder on ourselves for the wrong reasons—or no reason at all."

I don't reply to that. The cigarette burns down, smoke drifting out the window and dissolving in the heat. My temples ache, skull feeling compressed in a vice, jaw locking until my bones feel swollen under their taut tendons. The cracks of my lips caress the cigarette filter. I glance back at him.

"Someone holds my skin as collateral," I say. "Thankfully, I've grown to appreciate it—otherwise, this conversation would've been awkward."

Percy's face goes blank, and he presses his lips tight, chewing back his words. The lack of reaction gnaws at me. There's something buried in him worth prying open, worth digging into. I wonder for a moment whether a different response would change what I'm about to do to him. It wouldn't. His choices are already swallowed in this imminent collision between sentiment and afterlife. He doesn't get the luxury to deliberate his choices himself. He doesn't have any. That truth reinforces that what I'm about to do is right—there isn't an alternative that's better. It reminds me that everything is transactional. Whatever he thinks this is—whatever role he's reaching for—it's nothing but a frame, his way of shaping our proximity into some lucid sexual tension he believes will ripen into closeness.

He looks at me like that, and I want to get out of the car. His mouth presses to my cheek, tongue dragging wet around my earlobe. I exhale hard. Rage catches, burns through me. My veins prickle in icy rushes, then melt into a warm mist under my skin. The high surges. He mouths something I can't hear. My ears are vacant except for the single ringing pang reverberating in my skull.

I'm going to kill him.

He pushes off my chest and slips out of the car. The seatbelt snaps back against the doorframe. I watch him cross in front of the hood, the key fob spinning in his fingers. My hand slides beneath my shirt and I massage the scars carved across my raw stomach. Collateral. Whatever.

I watch Percy rummage through the kitchen cabinets, plastic spice jars rattling under his hand. I lift myself onto the marble counter beside the sink. The faucet drips in a thin stream, water pooling around the stainless lip of the drain. I glance around the countertop as he continues to poke through a cabinet. My fingers trace the counter, following flecks in the stone, feeling the tiny chips beneath my skin. On the stovetop, near Percy's hip, sits a bowl of cloves. They look more like charred bones—smoked remnants collected from a firepit. The backsplash above the stove is ivory with a patina trim, but the tiles bleed sickly green at the edges, as though algae were seeping from their seams.

Percy shuts the cabinet with a harsh click. The noise breaks my attention from the backsplash. He holds up a small jar of black vinegar. For a moment, it registers as blood. He unscrews the cap, takes a terse sip, then places it on the countertop. He winces and puckers his lips, shows his teeth, inhales the pungent odor, and licks the tart taste from his gumline.

"I read somewhere drinking black vinegar helps prevent cancer," he says, still squinting. "Preventing it, or something like that." He exhales sharply, as if to expel the aftertaste, then paces his breath with intention. "I'm not sure. But I guess it's for the *what if*. Same reason I pray sometimes."

All the people I've ever known that had truly taken care of themselves are dead. I don't tell him that. The switchblade in my boot digs awkwardly against my ankle. I cock my heel against the counter. It catches on the cupboard door and shifts it back into place. He doesn't notice. He turns to the sink and runs his hands under the water. Soap foams across his knuckles and he squeezes them dry between a hand towel.

"I smoke," I say. Killing yourself is the sincerest form of masturbation. His eyes skim over me. He smiles faintly, folds the towel, and drapes it across the faucet to dry.

I push off from the kitchen counter and move behind him, pressing my chest into his back, grazing the nape of his neck with my chin. My thumb digs into the muscle of his shoulder canal, massaging his taut skin in circles underneath my fingertips. I push him forward until his palms brace against the sink. His knuckles clench tight.

My hands worm under his shirt, dragging it above his sternum, tracing the outline of his ribs. They jut like worn birdcage wires, rough under my palms. I finger his oily hips, arching my fingers into his waistband. His hips scrape into the counter's lip, veins tightening through his arms. I hook my fingers around his belt buckle, tug, then bite at the back of his neck. His body stiffens, shivers. I lean lower, mouth grazing his spine, and unbuckle my belt—pull. His thighs flex against the lip of his jeans and leave impressions in his skin. His ass looks like makeshift belt notch, splayed raw and dripping buttery seepage from its puncture. Like my ego, it's run out of usefulness. My breath seeps into his skin as I chew down the protruding segments of his spine and strip off his shirt. My lips reach his hipbones, and I press hot against his waistline. The hunger climbs.

The switchblade slips free from my boot. My hand rises beneath his chin, prying his jaw open, my fingers hooking into his mouth. His jaw unhinges and lets my fingers enter, gagging in pleasure on the intrusion. His eyes water, and he loves it. I tilt his head back, bend his neck in a clean arc, jaw slack. My other hand crawls its fingers under his jaw, cupping his mouth, gliding the cold metal of the switchblade to his throat.

The blade clicks open, its edge pressing just below his chin. His body jerks—steel meeting flesh, and I press harder into his back. I guide my cock against his puncture, outlining his pucker with its head, then push—pressure clogging his tensing tunnel. It pulses around me, eroded, suctioning my bare skin. He grips the counter—arcs his back—push deeper. He offers a rapid, pained groan. Again—again—barely audible— my thumb pressing into his gumline, pressing down his tongue.

I wedge the switchblade under his chin, crank, like cutting chunks from a cheese wheel. His rectum tenses around my cock before loosening, the blood from his jaw slit leaks down his front, down my arms, and drips across his back, lubricating his asshole, wetting my cock. My cock flops like a flounder against my leg, released from its sanctum, fat and engorged in his fluids. He gags again, this time in pain, and blood sludges over his teeth. Blood seeps fast, a warm stream painting the marble countertop. The veins in his throat split open like tearing cloth seams. The blade rips stringy muscle tissue into coarse ropes, draining into a vicious flow from his jaw.

He convulses, spasms rattling his frame. I grip him by the hair, wrench his head back, taste the warmth spilling out of him. I hook my tongue around his and snake around the roof of his mouth. The blood smears my mouth, my cheeks, clownish streaks of color painted on by his collapse. The marble beneath him gleams red and spiderwebs veins in the stone—catching and framing the pool. His body shudders against me, heat leaving in waves.

I let his body slide down, leaving a smear against the counter. He crumples onto the kitchen tile, folding into himself. I pull my shirt over my head, peel off my jeans, and strip him the same way. Gripping his ankles, I drag him toward the living room. A trail glistens behind him— bleeding snail grease—slickening the floorboards. I prop him upright against a wall. His flesh hits it with a wet smack, clinging for a moment before slumping into place. He's still struggling—gurgling, choking—residual noises leaking out of him.

I leave him where he slumps, and I stagger down the hallway, my bare feet stamping footprints into the floorboards. The corridor is dim, breathing shallowly with me, and the floorboards fade into carpet as though the house is shifting underfoot. At the end, a door glows faintly at its base.

The garage exhales when I open it. A bare bulb dangles from its cord, swarmed by moths thrashing themselves against the light. Their wings snap. The light sways, illuminating a workbench laid out beneath it, cluttered in an altar of metal and rust—power tools crusted with grit. I move closer. Dust coats the handles of each tool. Their plastic bodies are brittle shells that crack under my fingertips, breaking like fragile exoskeletons when I squeeze them. A hammer is molded in dried flecks. A handsaw, its teeth jagged and dulled, lies waiting to gnaw through whatever it can bite. Pliers, warped with age, still flexing enough to pinch down and crank loose. A coil of wire, half-unwound with sharp edges, peeks from the corner. The nail gun sits farther back. It's heavier, electric—new. I trail my hand across them one by one, imagining each pressed into him, each leaving a different testimony on his body. The hammer could fold his bones in. The saw could open his seams. The pliers could strip his fingernails. All of them want a turn. When I choose, it feels inevitable—like a priest selecting his rosary, his cross, his word.

When I return, Percy is still alive, inching along his stomach, slow and futile, like a slug suffocating in his salt bath. I grip him beneath the armpit and hoist him up, his blood smacking streaks across my bare back, warm trails running down my spine and running down into my ass. I press him against the wall, body to body, our flesh clinging together into sticky putty. My own limbs shake from holding his weight. One of my arms braces against the wall while the other steadies the nail gun in the crook of his elbow. The trigger kicks—pop, hiss—and steel drives through him—erupts a stream. Again. His palm jerks as I fix it flat against the wall, fingers crimping like a dead spider. The sound repeats—pop, pop, pop— each strike threading him tighter, pulling muscle and tendon taut until they fray and give. His body buckles but holds, tethered to the wall in a crude lattice. His head droops, neck bending loose and lolling like a rotted branch. His skin holds onto the nails in snarled tangles—ripping but remaining stationary. The nails struggle to hold his weight. I fasten his legs the same, nails pinning thigh and calf until he hangs spread against the plaster. The wall accepts him. The floorboards beneath darken as his body weeps downward, a fountain guttering into its basin. I hang his body like an emasculated savior, and his limbs blacken the floorboards.

I tilt my head and study his eyes. The pupils track weakly, sliding toward the outer corners of their sockets. My fingers press along his cheek, noting the smoothness of the skin, still elastic with warmth. I run my tongue across the corner of his mouth, collecting traces of his fluids. He releases throaty gags as my tongue enters him further. I feel a coarse vibration deep in his throat, diaphragm spasming. I insert my fingers along the gumline, feeling the resistance of soft tissue against bone, prying his mouth open further like I'm impregnating his mouth in my juices. The jaw hinges wider under pressure, tendons straining at the angle. When I withdraw, I bring my fingers together. The surface is coated with clotting residue—blood thickening, granulating in the pores, tacky beneath the nails. A sample, adhesive, catalogued against my skin.

I step away from him and drift into the bathroom at the end of the hall. The oblong mirror above the sink reflects a distorted image of my sickened torso. My sternum juts forward, ribs flaring with every pant, each breath sharpening the outline until it looks more skeletal than human. The scars across my chest interrupt the reflection, cutting through the contours of my body, bending my limbs into unnatural shapes. I admire them—long cuts, thin and ropy, and jagged ones, raw as though they never healed. They form an index of what's been carved. Beyond record, they feel like altar markings, etchings across a surface meant for ritual. I could cling into their gashes, scoop my ejaculate—his ejaculate—through their trenches. Let it crust, harden in my crevices—mend my cracked porcelain and burn his grease into chalky chunks between my layers. The thought of melting into his oily semen stiffens my cock more.

A drop of blood breaks loose from my nose and spatters into the basin. Then another. Thin red threads trickle across the porcelain, veining the marble. I wipe my nose with the back of my hand and press the other against the sink for balance. My palm leaves a red print on the surface. Stark, declarative—a signature.

Blood travels down my chest in sluggish rivulets, gathering around the ridges of my abdomen, greasing my cock and coating it in a slop of lubrication. I see it as a varnish—a glaze poured over my vessel to seal it.

My breath clouds the mirror—heavy panting veiling the reflection in a dense fog. I raise the butt of my switchblade and bring it against the glass. The mirror shatters outward, shards falling in a ringing clatter. A shallow slice opens along my arm as I watch myself break apart into pieces with the shattered mirror. I crouch among the shards and collect them in my hands, stacking them. They grind and squeal against one another, edges sliding, rearranging themselves into new forms. I hold them to my ear, listening to the frictional whisper, as though the shards were conferring. The glass feels heavy in my palms. I stay in that crouch until my pulse levels, dropping into a dull, regular rhythm. Only when my breathing steadies, I rise and carry the fragments with me, stepping back toward the living room.

I arrange the shards in uneven stacks at his nailed feet, building small, crooked cairns. One by one, I lift them, testing placements across his body. A shard slips into his cheek—another props his mouth ajar between the gums. I drag one across the line of his thigh, splitting tendons and wedging the glass into the seam. I contemplate entry points for each shard. They need to catch me in their angles—my body mirrored through his, refracted on every surface, seen from all directions at once. A panorama of possession. Art imitating life imitating art, until the two collapse into one reflection.

I step forward and press my chest into his, tilting my chin to taste the blood dripping from the loosened hinge of his jaw. My hand steadies the switchblade beneath his sternum. The bone resists, then yields with a sharp crack. Jerking it back, I draw the blade downward, in precise sawing motions. Flesh peels in sheets, like cutting saranwrap. Behind it, the cavity swells forward, heavy with the weight of his sagging organs. I press my palm flat against him, restraining the collapse, preventing the contents of his innards from tumbling out by their strings for a moment longer. They loll against my pressure. The knife works in precise strokes, separating the cords that cling to his walls, clearing the cavity. Inside, his intestines are coiled structures tightening and loosening under my hands, as though the body still tries to protect itself. I pry them gently, methodically, feeling the knots yield one by one. Each opening is an aperture, another angle of reflection. The chamber reshapes itself around absence, and in that absence, I find the space I was looking for. I grip a section and cut the cord free from the contorted mess, folding it outward like a soggy stalk of celery, and rub my thumb through its wet channel. Loosen the bowel loop, pull the intestinal channel, finger the intact section further down. I press my fingers into the exposed hole, feeling the walls contract faintly around me, sucking my thumb as I push through the rank contents stuffing its tube. I release the intestinal orifice, and it pops a wet, slobbering pucker—nipping my slicked thumb. I twist the length in my hand, winding it into a cord, wrapping it tight around my forearm until it binds like a rope. The weight drags, warm and unsteady, seeping onto my skin. I lower it against my stomach, smearing its residue across the seepage already clotting around my soaking navel. The stains mingle, one fluid bleeding into another, indistinguishable. I pry the hole's lip open and descend the intestinal maw around my cock, squeezing its hollowed tract around my shaft. The wet inner sanctum oozes matter against my hips, damp residue clinging in sticky strands and clumping in my pubic hair. I exhale sharply, a tremor crawling through my shoulders, my joints locking with a sharp pull along my spine. My pelvic bones tense and quiver. I press forward into the disemboweled frame, folding my arms down as I slide inside his cavity. His broken ribs splay outward like wings, and I guide my shoulders beneath them, fitting myself into the husk as though it were prepared for me. The lips of his orifice lick my back, his incision wrapping my torso into him. I press my forehead to the wall beside his gored, torn-out neck, lips grazing the spill. The salt clings between my teeth, soaking into me, saturating my thirsty skin. My cock throbs inside his canal, thrusting deeper into his tissue and coating my head in his fecal mucus. My thrusting tightens and intensifies, coming closer. I pant into the gore of his shoulder and growl sharp into the maw of his leftovers, tearing loose before I clamp him back between my teeth. My mouth presses into him, lips dragging across the thin remnants of tissue still strung within the hollow, as though tracing the remaining strands that tether his form. I come vigorously inside his vessel, screaming pleasurable pain and aching in erotic pulsations. My body moans from the sexual exorcism, excising my seed and sealing it within him.

I crumple to my knees, shaking violently as though something has been torn from me. My breath rasps in broken gulps while I stare at the floorboards, watching them drink what drains from him, the planks gorging themselves. My skin tingles, and the force exhumed from me debilitates my ability to move. My legs buckle in a paralyzed stupor, and I slump on the floor, shaking like a sick newborn—spawn. My eyes bulge as if they urge me to let them split from their sockets.

My body is a vacated husk. I bathe in his black blood, pooled across the floor, and it slicks my skin in a tight suit. It crusts as it dries, tightening, sealing me inside. I tremble within it, bound in his residue. The casing hardens, stiff and fragile, cocooning me in its clammy sludge. I wait there, shivering, certain that when it splits, I'll emerge altered. Raw, unrecognizable, regurgitating his milky ejaculate over my flesh, new seed crawling out of this shell—into fresh form.

STANTON: HOOKY

"Let me know how it goes with Cameron," I say, eyes tracing the ocean of bobbing teenagers spilling from the front entrance, backpacks slung haphazardly, colliding with each other. Preston emerges, talking to a shorter boy, lingering at the top step for a moment. I urge him silently to hurry, but I'm also caught, curiously, in the opportunity of observation. He leans around and embraces the boy, separates, and hands him something from his backpack. I can't make out exactly what it is, but my mind fills in the gaps. Preston leisurely descends the concrete steps, glancing back at the boy a couple times. "I'll call you back when I've got a moment. I'm a bit preoccupied." I hang up and drop my cellphone into the cup holder.

"What are you doing here?" Preston calls, noticing the car. He leans in through the open passenger window, arms folded, chin resting lightly on them, and meets my gaze. Nervous, but not fear—something softer, more pleasant.

"I figured I'd pick you up for a change," I say, trying to sound casual, letting a grin lift the edge of my voice. "Unless that's not the cool thing to do. I won't be mad if you ditch me for the school bus."

He glances along the length of the car, waves to someone, then back at me, letting out a sigh. He swings the door open, drops his backpack at his feet, and fidgets with the zippers, fingers brushing the fabric almost obsessively—checking, confirming. I notice the way he watches his friend moving off in the opposite direction, his posture slight but betraying.

I flick on the blinker, signaling my intent to pull out. School buses hurdle past, teenagers litter the parking lot like crazed geese. I realize I might have to wait, let the current of kids thin, let the infant sea turtles make it safely to shore. The memory of why I never do this kind of thing floods back—it's a full-blown excursion.

"You don't have work?" Preston asks.

"I do," I say, "but I'm kind of on my own schedule today."

"And you wonder where I get it from," he replies, scratching the back of his head. I drum my fingers along the steering wheel, sinking further into the seat. "You can't be mad at me for skipping class when you're playing hooky from work."

"That's different," I say, peering out the window. I prop myself back into the seat, spot an opening, and turn the wheel to merge into the street. The car purrs as I press the gas. "I'm glad you were actually at school this time. I wasn't sure if I'd be driving home with an empty car."

"What do you mean?"

"You were ditching classes to go to those horror movies," I say. "I'm glad you decided to opt out of that endeavor for once."

"I haven't done that in a while," he says, tone wavering, uneasy. I don't know what that means in his timeline—days, weeks, months? I run through the last school voicemail I received. Could it really have been that long ago?

"Not that I support those adventures," I probe, "but why the sudden change of heart? I thought you loved those things—that you couldn't miss them for the world." I cock an eyebrow, glancing at him. His eyes are fixed out the window, avoiding mine. He seems distant, more than usual. I realize this is the first time in a while I've asked him about his life, and that's why it feels strange—unfamiliar.

"I don't know," he mutters, then pauses. "There were weird people that started showing up, I guess." He hesitates again, then turns to face me. "They didn't do anything, promise. Didn't say much either. But—you know your line of work. You can tell when someone's off. It felt like that. Like I was looking into this guy's eyes and there wasn't much behind them."

"It was a man?" I ask. He doesn't answer. A flush of concern spreads across my face and chills me. There's something more he's holding back. "You're sure no one did anything? Or said anything?"

"Yeah," he says, nodding.

"I'll take you sometime," I say, trying to lighten the mood. "We'll play hooky together one day after this case is closed. Promise."

"No, it's okay. I know you're busy," he replies, tone steady. I don't know if I should've said it, or if it's a promise I can keep. "I don't want to chance seeing him again."

"We'll do something else, then," I say, unsure how else to respond. I fiddle with the radio interface, noting the date displayed in its dim light. The station buzzes on, playing sultry jazz—a low background chorus to cover the silence between us. I guess I'm stopping by the theater tomorrow.

"I don't know why you'd want to do that anyway," he says, even and stern. The interjection catches me off guard. "Life's enough of a horror movie for you, isn't it?"

STANTON: PIG

I lick around the side of the cone, but the ice cream melts too fast, running in mint trails down the back of my hand and sticking between my fingers. The drone of passing cars rattles through the windows, scattering light across the dashboard in jagged, fragmented patterns. Summer heat waves warp the hood of the car like it's breathing. I toss the ruined cone out the window and scrub at the sticky stain with a napkin, my eyes locked on the theater entrance.

Several figures linger near the ticket booth, not quite natural in their movements. Others drift in and out of the nearby shops. The pornographic bookstore in the alley draws my focus. There's a neon sign depicting an anthropomorphic, sexualized deer wearing a mini skirt pointing toward the door. Even with the erotic displays censored, the homeless men shuffling past press their lips to the dirty window and rub at their crotches through crusted clothing.

It reminds me of my own teenage cruelty. We used to hurl ice cream remnants at the passed-out drunks by the pool hall and step on their cardboard signs. I'd like to think I grew out of it, but in moments like this, I feel the weight of it still. Karma isn't abstract—it lingers in the patterns and details you can't unsee.

I step out of the car and the discarded cone cracks under my boot. I glance up and down the street before crossing, then move onto the sidewalk in front of the ticket booth. A few younger men are in line, engrossed in chatter about the sequel to some low-budget horror movie I've never heard of. None of them interest me. I hover under the marquee, fists buried in my jacket pockets. The sun presses down, lacing heat around my throat, making my forehead burn. Sweat beads at my hairline, trickling down behind my ears.

A bell rattles in the distance. I turn toward the sound, near the alley's lip, and a man steps forward, a cigarette dangling from his lips. He rakes his fingers through his gelled, spiky hair, reinflating the crown of his sea urchin mane, and sparks a lighter. The flame dances in the reflection of his sunglasses. Something about him feels familiar. He rubs a scar trailing up the side of his neck, flicks ash to the sidewalk, and exhales a stream of smoke toward the rooftops. His cheekbones are sharp, features sunken, and skin rough—almost reptilian. I've seen him before.

"Excuse me," I say, pushing through the line. The moviegoers part with startled jerks. Several mutter annoyed hisses. I don't care. He removes his sunglasses and squints as I approach. A grin curves his lips, and he places an arm of his sunglasses between his teeth, holding their frame in place. "Can I ask you some questions?" I probe. He glances me over, nods once, and repositions his sunglasses on his nose.

"I need to know if you've seen someone," I say, unlocking my cellphone and scrolling to a recent photograph of Preston. It's his school portrait—teenage innocence draped in an oversized skull sweatshirt with a frayed collar—sporting a confident *cool kid on the block* grin.

I hold it up. The glare from the screen catches in his sunglasses. Preston's smile gleams back at me in an eerie contortion. "I believe he frequents the theater around this time. Have you seen him?"

"You're that cop, aren't you?" He tilts his head, and my memory begins flooding back to the grocery store. "I don't recall your name."

"I didn't give it to you," I reply. "Have you seen him—or anyone talking to him?"

"Is he in trouble?" His tone is pointed. "Or are you?"

"This is a waste of my time," I say, turning to leave.

"Does this have anything to do with those murders?" His voice stops me. His sunglasses hide his eyes, keeping his expression unreadable. "Have you taken an interest in that case too?"

"It's my case," I say. "What interest do you have in it?"

"Not the case," he says. "The person running it."

"Flattering, but that doesn't help me."

A silence settles between us as he steps closer.

"You know what the most fascinating example of mutualism in the animal kingdom is?" he asks, then drags on his cigarette, cheeks hollowing with the pull. "In my opinion, it's between tarantulas and frogs." He stops a few feet away, smoke drifting from his lips. He reeks of oil and meat. "Ants are drawn to tarantula eggs, which makes it difficult for the tarantula to leave the den and hunt—no protection for her young. Frogs, however, love ants. They'll camp out in the shelter of a tarantula nest, thrive off its security, and feed on the ants. That leaves the tarantula free to roam—to hunt. The burrow gives the frog protection from predators. See, there's this intricate, reciprocal relationship between the two. They're so different, and frankly I'm not sure they even like each other—but they can't live without one another. They rely on each other, whether they want to or not."

"You can save the ethology lecture," I reply. "I'm interested in people, not animals."

"I'm trying to figure out which you are," he says. "The tarantula or the frog."

"It doesn't matter," I reply, "either way, you're an ant."

"I would venture we've got more in common than you think."

He runs his fingers through his hair, fixing the spiked quills, then drags on his cigarette again. The hiss of embers fills the void of silence.

Then, my cellphone buzzes and a text from Preston illuminates the screen. I skim it, forcing my wandering thoughts back to why I'm really here. And I realize—I don't even know what I intended. Confront the men Preston described? Arrest someone? Fight someone? I feel obsessive—like the line between the role and the person is blurring until I'm not sure I remember what life is like outside of the uniform.

"He looks just like you," he says suddenly. "Is he your kid?"

"I promise you," I say, stuffing my cellphone in my pocket, "we are nothing alike," I say, voice flat, and walk away.

"I know you're not keen on discussing animal behavior," he calls after me, "but if you spend all your time in the pig pen, eventually you're going to get dirty."

PIERCE: UNDERTOW

Chief Cameron stares into his glass of bourbon, tracing the rim with his fingertip as we sit in silence. He brushes his fingers over his lips, opens his mouth as if to speak, then closes it again. I hesitate to interject, sensing he wants to choose the words that will express his rage with precision. I tap the closed file folder between my fingers. My reflection presses against the glass, either knocking or taunting—maybe both. I set the folder on his desk. He furrows his brow and finally turns toward it. I open the folder and start spreading the photographs across the surface.

"Stop," Cameron snaps. My fingers hover over a photo, obscuring a picture of spilled intestines. "What is this? What are you trying to do here?"

"Stanton has a theory—"

"I've heard your theories," he cuts me off, "your assumptions, all these ideas without any evidence. You're rehashing the same bullshit. I want concrete leads."

I purse my lips and look away, catching my reflection in the glass. I say nothing. Cameron rolls his eyes. I hear his glass scrape the desk. He swallows the last of his bourbon, sets the empty glass down, and leans back, chair creaking. I imagine him folding his fingers over his bulging stomach. My reflection fidgets, mimicking my movements. It doesn't reflect the sweat beading at my collar, the pounding headache rising behind my eyes. I wish I could mirror its empty composure. Should I have stayed in New York?

"What about Stanton?" Cameron asks, voice tensing, deliberate. "Does she have anything concrete, or is it all… existential musings?"

"I don't know," I say, glancing at him. His jaw tightens, the subtle warning before he decides whether to reprimand or patronize me. "No," I elaborate more definitively.

"I see." He tilts his head, watching me like he's weighing my answer. "What are you looking at?"

"Excuse me?"

"The glass panes," he says, tapping the desk with precision. His eyes drift past me, through the office windows, scanning some invisible corridor, then snap back. "Is there someone out there? Someone more important to you than this conversation?" The question isn't really a question. I freeze, caught in the gravity of it, like there's nowhere to hide. He leans forward, fingers splaying across the photographs, pushing them around the desk with calculated force. He isn't studying them—they're a barricade, a line drawn, a way to see how I'll react before deciding what comes next.

My phone buzzes in my pocket. I ignore it, but Cameron lifts his gaze, eyes sharp, ears attuned to the vibration. He tilts his head toward my pocket—an almost imperceptible order.

"You going to get that?" he asks. There's something in his tone— either tossing me a lifeline or a trap.

"Yeah," I murmur. I slide the phone from my pocket. The screen glows with a number I don't recognize. My thumb hovers, trembling. Cameron's stare is a vise, silent but deafening. I press the button, raise the phone, and cradle it to my ear, heart hammering.

"Detective Pierce," I answer. His words stumble over each other, desperate and jagged, and I raise a hand. "Hold on a second," I say, tapping the speakerphone button and setting the phone on top of the photographs. A static pause stretches, then a ragged hiss of breath fills the speaker like he's been running. "Can you slow down… repeat that?" I ask.

"It's Lee," he finally says. "From the garage—you remember me?"

"Yeah," I reply, glancing at Cameron. He leans back slightly, folding his hands and watching me more than the cellphone. "I have our Chief of Police here, Gus Cameron. You're on speaker. Is that okay?"

"Sure," Lee says. "I think I've found a vehicle. Matches the description you gave me. Front passenger side—completely caved in. Headlight's smashed."

"What's the make and model?" I ask, my pulse tightening.

"It's a hearse," he says. The word hangs, dissonant in the room. My eyes flick to Cameron, whose gaze is fixed, unblinking, on the phone. He knows—something is coming. He shifts, just a fraction, then checks me, measuring my expression, seeing if I'm ready. I am. "Remember those casket rollers I showed you?" Lee continues, voice low, careful. "He was waiting for them to come in before bringing the hearse in for maintenance. I pressed him enough, finally, and he admits—it's more than just the rollers. Says he'd been in an accident. Wouldn't say how—or with what. I didn't pry. Loyal customer. Figured I'd see it myself."

"What's the customer's name?" I ask, evenly.

"It belongs to Stewart," Lee says, as if I should already know him. "He runs the funeral home in town. Brings all his hearses here for tune-ups and repairs. Nice guy… but lonely. I'd be too, if I spent all day holed up in an office surrounded by dead bodies. You're probably familiar with the type."

"Did he act differently than usual?" I ask. "Nervous, jittery, or said something odd?"

"Not really," Lee continues. "He's always a little on edge, has that uneasy stutter, like he's nervous about everything. I chalk it up to age—or dementia creeping in."

"When did you last see him?"

"He dropped the hearse off about an hour ago. I told him it might take some time to get a proper quote." He pauses, voice tightening. "Looks like a pricey fix. Whatever he hit, he hit hard. I'll need to replace the bumper, all the wiring for the headlight, and—"

"Do you have an address for him? Personal and business?" I dig a pen out of my pocket and a scrap of paper from the desk.

"Sure." He rattles off the numbers and addresses, and I scrawl them down, my hand moving faster than my thoughts. "Honestly, I can't imagine he's up to anything shady," he adds, but his tone doesn't quite convince me.

"One more thing," I continue. "Did this man, Stewart, ever bring anyone else to the garage? Mention any friends, family, coworkers?"

"No, just him—always just him. I don't know if he's got any friends or family left," Lee says. "I don't think he has any employees, but I can't be sure. He runs a small funeral home—never a big client load. It's just been him, as long as I can remember. Hard worker. Though, at his age, I doubt he can keep it up alone for much longer."

"I'll be in touch," I say. "I need to record an official statement, and I'll probably have more questions. Thanks for your help."

"He tends to get wrapped up in his work," Lee adds. "Spends most of his time in the office. If you're looking for him, start there."

"I appreciate it, Lee." I hang up.

I slump back in my chair, heart hammering in my chest. Cameron doesn't move—his eyes fixed on the black screen. Then, a smirk begins to creep across the corner of his mouth. He pivots in his chair and rifles through the bookcase, pulling out another glass and the decanter. He almost tips over a book with his elbow, then pivots back around in his chair and fills both glasses. Still no words. My fingers itch for my phone, to call Stanton, but instead I find myself drawn to the photographs again. If this is our guy… what's the link? What am I missing?

Cameron measures the bourbon, savoring each drop as if it's a ceremonial act. I drift over the photos again, scanning, connecting dots that aren't there. The thrill drains. There isn't a clear connection. I thought everything would snap into place with a break. Nothing. Not even a farfetched connection. That's Stanton's department. I shove the thought down, clinging to the one thing I know—this is a step forward. Tangible. Real. Cameron pushes the bourbon toward me. The clink against the desk sounds loud in the tense silence. I wrap my fingers around the glass. And for a moment, just a sliver of awareness— drowning?

"And just like that?" I let the words hang between us. I don't know what they mean to Cameron, and honestly, I'm not sure what they mean to me. Something still feels off.

"I've got three of the finest Cuban cigars," he says, his eyes glinting. "But those are for when we've officially shut the books on this one. This is the lead we needed. Now it's just a matter of connecting the pieces."

"Yeah," I reply. He raises his glass, and I clink mine against it. He tosses his back and sets the empty glass down. I stare at mine for a moment, exhale sharply, and set it down—still full. My gaze drifts to the glass panes. The reflection I usually find there is gone. "There's still a connection we're missing."

"You're obsessing," Cameron says, leaning forward slightly. "That's always been a weakness of yours."

I say nothing. Am I supposed to believe an elderly man did this? Mutilated them like this? A lump forms in my throat, and I swallow hard, replaying the scene over and over. I feel magnetized to this case, and I wonder when—if ever—I'll be satisfied. Even after the case is solved, people still die. Chasing the next one offers a glimmer of redemption, but it's fleeting. No matter how many criminals are caught, the corpses keep piling.

"There's something else on your mind," Cameron probes, his voice softer. "And it's not the case."

The bourbon looks like molasses. I imagine it clogging my throat, my boots sinking into it, sloshing around, getting stuck. Looking at it makes me nauseous, like swallowing it would harden and plug my throat.

"Why did you choose this line of work?" I ask, uncertain whether I'm asking him—or myself.

"I don't think you choose it," he says, his eyes never leaving mine. "I think it chooses you. One way or another, it reels you in. Whether you intended to swim with the sharks or not, it finds a way to pull you under. And once it does…" he leans back slightly, letting the silence stretch, "it's almost impossible to escape. You get used to the current. Or it eats you."

"And what if you can't swim?" I ask, testing the waters of his analogy. "What if you find yourself drowning?"

"You're either in it long enough to watch yourself drown, or long enough to become the predator that eats the sharks," he says, pouring himself another glass. He replaces the decanter on the bookshelf behind him. "There isn't an alternative."

"Sometimes," I admit, "I feel like I'm drowning."

Cameron taps his finger against his glass, uncertain how to address that statement. He gazes through me, as if something beyond these walls has captured his vision. He stares into the full bourbon, silent, his mouth wincing in disgust, like he's just poured himself a glass of sour honey.

His cellphone rings, snapping him out of whatever trance he'd slipped into. Startled, he fumbles in his pocket and glances at the number—he must recognize it.

"Excuse me," he says, pressing the screen and raising the phone to his ear. "Cameron."

I stand from the desk chair and step out of his office, slipping through the cubical maze. I move past rows of desks and officers who are too preoccupied to notice. At the water dispenser, I pull a paper cup and fill it with cold water, glancing at the windowpanes, expecting to glimpse the reflection again—but it's still gone. The stillness soaks into my skin, the office reduced to a silent, moving cube. The voices around me are distant, and I feel trapped. I scan the windowpanes, then return my gaze to Cameron's office. He's pacing, rubbing at his forehead, mouthing something viciously to the caller. My skin flushes, heartbeat drumming against my chest, climbing into my core. I press my fingertips to my temples, trying to quell the growing ache. His expressions begin to dull. A stiff frown tightens his lips, the color draining from his face. His glass remains full. I finish the water, crumple the cup, and toss it into the trash. Cameron glances up, then turns to the bookshelf. For a fleeting moment, I think I see my reflection pass, but it's only a shadow of an officer walking by. He glances over his shoulder again, then returns to the photographs on his desk. I walk back into his office, and my boots are thudding inside my skull.

"I understand," I hear him say, his voice clipped. "I'm with Pierce now." I remain standing, vision swimming. The bourbon seems to smoke, cutting the air between us. "Yes." His jaw clenches. My skin burns— sweat soaking through my shirt. "I'm on my way."

"What's going on?" I ask, voice tight. He hangs up, placing the phone on the desk and glaring at it in silence, refusing to make eye contact. His fingers clutch the bourbon glass, knuckles whitening, contemplating it. He grips it tight but doesn't move. "Chief?" I push.

"James—" He swallows hard, the movement jerky, uneven. His eyes flicker to mine, and then back to the desk, to the photographs, to nothing. "It's your son."

STANTON: THRESHOLD

I cross the front yard. My boots sink into the wet lawn, crunching through soil and sodden leaves. The sprinklers haze the air in mist, the water droplets catching in the muted light, humming against the tension. A cloud rolls over the sun, dimming the scene, folding the concrete into deep, uncertain shadows. I step onto the walkway leading to the door and let my gaze trace its curve. It bends around the corner, linking to the driveway. When I look back at the path, a smeared, bloody shoe print catches my eye. It arcs across the concrete and trails through the grass, fading beneath damp blades and wilted leaves. Drops of gore speckle their edges, marking a grotesque landscape.

Police cars line the street, their lights flashing red and blue. The beams fracture across the garage door, spilling into the front entrance, bright and chaotic under the clouded sky. I pause at the mat, tracking the impression of my boots along the ground. Blood oozes from the doorframe against the corner of my vision. I reach for my sidearm, letting my palm brush its cold metal. The sting in my face radiates down my body and vibrates down my spine. My fingers tremble around the grip for a moment. Voices murmur through the open doorway in muffled chatter, but the sounds barely register. I drop my hand, slide into my pocket for gloves, and crouch under the yellow tape stretched across the threshold.

The gloves are tight, the seams biting into my wrists like razor wire. My gaze follows the trail of coagulating patches, tracing the flow down the hallway. The faint drip echoes across the floorboards— taunting. The wood seems alive, hemorrhaging in rhythm with the air itself. The floor bleeds. I draw a steady breath. The copper smell hits me, then the rotting of decomposing flesh. Each step forward is a negotiation with the house, the blood, and the voices. My footsteps seem to cling to the wood. What lies ahead calls me to notice it. I do. And I don't look away.

A forensic technician brushes against my shoulder, and I react instinctively, clutching his forearm. His eyes widen, body stiffens, and he skids to a stop, glaring down at me. I can feel the rigid outline of his bones through his sleeve. Then I notice my hands are trembling. I glance down at them, then back up, and release my grip.

"I want photographs of the footprints. Every single one," I hiss, teeth clenched so tightly my jaw aches. They feel fused together, muscles locked and rigid. "I want every inch of blood taken as samples—vacuum it up with your fucking mouth if you have to."

He doesn't respond, just nods, and continues out the front door.

I move into the living room. The kitchen lights slice through the gloom, illuminating the corpse pinned to the wall. The dripping grows louder—into an insistent, mocking rhythm. The victim's arms and legs are splayed, nailed through the palms. The nails groan under his weight, cracking paint, pulling drywall forward, tearing skin and muscle. He's been crucified. His wrists are lifeless, gray, flopping like pale fish. My eyes trace down to the chest cavity. He's been split open like a coconut shell, exposing creamy entrails from the orifice. Skin is peeled back and affixed to the wall with nails, fanned out in fresh bloom. The body is hollowed out, cut from throat to groin, like a suspended vestibule. His jaw hangs, shattered, toothy underbite exposed. His swollen lips are distorted with congealed blood. Shards of mirror protrude from the top and bottom lips, piercing his gums and fastened crudely within their lining.

"Fuck." My hand jerks back to my sidearm before my brain catches up. The bile in my stomach spikes into my throat when I recognize the corpse. The face—what's left of it—my lungs cinch shut. Heartbeat hollow—cavernous bellows beating the inside of my skull. If I don't get air, I'll rupture. Breathe. I claw past the holster, skitter through my pockets until my fingers snag my phone. I drag it to my face, nearly drop it.

"Chief," I choke out. The word breaks, but it's enough. "We've got another body. The victim is Percy."

Cameron's voice filters through, stretched thin like it's underwater. I count my inhale, grind my teeth until the tremor in my jaw dulls. I hear myself answering, but it isn't me—it's the orifice itself carrying the conversation. My own words don't belong to me. Exhale. Another phrase I can't remember.

"I'm on my way," I think he says—or I imagine it.

I end the call and shove the phone back into my pocket. My eyes stay glued to Percy's open maw, the echo inside growing louder than the background noise in the house. The noise dulls—footsteps, murmurs, radios. In my periphery, two uniforms slide through the patio door, strobes of red and blue sirens skating across their faces. My chest hitches. Their words start to make sense. Breathe.

"Out front, now," I snap, throat raw. I point hard at the door. "Lock down both entrances. When Pierce gets here, he does not cross the threshold. If he argues, hold him. If he pushes, detain him. He cannot see this." I sweep the yard, drag the patio door shut, throw the latch, and yank the curtains tight until the light dies. The fishbowl is gone—the glass shattered.

I turn toward the front door. It's a hive. Officers crowd the threshold, slipping down the hallway, taking positions at the entrance. Light burns across my face from the open doorway. I step toward them, then freeze—my phone vibrates in my pocket.

"Pierce," I answer. "Listen to me. You can't be here."

"What did he do to him?" he spits, words shooting through the receiver, and I can almost taste his saliva through the line. His voice is guttural, torn through a yell, bleating out and breaking loose in his throat. Behind him, his car windows echo the hollow roar of highway wind, swelling through the phone.

"Go home, Pierce." My plea curdles into a snarl. "If you cross this threshold, you aren't coming back."

The line dies. Silence—except for the hum of my blood under my skin.

I dial Cameron. The pounding returns to my ears, skull burning hot in panic. He answers, but I can't make sense of the words, or I just don't hear him at all—I only make out a shuffle, hiss, and whip on his end of the line.

"Pierce is on his way," I tell him. "This case is too close to home. We're out of time."

"I shouldn't be far behind," Cameron says, a door slamming shut behind his voice. "Keep Pierce away from the scene. We've got a new lead. Tracking down the Canine is all you now."

"I've got men at every door," I reply, then pause, the weight of it pressing in. "I'm worried about him, Chief. You know what this will do to him."

"I know." His tone dips, resigned. "I know you care about him, but don't let him take you down too. Pierce meets death with hurt. You meet it with passion. Use that. Don't let him drag you into the same well."

"Understood," I say, and hang up.

I lock my jaw and force my eyes on the body. The chest cavity yawns open, split open into blackened lips, and a hot surge of rage pulses beneath my skin. Cameron's words echo in me, dulling the fear in my stomach—shoving it lower, deeper. What replaces it is heavier, stranger. It doesn't disappear. It just changes shape—transcends to a new form.

I step closer until I can smell the salt in his blood. My hands bury into my pockets, and I study the hanging jaw. I tell myself it's restraint, though it feels more like surrender. The ears have been slit at the base, the cartilage pierced to embed mirror shards through and down into the jawline, locking them into place. Angled inward, they reflect his face in jagged fragments. Percy's face splinters—cheeks, lips, and eyes refracting from multiple angles, so the reflections converge. The shards catch more than his features. They hold an exposure outline of the Canine imposed in him, as if the Canine had stitched himself into the reflection. I glance to the mirrors wedged between Percy's gums, then to the ones jutting from under his fingernails and toenails. Each fragment throws back an angle of the victim, and—unavoidably—an angle of me.

For a moment, it feels as though the crime scene is turning me inside out, drawing me into the cavity with him. I picture myself turning, back facing his dissected cavity. The reflections crowd my vision, multiplying until I can't tell if I'm studying Percy's face or my own. My heart throbs against my ribs. I breathe through it, steadying, forcing myself back into my body. The scene is a design—a ritual of possession. The Canine's attempt to inhabit his victim—eat his way in and experience him from the inside out. I hold my ground, wanting to recoil. There can't be a difference between us if I let myself believe in what I see.

Pierce lurches through the doorway, and several officers lock his arms back, their hands strangling his elbows. I turn just enough to watch, lips pressed thin, refusing to move. One of the officers stumbles into view, clutching his jaw. A bruise is already blooming, blood welling from his lip. I don't move. Percy hangs above me, his body suspended like a deconstructed martyr, dripping.

Pierce's cry rips through the room in feral screeches. Then, his knees collapse, slamming into the floorboards, folding inward. Tears spill onto the wood and sink into its crevices. The officers go down with him, still pinning his arms, until his fight falters and his body immobilizes in their grip. They haul him back toward the entrance. I don't know what I'm supposed to do here. And the dripping is incessant.

Cameron peers in from the threshold, then steps fully into the hall after the officers drag out Pierce. His shoes clack against the floorboards. I glance at him only briefly before my gaze returns to the corpse. My mind scrapes for something—any lead that could point the way forward—but keeps circling back to the body dripping over me.

"Stanton," Cameron murmurs, hushed. His eyes follow mine, land on the corpse, and his expression knots, revolted. "Christ."

"What happens to Pierce?" I ask, still staring upward.

"He's being put on leave. He's going to have to turn in his badge and firearm for the time being. When the dust settles, we'll reassess." His tone is level, and it unsettles me. "I'll have someone follow him home, make sure he doesn't do anything rash."

"I'm worried for him," I repeat. My voice is flatter than I mean it to be. "What does a man do when everything he has is taken from him? What's left to do?"

Cameron doesn't answer. I don't expect him to. From outside, Pierce's voice tears out again—only now it's frayed, drying to nothing. Percy continues to drip, crimson ticking onto floorboards. For a moment, I swear its rhythm is quickening. My imagination is becoming unhinged.

"Pierce got a call," Cameron says, cutting through my fixation. "A lead on a vehicle from one of the Canine scenes. The one out by the highway—broken headlight, front end caved—"

"Yeah," I cut in. "I remember."

"A man named Lee owns a garage for specialty cars," Cameron continues. "He says the one he's holding is a hearse. The owner's an older man named Stewart. We've got his information. I'll track him down and have a talk with him."

"I'll do it."

He looks at me—irritation or worry passing across his face. His mouth shapes like he's about to argue, but he doesn't. Silence gathers. My mind circles back to the basement. That mutilation was different— calculated in a way the others weren't. The other scenes felt chaotic. The other locations were happenstance—less premeditated. The basement had structure.

"Do you have the files you pulled on the basement scene?" I ask.

"I told Pierce there wasn't anything useful in them," Cameron replies.

"I know. But something is off. It felt planned. Staged. I think we missed a connection."

He exhales. "The files should be in a folder in my office. I'll leave them on your desk. But first—follow the lead on that vehicle."

"Understood."

"Call me before you speak to Stewart," he adds. "If he's the Canine, assume he knows we're coming."

I nod, then glance back at Percy's body, dripping steady. "What do you think?"

"What do you mean?"

"About him," I press. "The Canine."

Cameron's jaw tightens. "I don't try to parse out the disputes between the Devil and God. I just clean up the mess after. That's all any of us can do. I don't see the purpose in pretending there's more."

"That's what you call this? A dispute?"

"It's not an agreement to let man have free will," he says, voice flat. "That's the most ignored fallacy."

PIERCE: ABSENCE

The room is cold and the blinds rattle in the draft. My shadow cuts across the window, blotting the light pouring in and silencing the streetlight's bleating hum. I part the slats with two fingers and peer out.

Two officers lean against their patrol car. One smokes, ember flaring as he jabs a finger into his partner's chest. The other shoves his wrist away, illuminated under the cone of the lamppost. The smoker stumbles, cigarette tumbling to the blacktop. They square off, arguing—too far to read their lips, but I'd wager I'm the subject. The smoker grinds the butt beneath his boot, pointing between the car and his companion. Then, he circles to the driver's side, opens the door, and slides in. Headlights flare. The second officer hesitates in the lamplight, weighing his choice, then climbs in after him. The cruiser pulls silently from the curb, tires creeping down the road until the taillights vanish.

I step back from the glass. My hand fishes through my pocket and finds the folded scrap I'd scribbled on earlier. The numbers are nearly illegible, but I squint until I make them out. I tap them into the glow of my phone. The screen's light washes over me, painting the room in soft white and drenching my skin. I pinch the device between cheek and shoulder blade. It rings.

I pour another finger of bourbon and roll the glass between my hands. The amber glow catches the lamplight. It burns a path as it descends my throat. Warmth spreads across my gums, sinking between my teeth until it feels like the liquor is nesting there. The phone keeps ringing. The burn climbs higher into my nose. I pinch the bridge, trying to keep it from flooding farther up. My eyes ache. Tears sting, dry, and leave a salty film in their sockets. Still ringing. I swallow again, hoping to soothe the rawness in my throat. It doesn't help—it only scratches deeper. My voice feels gone—not in volume but in resonance—like I lost its sound. Click. A beep cracks through the line and the flat signal of an answering machine buzzes.

"Hello, I—" My voice catches. I swallow hard, wetting my throat enough to push sound through. "I apologize. I know it's late. I don't think I can get to sleep without making some kind of arrangement." I stop again, searching for words that won't come. "These things just hover, you know? If you could call me back—" A click interrupts me.

"Hello?" The voice on the other end is raspy, older, but refined.

"Yes," I stammer, starting over. "I'm sorry. I know it's late. I need to make some funeral arrangements."

"I have availability in the morning, sir."

"Do you have availability tonight?" The urgency in my tone is more abrasive than I intend. "Now?" I nearly cut him off. There's a pause. I rein myself in, try to regain my framing for this. "It's been weighing on me. I'm losing sleep. I just need a moment of solace."

"I understand," he replies, and releases a reluctant, exacerbated sigh through the line. "Death is anything but an easy process. What time should I expect you?"

"Thirty minutes," I say, and hang up.

I pull open the bottom dresser drawer and finger through folded shirts. One ragged shirt is bunched in the corner. I peel it back and lift out a Glock 17. The serial number is filed off—a scar from a forgotten criminal. I consider it—exhale—then shut the drawer with a hard, decisive slam.

I rap my knuckles against the door. The lot is empty, blacktop glistening with oil streaks dotted across the painted parking lines. I glance around the building, examining its pockmarked bricks and stained pavement. Motor oil clings to the back of my throat like a bitter taste, hanging in the stale air. There's movement on the other side of the door. I jerk my head, listening. A light flickers through a window, shadow pressed thin against the curtain. It lingers there, swaying, arms stretched monstrously long—tubing folding like a worn out slinky. For a moment, it doesn't feel human. The shadow recedes. The doorknob rattles, caught in some awkward struggle. I raise my hand, almost out of instinct, as though to help. The door pulls open and light floods the hall, glossing over the shape until it sharpens into features.

His face emerges. Pale, wrinkled, skin folding in bunches, like a mashed plastic bag. The shadows between his wrinkles make his flesh look lumped and swollen. Beyond those folds, he's gaunt—bones protruding, skull fragile as if pieced together from broken pencils. He lets go of the knob and glances at my half-outstretched hand. I pull it back. The tension drains from his form, shoulders sloping into a permanent hunch. His suit hangs baggy, sleeves hanging around his wrists. Once it may have been cut to fit him. Now, it's lost shape and resembles a hollow barrel for his bones to clatter around in—fabric rattling loose around his form.

"Come in," Stewart says, motioning with a limp hand. His voice is husky, strained, and a wet cough follows close behind. I step into the hallway, fists shoved into my pockets. The corridor stretches back toward a kitchenette, where a coffeemaker and knife block sit floodlit beneath a fluorescent beam. The walls are wrapped in faux wood wallpaper that exaggerates the length of the space, making it feel like the hall goes farther than it does.

Stewart shuffles into an office. I pause in the doorway, eyes scanning the hall again, before the groan of his chair pulls me forward. I cross the threshold. He gestures to the seat across from his desk. The chair has a wooden frame with black cushions torn at the seams. The office is bare. White walls, bland except for the three canvases behind him and a few photographs scattered across the desk. The room carries a sterile weight, as if the air hasn't been disturbed in years.

His desk is gouged at the corners and the varnish rubbed dull. Dust rims the edges of the photographs, and their frames don't match. They don't look curated so much as left behind, like everything else in the room. His chair groans when he shifts his weight and the wheels creak on the carpet. It doesn't sound like a seat meant for work—more like an iron lung trying to hold him together. The canvases behind him pique my interest. Abstract—I can't place what they're intended to resemble. The colors swell and recede, breathing. They don't depict so much as perform. One spirals upward, seafoam frothing over a melting brown base, tendrils sprouting into something botanical. I realize my hands are knotted into fists again inside my pockets.

"What's with these paintings?" I ask, brushing my fingers across my lips before pointing toward them. Stewart's eyebrows lift. His gaze drifts across the canvases, his forehead wrinkling into shallow rows.

"They're abstract," he says finally. "Obscure. I like that. Leaves room for interpretation." His eyes flick back to me. "That's what clients want. Something they can make meaning out of." He folds his hands together on the desk, then adds, "I don't see much in them myself. But others—they've been eye-opening to them, in one way or another. The images that truly matter to me—those I keep just for myself."

I nod, but the words land strange, like he's alluding to something worth keeping out of reach. "I see," I say, tapping my fingers against the chair arm. The sound is muffled, dull. Behind me, the clock ticks, steady. Each second punctures the silence a little deeper. My eyes drift back to the second painting. A gray, furred shape claws its way out of a central void. The body seems animal at first, but its limbs bend wrong, too human in their articulation. The figure looks trapped, struggling to climb out—straining upward in silence. The longer I stare, the more I can't tell if it's trying to escape the hole or being dragged back in.

"What is it that I can do for you, Mr. Pierce?" Stewart asks. I realize I've been staring at the paintings too long. My gaze breaks. I fix on the corner of the room instead—plastic potted plant, cheap and lifeless. The clock ticks.

My lips purse. Heat bubbles under my ribs, rising. I keep tapping my finger against the chair arm. The sound feels necessary, like a way to fill the silence. When I look back at Stewart, my teeth grit together before I catch myself, easing my jaw so the tension won't show.

"What do you think happens after death?" I ask. My voice is flat, barely above a whisper.

"I think that's determined by your own faith," he says, his tone even. "Not just religious faith. Perception of our own virtue. In morality. That's what my clients tend to believe, at least. I don't have a definitive answer myself—nor do I attempt to have one. Whatever comes after must be better than what we endure here. Don't you think?"

"What if you kill someone?" I press. "Violently. Absent of morality, virtue, faith. Nothing behind it."

Stewart leans back. A pause stretches. The clock ticks. "I don't know," he says. "That depends on what you believe, I suppose."

"I'm asking what *you* believe."

His lips crease downward in an uneasy sulk. My eyes wander back to the canvases. The third one is rigid, streaks of paint forming something structural. A chair, or perhaps a throne. Its seat faces outward, arms spread as if beckoning me, urging me to sink into it. The canvas hangs crooked.

I break my eyes away, refusing to look longer. On his desk sits a phone beside an outdated voicemail machine, its bulb pulsing red. It doesn't surprise me—he's outdated too. The bulb pulses. The clock ticks again.

"I meant to put us on a pot of coffee," Stewart says, a smile carving across his lips. He plants both palms on the desk and pushes himself back, the chair rolling out from under. "Would you like a cup? It'll keep us bright-eyed while we page through the catalogs and make the proper arrangements. It can be quite a process for some people."

I nod. He rises and shuffles out. His footfalls patter down the hall, small and quick, like rodent claws skittering on carpet, then fade. Through the open door, the corridor looks darker than before. A sound carries from deeper in the building—metal against metal, something shifted across a counter. A container opening. The ticking swells in my ears. I ease my chair back, careful with the scrape of its legs against the carpet, the noise too loud in the quiet. Another clank echoes in the distance.

I stand and move around the desk, keeping my eyes on the hallway's dim mouth. A mound of papers clutters the desk. I finger through them first—bills, printouts, scattered emails—but nothing useful. I glance over my shoulder at the walls. Bare. Only the clock. Its hands circle steadily, but it seems to grow silent when our stare meets, as though it's holding its breath with me. I rub my fists into my eyes until it feels like I'm burrowing into their sockets. Salt stings, a thin film blurring the room. I slide open the bottom drawer. The hinges release a small, high-pitched chirp. I freeze, breath caught, listening. Somewhere down the hall, a grinding noise hums, faint but distinct. When nothing follows, I continue. The drawer holds spare file folders, but otherwise empty. The middle drawer is stocked with pens, boxes of paperclips, staples. Ordinary. Then the coffee maker coughs from down the hall. The sputter grows louder—a wet, choking rattle, filling the silence. I ease open the top drawer. More folders. Loose documents. I dig deeper. Then, my fingers brush something taut, wedged into the corner. A string. I tug it free and hold it up, staring, trying to assemble the pieces of what I'm looking at. It takes a moment to click, but when it does, it lands heavy— pressure pressing into me. Behind me, the clock hands groan. Tick. My hand moves to my sidearm. I unfasten the holster strap, my palm settling against the butt of the pistol, fingers tapping against the frame. The pot gurgles louder, choking itself in the hall.

"What are you doing?" Stewart fills the doorway, wiping his bony fingers in a damp rag. His pale skin catches the weak office light, and his mouth hangs open in an unsteady grimace. Not quite fear, not quite defiance—just the knowledge that he's too old and too frail to run.

I draw my pistol and train it on his chest. In my other hand, I lift the cord I've wound around my fist, raising it to eye level.

"What the fuck is this?" I spit, jaw tightening. Human teeth swing against my knuckles, threaded through a leather cord. A necklace.

"I—" Stewart stammers, his voice trembling. "I don't quite know." The rag slips from his hand, landing on the carpet. He raises both arms, palms out. The gesture isn't surrender—it's pleading. His head tilts, his eyes narrow—a posture meant less for cuffs than for execution. I drop the necklace into my pocket and step closer, the pistol shaky in my grip. From the hall, the coffee maker hisses once, then sputters out. The clock on the wall goes silent.

PIERCE: NULL

I knot Stewart's wrists behind his back, pulling the cord tight until it bites the bone. I push his head down and guide his frame into the back seat. He doesn't resist—just shivers, shoulders twitching like he's already conceded—subdued in acceptance.

I start the engine. The windshield wipers drag across the glass, smearing rain into slippery streaks. Each pass leaves more behind than it clears. The drizzle thickens, rattling on the roof, filling the car with its drumbeat. The headlights cut forward, the mist swallowing everything beyond. I ease us away from the building. The street spreads before me in sickly color, like tissue gone yellow with cirrhosis. My grip hardens—knuckles stiff, numb, ready to split the wheel under their pressure.

In the rearview, Stewart leans into sight. A sideways glance, then his eyes drift out the window. His mouth hangs open—saliva streaked with blood and unraveling in strands. It drips down his chin and into his lap. His lips twitch, shaping half-formed words, but he can't regain control of his jaw muscle. For a moment, it looks like he's speaking in gestures—strange contortions, too considered to be involuntary. I can't tell if it's muscle failure or mockery. Both? I'm imagining it.

Traffic thins as we push farther out, the interstate narrowing with the lack of flow. Rain hardens against the glass until I can't tell what's rainfall and what's insects hitting the windshield. Everything smears, indistinguishable, and they all bleed together—like everything comes from the same ejaculate.

The landscape begins to swell and grow, jagged shapes flexing up from the earth. Stone outcroppings jut like vertebrae, their ridges catching the light in bronze edges against a bruised cloud line. The mountains swell with shadow, wrapped in shawls of mud that cling heavy at their bases. Hardened stone markers expand into mountainous ranges. Their cavernous forms splinter into amber fangs and are outlined in bronze castings. The night blackens their sheen.

"What are you going to do to me?" Stewart stammers from the back. His voice scrapes against the rattle of rain, fighting to take vocal dominance. I can hardly hear his words. I'm surprised he manages speech at all—and surprised he'd want to.

"Shut up," I hiss, "or I'll throw you in the trunk."

Silence.

An exit sign appears under the headlights. Its numbers are nearly scratched away, corners bent, graffiti bleeding red across its surface. I take the exit, gravel spraying up as the car leaves the interstate, dirt and dust pluming against the chassis. The road ahead is lined with hollow stumps and rotting shrubs, their parched roots clawing at the earth like they're trying to hold on. The highway curves sharply, tightening as it leads straight into the dark maw of the mountain range. The air turns stale, humid, and the car tightens—feeling claustrophobic. Dust kicks up, flecking against the windows until the view muddies. Wind pushes against the frame, making the car tremble.

I drag a sleeve across my forehead, sweat beading from the stifling humidity, despite the rain. The road thins further, rock jutting through in uneven clusters. The tires jitter across stone, each bump vibrating through the wheel and into my arms. The whole car shivers as if it might shake apart before the climb is through, violently combating the terrain.

We reach a clearing, and I ease the car off the road. The mountains engulf us, the shroud of their shadows spreading wide, the moon breaking through clouds in slivers—silver moment, then gone behind the torrenting rain. Headlights cut into the open space, beams catching the suspended dust that drifts and swirls above the hood. I stare into the clearing, watch my breath plume, then vanish. The ridges loom in the distance, jagged silhouettes groaning against the horizon. Its unpromising form moans from its slanted silhouettes. The taste of muddy air settles on my tongue.

I step out and slam the door. The car shudders in response. My boots chew into the mud as I round the hood. My reflection undulates in the windshield, briefly swallowing Stewart's buckled frame from sight. At the rear passenger side, I catch my own face in the chrome handle. The metal warps me, and I can't tell if the reflection belongs to me or someone else. The thought stops me cold—only momentarily.

I open the door. My other hand slides the pistol from its holster, pulling it free, fingers tensing around the grip. *Is this what remains?* The question presses hard, then lingers without answer. I step back, raising the weapon, leveling it at Stewart's head. He stirs against the leather, shuffling to the edge of the seat. His gaze moves in either direction, scanning the mud-slicked clearing, then he bows his head, letting the rain drench him. He doesn't move to exit. Not yet. Hesitation holds him at the threshold of the vehicle.

"I don't know what I've done, but—"

"Get out," I cut him off, teeth clenched.

He spits rainwater into the mud and hunches out of the car, but his knees buckle, and he falls. He flinches against the chassis, cheek pressed to the metal, squinting up as I step forward and level the barrel at his forehead. I lower the weapon just long enough to draw a knife from my belt. His crumpled body shivers. With a quick slice, I sever the knot binding his wrists, then sheath the blade and raise the pistol back into place. Freed, he sags forward, palms pressing into the mud. He splays his fingers, leaving prints as he struggles to push his weight upright, frail joints wobbling like they might give out.

"Open the trunk," I order, tilting my head toward the rear.

Stewart stumbles along the car's side, leaving smeared handprints where he steadies himself. Rain spatters over us both, turning the ground to sludge. I follow close, pistol shaky in my grip. He fumbles with the latch. It clicks, then groans on its hinges as he forces it up. The lid opens wide, and its contents are obstructed from my view. He peers into the trunk and remains still, gripping the lip with both hands, staring down as though waiting for something. At last, he pulls a shovel free and props it against the taillight, then hovers again, reluctant.

"The tarp, too," I tell him.

He drags out a folded green tarp, fists clutching the bulk of it, and lets it slump against the bumper before it slides into the mud. Rain gathers in patches across the ground, darkening it in splotches. Each drop feels hot against my skin, sharp in the humid air. Stewart clutches the shovel, using it to steady himself. I seize him by folds of skin at the back of his neck, dragging him away from the car. My nails dig in as I drag him into the desolate landscape, gripping fistfuls of skin flabs around my knuckles. The tissue gives way, and a thin bleed runs down his throat. Several meters out, I release him and shove him forward. He stumbles, falls sideways into the muck, and catches himself with raw palms. The toothed rocks tear his skin open, blood lacing the creases of his hands. He stares at them, mouth open, and lets out a sharp yelp. It's either from the tenderness of the pain, or the sudden realization of how little time he has left—it's hard to tell.

"Dig," I say, keeping the pistol trained on him.

He wriggles against the mud, trying to rise, movements clumsy and half-stuck. The clearing stretches empty around us, echoing the vacancy in my own mind. My skull pulses. Pressure amasses behind my eyes, fluctuating into my jaw. My chest pounds, reverberations climbing into ringing in my ears. Every inhale feels choked by the thickness of the air, like breathing through an exhaust pipe. When I exhale, my body seems to wither inward. For a moment, the mountains wither with me, folding into themselves. A gust passes and cools the sweat beaded around my face.

Stewart presses the shovel into the earth, the blade biting shallow before it sinks. The sound is dull, metal grinding into mud that doesn't want to give. I watch him strain, his frail body shaking with the effort, and it mirrors the futility of all of it. The empty ground in front of us reflects the bareness of everything beyond this mud. Out there I've already been fading, a ghost among the side streets, a figure moving without weight. This moment feels smaller than it should be—like the end of a line that closes something behind me. No return. The threshold buckles under my feet. Nothing waits beyond it.

"I—I don't know what I've done," Stewart murmurs, forcing the shovel into the mud again. "At least allow me that."

"That boy was my son," I reply.

He stops moving. His frail body leans against the shovel, then turns just enough for me to catch the stunted grimace in his features. I step forward through the mud and press the barrel into his temple. The sagging folds of his skin sink around the steel. "You ripped his innocence apart," I say. "He was the last thing I had." He stares at the shallow mark in the ground, then back to the gun, considering what I'm saying— pausing as though the silence belongs to him.

"Our children turn from us," he says finally, voice breaking. "Feels like their nature, like they're born to do it." He sighs. "I don't know what he did to your child. I tried to help him, but some people are already gone from this world when they're born." I attempt to track what he says, but it comes out nonsensical, distorted—something. "I think he might have been like that before his parents died. I suppose trying was pointless.

I'll never truly know. But I did try. And somehow, I knew it would end with him. Just not like this."

I don't answer. The pistol trembles in my hand, heavy with more than weight. His words tangle and fall apart—lines I can't follow. It doesn't add up. My throat tightens. I swallow hard. He tilts his head, eyes searching me expectedly.

"I'm sorry," he stammers. He clings to the shovel, water dripping from his sleeves, his hair plastered to his forehead. "I see the pain in your face. That's what I've spent my life seeing—what people carry. I know I can't lift it from you. I won't try. On the next mortal coil, I hope you remember this. Maybe then I'll forgive you—I hope I can."

"Pain is knowing something is ugly and doing nothing about it," I say, finger tightening on the trigger, shaking. "This isn't that."

The gun discharges. The sound cracks across the clearing and rings through the canyon. Stewart's body collapses into the mud, body folding under itself. Blood sprays from his skull, pooling fast, bleeding into the broken ground. I toss the pistol. It sinks beside him, the mud consuming them both, folding over them in its slow churn. Rivulets spread outward in jagged strokes, and the mud drinks from his skull. It paints an abstraction of gore through the cracks and indentations in the ground. It stretches in interwoven patterns.

I don't care to make sense of it.

REMNANT

A piercing ring blooms at the base of my skull, licking the inside of my forehead, dripping from my ears. I blink against it, eyelids sticking, and tilt my gaze across the couch. Casey sits slouched at the far end, leaning into the armrest, cigarette in hand. Smoke wafts upward, dissipating toward the ceiling. The ash at the tip droops, begging to be flicked. Her face glows in the glare of her phone, imperfections of her pasty face sharpened by the stark brilliance. Her fingers flit across the screen, scrolling. She doesn't look up.

I force myself upright, arching my back. My spine cracks. My joints ache on their rusted hinges, every motion resisting, creaking. My body feels packed hard, firmed into a shell of pressure and tension. She either doesn't notice me or doesn't care. My stomach caves inward, compressing into itself, gnawing. I don't know how long I've been asleep, but if it's clawing at itself like this, I've been out for days.

"Casey?" The word grates out, rough. The shift of my body only drives the ringing deeper into my temples. "How long was I out?"

"Almost two days," she says, voice nonchalant, but shaded with something heavier—sullen. "You were kind of drifting in and out—I think."

She places the phone on the armrest and notices the ash piled at the cigarette's end. Flicks it—then realizes the ember stopped burning a while ago. She stares at it too long. Her tone changes when she speaks again. "I was worried about you. Usually, I'm the one who nods off, and you're the one keeping me from slipping under. You're the guy I rely on to make sure I'm still here—alive, present, whatever." Her voice tries to stay steady but wavers, delicate.

"Yeah." I rub at my forehead, grinding pressure into the ringing. The sound is dry in my throat. "Mackey hasn't come by?"

"No," she says, eyes falling back to her phone. Her voice dims into a mutter. "I'm trying to find new clients. I've been digging through message boards, forums, anything. I'm getting desperate. You remember the last time Mackey came by? He nearly beat me to death. I can't let that happen again—I might not get back up next time."

"Yeah." I nod, though the word is empty, just something to fill the space. The room is dim, moonlight leaking through the curtains, a sliver of light washing over our bodies. Rain patters against the glass, and the draft drags clammy air through the walls. The humidity crawls into me, tightening my joints and stiffening my movements. "Let me help, Casey," I say, tone flat, reluctant. "I haven't been in the skin game much lately, but I can open doors. Find clients." The words are supposed to sound like comfort—what I mean isn't the same as what she hears.

I don't care about her wellbeing. Not really. What I care about is the junk she funnels my way. If Mackey caves her skull in, I'll have to scrape together another source. That's the part that matters. Her body, her existence—they're secondary. And perhaps I've tricked myself into thinking there's more.

I've told myself she stabilizes me somehow, that her presence fills in the cracks. That's a lie I almost believe when I look at her slouched there, vacant but breathing. But it isn't her—it's what she brings. Her aloofness is useful. Her detachment keeps her pliant. She doesn't question. She doesn't leave. She crawls back no matter how many times the door slams on her. There's convenience in that.

I like that she still paws at me, clings to me, even through understanding the truth in front of her—that our relationship is nothing more than transactional. One day I'll fuck her just to prove I could. Just to see the look on her face, knowing it doesn't mean anything. If she wasn't riddled with track marks and chasing the next vein, she might have made a decent partner to some man. But that's not who she is. She's like a dog. Loyal, stupid, unconditional love for everything—for anything. You can kick her ribs in, leave her outside in the rain, starve her, and she'll still come back wagging her tail. Lucky for me, she's too fucked up for anyone to love her.

That's what makes her useful. That's what makes her mine.

No one else wants her. She's too rotted for anyone to bother. She's convinced herself Mackey's fists are proof of love, that my cold handouts are intimacy. She thinks her value lies in what she can perform—her mouth wrapped around Mackey's dick, doping me up, whatever. And she's right. That's all she's worth. There's nothing inside that husk of a body, nothing inside that skull, beyond what it can do for us.

Nobody gives a fuck about a junkie. Not her. Not me. The difference between us is that I understand that—I don't pretend otherwise. My value isn't in who I am—it's in what I can make people believe I can do. That's power—leverage. That's the advantage of knowing exactly how worthless you are.

"I'll start walking the side streets again," Casey says, scrolling absently. "Remember when we first met at that little hole-in-the-wall? That bar off the highway with the chili pepper lights—the one that always blasted mariachi music? We'd pick up men together. Somehow you could spot a queer in the closet from a mile away." She smirks, still staring into her phone.

"I remember," I say, lighting a cigarette. I feel this weird lightness in my chest. I scrunch my face and blow a stream of smoke across the room. I don't care to rehash it, but a trickle of fondness stirs in my chest—brief memory.

"Do you remember why we stopped?" she asks. The question hangs. I don't think she's really looking for an answer.

"No," I lie, hoping it will let the conversation die. My chest burns. It's the smoke—or it's that I don't want to revisit this. What would that get me anyway—other than wasted time.

"I remember how cold the bricks were against my cheek—against my broken jaw," she continues. "I'd stumbled into an alley downtown—drunk, sick, retching against a dumpster. And then these men cornered me. By the time you found me, I was sprawled in my own blood, trails running down my thighs. My legs were drenched, both sides, front to back. It felt like they'd torn me apart—cut me in half. I remember puking when I saw your jeans soaked in my blood. You didn't hesitate—didn't flinch. You didn't care—just hoisted me up and dragged me out." Her voice falters, but she forces it steady. "That's when I fell for you. Because no matter how fucked I was in that moment, you didn't treat me like something broken. You treated me like I was already a ghost, something that couldn't be broken any worse than it was. You've always seen me— past the damage, past the body. What has always mattered to you is the essence, not the disfigurement."

"Yeah," I say. "I remember." Smoke seeps from my mouth in another stream, drifting through the dim room. Casey sets her phone down, shifts closer, and settles against my shoulder. Her head presses into me, her fingers worming around my arm, clutching it like she's trying to anchor herself. The gesture drags Percy back into my thoughts.

"I think we should go," I mutter. "Line up a last round of clients, pull together a lump sum, buy a load off from Mackey—and then leave."

"What do you mean?" she asks, cocking her head up toward me. My cheeks suck in around their bones as I pull from the cigarette again, let the smoke burn deeper.

"Leave," I say flatly. I'm not done, I need a change of scenery— widen my scope, new stomping ground. "Start over—go to another state. New ground to work." Goosebumps rise across my skin. Burning flares in my chest, pustular, like my body's trying to warn me. Like some impending omen is seeping in under the blinds, crawling across the floor. My body doesn't want to leave—it wants to carry on where Percy left me.

So do I. The body knows better—it wants to keep me here, wants me to finish. Let the blisters burst. I don't care.

"You're serious?" Casey asks. The question lands more like disbelief than doubt. Her dazed expression drags on me.

"We get enough money to survive until we find new supply, new clients," I tell her. "Then we get a place. Start again." Inside, something claws through my gut, tangling a knot in my intestines. I try to reason with it—tell it that what I had with Percy can be replicated elsewhere, widened, transplanted. But my body won't listen. It doesn't want possibility. It wants what's already here. It wants to keep feeding.

"Okay," Casey says. "We can do that." She stretches up and presses her lips to my cheek—a crooked half-smile gleaming in my periphery. Then she folds back into the crook of my shoulder, eyelids heavy, head settling against me. I leave her there, caught between the urge to move and the paralysis that holds me. Soon she's drifting, drool beading at the corner of her mouth.

"I've got to go back to Stewart's place," I murmur. I lower her head from my shoulder and ease it onto the headboard. She nods drowsily, eyes already slipping shut, body sinking deeper into the cushions.

I step across the room, grind my cigarette out against the curtain, burning another hole through its fabric. Smoke scars layered over smoke scars. "Call me if you line up any clients you can't take yourself. I'll do the same."

The words taste wrong. Returning to selling myself feels counterfeit now, like slipping into a body that doesn't fit. My skin remembers Percy too clearly—the heat of it, the way he stretched open, the way he swallowed me whole. His memory clings into my pores, tacky and warm. My lungs ache like they're still filled with his breath. My body has learned what it wants, and it isn't strangers in alleys or men from bars. It's him—what he gave me, what he let me carve out, what he made of me. I don't know if I can restrain it. I don't know if I want to—normalcy is a rotted word. I've had Percy's taste—and it's buried in my body. And like the addict I am, there's no going back. I'll want it again, deeper, until I burn out on it completely—and the taste will remain an ever-parched thirst.

STANTON: VACANCY

"Shit." The word slips out sharp as I drop my cellphone back into the cup holder. Pierce still isn't answering—the absence presses on my chest.

I swing the wheel and coast up to the side of the funeral home. In the dark, the building feels half-erased—just brick edges catching stray light around a single window. Nothing whole. I open the car door and slam it shut behind me. It leaves a dew slick clinging to my palm. Rain has filmed the windshield, the car's skin, and now me. I wipe the moisture down my pant leg, already damp. My boots cut through puddles pooling across the lot, water whipping the blacktop as I move toward the entrance.

I knock—hard. The sound carries, echoing through the frame. Nothing. I shift to the glowing window and angle my eyes through the blinds. I can make out a desk, chairs, and framed photos. It's the kind of room that's arranged to look unremarkable, but the stillness inside hums uneasy. The blinds fracture my sight into broken lines. I can't pull the whole picture together, no matter how I tilt. Nothing appears amiss. Still, something feels off.

I step back into the grass, scanning the blacktop. The lot is empty, not even a shadow of movement. Oil slicks warp the puddles into iridescent swirls, colors splitting against the night.

Rain runs through them, distorting the reflection further. The chill that follows the wind jackknifes across the open expanse and cuts through my jacket.

I tell myself I'm searching for cause. Justifiable entry. Some anomaly I can put in words—write in a report. But it doesn't feel like that. It feels like circling a grave, like waiting for the earth to shift and prove there's something underneath.

No cars. No Stewart. Just structure holding silence.

I circle back to the door. Slam my fist into the wood again. Harder this time. The frame shudders with the blow. The sound carries through the hall beyond. Hollow, echoing, like knuckles on a casket lid.

"Hello?" I call. Still no answer.

I sweep the street with my eyes. Trees bend over the lawn, their soaked leaves drooping low, glistening from their rainfall coating. They look ready to collapse under the weight, ready to crash through the roof and completely dismantle it. Part of me hopes they do. The mistletoe chokes its parasitic limbs around the bark, strangling upward in a quiet coup. It's either a takeover or just blind growth. Either way, the building shudders, and I can feel something waiting behind those walls— something I could pin this case on if I could just pry it loose. I return to the car and pull out my phone, then dial the station.

"There's no one here," I say. My jaw is tight. "I need a warrant."

"I can get a warrant in an hour," Cameron answers, flat.

"Something isn't right here, Chief." I stare at the funeral home. Its shadowed bricks are steeped in unease. "From the descriptions we've gathered on the Canine—and the footage from the motel—this doesn't add up. Our guy doesn't line up as an elderly man. Stewart might be connected, but he doesn't fit. He isn't the Canine."

"We work off evidence, Stanton. Not assumptions." Cameron's voice carries a weightless calm that makes my skin crawl. "Our lead points to Stewart. There's nothing concrete suggesting anyone else is involved. If you think otherwise, I'll need a rationale and evidence. Prove it."

"I understand." My teeth grind the words flat. "I'll check his home address while I wait for the warrant. I'll need one for there too—assuming he isn't at either location."

"Careful, Stanton." I hang up before he can draw it out. I'm sick of hearing it.

PIERCE: FRACTURE

"He said he'll meet you at the marina at noon tomorrow," she says. I think her name is Cassidy, or Carrie—something like that. I try to retrace our conversation, but it slips. The high is depleting, leaving me vacant. My eyes comb the nightstand for more, even if it's just leftover dust, residue—anything.

My phone vibrates again, rattling across the wood. I watch it instead of answering. Then, I force my shirt closed, fingers clumsy on the buttons. My jeans are somewhere on the floor. My vision wavers, nausea climbing in hot licks up the walls of my stomach. My movements are sluggish, feeling submerged, as if I'm walking along the floor of a swimming pool and gasping for air underwater. I steady myself on the nightstand, palm flat, attempting to gain balance. I find my jeans, drag them up, tug the wallet from its back pocket. The bills inside are damp, curled at the edges. I thumb through, peel a wad free, and leave it folded at the foot of her bed.

My nose throbs. Blood wells fast, cartilage burning, and a drop darkens the carpet before I register it's coming from me. Another drop slides over my lip. I pinch the bridge, tilt my head back, wait it out. My breathing hitches in shallow pulls until the clot seals. The cocaine's cut too coarse—it slices tracks inside my nose, rivulets hardening.

"He charges as much as you?" My voice is hoarse. I scan the room for tissues, anything, but come up empty. I hold still until the nosebleed eases. My eyes wander back to her—pocked breasts, thin frame. Pickings are slim, it seems. A body is a body—I don't much care what genitalia are attached at this point. "What does he look like?"

"Yeah," she says. "He's scrawny, but attractive. Looks like he could use a few burgers. Walks around like the weight of the world's on his shoulders—kind of skulks around, always somber. Doesn't smile much—you'll know him by the hair. Spiked back, sharp, kind of like a porcupine."

"You got more of that shit?" The words scrape out in more of a growl than question. A pressure builds in my throat. Rage edging up with the dizziness. I swallow it down, taste copper at the back of my mouth.

"Sure," she says. Casey. That's her name. I tug my jeans closed, buckle, wipe at my nose, and feel the clot breaking loose. Blood streaks across the back of my hand, smeared dark along my wrist. Casey glances back at me as she disappears into the other room. Her voice trembles when she calls out. "It's just going to cost you a little more, okay?"

His words spool back through my head, cut off by the gunshot. I wish I'd held myself back just a second longer. Let him finish—let him unravel whatever he was reaching for—the shape of whoever he was pointing toward. Now, it's lost. Instead, all I see is the moment folding in. His skull breaking, caving in from the pressure of the bullet, splattering a bloody painting in the muddy canvas. The weight of him driven into ground, face gone slack, mouth sinking into the earth. That dull, vacant look—like he'd already left before I pulled the trigger. I can't scrub it out. The gravel tearing into his cheek, the smear across his eye. His body convulsing after the impact, nerves firing blind. What if it was someone else? That would mean that there's more than just Stewart. The gravel had scraped his eye out and wiped a cream streak through the mud. His skull sliced through his skin in fragments, regurgitating his inner gore. What if he wasn't the Canine? What if the words he was spitting weren't rambling, but reaching? What if I pulled the trigger on the wrong man?

"You alright, mister?" Casey asks, tilting her head. Her arm extends, shaky, a small baggie of cocaine pinched between her fingers. I break from my trance and trade it for a few bills.

"Yeah," I say, watching her tender fingers peel the money away from mine. Teal polish flakes off her nails, chipped down to nothing. I crinkle my brow and roll the baggie between my fingers. "Why do you do this shit?"

"Never saw much of an option," she says with a shrug. The strap of her bra slides loose on her bony shoulder, slipping down again no matter how many times she fixes it. Her frame looks skeletal—breasts tiny, nipples pointed and hard, poking against her bra as if they're staring back at me. "You know, things happen. You get pulled into places where there aren't other options. People like me—we don't get the luxury of alternatives." Her voice falters, then steadies. "Sometimes the sin of being born is enough to damn you inside your body. That's all it takes." She hugs her arms across herself, shuffling toward the dresser, staring at the carpet as she moves. "The way I see it, you either let yourself wallow in it, or you scrape together a way to make it feel like you're worth something. Even if it's only for a little while." She scratches at her cheek, glances back at me. "That's enough for me, I suppose."

I nod, but don't answer. My thumb digs at the edge of my nose, peeling away a crust of dried blood, tacky under my nail. My eyes blur, vision swimming like there's glass set into them. A pounding beats along the inside of my skull. For a moment I feel faint, body swaying, focus wavering and bobbing.

"What about you?" she asks, pulling a cigarette from its pack. She lights it, leans against the dresser, arms crossed. Smoke flutters around her, warping my view of her pasty cheeks. "Why do you do this?"

My cellphone rattles across the nightstand again. The name glows up at me. It's Stanton. I groan, shove it into my pocket, and drag my fingers back through greasy hair, matting it down. Strands curl down over my forehead, sticking in my sweat-soaked pores.

"The same reasons, I guess," I mutter. She exhales, the smoke drifting across her shoulders, dancing over her tight skin. "Everything I've loved has evaporated around me. Doesn't make sense to keep chasing the right thing when your conscience keeps its own body count. The only time anything feels good anymore is skin, fluids, junk. The rest of it—" I hold up the baggie and rub the plastic between my fingers. "—everything else dies."

"I don't think it's that bad," she says, tapping ash, then drawing again. The filter is stained with her lipstick, dampening a small wound pressed against paper. Smoke seeps out in ribbons. "I don't think you're that bad. You let it in, that's all. You drown yourself in it because you've convinced yourself it's what you deserve." Her tone is poised. She exhales as if she's thought this through a hundred times. "Nobody comes to me for my body. They come for escape. That's all this is. You're just like the rest—a few differences, I suppose. You want to feel sorry for yourself." She shrugs, like it's a diagnosis. "That's fine. Makes it easier to hide whatever really hurts." The words press into my skull until the ache flares and swells behind my eyes, like I'm being lowered into a boiling vat of fat. "It helps you cover up whatever pain—"

I clamp my hand around her jaw, fingers sliding to her throat, nails digging in. Her breath snags. She gags, her pulse hammering against my palm. Everyone is bathing in pain, consumed in pain—there isn't a moment that some isn't seeping from their pores—no one escapes it. The pounding in my temples drives through my skull until it feels like my own bones are splitting. My grip tightens. Her neck crunches under the pressure, foam bubbling at the corner of her mouth, and a wet gurgle loosens from her lips.

Then I release.

I stumble back, chest heaving, and she crumples to the floor. The cigarette slips from her fingers, rolling across the carpet, leaving a scorched mark as it burns itself out. A singed stench rises, the smell of charred hair lacing the air.

"Fuck—hey." The words spill out as I drop to my knees, crawling across the carpet, panic breaking through the blind rage. My chest heaves, each exhale blowing strands of her hair across her face. I rub my fists against my eyes and force them open again.

Her body bends into pretzel knots on the carpet. Her face is deflated—expression sags open, a line of spittle dragging across the carpet. Her tongue slumps out, limp against the carpet fibers. Her eyes bulge, glassy, as though straining to leave their sockets. Hair falls in loose strands across her face, fanning outward like roots veining through the floor. Bruises shift the color of her throat, spreading across her pale skin—a piercing swell of red, then deepening into purple. The discoloration spreads in blotches, stark against her yellowed flesh. I stare, waiting for movement, a sound, anything. Nothing. She's dead.

The phone vibrates in my pocket.

I kneel and fish through her pockets, peel back her bra strap, check along her body for cash or whatever she might've stashed. When I've stripped her of anything useful, I stagger to the bathroom. I press my palms into the sink, attempting to prop myself upright.

The mirror is caked in grime. My reflection comes back warped, blurred—unrecognizable. I splash water over my face, slick it through the grease in my hair, try to force it into orderly strands. It doesn't hold.

I return to the bedroom and sit at the edge of the bed, then tug my boots on. The laces blur in my fingers. I lift my head. Her body sprawls where it fell. Her eyes glare back at me—mocking. I pull my phone from my pocket. Stanton's name lights the screen in a line of missed calls. My thumb hovers. I can't do it.

STANTON: OBSESSION

I pull to the curb, idling a few feet from the driveway. The wipers smear rain across the glass, blurring the house. The lawn is bare—sprinklers ticking in lazy arcs, drenching soil already water-logged. Dead leaves mat the ground beneath a wilting tree on the corner. I kill the engine and step out, slamming the door harder than I intend, and push damp strands of hair behind my ears. I press key fob, it chirps, and the headlights flare briefly across me as I round the hood.

The trim and windowsills have been painted bright white, fresh and stark against the mildew-stained wood around them. Odd labor for a man Stewart's age. It seems like laborious work for an elderly man, unless someone else has been here. The driveway is clean, the yard too—grass cut even, the blades still clumped damp where the mower passed. A breeze rustles the leaves across the lawn and a chill bites into my cheeks.

I climb the steps and knock. Wait. The door holds its silence. My phone is a weight in my pocket—and for a moment, I consider trying Pierce again. Or Cameron—inform him I can't reach Pierce—hopefully he's heard something. I raise my fist again and strike harder, shaking the frame. My eyes stay on the door, as if sheer will could make it open. Still nothing. Someone has had to have heard from him.

But the thought sours. Something in me is screaming to stay away—that even another knock could fracture whatever fragile balance

I'm standing on. I tell myself I'm not fragile, that I'm not close to the edge, that I could step back whenever I choose. That this isn't something I can't escape. I've trained myself against fear. Haven't I? If I repeat that often enough, it becomes true. Or it's already a lie I've grown comfortable with. I stand there, fist hovering, pulse throbbing through it. The longer I wait, the more I feel like I'm practicing the lie.

"Looking for someone?" a voice calls from behind me.

I turn. A man stands at the mouth of the driveway, half-swallowed in the mist bleeding off the wet street. His figure is lean, face is gaunt, skin jaundiced and clinging close to bone. At first glance, he looks older than he is—youth buckling under sickness. A hood shadows most of his features. Black strands of hair are pasted to his forehead from rain. He drags from a cigarette, lets the smoke ribbon up, then flicks it into the street. The ember hisses out, then he lights another. His eyes don't shift. He doesn't blink.

I glance back at the door, then choose to descend the driveway toward him. My boots crunch against the wet grit, each step sounding louder than they should in the soaked air.

"I'm looking for the owner of this property," I say. I intend to sound official, but it comes out more rehearsed. "Do you know him?"

"You don't know who you're looking for?" His tone is offhand, almost mocking, like he already knows the answer.

"I'm looking for a man named Stewart."

"You looking to make an early appointment?" It's coy, almost lighthearted—but the delivery isn't right. There's something sharp underneath.

I push wet curls back from my face, and it hits me—I know him. The grocery store, the movie theater—it's the same man. He's thinner now—more ragged, sicklier, disheveled.

"You know him?" I press.

"I didn't say that." he replies.

"He owns a funeral home a few miles from here," I say, tightening my voice.

"It sounds like you're at the wrong place, then."

There's something performative in his cadence, something too measured. Like he's worked this scene over in his head, played it out before. I don't know if he's recognized me yet, but the unease in his tone says he knows *exactly* what he's doing.

The hood of his jacket gapes open as he shifts his weight. A black shirt sits beneath—red floral patterns climbing across it. The buttons hang loose halfway down. His chest is emaciated, skin pulled taut around the bone, and in the thin wash of streetlight I can trace scars etched deep. One curves up around his collarbone, pulling the skin into an unnatural line. My gaze drops lower, where the jacket hem lifts with the breeze. His waist is bare, lean muscle fading into the pale cross-stitch of scars scored across his hips. Old wounds. Long healed, but not softened. They look branded into him, like his skin is a coat sewn out of scar tissue. The rain slides over his skin, catching along the ridges of his scars before falling away. He doesn't flinch. He doesn't seem to feel the cold.

"Can I ask who you are?" I say.

"Sure," he replies, smoke drifting from his lips. "You can do whatever you want."

He drags again, cheeks hollowing, eyes fixed. I purse my lips, weighing my next words, contemplating my next move. My gaze flicks over the scars webbed across his chest, half-hidden in the dark. I try to imagine what could carve marks that deep into someone, what leaves a body so permanently disfigured.

"What?" he spits onto the sidewalk, then zips his jacket higher.

"Tell him I stopped by." I pull a card from my pocket and extend it. He takes it and briefly glazes over the writing, then flicks it into a puddle. The water swallows it, softening the paper until it crinkles into origami slush. I turn and walk back toward my car. Behind me, his cigarette hisses as it dies in the same puddle.

"Detective Stanton."

I stop, turn. His fists are jammed in his pockets, his shoulders slightly forward, rain streaking down the hood of his jacket. He follows me a few steps, then halts again. The way he says my name—he remembers me.

"I don't think you want to find who you're looking for," he says.

"Is that a threat?"

"More of an observation."

"And what exactly are you observing?"

"You." His tone doesn't shift—steady, even. "You can read a person by what they leave behind—their purchases, the little things they linger on, the way they carry themselves. You carry yourself like the world needs protecting from something only you can see. But it's just a costume. The intent beneath it is simpler. It's the thrill you get chasing something you'll never catch. Peel it back and it's nothing more than compulsion—a fix. At the end of the day, you and the men you chase feed off the same vein. The only way you get to save someone is if they're wounded first. But in the dark, when it's just you, you know you're not righteous. You're addicted. And that's the part I find interesting. You're not bad—not good either. Just tethered to the same hook as the rest of us. The difference is that you wear the lie behind your badge. Sooner or later, the rush wears thin, and when it does, what are you? Just another degenerate without the balls to admit it."

"You don't know anything about me."

"I know enough," he says. "You tune out everything else. You chase the obsession until it consumes you. And when you finally reach the end of it, you'll fold. Not because you're weak—but because you won't know how to live without it. We drown in our own mess—but we learn to enjoy it. What else have you got? I know you the same way I know myself. There's no depth here—nothing to figure out. We're both just circling the same drain, floating in our own filth, waiting for the pull. Drowning is inevitable—but at least we've learned how to savor it. It doesn't mean you're a bad person—it just means you've found a way to enjoy it."

I clench my jaw and hold his stare. Words don't come—maybe there aren't any worth saying. I think about handcuffing him, beating him—putting a bullet between his eyes. I want to—but I don't. My palm has drifted to the holster, thumb brushing the clasp. I stop myself. I turn away, jaw still grinding. I don't reply and head toward the car. I'm going to kill him.

STANTON: COALESCENCE

I ease the car into park in front of the funeral home. Before opening the door, I scan the mirrors, the windshield, the empty road—no lingering spectators, no movement. Just wet pavement glinting under the weak spill of streetlight.

I step out. The air is flat, carrying only the faint static of distant traffic. I pound my fist against the front door and announce myself. No one answers. The window still glows with its dull lamplight, but the room inside looks undisturbed—like someone left it this way hours ago and never returned.

I plant my shoulder against the door and drive weight into it, thrusting my shoulder into the wood. Once, twice. On the third hit, the hinges give. The sound is sharp and pitiful, squeaking like a nest of mice crushed in a rusted trap.

Inside—stillness. My hand drifts near my holster, fingers brushing the snap, though nothing stirs. The carpet crunches faintly under my boots as I step forward. The first room is an office, plain in its arrangement except for a row of canvases that hang along the wall. Abstract smears, crude colors bleeding in splotches that don't resolve into any pattern. They leer more than they decorate.

I start pulling drawers, rifling through folders, loose pages. Nothing. Outside, traffic hums by in low, distant tones.

The building itself creaks now and again, like it resents being intruded upon. There's a clock on the wall that's stopped ticking. I take it down, turn it over. No batteries. The compartment where they should sit is gone entirely—an empty shell. The silence deepens. I draw in a breath. A faint scent rides the stale air—coffee? The whole building feels trapped, floating in perpetual suspension. Caught between minutes.

I move back to the desk and study the framed photographs. Stewart, undoubtedly. Some are old, washed in black-and-white, the kind meant to dignify. Others are newer, though the years haven't been kind. In each one he's swallowed by clothing too large, fabric sagging like sheets wrapped around his body. His fingers are spidery, clasped together in bony mounds. None of it portrays the images I've built in my mind of the Canine.

My gaze wanders to the canvases. Smears of color bud into swirled swatches with no discernible shapes, seeping together across their surfaces. I don't know what I'm looking at—but I guess that's the point of obscurity. The last one snags my attention—it hangs crooked, just enough to look wrong. I step closer and lift its corner.

A photograph slips from behind the frame and lands face-down on the carpet. I crouch, pick it up. The image freezes me. It's the same office—same clock on the wall—hands locked in the same position. The angle is low, tilted, as if the camera had been propped against something. The frame cuts the tops of their heads. It's an image of two men. The first is the elderly man, Stewart, I'm assuming. He's sitting in his chair, arm looped around another man, snaking like a constrictor, hand hovering against his chest. It's almost sensual in nature. The other man's face is unmistakable—gaunt, yellow-tinged skin, hollowed eyes. The same one I've seen before. The same one following me.

My fingers tighten around the photo. I reach for my phone and dial the station.

"Chief," I say, voice clipped, "I need a squad car dispatched to Stewart's home residence immediately. I'm finishing up at his funeral home—I found something."

Cameron confirms, and I hang up.

The room is silent again, except for the faint blink of the answering machine. The red light pulses. I press the button. Messages begin to rattle through the static.

PIERCE: TETHERED

"You must be James?"

"Yeah," I answer. I scan the marina automatically as I approach him—boats shifting at their moorings, lines taut, water slapping in dull percussion. My head is pounding vigorously behind my eyes, pressure building like it's ready to split the bone, like my skull is inflating. My vision pulses with it, skin prickling pale, bloodless. I press my fingers through my hair, and it leaves a sticky residue of clumped sweat and grease. It clings under my nails. The color feels like it's been drained from my skin.

"You don't look like what I was expecting," he says, striking a lighter. I watch his hands cup the flame, the paper catching light, and the smoke unfurling.

Behind him, a boat drifts loose from its dock, engine sputtering, leaving a jagged wake. My boat comes into view when it pulls from the dock. It rocks softly against the piling, tether straining. The sight lands like an accusation. Part of me thinks about untying it, letting it drift out into nothing, untethered, and let the channel swallow it.

Salt air stings the inside of my nose, brine biting sharp into my sinuses. Somewhere farther down the docks an indistinct horn bellows, muffled behind incessant pigeons chirping. The birds choke out their throaty calls, and the sound cinches around my throat. For a second, I think I'm going to vomit.

He exhales. A line of smoke crosses my face—it's acrid and intimate. His eyes don't leave mine. He drags again, his cheeks tenting in, folding inward, skeletal. He'd be handsome if the structure of his jawline and cheekbones weren't so severely rigid and pointed, angles cutting into themselves until nothing soft remained. His collarbones jut, skin stretched thin across them. His eyes are ringed dark, like he's rubbed charcoal around them. At first, I think it's makeup, but then I realize the color has sunken deep into his pores. It's as if they're bruised—but set into him in a permanent ashen cast.

"What were you expecting?" I say, sniffing hard. I rub the back of my hand across my nose. The skin under my eyes sinks, weighted down into soggy sand dunes.

His shirt is black, stretched tight against his chest, fabric snug tight over the jut of his sternum. It clings around his waist but ends short, exposing his lower stomach and navel. That's when I notice the scars— jagged bands carved around his hips, raw in their shape, like barbed wire had been wound into him and pulled until it left its imprints behind. I wonder if they're self-inflicted or gifted by someone else.

"Bit more queer, I suppose," he answers, then drags from his cigarette. He passes it my way, the smoke trailing between us. I take it, pull deep, let the burn sear down, and flick the ash to the dock. "You look more like a lost dog," he says, eyes fixed on me. "Scrounging, hungry for whatever scraps you can get. Won't be long before your bones start showing through."

"You're one to talk," I snap, examining his wiry frame, ribs etched sharp against his shirt's fabric. He smirks, just a trace at the edge of his lips, and keeps staring. His eyes are hazel but dark—pupils wide, focus unnerving. Dilated yet sharp, like they're cutting straight through me.

"You a new client or a return customer?" he asks. "For Casey, I mean."

"I've known her," I mutter. "Still holed up in that same rundown place. The place looks as bad as she does now. Frail enough that if you touched her tenderly, you'd snap her in half."

"Yeah." The word slips out flat. He isn't listening—it's more like a reflex than a response. His gaze drifts out across the docks, following the rise and fall of the boats. I feel myself start to fade too. The nicotine buzz whirs low in my skull, tilting the edges of my vision. For a moment, the docks melt into the mountains and their stillness drips through my imagination—ridges dissolving, hardening into crust. Stewart's head coated under wax, arms sealed stiff, the pistol encased in resin. I shake it, flick the cigarette, and hand it back to him.

"Casey says you've got a place?" he asks.

"Yeah," I mutter. The word comes out hollow, my head still snagged in the melting mirages. The water slaps softly against the dock, but in my ears it drains like something emptying out of me. The hulls grind against the piers, their metal-on-wood clatter warped, disturbed. If I let my focus linger, the docks start shifting—boats buckling into shapes that don't belong, their lines blurring into some half-formed creature.

Stewart's skin, slick and rubbery, weeps through the algae as if he'd been dredged up from below. The hulls become muscle, splitting into withered flesh, pale hairs flicking in the wind like nerve filaments. I bite down on my lip, tracing the patterns until they almost make sense. Stewart's last words cut through me again, echoes branding themselves deeper each time.

"I'll call you," I blurt, cutting across the image before it solidifies. "There's something I've got to do first. Then I'll call."

"Whatever," he says. He rattles off his number, detached and monotone. I pull a pen from my pocket and scrawl it across my wrist.

"I shouldn't be too long," I add, though I don't know who I'm reassuring—him or myself.

"There's something I should take care of anyway," he replies.

He takes a long drag, the ember lighting his face in quick, skeletal relief, then turns down the marina. I watch him go. He slides his phone out, dials, holds it to his cheek. I start back toward my car, but something tugs in my chest—a snag pulling against my breath. Something is wrong here. His vacancy isn't just in how he looks or how he carries himself— it feels staged, like an inhuman shell built to pass as ordinary.

I rub both palms down my face, dragging sweat into my pores, my skin slick and raw. My head throbs hotter. When I glance back, he's reached my boat. He stands at the dock's edge, staring up at it with a stillness that feels intentional—like it's familiar to him. He looks down, dials again, waits. No answer. A beat passes. He dials again. Someone isn't picking up. The breeze kicks, lifting his matted-back, spiked hair. I've seen him somewhere before. I know I have.

VIOLATE

I slam my knuckles against the door again. Silence. This isn't like her. I thumb my phone and dial. From inside, faint and muffled, her ringtone hums through the wood. It sounds distant, like it's coming from under the floorboards, swallowed into the void of the apartment itself.

The sun bakes the back of my neck, boiling through skin that's already blistered. I scratch hard until flakes peel under my nails. Sweat slips down my scalp, greasing the spiked strands until they collapse into limp curls across my forehead.

Something's wrong.

"Casey?" I bark louder, slamming my fist harder, the wood shuddering against its frame. No answer.

The knob sears into my palm when I grab it. Sweltering hot. I turn it, testing the door. At first, it refuses, locked, but when I force my shoulder into the door, it jerks open with a long squeal, hinges crying like wounded animals. Inside, the air is stagnant. Curtains beat rays of sunlight into the gloom, pale stripes cutting the apartment into pieces. Dust hangs in the beams, drifting in the stillness. The silence is cavernous, broken only by the faint hum of traffic rumbling in from outside—distant horns, engines coughing, all warped in a low drone.

The place looks the same: half-rotten takeout cartons bloated with grease, laundry hardened into stained bunches across the floor, clutter mounded in corners. But the stillness makes it unfamiliar.

I move deliberately, each step sinking into the carpet. My hand brushes the wall, fingertips slick with a clammy dampness that clings to the paint. At the bedroom door, I lean into the frame. Darkness stretches inside, heavy and unbroken. Something clumps against the far wall. A shape—indistinct and motionless. My hand gropes for the switch. The plastic clicks, and the bulb sputters before blazing to life. The shape resolves and the room lurches—the tumor bulging on the floor coming to life under the glow.

Casey.

I kneel over her body and press my fingers into her forearm. The skin is stiff, cold—like the chill doesn't just sit on the surface but radiates from within, freezing her from the inside out. I brush her stringy hair back from her face, curls plastered in sweat against her cheek, and push them from her eyes. They're pierced open in a blank stare across the carpet. Her mouth hangs open, lipstick smeared and fading into a pale, indigo tint. Her flesh looks like it's collapsing inward, beginning to shrivel into dried husks.

There's a rigidity to her chest, a density that wasn't there before. I press lightly, testing it, tightening my fingers around her breasts, curious. There isn't any purpose to it—other than I'd never felt her like this before. Death has stiffened her, reshaped her—turned what had been pliant into something calcified, foreign. I can't help but wonder if it's the body hardening, or if she had always carried this firmness and I just never bothered to notice.

I lower myself until I'm sitting beside her, adjusting her torso until she leans half-upright. Her head lolls sideways, eyes still vacant, mouth still open. I press my fingers to her lips, prying them wider, her chapped skin cracking against me. Her teeth are faintly visible in the dim light, and for a moment it feels like she's trying to say something, though the sound never comes. I stare back into her gaze until I feel myself sliding into it, as if her emptiness is dragging me with it. Her eyes are in a trance, looking back at mine. I feel like I'm swimming down into one too—starting to disconnect from my own body and into her, into the floor. It's unsettling—that pull. Things shift too easily. I don't like change. What worked about her, what mattered, was the simplicity. Casey didn't need to think, didn't need to parse meaning out of anything—she existed, she followed, she filled in the space. She didn't complicate things. That's what kept her useful. That's what kept her mine.

Percy had that too—or at least I thought he did. Detached, unflinching, as though even the act of burying his mother hadn't pressed a mark of remorse into him. That ambivalence excited me. I thought it meant permanence. But then he shifted. And now Casey's body has shifted too, turned alien, no longer the same.

I lean forward, studying her face one last time, sinking deeper. My breath fogs over her open eye, and I scrunch my lips into a pucker over its surface. I trace my tongue in ringlets around her socket, lightly sucking. I'd imagine the texture to resemble a lubricated grape—it doesn't.

I don't like change.

Can Mackey kill someone he claims to love? Of course he can. He proves it every time he beats her bloody and keeps her crawling back. That's the difference—he keeps her on track. That's what love is: discipline, submission. He knows it. I know it.

A line of spit slips from my lips, catching in her lashes before stringing down her cheek. I slide my fingers free of her mouth and let her head sag forward, chin sinking against her chest. She collapses into herself like a broken doll.

I pull my phone from my pocket, scrolling through recent calls. Her name flashes yesterday evening—right before meeting James. My head is pounding and starts churning into a carousel. His demeanor lingers in me, the way he trembled, preoccupied, his voice fraying at the edges. I'd chalked it up to withdrawal—his hands shaking, his body trying to crawl out of itself. But it doesn't quite connect. Something is missing.

Whatever. It doesn't matter. I'm going to kill him, anyway.

In the meantime, I need to decide what to do with Casey. Dead weight, but still mine. This pushes our relationship into new ground— territory neither of us signed for, but I'll carry it anyway. Stewart, though… Stewart's different. He loves me like a father and like a lover. No one else has ever filled those roles—not even close. That's what makes him useful. It's time I treat him like what he is—and use him as both. He'll know what to do.

Stewart still hasn't come home. It gnaws at me—it's not worry, not longing, it's just the strangeness of not seeing him for this long. The house feels wrong without him breathing somewhere inside it.

I open the refrigerator and stare into the dim light. A plastic container of fruit sits shoved to the back. The skins have collapsed, shriveling into themselves, their bodies crowned with a coat of white fur. Mold webs across them in a soft, suffocating net, like a mossy mesh clinging around their edges. The air inside the fridge stings faint and sour. I close the door before it spreads too far up my nose.

On the stovetop, a pan has been left behind. Its center is smeared in a hardened pool of grease, amber-colored, congealed into sap. Food scraps lie sealed in it like prehistoric insects. The edges of the pan are blackened, as if it hasn't been properly washed in weeks. The window over the sink is cracked open. Outside, the air is heavy, soaked with summer heat. It slides through the gap in humid gusts, clinging to me, turning the sweat on my skin sticky and persistent. The curtains stir lazily in the draft.

On the table, a newspaper sits folded in half. I thumb through the pages—stories already old, the date almost a week past. He hasn't been here in days. Not just out, not just working late. Gone.

I move through the threshold into the living room. The carpet crunches faintly under my boots. The television is on, but it's nothing— rosy caricatures pulsing in and out, weak color flickering as the bulb strains to keep alive. No sound, just the faint electrical hum, the glow painting the walls in dying pink. Dust hangs in the air, drifting in the screen's light like ash. The silence is strange here. Not true silence, but the kind that comes when a space has been emptied. The cracked window rattles against the frame, tapping steady, a faint pulse that fills the quiet. The house feels stripped to its bones.

I walk back through the kitchen, my hand trailing across the counter, over the grooves and chips worn into its surface. The whole place feels like it's rotting, like it's been abandoned longer than it has. It's as if Stewart had been emptied out of it piece by piece, leaving only the blueprint of a life, hollow and dry.

I don't linger—there's nothing here but echoes. I leave.

I knock again, harder this time. My knuckles dull themselves against the wood, like I can hear my bones. No one answers.

The blinds breathe light in pale slats, leaking from the office. He's here. Or should be. Stewart doesn't wander. Men like him calcify in place, rotting in the same chair until they're pried loose. If he's not at his house, he's here.

I look across the lawn. Strips of grass lean in the breeze, blades bending like spines mid-collapse. The trees are worse. They stoop under their own rain-fat leaves, branches crumpling like sickly arms ready to give. I always imagine them snapping all at once, folding down onto the roof. A casket cracked open by oak and elm. Patrons already waiting inside—no transport necessary. It'd be good for business—better yet, no one would have to collect the bodies.

I put my hand on the doorknob. The brass is chipped and scabbed, lacquer peeling like skin. Cheap, tired, and over-handled—kind of like Stewart. I try the knob. The latch catches, loosens, and the hinges wail, then die down to a thin, abhorrent gasp.

Inside, the air sits heavy. A faint musk of old coffee clings to the walls. Two sources of light spill into the hall: one from the office, one from the kitchen. Both steady—Stewart never leaves lights on. My shoes shift across the carpet. It's patterned in pale flowers—petals dulled into stains. Each step drags their shapes into something darker, like they bruise under my heels. I lean into the office doorway. The desk slumps in its corner, papers stacked. The chair is empty, but it feels warm, as if the lingering ghosts have been keeping it warm for me. Otherwise, nothing seems out of place.

I keep moving down the hallway. The kitchen waits at the end of the hall, lit too bright, like it's on display. On the counter: two ceramic mugs, empty, untouched. Beside them, a full pot of coffee inside the machine. I touch the glass. Cold. Hours gone, maybe longer. I stand there with my hand still on the pot. The handle feels greasy, like it's been clutched too long, too tightly. A thought wedges in—two cups, one pot. He was expecting someone.

The window above the sink is cracked open, letting in the afternoon heat. It licks at me, humid, sticky, crawling into my pores. The curtain flutters against the sill, brushing back and forth like it's breathing. A faint creak runs through the frame, and I notice dried rainwater splotched around the windowsill and trailing down the wall.

I glance back toward the hall. The light feels heavier now, stretching its glow toward me, trying to herd me back to the office. The office glow widens as I approach, swallowing the shadows. My hand grazes the wall. It's warm. He's not here—but it feels like something's waiting for me.

I peer into Stewart's office, scanning the room left to right in the pale glow. The canvases hang crooked behind his desk—warped abstractions he called art. I've always liked them—liked not knowing what they meant. Meaning ruins things. Meaning changes relationships. Best to leave them obscure.

The answering machine pulses red, blinking fast, steady—like a vein throbbing in the dark. I lower myself into his chair. The wheels creak as I roll over the carpet, the sound small but sharp in the silence. The first messages stammer out the usual chorus. Prospective clients with their rehearsed grief, sob stories stretched thin, voices trembling in forced tremors. Sometimes there's a good one—something violent, an accident, a face mangled beyond recognition. A client, whose loved one had been in a fatal accident, had once asked Stewart: *can you make a mutilated face look normal?* Stewart had told the caller, flat: *there's no such thing as normal.* They hung up on him. I liked that. The next message plays, and I immediately recognize the voice.

"Hello, I—" he breaks, swallowing air, then pushes through. "I apologize. I know it's late. I don't think I can sleep without making some kind of arrangement." Arrangement. He lets it hang there, his tone bending like he's forcing sincerity, but it curdles in my ear. "These things just hover, you know?" A pause. An ulterior motive pushing under the words. "If you could call me back—" The message cuts off.

Hooks rake through my skull, thoughts catching sharp on themselves. I see Casey slumped where I left her—her body a ruptured bag, contents pressed and leaking through seams. My breath ratchets up, chest hammering, air bursting through my nose—hyperventilating. I swivel toward the desk drawer.

I know what's supposed to be there. I've run the scenario a hundred times. A failsafe I could lean on, something to confirm suspicions when it came. I figured I'd see it coming when it eventually transpired—I hadn't anticipated an interloper. I yank the drawer open, paw through it, tearing papers out in fistfuls. They scatter across the desk in crumpled stacks and rips. My breath chokes up in my throat raw. I rake through again. Harder. Nothing. Just clutter. No necklace. If James did something to Casey, did he do something to Stewart too? What's his motive here—what's the connection?

I stare at the carpet until its flowers blur into teeth. My mind replays James's shaky posture, his withdrawal tremors, the way he tried to hold his voice steady. Did he take it? If so, what does he want with it? What does he think it means? I inhale deep, lungs aching, trying to still the beat in my chest. It doesn't work. The thought rattles too fast, too loud. Whatever. Fuck it. The answer doesn't matter. I'll throw the fucking beartrap in his den.

STANTON: DISSOLUTION

I push open the café doors and the bell above me shrieks in a thin jangle that feels louder than it should. The smell hits—burnt beans, sour milk dried on the counter, sugar hardened in its jars. The place is nearly empty. A single barista slumps behind the register, dead eyes scanning their cellphone. The rest is silence—chairs stacked, booths vacant, nothing alive but the low gurgle of the espresso machine in its death rattle.

Then I notice Pierce slouched in our usual booth. I move across the floor, rubber soles squeaking faintly against linoleum. He's hunched, forehead buried in his palms, fingers knotted in clumps of hair. The strands are wet, plastered flat to his scalp with sweat. His skin is pale, almost gray, like the color has been leeched out of him. His collar gapes open, tugged sideways, edges stained with mud. My eyes trail down—his pant legs splotched too—dirt crusted into the seams.

I slide into the booth across from him. The plastic seat groans under my weight. He stirs, becoming alert, like the noise cuts him open. He lifts his head and his eyes catch mine. Drooped, glassy, his lids half-sliding back into sockets—etched with gray hollows. Wrinkles ridge the skin around them, harsher than the last time I saw him. He looks older, worn, eaten from the inside out. His hair is parted wrong, strands jutting sideways, some sticking across his forehead. His jaw is rough, stubble thick across it—he hasn't shaved in days. Buttons hang loose down his shirt. Beneath, a nest of damp chest hair clumps together. Tangled in it, a gold cross dangles on its chain, crooked, catching the café's sickly light every time he shifts. The whole picture fits together but not cleanly—it's disorder soaked into him. Not accident, not chance. It looks lived in, scarred into his pores. He doesn't just look exhausted—he looks excavated.

He opens his mouth, lips pursing like he might speak. But nothing comes out—only a sound caught in the back of his throat as he swallows hard. I lean forward and press my palms flat to the table.

"I've been calling you for days," I hiss through my teeth. Compassion feels like the appropriate mask, but it won't fit. This isn't concern—it's obstruction. Pierce is slipping into liability. "Where the hell have you been? What's going on?"

"I think I fucked up, Stanton."

The words hang. I don't answer—not yet. I know exactly what he's talking about. I want to hear it raw from his mouth, not dragged out. I keep my eyes locked on him. The waiter appears, sets down two mugs, and greets us. What's that say about us that we don't need to order? It just arrives. Ritual. I lift mine, sip from the rim, and the steam rises. Across from me, Pierce doesn't touch his. He just stares down at the mug like it's a freshly dug grave.

"Look," I break in, steady but clipped. "Whatever it is, we'll figure it out. But for your own sake, you need to step back. Stay off this case."

"I don't know if there's another option."

"I know about the call," I say flatly. No pause—no room for retreat. He doesn't flinch. "I found this in Stewart's office." I slide the photograph across the table. His eyes fix on it. I point at the younger man in the image. "I think this is our guy," I tell him.

Pierce doesn't move. Color drains from his face until he looks washed-out, almost translucent. I catch the tremor in his arms—like he's trying to lift them, but the command won't follow through.

"The pool case drove me somewhere I didn't think I could go. Back then, I had things to lose. And I lost them—nearly all of them." He stares at the rising steam until it thins and disappears. He still hasn't touched his coffee. "Now, there's nothing left. That makes this easier."

"What did you do?"

He drags his eyes up to mine. "I don't need a badge to close this."

My chest knots. "Pierce," I press, voice tightening, "what do you know?"

He doesn't answer. His wipes his fingers across his eyes, smearing sweat. He pulls in breath, then lets it out in a measured stream. A foul odor carries across the table, sour on the exhale. He glances at me, then down at the coffee, and lets a crooked grin hook onto his mouth as he returns his glare to the photograph of the man. Nervous—like he's on the verge of speaking. There's something clogged at the base of his throat, pushing to surface. He swallows it down, hard, and buries it.

"Give me a little more time," I say, voice straining. "We have to do this the right way."

"Like I said, I don't know if I have much of an option." He pushes himself up from the booth, shoulders unsteady. I weigh my options. "I have to make a call," he says. I don't move. Don't try to stop him. I let him shuffle past me and out the door. The bell above the café jangles, then dies away. His coffee stays untouched, a placid surface barely rippling in the mug. I stare into it. The reflection bends, fractured in the liquid's sheen. I tell myself I don't regret the things I do—or the things I leave undone. I find the words to justify keeping the fire lit. But the longer I watch that bending reflection, the harder it is to believe myself.

BLOODLINE

I bend down and inhale a line of crushed junk off the coffee table. The burn scorches my sinuses, tunneling thorns into the back of my skull. The television drones—its chatter tinny, electric, insectile. The screen writhes in crimson eruptions, a void bleeding outward and folding back in on itself, like a flower eating its own petals. The glass surface isn't reflecting light anymore—it's swallowing it. Flies orbit the glow, drawn into the heat of the fleshy abyss.

I try to blink it back into coherence, but my vision films over—dew across the lens, edges softened, wetted in seeping reds. My phone rattles against the table, skittering like it wants to crawl off the edge. The number is unfamiliar. My groin knots, itching, and I know it's James. I've grown sick of the guessing games, but I'll keep playing them until they break open. Either he's an admirer of my body, or he's a vicarious heretic to my transcendence. I don't know which would excite me more.

"Yeah," I mutter. Too fogged to shape a proper greeting. My head is a cauldron of collusion—thoughts a bubbling cesspool that's bursting and seeping over its rim. None of them separate—they're all one boiling sludge.

"I'm going to pick you up at noon from the marina. That gives you two hours." James says. It crackles down the line like barbed wire tightening in my ears. He forces the words through as though he's got a boot crushing his throat. It should sound commanding. Instead, it trembles between demand and hesitation. The attempt at poise in his directness would be attractive had he committed to an abrasive tone. Regardless, my cock stiffens at the thought of it—the thought of his smoker's rasp sanded down into something raw, demanding me to beg. I knead my palm into my crotch, like folding dough, letting the voice push heat through me.

"Sure," I answer, eyes dragging toward the wall clock above the kitchen doorway. Time has melted, days bleeding together. There's an etched design between the numbers that leer back at me, sneering—like time is taunting me. I narrow my eyes and realize the hands aren't moving. "I'll be there," I say.

"Good," James replies. A pause. "Don't bring anything. I've got plenty."

The line clicks dead, his breath dissolving into static. That last phrase still hums in me, ominous in tone—though I can't tell if it was deliberate or if I'm just stitching meaning where there isn't any. The amphetamines splinter out through the veins winding my arms, tiny detonations firing in their channels. They tingle and quake in my flesh until my skin feels tight on the bone. A groan slips out, sharp and raw, and I hate how exposed it sounds in the empty room. I hate giving away that palpable rush, that intense fracture of pleasure so blatantly. But the disdain subsides instantaneously whenever another rise arouses me. It always does. Another itch climbs up before the first has time to evaporate within me.

I shove my palms against the couch, rising in a sway, and the pressure forces another barb of chemical light through my hands, streaking up my arms and settling in the pit of my stomach. The scars along my ribs burn erotically, as if the drug is caressing them from the inside, teasing the crevices carved there.

The television screen drips at the edges, colors melting into each other until the picture turns gelatinous. A wobbling mass—soluble, edible, obscene. I think about lying down in its gummy slop, letting it fold over me until I'm swallowed. Instead, I stagger down the short hall to the bedroom. The lamp on the nightstand hums in radiance, its glow soaking the walls.

I pull open the drawer. My fingers clatter through its clutter, fumbling, pawing, until they find my switchblade wedged in the corner. My hand tightens around it as I drag it free from its little holding cell. I crouch, find my boots, and slip the knife into the lip before zipping the leather snug against my calves. Breathe. Lighter. Cigarette. Ritual.

James jerks the car into a space a few meters from where I'm hovering, nearly clipping the concrete street marker on his approach. His driving tells me more than his words—unraveled, impatient, hunting for something to crash into.

I take one last drag from my cigarette and grind it beneath my boot. The marina air clings wet to my skin—reeks of algae, salt rot, fish guts swelling in the humidity. The water slaps against the docks in uneven percussion. Fiberglass hulls clatter into their pilings. Above, seagulls turn in relaxed arcs, wings cutting through the haze. I imagine them conspiring.

James rolls down his window and motions me over. I shove my fists into the pockets of my leather jacket and cross to the passenger side. The reflection that stares back from the window catches me—more gaunt than usual. Objects in the mirror may be more emaciated than they appear. He doesn't seem to care.

I open the door. My shirt clings damp to my torso, fabric stretched taut against ribs that jut and pop against the cloth. The hem rides short, barely grazing my navel, frayed and torn along the cage of bone. My body presents itself whether I want it to or not—hunger sculpted in skin.

When I slide into his car, the seat groans beneath me. James glances over. His eyes mull over my body and linger too long. He comments on it—on the shirt, my frame—how I look. His words are dressed like observations, but I hear the calculation underneath. He's turning me over in his head, weighing femininity against masculinity, trying to spin some narrative that makes what he wants acceptable. I let him think it. Let him scramble for the language. He wants a reason— some justification to fuck me without breaking his own illusion.

"I can lie to you if you can't convince yourself," I say, cocking an eyebrow, smirking. I pitch it coy on purpose—I want him to want to fuck me. A hollow vacancy floods my gut all at once. Either I'm high, aroused, or some queer braid of both—I can't tell. He cracks an inauthentic smile. Something hides behind it, tucked deep in the curve of his lips. I've seen that expression before—somewhere else, in some other face. It alludes—I can't place it. He remains silent.

"Where are we going?" I ask. The car rattles as he jerks it across the gravel, tires spitting stone, careening out of the lot. The marina falls away behind us. I roll the window down and let the wind slap across my face, pattering through the spiked strands curling back against my scalp.

"It's a vacation home," he says finally. "Something secluded. Nice view. I haven't been in a while. It was my ex-wife's favorite place. I never cared much for it."

I let the words hang, then tilt my head toward him, cheek angled into the rush of air. "Is that why you're into this?" My hand dangles loose outside the window, the gust streaming along my arm like it wants to peel my skin back. "You've got to siphon affection from somewhere else?"

"Guess so." His tone is dismissive, detached—insincere, or just unsure. "Haven't been there since the divorce. She died, though, so now I guess I've got to do something with it."

My focus falters, wavering. His voice blurs into the same dull chatter men always pour into me—snippets of drivel I've heard a thousand times before. Sunlight needles through the window, soaking into my tender skin until it burns.

The car veers, jolts. He turns us off the main drag, steering onto a road that winds away from town. Each curve churns my stomach, pitching it in nausea—I feel like a gutted hull. I try to keep track of the route—landmarks, direction, anything—but dizziness knots in my skull, loosening my grip on the map I'm building. The landscape outside warps unfamiliar. I don't think I've been here before. If I have, the memory's been swallowed—blurred out like everything else that burns away. The road keeps bending, sickening switchbacks that tilt my insides. My vision swims. I shut my eyes and sink back into the seat. The heat gnaws at my temples, pressing down until all I can hear is my blood pounding in my skull.

"What happened to you?" James probes. "What gets someone into this kind of life?" His tone is genuinely curious—and I sense a hum of sorrow too.

"Both of my parents are dead." I rub at my temples, retreating deeper into the shadowed interior of the car. "That doesn't explain anything, but it's the kind of excuse you're looking for, right?" I blink hard, vision recalibrating as I pull away from the relentless glare outside. "Truth is, I think I was born with this. I would've ended up here no matter what, one way or another."

"What do you mean?" he presses.

"I don't see things in the same lens other people do. Of course, I can't know for sure—none of us can—but when I watch people, hear what they say, there's always a gap—I don't understand them. I can mimic it, sure—adapt to their mannerisms. But the substance isn't there. I don't have the same experiences they do—it's like I'm lacking something." My eyes follow the road narrowing ahead, cutting into the mountainside as the car begins its climb. A sharp curve jolts me sideways, pressing a warning into my chest. "I find connections in other ways," I go on, slower now, the words breaking into longer pauses. "This, right now—sex—

that's one way. The drugs—that's another. They fill in the gap. Not perfectly, but enough to bridge it for a while. At least I can pretend like I understand." The road bends again, slanting upward into a mountainous range that stirs something in me, an echo I can't place. It's familiar. My body feels it before I do. A pressure rises in my sternum. "I think people like me don't have a choice," I murmur. "It's a black and white path for me. Everyone else—" I watch the windshield and trace the blur of trees and sky behind my vision. "They've got life in color. I don't."

"I don't know as that makes much sense," he admits, dragging his response out like he's trying to force understanding from the words. "Either way, you're cheating yourself."

"Yeah, well." My gaze drifts out the window. The guardrail dips low, the cliffside yawning open beyond it. Waves slam into the rocks below, white spray clawing upward as if it's trying to reach the road itself. The blacktop narrows tighter, the space shrinking. "Does it really matter?"

"Everything matters." His voice roughens, husky, almost collapsing into a groan.

I don't answer. It's not so much a lack of words—I can feel a retort pressing at the back of my throat—but I succumb to the prickling rush climbing my nerves, swallowing them whole. I let out a sharp exhale. James glances my way. His expression caves downward, jaw rigid. In the blur of my periphery, I can't parse whether it's rage or fear. Maybe both— or they're the same thing. Whatever. My cock is hard—pulsing against my zipper like the blood pulsing through my heartbeat.

The road keeps climbing, blacktop narrowing, the guardrail hugging a sheer drop. Waves shatter against the rocks below—spray clawing upward like icicles spiking from the undertow. I feel them under my skin, fingernails dragging along my veins.

Then the road breaks open. A dirt turnoff veers left, choked with foliage drooping low, branches curtaining the entrance in a heavy arch. James jerks the wheel, guiding us off asphalt and onto gravel. The tires clatter over stone, the suspension groaning as the car lurches upward again. The foliage swallows us. Shadows whip across my face, blinding, then parting, then crowding close again.

I press down at my crotch, forcing my palm hard against the swell. I'm trying to drag my focus forward, out through the windshield, but it slides sideways, collapses inward. Clammy heat spreads like butter in my forehead, sweat leaking from my scalp. The pieces grind together in my skull.

James's jaw flexes, muscle twitching, sharp enough to cut through skin. His hands clench tighter around the wheel. I watch him—and it's like watching Percy's face decayed forward in time—same bone structure, same stubborn set of the jaw, but boxier, calcified by age.

The realization comes in me like a feverish collision of everything I've carried: Percy's mouth, Percy's eyes, his sounds buried in my thighs— and now, refracted in the driver's seat, in this older body—steering us deeper into the trees. My cock jerks against my jeans at the same moment my throat cinches shut. A rush of arousal and dread tangles in my gut.

I rub both palms against my thighs, smearing sweat into denim. My ribcage feels like it's cracking open, prying wider. His profile is distorted, thickened with years—but it's Percy's all the same.

The thought rips through me and leaves a ringing echo. I feel myself slipping. The air in the car is humid, strangling. The foliage crowds tighter overhead, branches scraping the roof. I've been here before. I turn my face back toward the windshield, but the image is already burned into me. Hot. Permanent.

He's Percy's father.

VIATICUM

What's a man capable of in the shadow of his dead son?

It's been too long. I sag into the couch cushions, the springs groaning under my spine, eyes fastened to the painting. I've studied it enough times to know every torn contour of the carcass—of Percy's body. But still, it feels new—his wounds flowering fresh each time I look. It's an altar now, a deity, a rosebud split wide, gleaming with the lacquer of congealed wetness, the defiled wounds of Percy's beautiful body. Pull back his skin flaps, like stretched saranwrap, and fornicate my tongue in his webbed muscle—bury myself inside his peeling meat until the sanctum folds shut over me.

"You want a beer?" James asks, his voice cutting through the thought.

I blink, catch a string of spit from my mouth. The saliva beads at my lip and stretches when I wipe it, smearing down my chin in a wet, tacky streak. The air conditioner kicks alive overhead, churning into a low sputter.

"Sure," I say. My voice is sluggish, cracked, but I manage to tilt my head toward him, meeting his outline where he stands. My neck creaks against the headboard as I roll it back. He moves to the refrigerator. When the door opens, a stark white glow spills into the kitchen, cutting his silhouette sharp against it. His shoulders hunch forward, head ducked, and he rummages through the refrigerator—fishing around like he's examining deeper. The fridge is near-empty. Its light makes that absence loud. Finally, he pulls two bottles from the bottom shelf. Their dark glass sweats in the heat, droplets sliding down their sides, pooling into small, trembling rings when he sets them on the marble counter. He doesn't move to open them—instead, he just stares. His thumb rubs at the glass—tensing, circling, as if carving invisible grooves into the condensation. Over and over. Patient. He looks almost hypnotized by it, like the act itself has weight. I watch him from the couch. I can't tell if he's praying, remembering, or just lost in the sound of his own breath. I want to see how long he'll stand there, circling that thumb around and around, as though the answer is hidden under the glass and he's trying to rub it out.

"It looks like my son must have beaten me to them," James says finally, speaking from the corner of his mouth. His eyes don't leave his thumb, still tracing circles in the sweating glass.

I tilt my head back toward the painting. Its surface swells, paint thickening, colors clotting into dollops of tissue. What should be canvas puckers inward—shaping itself into a dehydrated rectal cavity—an orifice collapsing, wilting, hungry.

"He was the only one of us who'd leave leftover beers," James continues, his voice hollow, metallic, carried like it's echoing out of a drain.

Was. I latch onto the word.

"Was?" I ask, questioning the tense of his words.

He doesn't answer. A drawer slides open—metal grinding against metal. Then the sharp hiss of caps snapping free, fizz crackling as carbonation escapes. The sound fills the stillness. Bootsteps cross the tile, growing louder, heavier, and then his arm extends into my line of sight. He holds out a bottle, trembling in his hand. I take it, sip from the rim, and let the question dissolve on my tongue. The bubbles die in the amber. His throat contracts audibly as he takes a long pull. Then his boots scrape back, returning to the kitchen. I swirl the bottle in my palm. The liquid sways, the painting breathes.

"It's a weird painting, isn't it?" I murmur. The strokes seem to peel under my gaze, layers unfurling away from themselves. I imagine digging in, flaking pigment under my fingernails, and pressing it into my skin until the canvas is inside me. It moans—he moans. Its haunches are bound, and I can almost feel the ropes constrict my wrists and ankles. Unwrapping my flesh like I'm a forgotten hard candy—sucker. My breath sounds like turbines whirring in my chest.

I turn back toward the kitchen.

James stands there at the corner of the kitchen bar, hand trembling around a revolver. The muzzle points directly at me, his fist white-knuckled around the grip. His fingers quiver, one hovering over the trigger, waiting for permission.

I don't speak. I don't move.

I watch him step out from behind the counter, gun first, the weight of it dragging his body forward. My beer fizzes faintly in my hand, a dying hiss that mirrors the sound in my head. I tip the bottle back, finish the remainder in one long swallow, then set it gently on the coffee table. The hollow clink rings loud in the silence.

Behind me, the painting breathes.

PIERCE: PENANCE

I level a snub-nosed .38 revolver on him. My grip trembles, but I lock my arms, sight trained on his chest. The sound of my boots carries, seemingly reverberating, drowning out the drone of the air conditioner. I move out from behind the counter, the revolver steady in my hands. He finishes his beer in one tilt and places the bottle down with a measured finality. The glass sweats across the table's surface, leaving a slick ring in the wood. He doesn't flinch. Doesn't speak. His face is flat, unreadable—like he's somewhere else.

"It's not my service weapon," I say, voice hoarse. "But it'll do."

"You're going to shoot me?" I'm not sure if it's meant to be a question or an observation. He straightens his back against the couch and gestures, waving me closer.

I move, cautious, circling the coffee table and moving toward a wicker chair in the corner. It groans when I drop into its frame, leaving several feet between us. Close enough to smell the residue of beer on his breath and the sweat on his shirt. He runs his fingers back through his hair, pressing down the spiked strands that spring loose around his skull. His nails scrape his scalp, and he looks more like he's performing than adjusting—showing me how little this moment unsettles him. And my hands keep shaking.

"Did you kill Percy?" I stammer, jaw rattling.

"I'm guessing that question means you did something to Stewart," he says coolly, sidestepping the question. "Did you kill him? Casey too?" His tone flares, sharp with irritation, but his body is unnervingly steady. He rubs his palms against his thighs, then hooks them on his knees, fingers tensing around the fabric. My vision throbs, the pressure behind my eyes building until the edges blur. His composure is disconcerting, and I question the very sequence of things—the continuity of his choices from one moment to the next, especially staring down the barrel of a gun.

"I need to hear you say it," I snap, hissing through clenched teeth. I know what he is—I know he's the Canine—but Stewart's decrepit corpse won't leave me. His face caves in, mesmerizing my nightmares in haunting, chaotic visions. I need a definitive answer to make this judgment.

"You ever feel like you were born in the wrong body?" he asks, even and detached. "Off subject, I know. But if this is our last conversation, seeing as how much you've been through—how much you've seen, I want to know. Seems like anyone else's answer would be trivial at best."

I grit my teeth, silent.

He leans in, voice flat, calm. "No? Don't tell me you're the religious type—you believe in God? It's easy to believe in something otherworldly when you don't have much going on, right? People console themselves with it—say their suffering happened *for a reason*. You think any of this is ordered? Purposeful? The lie is easy to fall into, isn't it? The idea that someone's keeping score—intentional with suffering. Because if suffering has no meaning, well, nothing actually matters, right? But you, James—" his lips crook faintly, taunting me— "do you think any of this happened *for a reason?*"

I swallow hard, my throat worms, but nothing comes.

He continues, leaning in closer. "See, I don't think so. I think you're like me. You can't make it add up. You keep trying to force meaning into the void, but it's empty. And if there's nothing, then all your rules collapse. Your badge, your cases, your conscience—it's all a bluff. The only question that matters is whether you'll put the gun to your own head. If not, then stop pretending you're anything but a hypocrite."

I can hear my pulse in my ears, drowning the room, rattling the gun in my hand.

"Alright." He sits back, voice even, steady. "Answer me, and I'll answer you. Back and forth until you get tired, had enough, or whatever. Then, that'll be it. That's fair, isn't it?"

My voice claws its way out. "No," I choke out. "It didn't happen for a reason."

"Now we're getting somewhere," he says, sliding a crumpled pack of cigarettes from his jacket pocket. The motion jolts me—I edge my finger further along the trigger, tightening—but I hold steady. He notices, smirks faintly. "Relax. I figure you won't mind if we share one last smoke, right? Indoors, since I don't foresee us making it out to the deck together." He gives me a minute to object. I don't. He shrugs, flicks his lighter, and drags the cigarette to life. The ember flares, smoke unfurling between us. A burnt, acrid stench settles into the room. "You know," he exhales, a plume veiling his face, "I pictured this playing out differently. I'm guessing you did too." He taps ash into the carpet. "Shame, really. I could've done so much more—"

"Did you kill Percy?" I cut him off, voice raw.

He eyes narrow and he licks his teeth, as if tasting the words. "On the record… or off?"

"I don't need a badge for this." My grip hardens on the revolver.

"I thought he was different," the Canine says, dragging hard on his cigarette. Smoke streams from his mouth in ribbons. "Really thought so. The way he carried himself, the pauses in his voice, the little gaps in his mannerisms—it felt off from the others. I liked that. There were overlaps between us. Similarities. He had this vacant look at the funeral— your ex-wife's, I'm assuming. Like he was there and somewhere else at the same time. That drew me in." He flicks ash onto the carpet. "It's my fault for mistaking that vacancy for honesty. If he'd been more upfront, he would've vanished into the background with everyone else—just another blurred face I'd never remember. Instead, he gave me something to work with. So yes—it's partly my fault. But it's his fault too." He taps ash into the carpet again. "Did you know he was queer?"

"It doesn't matter," I mutter.

"Sure," he says, smoothly, cocking his brows up with the response. "He walked himself into it, like all the rest of them did. People are all weak behind the masks they're constantly transitioning through. They're all people susceptible to being devoured, so you can't be wrathful when someone takes advantage of the opportunity. Percy was no different. They all end the same way." He crushes the cigarette into the arm of the couch, leaving a blackened crater in the fabric. His voice lowers—careful, final. "Most people stagger through life convinced they were born in the wrong body—clawing for some shell to crawl into, some mask to parade as truth. It's pathetic. At least I'm not deluded. I don't need a disguise. I know exactly what I am. And I relish it."

His gaze lingers on the ash smear seared into armrest. When I don't answer, he lifts his eyes slow—deliberate—until they lock hard into mine.

"I killed Percy."

I pull the trigger.

CHOICES

Revolver—click.

The empty sound drifts through the room—false start.

My fingers snap to my boot, jerking the blade free. The switchblade finds the soft hinge of his kneecap. I drive it in deep. Cartilage crunches, tendons snaps—his whole leg spasms like a severed cable. His mouth drops open, but shock strangles his throat. My elbow catches his jaw, rattling his skull sideways. He crumples, the revolver tumbling from his grip. His body jerks across the carpet, spasmodic, as if wires inside him have been crossed. He reaches for the blade with locked, tense hands—the metal protruding from his knee.

I kneel, grip the handle, and twist with methodical precision, gouging chunks from his cartilage. Steel grinds against bone and saws through his tendons. He releases a guttural choke, spittle frothing red from his lips, lacing the carpet in wet veins. Blood spits upward—arcs, soaking into the bristles, staining the floor in a fresh scripture. His ruined leg collapses dead. The other thrashes, beating at the ground, desperate, as if it could drag him away. He crumples into himself. Fetal, forehead pressed to the carpet, body shuddering—nerves stripped bare. I rise and grab the wicker chair waiting by the wall—then drag it across the room, scraping a low hymn through the fibers, and setting it before the painting.

Percy's body stares back from the canvas, torn open, wounds budding—a shrine that breathes with me. I seize James by the collar and haul him upright. His body resists in spasms, jerks, and reflexes. I haul him into the chair. He folds there, head lolling, limbs dangling over the arms. His dead leg dangles like a snapped matchstick and drips steadily into the carpet. The other twitches, convulsing uselessly.

Now he looks right.

Set beneath the painting, beneath Percy's altar, his blood soaks into the carpet like a sacrificial lamb. The broken man propped before the carcass consecrates me—an immolation arranged for the only thing that's ever mattered to me.

I crouch, lift the revolver, side out the cylinder. Empty. The chambers spin hollow, mocking him. I cinch the revolver in my waistband and give him a smirk before heading down the hallway. I let his cries chase me—thin, shrill, collapsing into themselves, like a drowning animal—a dog whimpering through its teeth.

When I return, he's trying to lift himself, trying to climb back up. His shoulders shake, his palms shove against the chair arms, and his good leg quivers from his shifting weight. Futile. He falls back into the chair and his head sags back, eyes glistening, lost. I stand over him. The painting looms behind, salivating over my shoulders in my imagination—colors peeling back into meat, into tissue, into Percy. His presence breathes through the walls.

I push my hand through the back of his hair, snagging a clump between my fingers, then lean in close and whisper into his labored breath.

"I never liked guns much," I say, then begin untangling a coil of rope wound around my knuckle. The fibers itch across my skin—rough, frayed. I loop it over his wrists and yank until it bites, veins blanching under the tension. His groan leaks through his teeth, low and guttural. I lean to his ankles next—cord taut, knot pulled hard until his legs jerk limp. "I've always found guns too unpredictable," I go on, murmuring in his ear while I thread the rope tighter. "And that's fair. Because you're taught the same ritual over and over—always clear a gun before you use it, check the chamber before you hand it off, check it when you pick it up, check it again just to be sure." I lean close, throat tightening as I spit mucus on his shoulder, then drag the back of my hand across my mouth. His skin tenses under the spatter. "Feels pointless—until the one time it isn't." I pull back and meet his eyes, scan them back and forth, and offer a coy grin. "This is one of those times." I cinch the last knot and slice the remainder of the rope free, leaving him bound against the wicker frame. His arms splay awkwardly, his fucked leg dangling like a rotten fruit.

"Percy brought me up here once," I say, stretching out the cord, savoring the way his eyes tremor at the name. "I doubt he ever mentioned that to you. He was looking for a bottle opener, opened the wrong drawer." My lips curve slightly at the memory. "Turns out he had a strong aversion to guns too. I got a whole discourse about it." I slide the rope across his chest, hissing against fabric as I pull it taut. His breathing rasps louder, pained. "He hated that you kept them loaded, lying around all the time. Said it made him nervous." I wind the final length between my fists, then push it into his mouth, wedging it deep between his teeth. His jaw resists, then slackens. I knot it behind his skull, forcing his bite into the threads until his lips bruise against the coarse fiber. His muffled grunt vibrates through the rope.

"He unloaded the rounds," I say, crouching beside James until we're eye level. His breath stinks of iron and pain. "Told me his old man taught him plenty—how to pitch a tent, bait a hook, load a gun, hunt. All the basics. He had this catalog of things you'd drilled into him. Things that piqued my curiosity." From my jacket lining, I pull a small cardboard box. It rattles in my hand as I shake it—its interior compartment sliding from the container. I set it at his feet and sift through the contents. "Looks like you were prepping for doomsday with all these boxes of ammunition. Percy said you had enough to last through the year—depending on how angry you got."

I take the revolver, open the cylinder. One by one, I drop the .38 rounds inside. Metal kisses metal. First. Second. Third. His eyes flare, veined red, rimmed wet. His ruined kneecap leaks through the denim, soaking into a pool that clots black on the carpet. The stain spreads to the box, darkening its edges like char. I click the chamber shut. The sound is crisp. His groans pitch higher, breaking into shrill strains. I pause, watching him struggle against the rope, his face contorting. My mouth waters.

"You know the one thing I appreciate about you?" I continue, sliding a cigarette from the battered pack in my pocket. My fingers fumble with the cigarette before I get it lit. "It's your intensity. You don't pretend—nothing about you is hidden." I hold the revolver steady in one hand, lighter in the other. The flame flares. The cigarette catches. I drag smoke deep and let the ember crackle alive.

"Most people wear masks. Pretend they're something they're not. They think that's strength. But you—" I exhale across his face, smoke veiling his eyes. "You don't bother. That makes you dangerous. It makes you honest. And I admire that. If you weren't so fucking damaged, this would've played out differently. You'd have come at this with a clear head." Ash drops, scattering over his jeans. His jaw strains against the gag. The threads start to slip, his tongue working against them—pushing, testing. His muffled sound leaks through. I sit there smoking, watching.

I clamp his skull between my palms—cigarette smoldering in one hand, the side of the revolver grinding into the flesh of his cheek in the other. I drag my tongue across his ruined lips, up the ridge of his face, tasting the mix of salt, copper, and fear. Then I pull back and let out a long sigh. My head dips, eyes fixed on the floorboards for a beat before I look back at him. I let him see it—how empty this feels—just the flat contempt I hold for endings themselves. Finality bores me. Death isn't a climax, it's a letdown.

"I told Casey once that I don't think we have much choice. We don't make our beds. Someone else builds them, shoves us into them, and orders us to lie still. You can resist, but it doesn't matter—sooner or later, someone beats you down until you can't stand again. And sometimes, even when you *do* submit, even when you *do* play along, you still get broken. There's no safety in obedience, just delay." I pause, my cigarette drawing a faint smoke trail between my fingers. I lift the revolver and press the cold barrel into his temple. "Choice is the lie. The floor is the only truth. It's not *if* you end up there, it's *when*. Some of us sooner, some of us later. I only wish I could've given her a cleaner sendoff." The gun digs harder into the sweat along his temple, skin denting under the steel. "But like I said—we don't get to choose."

STANTON: PENUMBRA

The desk lamp hums faintly, its bulb throwing off a weak cone of yellow that pulls starving gnats out of the dark. They flit and smack against the shade, sizzling their little bodies when they drift too close to the heat. Their shadows inflate grotesquely on the paper cover, twitching as they stagger around its edges. Outside, rain pounds hard against the glass, sheets sliding down in warped distortions that cut the streetlights into bleeding streaks.

I lower my eyes back to the folder spread across the desk. Photographs line the page protectors—basement concrete, water stains, shattered glass scattered across the floor. My pencil taps against the edge of one photo as I study it again. The setting is wrong. Different. The earlier murders bled into the victims' own spaces, familiar environments that aided in confirming their identities. Nothing in the basement ties to the victim. Which means it wasn't circumstance. It was chosen. Selected deliberately. I flip to the next photo, tracing the cracked plaster along the wall. What was he doing here? Why abandon the pattern? The Canine isn't careless. He guided the victim here. He staged this. But the logic tangles the more I chase it—the randomness feels designed. A rift in his own system. What's the connection?

"Stanton." The voice snaps me from the spiral. I lift my head. An officer stands in the doorway with a binder tucked under his arm.

"These are the remaining files on the basement incident. Looks like there isn't much of value. Old newspaper clippings, neighborhood crime reports, a handful of profiles from other investigations. Nothing Cameron didn't already flag."

"There may not be anything worthwhile," I answer, keeping my eyes on him, "but I'll confirm that myself."

He shrugs. "Cameron must've forgotten you asked for them. Just let me know when you're through, I'll get them refiled."

I nod. "I appreciate it."

He sets the binder down, the weight of it thudding dully against the desk, then turns and disappears down the hall. The rain keeps hammering. I drag the binder closer, fingertips lingering over its worn edges. The gnats keep orbiting the bulb, burning themselves like they have a death wish.

I gather the photographs into a neat stack, close the folder, and pull the binder toward me. I flip through file after file—homicides, scattered assaults, neighborhood crimes. None bear the Canine's signature. No connective tissue. Just noise.

Next come the real estate listings, sheets of sales data, and parcel maps. Then, local news articles clipped from neighborhood columns. I skim them until one catches my interest: a community piece, glossy in its triviality. A house decorating competition. In the foreground, a beaming couple poses with their son—holiday lights draping behind them, ornaments cluttering the yard in gaudy precision. The house in the background, unmistakable—the same one where the basement crime scene was staged. The clipping is dated fifteen years ago. My eyes snag on the boy. His face is familiar.

I set the clipping aside and keep digging. Another article surfaces dated ten years ago. A missing persons notice—written almost like a milk carton report. Same boy. The photograph is unmistakable. I keep going. One final clipping stops me. A husband and wife found murdered— described in such grotesque detail that I wonder how it ever made print in a mainstream paper. The date is also ten years ago—only months before the missing persons piece. And then it clicks. The boy's face. The persistence of it, why it's been haunting my recognition.

I reach into my jacket and pull out the photograph I took from Stewart's office—Stewart with his arm draped around another man. I lay it side by side with the missing persons clipping. The years have aged him, hollowed him, but the bone structure doesn't change. It's the same man.

I lean back. The gnats that had battered themselves against the lamp are gone, burned out or fled. The shade stands bare now, its glow unbroken. Rain ricochets against the window in steady percussion, blanketing the office in a bleak shroud.

My phone vibrates in my pocket. The sound feels abrupt, jagged against the stillness. I pull it out and press it to my cheek.

"Stanton," I say. Sirens wail faint in the background—urgent, raw.

"It's Pierce," Cameron says.

STANTON: SEVERANCE

I hover over the wicker armchair. The thudding in my chest rises into my fingertips, trembling there, like my body isn't mine. It's part of the scene. My shoes stay pinned to the carpet, rooted in place.

His body leans forward, ankles lashed to the chair legs, kneecap draining down his jeans from a weeping, concave gouge. It soaks into his sock before dripping into the dark pool gathering beneath him. It's already begun to crust at the edges, thickening into tar. The air tastes of it—salted iron clinging to the back of my throat. His arms are wrenched behind the chair, rope biting into the skin until it split—until abrasions carved ridges into his flesh. His hands look foreign—bloated, waterlogged, the pink flushed out.

The entry point was close range. I can tell by the cavity—wide and crude—a crater blooming where his head had been. The wound is rimmed in swelling, clotting blood frothing inside until it stiffens into silence. The exit wound sprayed outward across the wall and carpet, a crude mural of arteries bursting. Red strands spindle to wiry graffitied webbings across the carpet, veining outward until they dissolve into faint mist.

The remains of his ear dangle like wilted petals, a rubber carnation split into strips. They dangle from the mangled seam of his neck, dripping into the collar of his shirt. The fabric soaks it up greedily, turning the threads into a black paste that spreads across his chest—the stain looks like it's still growing. It starts to look less like evidence and more like a message. The thought creeps in. This isn't just for ritual—it was for an audience. And I'm the only one left in the crowd.

"Photograph the painting," I snap. The forensic technician mutters something low, indecipherable, before slipping away to fetch his kit. The dripping persists in the background, steady as the ticking of a clock, but the blood itself has gone rigid, stiffening into clots. I break my stare from the body and pivot toward the canvas.

The technician returns, camera dangling between his fingers. He doesn't raise it right away. Instead, he stands there at a distance, staring with me—like he's weighing how to frame it, or whether he even wants to.

I step closer. The movement pulls taut through my body, fingertips brimming with pressure, footsteps dragging against the carpet. The painting pulls me in. Outside, sirens strobe through the glass panes. Their red and blue beams pour over the room, over the canvas, drowning it in nauseous light. The paint strokes mutate under the influx—warping, shifting. The reds sear first—blistering, kiln-hot, like I'm pressed against the carcass—or inside it. The whole painting seems to radiate heat. Then the blues crash over it, rigid and cruel, sliding icy ridges down my spine. I feel like I'm shivering in a meat locker, dry ice pressed against my bare breasts. The carcass burns and freezes at once. The blood drips. The camera flashes. A brilliance of white obliterates the image for a moment, leaving it seared onto my vision.

When it fades, I trace the lines again, this time around the ribcage. Its curve is precise, methodical. The hooves are bound, the body stretched taut. The layering of strokes mimics a hide in their thickness—paint hardened into the suggestion of leather, skin stripped into texture. I squint, trying to force it into recognition. The gore smears its identity, but the bulk, the shape, the geometry of the bones—bovine, I think. A cow, or something close to it.

"It's the Canine," I say. Cameron's footsteps drag in behind me, approaching from my periphery. He hovers, hands knotted together, his mouth wincing through half-formed expressions that don't survive long enough to turn into words. His eyes land on Pierce's body, linger, and his lips pull back in a faint grimace. He looks like he wants to reach out, cover the man's body, but he can't bring himself to. His fingers keep fidgeting instead.

I don't move. I clench my jaw tight. My gaze doesn't leave the painting. My fingertips are swollen with pressure, as if the blood inside them wants to burst—stain the canvas and add some strokes. The steady drip behind us continues—carving in deeper, heavier.

"We can't conclude that definitively, Stanton," Cameron blurts—more comfortable making eye contact with a corpse than me. He's dismissive, ignorant—offensive in his cowardice. He doesn't see it—doesn't *want* to see it. If I'm being honest, there's no one left I can trust—everything else has gotten in the way. The heat spikes through my fingertips, boiling under the skin until I feel like they might blister open. My face burns red, fury climbing my throat, threatening to spill out and drown him where he stands. My face flushes, teeth grinding until my jaw aches. I don't feel like I'm standing in the room anymore—I feel like I'm burning through it.

"I'm telling you, Cameron." I hiss—the words rip from my throat. "It's the Canine."

"The method, the weapon, the lack of attention to detail," Cameron drones, each word thinning as if he already knows I'm not listening. "It doesn't add up. I know you want to close this case, but you're wading into murky waters. If you start tying everything to the Canine—"

"Then who?" I cut him off, teeth bared, spitting. My vision buckles, swimming under the swell of tears I refuse to release. "How do you explain this? What fucking story are you going to tell yourself tonight that'll let you sleep."

"I know you were close to Pierce," he says evenly, as if pitying me. The softness makes me want to put a bullet in his throat. He hesitates, his jaw tightening, like he's considering whether he really wants to say what he's about to say. The blood drips again. "In this line of work," he adds finally, "almost everyone is an enemy. Few people are friends."

That's it. The pressure fissures up my skull until my head feels split in two. My eyes are blurred glass, dew clinging heavy. My hand moves on its own, dragging along the holster, closing around the leather strap. The gun hums against my palm, waiting. Cameron's face looks vacant, his lips sagging in crooked hooks, his wrinkles caving into gorges.

I drag my stare back to the painting. The carcass pulses, swells, opens like a wet, endless gash. It dares me to step through—to give up the illusion that anything matters. My fingertips go dead, my breath turns jagged, and in the silence, I realize the dripping has stopped.

"Fuck this." My voice splits the stillness like a gunshot. I tear the badge from my belt and fling it into the blood pooling in the carpet. It lands with a slap and disappears in the clotting muck. I grind my heel into it as I shove past Cameron. He's not part of this anymore. None of them are.

SCARS

A piercing wail gnaws through the ceiling, reverberating like a submerged siren. The low hum rattles through my bones, vibrating them into indulgent quivers. I'm perched on a cold metal stool. Its sheen is scuffed with hairline scratches, and my thighs stick to its edge—I can feel the tacky rim biting into the backs of my legs. The counter in front of me gleams stainless steel—my reflection warps across its curve like it's hiding in a funhouse mirror, bent into distortion. My face stares back crooked, skin and bone stretched out of proportion. I drum my fingers against it. The corded phone waits, bolted to the wall, plastic chipped and cord warped in limp spirals. Its paint has flaked off—chips pooled into the corner of the counter like it's been molting.

The air is stale and metallic—heavy on my tongue. The bricks around me glow yellow under the fluorescent tubes, radiating a sickly fever dream staleness. I imagine pressing my mouth to them, letting the dirt and chalky industrial grime line my tongue, coat the roof of my mouth and fuzz my gums. I'd taste the building's history—every exhale trapped in this cell of a room.

The wail subsides, replaced by a grinding scrape—metal dragged on metal, bolts resisting. The cage door opens, then boot heels. The guard steps in, waving someone forward, his face carved into indifference. He jerks his head, and a man in an orange jumpsuit shuffles through the frame, bowed head with greasy strands veiling his face and matted across his forehead. The jumpsuit is spattered down the front with stains—food, piss, spit. His wrists and ankles rattle with shackles. His posture is curious—boyish, almost childlike in its slump, but weighted as though every limb has been filled with sand.

When he tilts his head toward the guard, I notice the back of his scalp—patches hacked out crudely, tufts jutting like mange on a dog, jagged and uneven—a mutt gnawed bald in clumps. The guard guides him toward the glass partition, gesturing at the stool opposite mine. He moves, clumsy, as though he's being steered on puppet strings. His shackles chime with his steps—like a fiendish windchime.

He sits. Metal shrieks against concrete. He lifts his head just enough. There's a dazed vacancy in his lips, like something is moving through him. His body jerks sideways, then back, head darting like he's trying to follow something spinning above us—eyes skittering across the room as if following a specter circling him. His lips are moving. The shapes they form are grotesque—flapping, fishlike, gasping. It looks absurd, but there's a rhythm to it, like he's carrying on two conversations—one with himself, one with something else I'll never see—a conversation I'm not invited to.

I tilt my head, studying. The scruff on his chin is black with oil—it's curled and filthy. His breath fogs the glass with his twitching, leaving smudges that warp his already crooked face into something less human. I find myself fascinated—not by him, but by the thing animating him.

I lift my receiver. The phone is sticky with old sweat, its ridges greasy from being caressed by too many hands. I pin it between my cheek and shoulder, then rap my knuckles against the glass. The dull thud catches his attention. His eyes flick from the pane to the phone, then back to me. For a moment he looks confused, as though he's forgotten what it is. His lips twitch again—one last phrase tossed at the phantom. Then, with a jittery hand, he lifts the receiver, still twitching. After a moment, he reaches for the receiver, angling it into the crook of his jaw. His eyes meet mine, watery and distant, yet piercing in their emptiness. I smile faintly, more to myself than him, at whatever this is—conversation, confession, communion—it's mine.

"Who—" he stammers, the words catching on his tongue, "who are you?"

"An admirer, you could say," I tell him, voice restrained. "I've got some questions for you, if you'd entertain me."

"I—I don't know you," he mutters.

"I know you," I say. "I've followed your case for a while."

He doesn't answer. The room buzzes with the murmur of guards somewhere beyond view, their indistinct chatter sloshing in the corners of the room like background static.

"How many dogs do you think you killed?" I ask.

His mouth trembles. "I don't remember."

"What about people?" My tone drops further, a hush that feels pressed against the glass. "You ever kill a person?" I lean forward, elbows scraping the counter's steel, my eyes drilling through him, waiting.

His head shakes, quick and jittery, like it's not entirely his choice. Drool glosses from the corner of his mouth, fattening into a sticky line that rolls down his chin. He bows his face toward the floor. The spasms twitch through his body like static shocks, his eyes drifting, unfocused, sketching invisible patterns across the concrete. The tension clings to him, inflates around him like a film of air. He shakes his head again, slower this time, but I can't tell if it's denial or compulsion.

"We have a lot in common," I murmur, letting it slither out. "I'll admit, I was envious." My tongue sweeps over my upper lip as I study him, glazing over the fragile lines of his collarbones beneath the jumpsuit. "Why did you remove their teeth?" The whisper barely crosses the receiver. I stretch my fingers across the counter, tapping, then crawling upward toward the glass. They flex in arachnid arches, joint by joint, until my palm presses flat against the barrier. The print smears greasy across its surface, leaving a cloudy trail behind. I drag it down, streaking the glass until it drops back to the steel, leaving snail trail residue. "What was the purpose for you?"

"I—I—" he stammers again, his throat convulsing as though his words are being strangled on the way out. "I wanted to make them beautiful," he blurts, the sound breaking into a childish snarl. "I wanted to return their innocence, back to when they were small. I don't think they're meant to have them. Teeth don't belong there. They only grow them to protect themselves, because the world cages them, abuses them. To remove them is to undo that, to return them back. It's freeing."

"From another perspective," I say, "it could be seen as something else. Not just restoration—but control." A pause lingers between us. I feel the weight of his confession settle, warped but almost tender in its own way.

His fingers wind the phone cord tighter and tighter, weaving shame through its loops. And I see it now—it isn't fear that stains his eyes, it's the humiliation of being misunderstood. His intent construed as vile when, to him, it was divine. He wanted reverence but found only revulsion. That degradation clings to him, and for a second, I almost want to hang up—to leave him drowning in it.

But I don't. I lean in instead, my voice lowering to something near reverence. "Think of it this way—you weren't only giving them something back. You were stripping them of their only defense, the single part of their bodies that were still theirs to command. In taking that away, you dictated what remained. Their loss became your possession. And in that act, you weren't just remaking them—you were remaking yourself. That subtraction fed into you. It makes *you* the beautiful one."

"I think people who contrive things like that aren't much of people," he says finally, his voice wobbling but firm in its intent. "It doesn't mesh with human nature. People don't strip the weak for their own benefit—monsters do. What you're describing… it sounds like you want to play God. Crawl around inside someone else's skin, just to see how far you can push it."

"You're preaching from behind bars," I answer, teeth grinding, "while I'm on this side of the glass. What does that say about my character?"

"I don't know as it matters," he mutters. His eyes narrow into squints as he rubs hard at his temple, refusing to meet my gaze.

I lean back, trying to smooth my composure, but a ripple of unease worms through me anyway. My skin feels hot, burning at the edges. I don't get flustered—ever—but the divergence nips at me. We walk parallel paths, he and I, yet our ideals veer in violently different directions. The friction scalds my thoughts. I exhale, fogging the glass, leaving a smeared mar—like evidence of a lapse. I hadn't intended to follow this route. Reel yourself in.

"Detective Stanton led your case," I redirect, steadying my tone. "You ever meet her?"

"Yes," he nods, voice low. "A while back. She interrogated me when I was first taken in—before the medications. Schizophrenia wasn't managed then—still have difficulty sometimes. I can't recall much of what I said, not clearly. I wasn't—wasn't stable." His voice hitches, and his eyes lift—but not to me. He's glaring off at something across the room, something I can't see. "I do remember her well, though." His lips edge upward. "Especially her smell."

"What would you do to her," I press, voice low, "if you weren't locked in here?"

"I don't need to do anything," he says flatly. "People like her implode on their own. It would be criminal to interfere with that." He pauses, dragging his fingers across his eyes, then claws at the sweat-matted patches of hair along his scalp. When he looks up, his gaze locks into mine—steady, fevered, almost like he's daring me to understand.

"Listen," he goes on, sharper now, "you're obsessed with control. You salivate over every chance to bend the pieces, to strip everything away. But the real power isn't in taking—it's in watching. Sometimes the strongest form of control is restraint. Doing nothing. It's more gratifying to see someone unravel themselves, to collapse under weight you never even had to touch. That's the purest kind of manipulation. The implosion lasts longer when you let them walk into it on their own."

The answer needles me. It's not what I wanted. I was expecting something blunt, something tangible—validation for the direction I've always known I was headed. Instead, his words crawl with ambiguity. I study him across the glass, searching. And beneath the jagged edges of his voice, I see it—remorse, sour and festering. It sickens me—and still, I feel it stir in my gut, tempting. The restraint gnaws more intimate than the violence.

"If you could keep going," I murmur, leaning in close to the receiver, "if they hadn't stopped you—what would you do?"

His lips twitch, and a warped grin pulls across his face. "Step on the landmine," he says. "Even implosions need a trigger."

He knows what's coming—embracing it even—because this is how things are supposed to go. I'm glad he can't see it from my vantage point—can't share in the clarity of it. He's had enough—already racking up credit for bodies that weren't his, claiming echoes of work that belonged to me. I'm not jealous—the spotlight was mine from the beginning. Whatever. I cradle the phone back into its slot and leave.

The automated gate rattles behind me. Out in the dusk, the prison looms with its perimeter lights still dark, the last spill of the sun flattening across the razor wire. I fish out my cellphone, thumb through the *received messages* text log until I find her number buried back in some previous messages. I tap it. The dial tone hums in my ear. The air carries a shift— the day's heat thinning into something cooler. Summer is giving way, collapsing into the chilled throat of autumn. I light a cigarette, drag deep, and let the smoke bleed out slow from my mouth. The prison lights flare alive behind me, a ripple of fluorescence across the concrete perimeter, flooding the walls in stark white. My shadow detaches, stretches long across the ground, climbing up the side of my car—floodlit, skeletal, empty.

The phone clicks alive.

"Detective Stanton," her voice answers.

"I figured out which one you are," I tell her, grinning faintly through the smoke. "You're the tarantula."

STANTON: ECHOES

I drape my jacket over the kitchen stool and circle the counter. The fan ticks overhead, stirring lazy currents of air that move the heaviness in the room. I run the tap, fill a glass, and pull open the refrigerator door. The shelves gape, nearly empty, except for several greasy pizza boxes—cardboard sagging and furred in yellow mold. A sour odor clings to the plastic walls. I stand there, staring into it, and realize I can't remember the last time I was home. I don't remember ordering pizza.

I lean over the sink and swallow the water too fast. It shocks cold down my throat, pooling in my stomach like ice water splashing against raw skin. My whole body feels withered, eroded from the inside out—nothing but coffee and adrenalin—stretched past breaking.

A faint hum interrupts me. At first, I mistake it for the fan. Then I see my jacket shuddering where it rests on the stool, vibrating. I cross the kitchen and dig into its folds, fingers closing on the phone. Its screen sears in the dark: *Unknown Caller.*

The glow makes my eyes ache. I swipe and lift it to my cheek.

"Detective Stanton," I answer.

"I figured out which one you are," a voice says. Calm, steady—almost playful. "You're the tarantula."

My hand goes rigid around the phone. "What do you want?"

"Not curious?" he presses. "You're not going to ask me why?"

I don't answer—I listen to the receiver static and his controlled breath, trying to anchor myself into something solid.

"I'm the frog," he says, taunting, "because you're waiting for me to enter your burrow. Until I do, you're worthless. Just sitting there at the bottom of your hole." Static—muted breathing. "We need to talk," he continues, his words dropping like weights into the quiet. "Or at least— that's where we can start."

"What do you want?" I repeat, and a quiver slips into my voice.

"I'm doing this for you," he replies. His tone dips low, intimate, like he's confiding rather than threatening. "How do you feel about closing doors?"

The question lingers, heavy, and I feel my throat tighten. The room seems smaller now, as if the walls are folding inward with the weight of his voice. My pulse climbs into my fingertips, swelling hot and uneven. I press the phone harder against my cheek, as if the pressure might hold me together.

"Where are you?" I hiss, teeth clenched.

"There's a bar a few miles off the interstate," he says, smooth. "You know the one. You went there during the investigation—one of the Canine scenes." He pauses and I can feel his breath—like he's already in the room with me. "You're going to meet me there. Back patio. Ten o'clock tonight. Got it?"

"And if I don't?"

"You will."

The corners of the kitchen seem to darken. Shadows bleed outward, birthing shapes where there shouldn't be any. Through the glass in my hand, they writhe into grotesque forms—limbs unfurling, torsos gasping for air. They scale the backsplash, drip down the tiles, pool along the counter until they're creeping toward me in a rolling tide of mist. The phone trembles against my palm. My mind tries to tell me it's a trick, nothing but fatigue and suggestion, but the tide clings to my skin. It seeps into my fingers, slick and cold, wetting my flesh like it belongs there.

"I read a case file once," I say, forcing the words out through my teeth. "A husband and wife—found brutalized, grisly beyond reason. It wasn't just violent—it was grotesque, staged in ways I couldn't rationalize. The kind of thing you can't invent. Too bizarre for accident. Too methodical for chance." My throat tightens, but I press harder. "It didn't look random. It looked planned." I leave the words hanging, waiting for him to bite. Nothing. Just that steady, needling breath soaking into the line. Mingling with the static—feeding the silence. My grip tightens on the phone. "Did you murder your parents?"

"No," he says. It sounds honest. "Though with how obscure it was, I don't venture you believe me. It doesn't matter either way. I'm not keen on mysteries myself." He pauses. I hear the faint hiss of a cigarette, the draw in his lungs, and the smoke dragging out between his teeth. The ember crackles. Another pull. Another exhale.

"I had this fish once," he goes on. "Carnival prize, I think. Big thing, big lips—reminds me of you, actually. We didn't have a fishbowl. The closest thing was this artisan vase. It had warped glass with melted sand patterns—difficult to make anything out through the colored glass. One day, my mother knocked it over and the vase shattered on the floor. I imagined the fish flopping, gasping for water—but she said it didn't. She said the shards punctured it—instantly killed it."

The reflection in the glass shifts. A figure stretches itself loose in the dark, rolling its shoulders, its glare cutting into me. The same one from the bedroom. Watching.

"You see, it reminds me of you in other ways too," he continues, voice even. "It swam around in the darkness of this vase with some prior understanding of the world. The darkness seeps in, and the fish soon finds it's lost sense of its bowl, of its own size, and there's nothing left for the fish to do but eventually hit the edge." A drag, smoke hissing.

My pistol is already in my hand, raised, trained on the figure creeping closer, crouched and slinking across the counter's edge.

"The bowl wasn't knocked over," he says. "The fish had no option but to break it."

"What does that say about you?" I press. The figure breathes with me. My thumb cocks back the hammer.

"This isn't about me as much as you want it to be," he replies, almost smug.

"I'm going to kill you."

"What are you going to do after you do?"

"Retire." I hang up.

I shove off the counter and knock the empty glass, sending it crashing against the floor, splintering into fragments. My breath is ragged as I crouch, fumbling clumsily across the tile, pistol still clenched in my hand. I sweep the shards into a pile with the edge of my boot and flip on the kitchen light. The figure is gone. Only my shadow bends across the tile.

"Mom?" Preston's voice pulls me back. He's standing at the foot of the counter, thin and pale in the kitchen's light. His eyes catch the pistol in my grip. "Everything okay?"

"Yeah." I force a smile, though my knuckles are bone-white around the gun. I slide it back into its holster and snap the strap shut. "I dropped a glass."

He doesn't move, just stares. "Are you going somewhere?"

"I have to go into work," I answer, already pulling the dustpan and broom from under the sink. "Will you do me a huge favor and help me clean this up?"

"I need you to stay home," Preston says. His voice cracks at the edges, a quiet plea hidden under practiced steadiness. "I'm sorry if your credit card bill is a lot, I've been buying pizza for me and Lainey. There isn't a grocery store close enough."

"That's fine." I try to soften my voice, shape a smile for him, but it doesn't land. "Get whatever you need. I trust you."

He shakes his head, eyes fixed on the floor. "It's not that. I can't get Lainey to go to school. And I can't go either—I've got to take care of her. She cries at night—most nights. I hear her sobbing through the walls." His voice falters. "I don't know what to do."

The broom bristles drag shards into the dustpan. I crouch, picking at the smallest pieces with my fingernails until they scratch into my skin.

"I need you to stay home," he says again, quieter now. "Please."

I set the dustpan on the counter and lean the broom against its lip. My chest knots as I cross the kitchen, stand before him, and pull him into an embrace. He's taller than me now—by an inch, maybe two. His cheek burns against mine, and I feel the quiver in his shoulders. When I pull back, I grip his arms tight, searching his pale eyes. He looks worn, older than he should.

"I'll be back soon," I tell him. My voice doesn't sound familiar. "There's something I have to take care of."

We stand there in the kitchen—broken glass still glinting at our feet. I grab my jacket from the stool, slide into it, and leave.

STANTON: COLLATERAL

I sit at a wrought-iron table on the patio. Rain claws at the awning, its drumming relentless, trickling rivulets down the corrugated sheet metal. The runoff carries a faint aroma of wet rust into the night air, damp and close. Humidity clings to my skin. I tap a finger against the table—fingernail clicking out a shallow rhythm. The surface is scratchy, abrasive, and the pulse of it shoots up through my nailbed, syncing with the rain and with the drumming in my chest.

I glance around the patio again, then back through the glass doors. Nothing. Just the hum of low voices, bodies shifting, silhouettes slipping across neon light.

The patio is strung with chili-pepper bulbs, cheap plastic domes glowing weakly against the brick walls. They flicker in irregular pulses, casting halos across the wrought iron and mottling the concrete floor. It should feel open—the air moves, uncontained—but instead it feels close, tightened, like the space itself is narrowing around me. The lights flutter against my hands and fingernails, then stretches over my skin until it looks as though I'm glowing too. I scan the bar again. Still nothing. I draw a cigarette and light it. The flame breathes at the tip, licking the paper, and pulling oxygen greedily from the air. For a moment, everything goes quiet—the chatter blotted out, the rain receding—until the lighter's click extinguishes the silence.

The drone of voices resumes, muffled, anonymous, filling the gaps in my mind where thoughts rattle too loudly. I inhale. The ember brightens, flares. Smoke folds through my vision, smearing it in a film of haze. I catch faint strands of mariachi music drifting through the bar—the sound tinny, looping, working its way into my head until it throbs in my temples. The temperature climbs. My ears fill with heat. Check again.

And then—there he is. Leaning across the bar, lips shaping words I can't hear. The bartender listens, nods, reaches for a bottle. Liquid tilts into a glass. His jacket—black leather—bends at its edges, the folds sliding across the bar like the fins of a filleted stingray dragged up from the dark. He hooks the drink into his hand, pivots, and pushes off the counter.

I watch him cross the floor. The glass door groans open under his palm. I look away—pretend distance, control—but I feel him before I see him. The weight of his attention draws across the space, fixing on me. He pulls out the chair opposite and slumps into it. The wrought iron groans, his clothes giving a sodden exhalation under his weight. Rain still clings to him and drips from his hair.

I don't meet his eyes right away. I hold the cigarette at my lips, letting smoke veil the gap between us. But I feel him watching. I feel the smirk crawl into his cheek, slanting upward, daring me to acknowledge it. When I do, when our eyes lock, he's already leaned back, casual, tongue massaging his front teeth like he's savoring the last trace of a meal. The expression that sits on his face is closer to a snarl than a smile.

"I know it's a bit different from what most men prefer," he says, glancing absently around the patio. His hair spreads back in black quills, damp with rain, soaking in the bouncing neon. He pushes back damp clumps, and plastered strands curl in gummy arcs over his forehead. "But we'd both agree, wouldn't we? I don't quite belong in that category."

"No," I answer flatly, my gaze locked on the deep hazel swirling in his eyes. Yellow streamers burst outward, diluted in murky pools of swamp water brown. I drag from my cigarette, hold it, then let the smoke slip out the corner of my mouth. He fishes in his jacket, produces a crumpled pack, and sparks his own. The lighter hisses, flame lapping up hungrily. For a moment, the world pares down to that small fire—its groan, its rasp. Then the chatter creeps back in, a backdrop of muffled horns and tambourine. "Either way," I mutter, "this isn't the scenery I pictured for this."

"Stanton, that sounds so definitive," he says, his tone carrying a mock-whine, "you say that like you're not thrilled to see me again." A drunk couple stumbles past, lightly knocking into the table, laughter spilling as they stagger off.

"Can't say I am."

"And what did you envision, exactly?" He flicks ash, eyes narrowing in amusement. "Whatever *this* is?"

"I don't need a badge," I hiss, the words tearing low from my throat. "If anything, it only gets in the way." I flick ash down onto the wet concrete, my other hand drifting across my thigh, pinky grazing the edge of the holster.

"I thought we'd at least start with pleasantries." He tilts a brow, smirking through the smoke. He drags from his cigarette, cheeks hollowing as his lips purse against the filter. "No?" His squint sharpens, then he exhales a stream toward the patio air, surveying the crowd through it—bargoers clinking glasses, slurring laughter, oblivious. His eyes cut back to me—hungry, certain. "Here's the thing, Stanton. You're not Pierce. We both know that. And it's not because you're more grounded than he was. If anything—you're a bit more unhinged. And that?" he leans back, smoke disfiguring his grin. "That's the part I think I'm really going to get to like about you. The unpredictability."

I slide my hand further down the holster, thumb flicking the snap loose. He dips a fist into his jacket pocket, the leather creasing, bulging with whatever he's palming. The wrought iron beneath me is icy, grounding me for a moment, while the rain outside thins to a faint hiss. Neon chili pepper lights jitter above us, casting fractured colors across his irises like a broken kaleidoscope.

"I don't know how a man could do what you did," I say, voice low, teeth clenched.

He nods faintly, lowering his eyes as if considering it.

"Your son's cute," he says. "Little young for me. But under the right light, right conditions? Doesn't take much imagination." The ash clinging to the end of my cigarette breaks, fluttering onto the table, scattering like dust across the iron mesh. "Wild story, too," he goes on, grinning. "Ran into him at that theater—you know, the one always showing that bottom-barrel horror garbage. But, to get to the point—"

He leans in, voice dipping to a murmur. "I think your boy might be a little queer." He draws the lump from his pocket—just a phone. Its screen flares alive, blue light carving through the dark. He tilts it toward me, the glow catching my face. "You can tell by how he texts," he says, almost gently, before flipping it back and sliding it into his jacket.

My temples burn, a pulse searing hot and fast, and my fingers lock rigid around the grip of my holstered pistol. The rest of the patio dulls into static, voices warped, music fading into a shrill pitch behind my ears.

"I know you're the Canine," I say, grinding my cigarette stub into the plastic ashtray. My voice cuts flat, absolute. "I'll kill you."

"Sure," he says, dipping his head in an exaggerated nod. He drags hard on his cigarette, then spreads his arms wide in a mock invitation. "Go for it. I'm all yours."

My fingers tremble against the pistol grip, joints locking so tight it feels like they could splinter with the slightest twitch. A gust cuts across the patio—sets the chili pepper lights swaying, their plastic skins slapping together in hollow little smacks. He lowers his arms, leans in, smoke wafting from his lips. I can't move.

"Here's the thing, Stanton," he says, voice rolling into a raspy calm. "You're not like James. He let this consume him—let me consume him. If it hadn't been me, someone else would've found their way inside, peeled apart that soft interior, and torn it completely out. I just wish I'd had more time to do it properly." His eyes glint. He knows what he's doing—the nerves he's touching. "You?" he continues. "You get off on this—our jargon, our weird connection. Once this ends, you'll have nothing—and that terrifies you. We're the same in that way. Your husband, your daughter, your son—they're all caricatures. You keep propping them up in the background like faded cardboard cutouts to pretend you've got a decent life. But this is all you've got. Same as me." He grinds the cigarette out in the ashtray. The ember dies in a hiss. "The only difference," he finishes, leaning back, voice flat, "is I'm comfortable in the bed I made."

I don't respond. And then it hits me—it's not that I can't move. I don't want to. The background noise cascades through my skull—bursts of laughter, the clink of glasses, the scrape of wrought iron. All of it washes into a dull roar behind my ears. My jaw clamps shut until it aches. He's right.

"How did you get those scars?" I ask, tipping my chin toward his collar.

The chili pepper lights flicker across the marks cutting jagged lines up his neck and into the fabric of his shirt. He touches them absently, fingers grazing the grooves, then tugs at his collar, exposing the wreckage along his shoulder. The scars pucker under the dim glow—some are shallow slices, others are carved into deep, gouged valleys. One rakes across his shoulder blade so wide and ragged it looks like a bear had clawed through him, fissures thick and raw even after healing. He stares at it too long, then presses a fingertip into the crevice, dragging sweat across its lip as if testing the depth.

"We're just getting to know each other," he says, casual. He pauses. A bead of blood blooms in his nose, trickling down over his lip and streaking across his teeth. He licks it lazily, dragging his tongue over the red stain. His smile shines wet and feral. "When I walk out that door," he asks, "are you ready to start this all over again?" He smirks wider, blood slicking his front teeth.

"I'm ready to plaster your skin across the floor."

"Call it collateral."

EPILOGUE

"Shit."

The word leaks through my teeth as I press the back of my hand to my nose. Blood smears across my fingers in long streaks, tacky, crusting as it dries. The metallic tang seeps into my tongue as I breathe. I keep walking down the blacktop, leather jacket rubbery against my skin, the night air clinging to its seams.

Up ahead, a car idles just beyond a gas station. Its headlights are dimmed to a faint glow, spectral in the dusk, hovering like twin eyes waiting to swallow me. The engine hums, low and guttural, choking on itself.

I pass the oil-slicked pumps, neon halo buzzing overhead. The sign bleeds maroon light down the sidewalk, pooling into the rain-pocked pavement, painting it in stains that look like old blood. My shadow stretches long, warped, as if it doesn't quite belong to me anymore.

At the car, a figure shifts inside. A shadow raises its arm, sliding across the passenger seat, fingers hooking the lock with a dull click. I circle the hood, cross in front of the headlights—they wash me in their sickly glow, a ghost skinned raw—and slip into the passenger seat. The door closes with a muffled thud that feels louder than it should.

The windshield is veined in water droplets. They shiver from the engine's vibration, streaking downward in crooked rivulets, scattering my reflection into fragments. I catch myself multiplied in them—skin in shards, bone in distortion—like I'm already dissolving. I crank down the window, fishing out my cigarette pack with the other hand. The pane grinds, stuttering, and damp air rushes in. Droplets cling to the edge, crawl down my forearm, and sink into the leather, spreading cool patches against the heat of my skin.

I light up, drag deep. The ember flares. Smoke churns out of me, dense enough to make its own weather. It drifts through the car, hooks around my face, and clings to the glass before leaking outward. It rises into the night air and disintegrates—gone as quickly as it came. I lean back. My arm hangs out the window, cigarette glowing in the dark. The figure beside me doesn't speak. Neither do I. The engine keeps buzzing, and the road ahead waits—blank and endless.

"Did you kill her?" he asks.

I let my back sink into the leather, muscles loosening in a feigned ease, eyes fixed on the vacant street ahead. Pressure builds behind my nose where the clot has swollen—like my organs are pleading to be torn free from their cage. Above, a streetlight sputters over a graffitied stop sign, its surface tattooed in crude stencils of fangs, claws, and curving lines that look half-symbol, half-doodle. I tap ash against the window. The embers fall in burning flecks, sticking to the wet glass like black snow.

"I need to know," he presses. His voice has dropped lower, its edge more frayed. "It's getting complicated. They're starting to notice inconsistencies in the evidence. Inconsistencies I created."

Out of the corner of my eye, I see his face tighten, cavernous wrinkles folding into a sneer. His jaw clenches hard enough that I imagine the bone splintering, teeth snapping upward through his skull, puncturing his eyes like sprung bear traps.

"I still need you. On my terms," I answer. My voice comes flat, almost calm. The blur of chili pepper lights still lingers in my vision like ghosts—an afterimage of the patio, a memory burning behind the eyes. "You chose this. Now you're going to eat it, too. You either go down for covering my tracks, or you go down for covering your own. Everything else—" I drag in smoke, then let it leak out between my teeth. "—is just an amusing way to delay what's inevitable."

I turn to meet his gaze, cocking my head slightly. His thumb keeps circling the gearshift, tracing the knob in compulsive, endless loops. The cigarette smoke thickens between us, stinging at the corners of my eyes. It's time to wrap this up.

"There's always a way out," he says, voice faltering. "I just haven't figured it out yet."

"There's never a way out," I answer, steady. "But if that's what you need to tell yourself at night—after tucking your kids in, pouring a couple bourbons, staring at the wall—then by all means, cling to it. Revel in the fantasy."

His eyes flick nervously between the steering wheel and the window, jerky, uncertain—like he's not sure what comes next, or if there *is* a next.

"I can disconnect Pierce's murder from the other Canine cases," he blurts, pushing forward. "Too many inconsistencies to bind them together. The only real overlap is his son, but even that doesn't hold—there isn't enough to tie him directly. Not enough to link him to the Canine."

"I want my hearse back, too," I say. Percy's splayed body flickers in my mind—pinned wide against the wall, gouged in carvings, my fingers buried in his ejecting seepage like tearing open a ripe apricot.

"If you keep going, I can't guarantee I'll be able to continue." His voice wavers, breaking under its own weight. Sweat beads along his hairline, rolling his wrinkles and pooling in the creases around his eyes. "I'll do what I can. That's all I can promise."

I shove the door open and slam it behind me. The force reverberates through the frame. I bend back into the window and perch my elbows on the sill. I take one last drag and grind the cigarette into the dew-lined trim. It hisses and steams, smearing tobacco innards into the metal. Smoke lingers between us. And through it, I watch him tremble—hands kneading the fabric of his pants, trying to press his shaking into submission. His gaze lifts to me, glassy as though he's staring straight through my body and into some hollow expanse yawning behind me. I imagine pressing his throat under tire treads, flattening him into the highway's molten skin. Roll his corpse into mulched carpet fibers, recycled into a singeing, tightening noose. I wish I'd watched the liquor store burn.

"If it makes you feel better, Cameron," I murmur, voice low, "someone's holding my skin as collateral, too."

ACKNOWLEDGEMENTS

I would like to thank everyone that didn't want me to write this book.
It was a good motivator when too often I didn't give a fuck.

Damian Pryce is a mental health therapist, punk rock devotee, and horror junkie who writes at the edge of obsession and flesh. *Canine* is his debut novel, an extreme horror descent drawn from semi-autobiographical experience and the intrusive thought patterns that come from living with obsessive-compulsive disorder.

His introduction to transgressive horror came through the work of Dennis Cooper, whose unflinching prose showed him that disturbing thoughts could become art rather than exile. Influenced by Cooper's writing, the body-horror cinema of David Cronenberg, and the industrial soundscapes of PIG (Raymond Watts), Pryce crafts stories that blur psychological dread with visceral extremes.

With *Canine*, he wants readers to feel the disorientation of addiction, the tension of mystery, and the gut-churning disgust of gore pushed to its limits. He lives in Tucson, Arizona, where he balances his therapeutic work with his life as a self-described "dumb twink" who somehow ended up writing splatterpunk instead of starting a band.

Email: bloodprycebooks@gmail.com
Facebook: https://www.facebook.com/bloodprycebooks/
Instagram: https://www.instagram.com/bloodprycebooks/